Telescope

Jonathan Buckley

TELESCOPE by JONATHAN BUCKLEY

Published in 2011 by
Sort Of Books
PO Box 18678, London NW3 2FL
www.sortof.co.uk

Distributed by
Profile Books
3a Exmouth House, Pine Street,
London EC1R OJH
in all territories excluding the United States and Canada

10 9 8 7 6 5 4 3 2 1

Typeset in Palatino (9.5/14) to a design by Henry Iles

Printed in the UK by Clays Ltd, St Ives plc
on Forest Stewardship Council (mixed sources) certified paper.
336pp

A catalogue record for this book is available from the British Library.
ISBN 978-0-95630-862-7

For Susanne Hillen and Bruno Buckley

Telescope

Jonathan Buckley

No man ever came to an experience which was satiating
Ralph Waldo Emerson

1

Charlie thinks he has found the right person: Ellen Symons, forty-two, professional carer, recently separated, obviously capable, immediately likeable and available right away. Janina thought she was lovely, says Charlie, and we both know that this is an adjective used sparingly by Janina, and very rarely upon first acquaintance. 'What do you think?' he says, producing a photo. The face is plain and pleasant enough, but I can't say that loveliness radiates from it – she looks kindly, slightly bemused (understandable, in the circumstances) and extremely tired. I'd have guessed somewhere nearer fifty than forty. If he's happy I'm happy, I tell Charlie. He's definitely happy, he assures me: Ellen was their clear first choice. It turns out, however, that she's the only choice. Candidate number one, upon being shown a snap of the invalid, said 'I'm sorry, no, I can't,' and departed so quickly it was as if Charlie had pulled down his pants in front of her. The next put her hand to her mouth and said nothing for a full minute, before similarly excusing herself. Another suggested that, in view of what was being asked of her, the remuneration should be revised upwards to the tune of one hundred percent. Only

Ellen passed the test of full disclosure impressively. 'Gosh,' she murmured, but regained her balance right away. Within a minute they were discussing the arrangements. Janina brought her upstairs to see the room that would be hers and the room where the patient will die. She stayed for coffee.

My new lair has been decorated and shelves have been erected. Not enough shelves – a lot of stuff will have to go into the loft. Can't complain, however. Charlie has a photo of the room, and it all looks very nice. If I change my mind about the white, some colour can be introduced – Janina thinks it's too cold, but if white is what I want, white it shall be. He even has a photo of the view from my future window, and this looks nice too: fields, distant low hills, a lot of sky. Janina is taking care of the logistics of the removal. She'll oversee the packing, the re-routing of the mail, meter readings, and so on. 'My wife could have run the Berlin airlift single-handed,' says Charlie. He collects a takeaway and we watch TV for a couple of hours.

Goodbye to Sandra, and not a wet eye in the house. 'I'll miss you,' she tells me, giving the pig-sty one last long look of farewell as she buttons her coat. Next week she'll be attending to the needs of a decrepit old gentleman in Forest Hill: there'll be some incontinence to deal with, and she's expected to push him around the streets for an hour or two every day, but she's not anticipating any behavioural issues and the pay is better. He used to have a big job in the City so he's got a bit of cash stashed away, but he's gay so he's got no children to look after him, which she thinks is one of the sad things about being that way, when you get older and there's no kids to look out for you. Yes, gay isn't the right word, I sadly concur. She's glad I'm moving to the semi-countryside. 'Fresh air, a change of scene, having the family with you – it'll be better than here,' she says. I'm sure she's right, I answer, before presenting the final envelope. Assessing the size of the bonus by touch, she wishes me good luck. 'Thank you,' I say. I promise I'll write to her. 'That'd be nice,' she replies. From the door she gives me a wave, like a released prisoner at the gates.

An operatic dawn to welcome me: pale peach sun behind miles-wide rungs of amber cloud; fields and trees daubed with diluted honey; in the background, low undulations of indigo hills; jubilant blackbirds. At 5.30 a.m. a garage door slides open as smoothly as an eyelid, releasing a vast black BMW, the first commuter out of the blocks. A few minutes later there's a Mercedes sliding down the slipway of a long stone-paved drive, turning slowly onto the empty street. It's another hour before the station-bound people appear in force: a sudden posse, mostly men, moving right to left. There's even a wife in a front garden, waving the spouse on his way. By 8 a.m. the flow has ceased, more or less. Some smaller cars, driven by women, take to the streets; half a dozen buggy-pushers pass by; the chug of a digger begins, on a site that would appear to be a short distance beyond the right-hand limit of the visual field.

A tractor, listing severely, traverses an expanse of soft dun soil. With not a thought in my head, I'm watching it return when Charlie comes in, bearing breakfast. I assure him that I slept well, which I did. Charlie reiterates that I must treat the house as my own. 'We don't want you spending all day up here,' he says, and at this moment there's a knock and in comes Janina, smiling with such delight you'd have thought she'd feared she might have found me dead in my bed. Behind her stands my hired companion.

Ellen is a considerably larger lady than I had imagined from the photo, and the eyes, dark grey, have a less weary cast than they did in the picture. The slabby upper arms are squeezed by the sleeves of a dress that's patterned with flowers in various shades of lilac, mauve and purple; big white buttons hold it tightly to a big white chest. The shoes aren't right for the ensemble: block-like black things with a ridge around the toes and thick crepe soles – nurse's footwear. It's evident that my mugshot didn't do me justice either. 'Pleased to meet you, Mr Brennan,' she says, blinking too rapidly. 'Oh Christ,' she's thinking, 'this chap looks like something that's melted.' Charlie is pushing a chair forward for her, and she glances at it as if having to remind herself what a chair is for. Janina withdraws. 'Not looking my best today,' I say to Ellen. 'You won't mind if I don't kiss you?' It will take her some time to adjust to the mumbling, but she gets the gist and gives me a queasy smile. Charlie remains with us for ten minutes, having sensed that Ellen may be regretting her decision. Taking charge, he runs through a brief agenda of housekeeping topics: the medication schedule, questions of diet and hygiene. Could the furniture, he asks me, be redeployed in ways more useful to me? All is hunky-dory, I reply. Ellen has the look of a learner driver on her first lesson, waiting for the instructor to turn the ignition key. When I request sandwiches for lunch she concentrates as though committing a code number to memory. If I need anything, I'm to use the buzzer. 'Anything at all,' says Charlie, with much nodding from Ellen.

On the stroke of 1 p.m. Ellen is at the door with a plate of sandwiches. Cheese and bread have been aligned to a tolerance of one millimetre, and the butter has been spread evenly and thinly into every angle of every slice. 'Is there anything else I can do for you?' she asks. 'Shall I stay for a while?'

There's a wariness that suggests she's been warned of a brittle temper. 'I'm fine, thank you,' I reply. 'You're sure?' she asks. I tell her that I am quite sure, and she leaves it at that. At three o'clock, on the dot, she's back: she helps me get up, freshens the bed, dispenses the pharmaceuticals, brings over a couple of books. A tautness around the mouth and jaw betrays the effort of suppressing repugnance; she doesn't chatter. Talk is limited mostly to discussion of the evening meal, which is brought punctually at seven, with a big mug of tea made exactly to specifications. She smiles as she places the mug on the table, remarking that she's never known anyone drink tea so weak. It was like making a martini, she says: she just introduced the tea to the water for a second, like letting the gin get a sniff of the vermouth. She glances at me, trying to assess my reaction. You have to look hard to read my face, because the skin isn't telling you anything, and she can't be sure that her familiarity was appropriate. I begin to understand why Charlie was so taken with her. 'I have a refined palette,' I inform her. I suspect she hears: 'I have a fine parrot.'

At ten she comes to wash me, our last interaction of the day. Very lightly she runs a flannel over my skin. I can see her, reflected in the taps, turning aside as if for air. 'Is this all right?' she asks from time to time. It is: she performs the task with the concentration and delicacy of a bomb-disposal expert. When she closes the door she does it as softly as you'd close the door of a room with a sleeping baby in it.

An ironing board, with an iron on it, has been standing in the bedroom window of a house across the street for three full days now. From time to time I see someone in there; at night the curtains are closed and a light shines through them – so the room is being used. The head of the bed is against the far wall. So, as they lie in bed, looking towards the window, the occupants see the iron standing to attention, awaiting its next pile of clothes. Depressing.

Again the dream of the walled lawn – the third or fourth time in the past month. As it begins, there is a strong and pleasurable sensation of recognition, but I have no idea of what is going to be seen. The centre of the scene is a sizeable and irregular area of grass, cut as closely as a bowling green, with a high brick wall around it and trees rising behind. It is dusk, and it appears to be a warm evening: people in summer dresses and short-sleeved shirts are standing around the edge of the grass, talking with the air of guests who are waiting for an event to happen. Someone or something is going to appear over the lip of the slope that falls away at the far end of the green, where previously there had been a wall. Beyond this slope can be seen the lights of a town, not far away, but full night has fallen there, while on the lawn it's still dusk. Nobody arrives; nothing happens. In a murmur the people continue to talk; the atmosphere of anticipation leaks away, but everyone seems perfectly content to remain there, talking in the constant dusk. A feeling enters the dream: it seems that whatever was going to happen has in some way, imperceptibly, happened. The trees look like oaks; sometimes there's a tent, a white marquee, which has the aura of a memory, but I don't think I've ever seen it.

When Ellen comes in I ask her: 'Do you have interesting dreams, Ellen?' She is a little surprised, perhaps by the question, perhaps because I've used her name for the first time. She's been calling me Daniel for a few days now.

'Not often,' she replies. 'Shops. I dream about shops quite a lot, and buying food I don't like, or clothes that aren't right. They're not the right size, not the right colour or something, but I have to buy them for some reason.' I can tell she can tell that my face is smiling as clearly as is possible for it. Recently she dreamt about being alone at night in a supermarket where the aisles were so long she couldn't see the end of them. She was walking and walking and walking, pushing an empty trolley, and there was hardly anything on the shelves, just a can here, a box there, a few bottles. 'It was so boring I couldn't bear it,' she says. 'I bored myself awake.' Here I laugh. The sound is more like a cough, but she knows it's a laugh.

I show her what I've written, about the people on the grass. 'What do you think it means?' she asks and I start to tell her that it doesn't mean anything, that it's just something that happened in my head – but I'm incomprehensible, so I write it out for her. 'You see wonderful things when you're asleep,' I say to her, 'but you aren't really seeing, are you? It's enjoyable, but it's not really you that's enjoying it.'

She frowns. 'I don't know about that,' she says, 'but I wouldn't mind having dreams like I used to have when I was a girl. But your brain's losing its fizz when you get to our age, isn't it?'

'Try these,' I suggest, tapping a bottle of tablets, and for a moment, I'm sure, she thought I meant it.

What have we learned today? That it was in the Harajuku district of Tokyo, in the mid-1990s, that young people first began to combine elements of traditional Japanese dress – the *kimono*, the *obi*, *geta* sandals – with custom-made clothes and cast-offs and designer gear. One of the multitudinous styles that arose at this time was *decora*, in which clothes were hung with toys and plastic jewellery that made a light noise as the wearer walked. Also popular was the 'elegant gothic Lolita' look, which added black lace, corsets and other vampy accoutrements to the well-established 'Lolita' style. Many young women modelled their attire on cartoon characters such as the Sailor Senshi of *Sailor Moon*, one of the most successful creations in the 'magical-girl' sub-genre of *anime* and *manga*, in which young girls combat the forces of evil with their superhuman powers. Here's a twenty-ish girl wearing a red tartan mini-kilt, fat-soled red vinyl boots, a faux-leopardskin stole and a T-shirt hooped with bands of a dozen different colours. Another photo shows six young women who appear to be going for a paedophilic group-sex fantasy kind of look: pigtails; tiny pink miniskirts; huge shaggy boots; hooped candy-bright tights; supertight Minnie Mouse T-shirts. The monthly magazine FRUiTS, established in 1997 by photographer Shoichi Aoki, is essential reading for those interested in the latest developments in Harajuku.

Janina brings me the phone – it's Stephen, with an incident. A profusely bearded man, wearing a full-length black cape fastened around the neck with a thick golden chain, climbed aboard the bus this morning. This gentleman was also wearing, on this blustery and overcast day, a huge pair of sunglasses, of a style one would associate with Jackie Onassis. And he was sucking on the stem of a pipe. There was no pipe – just a stem. Cape-man sprang on board, and inevitably planted himself next to Stephen. He removed the sunglasses, turned to face Stephen, and smiled benignly. He wanted Stephen to understand that plumes of some ethereal substance – invisible to all but this improbable adept – were dancing on the heads of everyone around them. The reason he had seated himself next to Stephen, he explained, was that Stephen's efflorescence was a remarkable bipartite thing, with one large indigo plume and a much smaller scarlet one alongside. Such bifurcated head-flames were very rare, and in all the years that had passed since the man was granted the gift of being able to discern the plumes, he had never seen one of such beautiful colouration. 'Very, very lovely,' he said, and then he removed himself to the upper deck.

'Remember the mauve lady?' asks Stephen. Indeed I do: the woman with mauve shoes, mauve tights, mauve coat, mauve dress, mauve plastic bangles (about twenty of them), mauve earrings, mauve eye-shadow (lots of it). Having sat beside him without comment all the way from Oxford Circus to Brixton, she suddenly asked, demurely, sweetly: 'How old do you think I am?' Stephen, knocking ten years off the lowest plausible age, answered 'Sixty?' The old lady blinked, as though he were a doctor who'd just broken the news that she was going to expire within the week, and yelled to the driver that she wanted to get off, right away.

Wafts of slow thick drizzle since reveille; the sky a panel of old zinc across its whole extent; fields obscured by grey wash; hills invisible. Janina brings the telescope that my parents gave to Peter for his tenth birthday. 'I thought this might be useful,' she says. I thank her, thinking: 'For what, exactly?' Putting Peter's book of British birds on my table, she tells me there are herons down by the stream. For more than an hour I shun the thing, but then I find myself scanning the farmland and soon, in a gap in the mist, I spot a fox, rain-blackened, dithering on the edge of the copse. For a whole minute it stands there, considering the dullness, before retreating to the under-growth. A Land Rover emerges from between the hedgerows of the lane to the farm: when I get it in my sights I see the driver, a middle-aged man, being harangued by his passenger, a scrawny gent in his seventies, who brings his face to the windscreen and bares his teeth at the murk. The woman who waves goodbye to her husband every morning emerges from her house, with trenchcoat belted, huge umbrella aloft and a scarf over her hair – not a look one sees very often nowadays. A heron flies over the hedges on the south side of the farm. Later there's a glimpse of a raptor – a kestrel, I think. In the direction of the ridge there is now the beginnings of a fissure in the cloud, a streak of paler greyness like a trickle of meltwater seen through thick ice. Here, however, we have rain: the quiet chortle of water in the drainpipe is the only sound, other than the occasional evidence of Janina about her business downstairs. Oh yes, there can be no very black melancholy to him who lives in the midst of nature and has his senses still.

Janina and Charles, Ellen reports, would like me to spend more time with them. Perhaps this evening we could all eat together? I appreciate the offer, I answer, but this evening I have other plans. She tells me how much she likes my brother and his wife: they've really made her feel like one of the family. I'm very pleased to hear it.

'Perhaps tomorrow evening?' she asks.

'Perhaps tomorrow evening what?'

'You could come downstairs.'

'We'll see.'

'They really would like it,' she goes on. There's more on the kindness of Janina and Charlie; much use of 'really'.

'They are saints, but I'm tired,' I tell her. 'Please leave me alone.' She goes without a word, like an actress following the director's orders.

The state of Minnesota has some 15,000 lakes and its name means 'sky-tinted water'. ('From the waterfall he named her, Minnehaha, Laughing Water.') The state bird is the Common Loon, *Gavia immer*, otherwise known as the Great Northern Diver. The state butterfly is the Monarch, the state fish the Walleye, and the state flower the Pink and White Showy Lady Slipper. A roll-call of eminent Minnesotans: Bob Dylan, F. Scott Fitzgerald, Judy Garland, Charles Lindbergh, Prince, Charles Schulz.

By way of an apology, I ask Ellen if her accommodation is to her liking. 'It is,' she replies, briskly removing the sheets from the bed. Eye contact so far has been perfunctory. She tells me that she and Janina are going to redecorate the room at the weekend.

'So you're not planning on leaving before me?' I ask.

'No,' she states. 'I'm not.'

I ask if the music bothers her.

'Sandra warned me,' she answers.

I'd had no idea that she'd been debriefed by her predecessor; I want to know more.

'She said you like to have noise around you,' says Ellen.

'Noise?' I roar, faux-furious, but as I'm making the sound I realise that only I can tell it's fake. 'It's Scarlatti, for crying out loud.' This comes out as gibberish: the ulcers are making a hash of the enunciation.

'What?' asks Ellen.

I point to the CD box. 'What else did Sandra tell you?'

'Nothing much,' says Ellen.

This cannot be true. 'Tell,' I say.

'She said she could never understand how you could read with a radio on, and another radio blaring next door.'

I point out that when you walk down the street there's stuff going on all around you: people talking, music coming out of cars and shops, and while all that's going on you're seeing adverts and glimpses of newspapers and magazines and TVs in shop windows. 'Think of it as an indoor street,' I tell her.

It takes a while for me to say this, and Ellen listens attentively, frowning, as if listening to someone to whom English does not come easily. When I've finished she says: 'But you don't read in the street, do you?'

'OK. But you read in the park, no?'

'Suppose so,' she says, unpersuaded, smoothing the fresh bedlinen.

'Sandra hated this stuff,' I tell her. She knows Sandra hated it. 'What about you?' I ask.

'Sounds like a mad person throwing cutlery down the stairs,' she says. 'I'll go and get your breakfast.'

Ambroise Paré on the meaning of dreams: 'Those who abound with phlegm dream of floods, snows, showers and inundations, and falling from high places . . . Those who abound in blood dream of marriages, dances, embracings of women, feasts, jests, laughter, or orchards and gardens.'

The quartet dines together, and Charlie produces a fine bottle of Burgundy to mark the occasion. I dribble profusely; the food – a nice-looking assemblage of chicken fillets and pine nuts and raisins and rice – tastes of oatmeal. Ellen cuts up my portion of meat with the minimum of fuss. Conversation sporadic and unrelaxed; I'd rather be in my room. Charlie is giving Ellen a summary of his day at the office when the doorbell rings. Janina answers, and returns two minutes later, nicely flushed. The caller was some horrible woman who wants to become a local councillor, she says. There's a rumour that the council is going to be taking a lot of asylum seekers, and this woman thinks our money should be spent on better things – things that benefit us, the community. Janina called her a Nazi and sent her away with a flea in her ear. 'There are so many people like that around here,' Janina informs Ellen. 'They want the government to crack down on the immigrants, but they're happy to pay a Polish girl a pittance to keep their house spick and span.' Charles gives her a light slap on the shoulder. 'That's my girl,' he says, pulling a face of comic alarm. 'My wife likes a scrap,' he says, 'but I'll do anything for a quiet life. Mr Risk-Averse, that's me.' Janina says this isn't true – he'd taken risks with the business, and they'd paid off. A brief passage of affectionate bickering ensues, for Ellen's benefit.

Ellen out for an hour in the morning, to meet Roy, the ex-husband. They have one or two things to discuss; nothing major, she says. She suggests that I might like to sit in the garden, as it's such a nice day. I stay in my room instead, reading in the chair by the window. At twelve I see Ellen at the end of the road; viewed through the telescope, her face suggests that the encounter has not gone well. 'Everything OK?' I enquire, when she brings in the lunch.

'Fine,' she says.

'Not how it looked,' I say.

'That's just the way the face hangs,' she answers. 'It's all going south.'

'Tell me.'

'There's nothing to say.'

It's obvious that she and Roy argued. 'Tell me, please,' I wheedle. 'Come on, tell me,' I go on, irritatingly.

'That's enough, Daniel,' says Ellen. 'Behave.'

Tanizaki writes that the Japanese sensibility prefers tarnished silver to polished, the shadowy lustre of jade to the crass glitter of precious stones. The gold decoration of Japanese lacquer-work, he says, must be seen in candlelight, not in the glare of electricity.

Ellen is drying my back and I notice, reflected in the window, her gaze slipping over the skin. A wince of pity, and I can almost hear the question being whispered: 'I wonder who you'd be if you didn't look like this?' Answer: 'Well, I wouldn't exist, would I?'

I tell her about the count and countess, a long time ago in Italy, who had a daughter who was a dwarf. They raised her in a house in which all the staff were dwarves, and never allowed her out, so she grew up thinking that her parents were giants. Not sure if I've read this story or made it up. The former, I think.

A call from Celia, with some good material. Two weeks ago, coming out of a café, she encountered one of her former students, who told her that he had just seen the worst painting in Italy, maybe in the whole world. It was on show in a church not far from where they were standing; the next day, Celia dropped in to take a look. The painting was astonishing: displayed under a spotlight in a room off the sacristy, it showed a life-sized, blue-eyed and rather sexy Mary in a clinging blue robe, with masses of lustrous hair in a style reminiscent of Rita Hayworth in *Gilda*. She was holding the baby Jesus away from her body in a manner that probably was meant to signify that the Holy Mother was surrendering her beloved Son for the sake of humanity's salvation. Instead it made her look like a young woman who didn't much care for kids and was passing him back to his mum. On her way into the church Celia had passed a man who was sweeping the steps; she noted the shabbiness of his outfit – a red jacket with a rip in one shoulder, loose black jeans that ended an inch or two short of elastic-sided boots, one of which was losing its sole. When she left he was still there, and now she noticed the tin on the top step. A card, resting against the tin, advertised the man's availability for work and the hardships of his family. Hearing the rattle of the coins, the man stopped sweeping, smiled widely (exposing some horrendous dentition; he was about forty, she reckoned, but his teeth – or the minority that remained in situ – looked like things an archaeologist might dig up), and shouted at her: 'You like this?' Having no idea what was meant, Celia smiled. The clarification was almost immediate: 'This church? It is beautiful?' he proposed, jabbing his broom in the direction of the doorway.

'Yes,' Celia lied.

'English?' the man loudly enquired, with another smashed smile.

'Yes,' said Celia, becoming a little disconcerted by the man's eyes, which were flickering about as if distracted by an insect.

'Vivien Leigh,' he announced. 'Beautiful.'

'Yes.'

'English.'

For a moment he seemed to be hoping that Celia would have something to add on the subject of Vivien Leigh, but he swiftly moved on. 'Margaret Thatch. What you think of her?'

'Ghastly.'

'What?' he shouted, not with incredulity, but as if they were talking on a bad phone line.

'I don't like her.'

He nodded; it appeared that Celia was scoring satisfactorily. After the eyes had performed a few more high-speed manoeuvres he enquired, with another capacious smile: 'London?'

'I am from London, yes. But I live here.'

This last item of information seemed to strike him as an irrelevance. 'Craiova,' he responded, jabbing a thumb into his chest.

'Your name?' Celia ventured.

As if both wounded and perplexed by this reply, he blinked at her for a few seconds, then bawled: 'From Craiova. I am from Craiova. You don't know Craiova?'

'No, I don't. Sorry.'

He gazed at the head of the broom, as if to say that he'd become accustomed to the ignorance of people in this city but had imagined that Celia would prove to be a better class of person.

'I'm sorry,' said Celia, putting out a hand, 'but I have to go.'

'You live here?' he asked.

It took several more minutes to get away, but yesterday, being in the vicinity of the church, she found herself taking a detour and there he was again, sweeping the litter-free steps, in the same clothes as before.

As Celia deposited her coins he raised his broom in salute. 'Thank you,' he yelled. As before, he presented a broad and hideous smile, but in his eyes there was not the slightest sign of recognition. The ensuing exchange seemed to prove that he had no memory of her – it didn't simply follow the same format as on the previous occasion, it followed a script that was almost identical. Again he told her where he was from. Celia now knew the name of Craiova, but he registered no surprise or pleasure at her familiarity with it. Expectantly he squinted at her, as though to say that he had done his part in carrying the conversation this far, and now it was her turn to take the lead. A question came to mind – 'What is your name?' – but Celia didn't ask it: his eyes, now fixed on her, were desperate and dim-witted. Wanting to get away, immobilised by guilt, she returned his smile. 'I have to get back to work,' she said.

With a grimace, as if rummaging in a basket of barbed wire, the man thrust a hand into a pocket of his jacket, from which he took an envelope. He withdrew a photograph of a woman and two small children sitting at a table in front of a curtain-less and greasy window. 'Mine,' said the man, presenting the photograph for five seconds. The woman and the children all had short, straight and very dark hair, and they sat as though posing for a photograph that might be produced to persuade a possible benefactor of their good character. 'I need work,' stated the man, putting the picture away. 'Where is there work? I do all things.' Celia suggested that restaurants often needed help in the kitchens; she named three or four that came to mind. 'Where are they?' he asked. She tore off the margin of her newspaper and wrote the addresses. He scrutinised the list; his eyes almost disappeared under the buckled brow; the lower lip jutted upwards, covering the upper. 'They need people?' he asked. An unequivocal guarantee seemed to be required, but Celia could say no more than that it was possible. This answer elicited a long stare, within which, momentarily, there rose an angry and obtuse puzzlement as to why she should be fobbing him off with something that fell so far short of adequacy. 'I'll try to think of some more,' she said. Giving the top step a perfunctory sweep, he nodded, as if to say he didn't believe her. 'I have to go,' she told him, ashamed and annoyed at feeling ashamed. At last the man said: 'For sure.' He resumed his sweeping.

Now Celia can't get his face out of her mind, and she has nightmares in which he's following her, unhurriedly, implacably, all over the city and out into the hills.

The city of Craiova occupies the site of the Dacian and Roman city of Pelendava. Formerly the capital of Little Wallachia (Oltenia), it is now the capital of the county of Dolj. Its population has increased more than fivefold in the last eighty years, to around 320,000 inhabitants. *Besides historic sights, there are architectural and art monuments that lure the tourist to Dolj. A stroll through the Romanescu Park becomes compulsory*, it says here.

Ellen tells me that she didn't know there was a sister until yesterday, when she rang. She reads what I've written. 'I'm looking forward to meeting her,' says Ellen. 'Janina says she's quite a character.'

'I bet she does,' I answer. To the quizzical look I respond with a promise to tell her more. 'I'll write you the life of Celia. Edited highlights. And in exchange—'

'There's nothing to tell that you don't already know from Charles,' she says, and with the next beat she changes the subject. 'Why don't you come out into the garden? The only way the neighbours could get a peep is if you're lying in the middle of the lawn. Even then they'd have to hang out of an upstairs window.'

'I'll consider it.'

'That's what you always say,' she says, picking up my stick. 'Today's the day. Let's move.'

'Carpe diem, eh?'

'I have no idea what you're talking about, Daniel, but you can explain outside,' she says, offering me a forearm to grasp. She's very strong. Grabbing the bar of a ski-lift, I imagine, is a similar experience.

Janina awaits on the terrace, with a jug of home-made lemonade and three beakers. She is, it has to be said, looking lovely. The hair is gathered back in a crimson scarf, so the neat little ears are on show, and she's wearing a thin black roll-neck top with a pair of black jeans that are nicely tight around the thighs. Espadrilles, black, round off the outfit. This is how Janina dresses for the garden. Some women go to the opera looking more slovenly. The exposed areas of foot and ankle are smooth and shapely and a shade more tanned than I think could be attributed to late-spring sunlight. I suspect some sunbedding goes on, after the gym. Does Janina have too much time on her hands? Five half-days of admin work at the college are perhaps not enough.

She tells a nice story. An eight-year-old girl – the daughter of a colleague – comes home from school last week and tells her mother that they'd had a very odd supply teacher that day. She'd asked the class how many bedrooms they had at home. One kid wasn't certain if it was eight or nine. Another wasn't sure how to count the rooms, because sometimes daddy sleeps with mummy, sometimes he sleeps in a room downstairs, and sometimes he sleeps with Milva, the lady who lives with them and picks her up from school.

A parcel arrives. When Ellen brings me my tea I am in my chair, with the new book on my knees. I turn the pages: a photo of clouds; a photo of a street scene; a photo of a couple on a beach; two boys standing in the middle of a road; flowers; a boy and a girl on a path; a naked young woman, bound and gagged, in a car; a naked young woman holding a stuffed lizard to her chest; a naked young woman, bound with rough rope, seated on rough matting. I linger on the last; Ellen observes.

'Are you trying to embarrass me?' she asks.

'Not at all,' I answer. Were my face more mobile, it would have betrayed me; I think Ellen doesn't believe me anyway.

'So what else did Sandra say about me?' I ask.

'That you were a difficult sod, and you were forever playing music she didn't like,' she answers.

'I'll turn it off,' I offer.

'I'm getting used to it.'

'I'm going to tell you all about me and Sandra,' I say.

'OK,' says Ellen, as if I'd said something like 'I'm going to read the newspaper.' She picks up the packaging from the floor, where I'd dropped it. 'Where do you want your tea?' she asks.

Beneath the Lenin mausoleum there was once a laboratory in which a hundred embalmers worked on perfecting their craft. To each was assigned a corpse, and every corpse had its own rubber bath. Imagine it: dozens of dead men bobbing about underneath Red Square.

Before she came to look after me, Sandra's last salaried job had been in an old people's home, a bad one. 'The people who ran it, it was just a business to them,' as she told Charlie. 'They didn't care about the old ones. It was like we was just keeping them in storage until it was time to bury them. But do as you would be done by, Mr Brennan, that's what I've always said. We all get old. It's a bad thing, but it's going to happen. The alternative is a whole lot worse, that's what I say.' The reason she couldn't produce references, she informed Charlie, was that she'd been forced to leave. Some of the staff used to treat the old people harshly, and Sandra had put a few backs up when she argued about it. Then she saw one of the supervisors giving a lady a plate of leftovers to eat. 'She's a hundred years old, for fuck's sake. She can't tell the difference,' said the supervisor, so Sandra reported her and the next thing she knew she was being given a bollocking for not being a team player and she was telling them where they could stick their job. Sandra's straight talking made a good impression on Charlie, as did her honesty when shown the portrait: 'That's a shock, Mr Brennan. I've seen some things, but nothing like that. I'm a bit at a loss, to be perfectly frank.' This was one of Sandra's favourite phrases: 'This stuff's overpriced, to be perfectly frank'; 'I'm feeling a bit under the weather today, to be perfectly frank'. From time to time it could get on one's nerves, to be perfectly frank.

(Honesty was not one of the virtues of Sandra's predecessor (name withheld). Small fluctuations in the household outgoings made me suspect that when she was shopping for me she would pick up a few items for herself and add the costs to my bill. Once, the week's expenditure was so much higher than normal, and so implausibly explained, that I took a look in her bag and found half a dozen unopened packets of cigarettes; when I asked for the receipt (it had mysteriously vanished), she wanted to know what I was implying. It wasn't worth the fuss of an accusation, but now she knew I didn't trust her. In the following weeks she would sometimes leave receipts for inspection on the kitchen table; she regularly hinted that she would be leaving me some time soon. And she did leave soon, and abruptly, after an incident that occurred on a hot day in July. She had returned from the shops sweating so heavily that her T-shirt was piebald and her sandals squeaked. 'My hair looks like seaweed,' she said. 'I can't walk around looking like this.' Because she was meeting her sister later she'd bought herself a new T-shirt while she was out; she took herself off to the bathroom to change. Passing the bathroom on my way to the adjoining toilet, I gave the door the gentlest of pushes and it opened an inch or two, disclosing my helper, towelling a foot on the edge of the bath. My appearance was unnoticed for a fraction of a second, and it's remarkable how much information the eye can process in so brief an interval: the triangle of springy black hair, beaded with water; the soft triple fold of the belly; the little dimples on the inside of a thigh, as if the flesh bore the light imprint of fingers; the shimmer of hairs on the edge of an arm; a breast, long and pale, dented against a knee. Conditions were perfect for the presentation of the female form unclothed: bright sunlight through stippled glass; the merest tint of green imparted by the foliage of the chestnut tress in the courtyard; the enamelled surfaces animated by leaf-shadows. Seeing me, observing the avid nippleward gaze, she straightened up, furious, pulling the towel to her neck. 'What the fuck do you think you're doing?' she yelled. My apologies, when she emerged, were profuse. Seeing the door ajar, I told her, I'd assumed she wasn't in there. 'And where exactly did you imagine I was? I'm either in here or out there with you, aren't I?' She had a point, of course.)

To return to Sandra: she'd had plentiful experience of cleaning the catastrophically unhygienic, spoon-feeding the almost dead, keeping company with people who could not remember who she was from one day to the next. The body in collapse was a challenge at which she would not quail, but a messy domestic environment was something she could not abide. Sandra liked to run a tight ship: books belonged on shelves unless currently being read; magazines, once read, belonged in the bin, likewise newspapers on the day after publication; floors were surfaces to be walked on, and should be left uncluttered; the toilet cistern was not to be regarded as an ancillary bookshelf; food-preparation surfaces were to be kept clean and free of printed matter. She saw as squalor what I saw as merely light disarray. (Charlie sympathised with her. 'When Danny was a teenager his room was a pit,' he told her. 'You have to think of it as a kind of protest,' he said. Maybe, Charlie, maybe.) And it must be recorded that, as with Ms X, matters relating to female nakedness were also the occasion of controversy. The first time she came upon me *in flagrante* with my computer Sandra backed out of the room promptly, and nothing was said about it. At the second offence I asked her if she was shocked and she confirmed that she was. I remarked that the young woman on the screen evidently had access to some remarkably efficient depilatory products, which perhaps might be of use to me, as razors were too clumsy for the crevasses of my face. This did not amuse. 'I wish you wouldn't, when I'm around,' she said. I agreed to keep my browsing decent whenever Sandra was in the flat, and I honoured that agreement, but there were other incidents: a magazine uncovered during one of her bouts of tidying; a picture that fell out of a book; an envelope ripped when the postman crammed it through the letterbox, disclosing its indecent contents. Entering my bedroom, I saw her lifting a magazine off the floor as if it were a dollop of week-old afterbirth. Her distaste and her disappointment in me were very affecting. 'It's a weakness I have,' I confessed. 'I have tried to live like a brain in a jar, but I am a backslider.' This did not get a laugh either. She was angrier than she was allowing herself to appear. In an empty gesture of resolve, I surrendered the offensive publication to the recycling bin. 'Maybe it'll be reborn as a flyer for the Jehovah's Witnesses,' I suggested. Again, no laugh. Rarely did she find anything I said funny. We were not ideally suited to each other.

'This isn't news, is it?' I ask Ellen, after she's read it. 'Sandra had told you, hadn't she?'

'A little,' she says.

'Does it bother you?'

'A little.' But she appreciates my honesty, and thinks that some of it is quite nicely written. 'I can almost see her,' she says.

'So can I,' I say. I close my eyes and grin.

'No more of that, Mr Brennan,' she orders, pulling back the sheets. 'This came for you,' she says, handing me a flyer from Stephen, for a season of cult Japanese movies. *Stray Cat Rock: Sex Hunter* seems promising: 'a blaze of knife fights, jeep chases and LSD-tinged nightclub sequences'. Also intriguing is *Female Convict Scorpion*, an 'exploitation classic, an art-house wonder and a feminist movie all rolled into one.' Both are trumped, however, by *School of the Holy Beast*, described here as 'an unholy mix of sex, comedy, drugs, flagellation, horror and political commentary.' Now available on DVD. 'Perhaps I'll order it,' I remark, showing her the advertisement.

'Ho ho,' she says, easing me out of bed.

Stephen, I explain, is the Number One friend, and he'll be visiting us soon. 'Shall I tell you about Stephen?' I ask. 'There'll be nothing about naked ladies, I promise. Shall I do that?'

'If you'd like to,' she says.

'Yes, I would like to. If you'd like me to.' I reply.

'Yes, I would,' she says.

'Now, are you just saying that, Ellen? Are you humouring me? I think you are.'

'No, Daniel, I'm not.'

'I think you are.'

'No. I'm not. I'd like to hear about him. And you.'

'Are you sure?'

'Quite sure.'

'You're not just being nice?'

'No, Daniel. I'd like to know.'

'I think you're just being nice.'

'OK. That's enough.'

2

When the face started to sprout and the limbs to burst into bud, a diminution of my social circle commenced. Several classmates did not respond well to the deterioration of the façade, and – despite my assurances to the contrary – behaved as if the condition might be contagious. Most made an effort to mask their queasiness, but rarely with complete success, and I admit that, upon perceiving what I took to be intimations of aversion, I often took the initiative and began to withdraw. Also to be considered is the simple matter of my becoming unfit for the more boisterous modes of schoolboy interaction – football, for example, was an unwise pursuit when the physique was developing in ways (warping of the skeleton; weakness of major bones) that were unconducive to sporting endeavour. Did I make the situation more difficult than it might have been? Possibly. I don't know. All I can say with certainty is that, were I to enumerate the friends I had at the age of twelve and those I had at the age of, say, seventeen, the former number, though small, would be considerably larger than the latter. The latter, in fact, would be approximately one (excluding Celia), and that one would be Stephen Siveter.

The images that have endured most strongly from Stephen's early childhood, he says, are of his mother and father looking at him across the room, or across the table, or from the kitchen window: looking at him lovingly, gratefully even, but as if they had been entrusted with the care of something that had come into their lives inexplicably. This was in part because, having long passed forty, they had almost reconciled themselves to being childless when suddenly, against odds that doctors had warned them were more or less the same as the odds against their meeting Elvis at the supermarket, Mrs Siviter found herself pregnant, and in part because his resemblance to them did not extend much beyond his having eyes of the same hazel hue as his mother's, and a head that from certain angles had something of the shape of his father's. Mr Siveter – a builder – was a powerful little man, with biceps like coconuts, a neck like a rhino's and legs as bandy as a jockey's but three times the circumference. Mrs Siveter, in her own words, was not a lady cut out for ballet; I remember her lifting with ease, one-handed, the end of the huge settee. But Stephen was a spindly lad and remained a spindle despite his mother's unending campaign to put some more substance on his frame through a diet that was heavy with sausage and potatoes. The differences of temperament between parents and child were as striking as the physical discrepancies: Mr and Mrs Siviter were an ebullient and energetic couple, whose idea of fun was a day spent sanding floorboards or taking a ten-mile hike (the family holidays were as gruelling for Stephen as a secondment to the Territorial Army); their son, however, was placid, slow-moving and thoughtful. When Stephen was born there wasn't a book in the house, but by the age of seven he had acquired such an appetite for information, and such powers of concentration, that he was content to be left in his room with his books for hours at a stretch. He was, said his father proudly, a bit weird. This was one of our classmates' favoured epithets for him too, but in their case there was little affection in it. His appearance – scrawny; over-sized incisors; disproportionately large head; horn-rimmed glasses – was the object of much comment, and his failure to even dissemble an interest in any kind of sport assured him of more or less comprehensive unpopularity among the boys. But, more than any other trait, what sealed his position as the class's second-ranking oddity was that he had never made the slightest effort to disguise his eagerness to learn. Even some of his teachers were concerned that Stephen's pursuit of knowledge might be a little too single-minded. He needed to cultivate a few non-academic interests, his parents were told, but Stephen regarded hobbies as a waste of reading time. And once Stephen had read something it was lodged in his brain as securely as downloaded software. Consequently, he achieved marks that put him in the top three places in every subject. (When the time came to decide whether he was going to specialise in the sciences or the arts, he made his decision (hearing no inner voice) simply by totting up his marks, which tilted the balance by a percentage point or two in favour of the latter.) 'King of England in 1350?' – the Mekon could tell you in an instant. 'Population of Hong Kong?' – a cinch for Mongo the Memory Man. 'Formula for phenylalanine?', 'What's the world's deepest lake?', 'What's a cosecant, for Christ's sake?' – just ask The Brain. Exams for Stephen were a pleasure, an opportunity to release all that pent-up knowledge. Sitting an exam was like running down a mountain, he said.

Although his idiosyncratic features disqualified Stephen as a lust-object in the eyes of the girls, his intelligence earned him a degree of respect from a few, which, when blended with the sympathy stirred by the treatment he received from so many of his male classmates, produced a genuine liking in one or two cases. Melanie Watts, the semi-Belgian girl who kept him off the top spot in French, and Jenny Oakes (called Jenny Bloke because she was good at physics and maths, and was far from pretty) – they both had a soft spot for him. The one girl that Stephen liked more than any other, though, was Celia. 'She's bloody terrific,' he said to me once as Celia left my room (the frankness and the rather quaint usage were both characteristic; in his dress sense, too, Stephen was anachronistic – how many teenagers in south London wore brogues by choice?), having loaned him an album she'd recently bought (The Ramones?). Holding the album with care, he gazed at the closed door as if contemplating the radiant after-image of Celia. 'She is just great,' he murmured, dazed. 'Will C be in?' he would ask when invited round to our house – not that his acceptance was dependant upon the likelihood of Celia's being present, but the possibility of a conversation with her would definitely improve the quality of the afternoon. Celia was predisposed to be fond of Stephen simply because of his fondness for me, but she also recognised in Stephen a fellow smart-arse (to quote Charlie). Later, she was to esteem him for his refusal to consider his future in terms of a career. The very word 'career' had the same effect upon him as the words 'golf club' or 'Conservative Party'. He despised the idea of defining one's life in terms of what one does for a living, of 'forging a life for oneself', as he once put it – a phrase that Celia liked to quote (as if citing Jean-Paul Sartre) to Charlie, who, having no truck with smart-arsed word-play, refused to see even the tiniest particle of wit of it. For her fifteenth birthday he bought her a Tom Waits album. When she kissed him he blushed like a radish, then said: 'Another, if you don't mind. I paid good money for that.' It would have been not long after this birthday that, teasing Celia about a boy in my class who'd sent her a Valentine's Day card, I let slip that Stephen fancied her too – at which Celia burst out laughing.

'What's funny?' I asked.

After a pantomime frown, she stated: 'Stephen does not fancy me.'

'I think he does.'

'Of course he doesn't.'

'Why "of course"?'

'Come off it, Dan.'

'No, I mean it. Why "of course"? He thinks you're fantastic.'

'Of course. I am fantastic. But Stephen is not interested in me. Not in the way you mean.'

'You sure?'

'Positive.'

'I think you're wrong.'

'I know I'm right.'

'How?'

'Because he's not interested in any girls. He's gay, you prat.'

'Really?'

'Bloody hell, Dan. Yes, really. It's obvious.'

'How?'

'I can tell.'

'How?'

'The way he looks at me. The way he looks at girls and the way he looks at boys.'

'He's never said anything.'

'There are good reasons not to, aren't there? I bet his folks would go bananas, for one thing. Or maybe he doesn't know himself.'

'Or maybe you're wrong.'

'No, Dan, he's gay,' said Celia with immovable firmness, as one might tell an infant that playtime is over.

And of course Celia was right: Stephen was gay, even if he didn't yet know it. (Another year would pass before Stephen acknowledged it as a fact, to himself, and he didn't acknowledge it to me until a short time before the 1979 election (gloomy about the way the campaign was going, he turned off the radio and said: 'I have something to tell you . . .'), though he'd begun to wonder about his orientation (as he told me on the evening of the confession) during the 1976 Olympics, when the male high-board divers had worked for him in a way that none of the girl gymnasts had.) Her speculation as to how Stephen's parents would react, however, proved to be inaccurate. For a while they had carried on as if they believed that Stephen was simply too involved in his homework to be messing around with girls. And I think that, as it became clearer that their boy was in fact resistant to the allure of the feminine, they then persuaded themselves that he might be effectively neuter, taking as proof the fact that his only close male friend was a boy so peculiar-looking. In time, though, they must have had their suspicions about their son's proclivities, and Stephen knew that a declaration of the truth would require some realignment of the parental attitudes. It wasn't that they regarded a failure to be heterosexual as an unpardonable offence against the natural order (unlike the parents of one of Celia's classmates, who refused to talk to their daughter for a full decade after she'd clarified the reason for her apparent lack of success with boys), but it was apparent that they were less than entirely comfortable with queerness. It had for a long time been noticeable, for example, that they were irritated by Frankie Howerd, Kenneth

Williams and other performers of that ilk. So Stephen was content to postpone for as long as possible the moment when the household would have to adjust to having an avowed homosexual in its midst.

During all the years that he lived at home the moment for full disclosure never arrived. Avoidance of the issue finally became an unsustainable strategy in his second year at university, when he fell for a Californian exchange student. Out shopping with his mother, he told her that he'd be going away for part of the summer vacation; to Greece; with a fellow student; called Allen. At this news his mother merely nodded and smiled, a little saddened, powerlessly acquiescent, but as though all she'd heard was that Stephen would not be coming home in July. When, a day or two later, Stephen asked her what she felt about it, she admitted that she'd never get used to the idea that she was not going to have grandchildren, but that she would always be proud of him. (More than once she told him that she was delighted he had the brains to better himself. 'She's more of a class traitor than I am,' said Stephen.) But his father, she warned, hadn't come to terms with the situation. And to this day his father's acceptance is perhaps still only provisional. Sometimes – should Stephen happen to remark on the attractiveness of an actress on TV, for instance – he thinks he sees in his father's eye the last low glimmerings of the hope that his son might one day recover.

My relationship with Stephen was a case of friendship at first sight, and it began on the first day of his first term at my school. I had been at the hospital for a review the previous week; they were going to excise some lumps from the arms. It was lunchtime, and I had settled myself in an angle of the low wall below the chemistry lab. The angle was in sunlight most of the morning so the bricks were warm by one o'clock, and I liked to tuck myself into the corner to read. Stephen was standing outside the lab, pressing his face to the window to get a good look at the benches and racks of equipment. 'Nice set-up,' he remarked, as if he thought I was the person who'd paid for all the kit. The school he'd come from was rubbish, he said, still at the window. He sauntered over to the angle; leaning against the wall, he surveyed the playing fields. 'This is good,' he said. Then, swirling a hand in front of his face, he asked right out: 'What's the story with the mush?' So I told him what the story was, and when I'd finished he looked me steadily in the eye and said, after a lengthy and thoughtful pause: 'Bollocks.'

'Quite.'

'So they never go down?'

'Nope.'

'Not ever?'

'Not ever no how. But the docs can lop some of them off.'

'And then?'

'New ones grow.'

Again he looked at me and again he said, with extra force: 'Bollocks.' This was, we agreed, as much as could usefully be said. Then he asked: 'What you reading?'

(It was *Fahrenheit 451*, which he'd read already; *Brave New World* was better, said Stephen. I seem to remember discussing *Brave New World* a week or two later, on the slope above the football pitches ('the grandstand of the incompetent', he called it); this, I think, was the hour in which the nickname 'Bleb' was conceived, a nickname at which Charlie – missing the point – took some offence, believing that it constituted collusion in the cruelty of the likes of class thug Vincent Draper, to whom I was 'Grape-Face' or 'Pig-Tits'.)

So: 'What are you reading?' asked Stephen, and I can still feel something of the refreshment of being regarded by that calm yet tightly focused gaze, as if the disfigurement, having been discussed, had become invisible. Already I was used to people giving the impression, when they looked at me, that they were striving to peer through the face, as if the eyes were peep-holes through which – if they looked carefully – a small and vulnerable creature could be discerned, scurrying around inside.

Here, it occurs to me, is as good a place as any to bring in Miss Anscombe. Fifty-ish, cylindrical of torso, with ankles as wide as pint glasses, Miss Anscombe arrived at the school a year after Stephen, as a replacement for Mr Gidley, who had been arrested driving on the wrong side of the road in the middle of the night, at about 10 mph, and very much the worse for wear. Stephen and I were soon entranced. Miss Anscombe's lessons were purposeful and fast-moving, with high-quality slide shows and a leavening of deadpan sarcasm, but even better than the lessons were her field trips. The first was a day's excursion to the Sussex Downs. While the rest of the class trooped up the hill in the wake of the other teacher, Miss Anscombe loitered with Stephen and myself at the rear of the column, pointing out the salient features of the terrain. I see the three of us, sitting on a hummock, facing a slope on which the grass has a pleated appearance (soil-slip): her hands mimicked the curve of the scarp, and she talked as if she could see the surface of the earth buckling and falling before her eyes, like a time-lapse film in which tens of thousands of years were compressed into seconds; she held a lump of flint in her palm, stroking the stone as if to make it purr. She made a greater effort than some of her colleagues to act as if all of her pupils were equals in her eyes, but she had immediately taken a special liking to Stephen. 'He's Oxbridge material,' she had told his mother emphatically at the end of his first year at the school, and Stephen's decision to read anthropology at university was largely attributable to the advocacy of Miss Anscombe. (Miss Anscombe was a snob, and there was a suggestion, in the way she announced this to Stephen's mother, that she feared the boy might be dispatched to the factory floor if she didn't campaign for his further education; his mother, Stephen recalls, was thrilled and slightly alarmed by Miss Anscombe's verdict, as if her son had been singled out by a recruiting officer for the Jesuits). Handing back an essay on Saharan oases, she told him that anthropology was a subject to which he should give the deepest consideration (her exact words, delivered in the tone of a judge giving advice to a jury), because it had become apparent in the course of the year that what principally interested him was not geology or weather or vegetation but people and the way they lived. The oases essay was quite brilliant, as had been his essay on the Inuit; his essays were always remarkable when the topic touched on unfamiliar cultures. She loaned him a book by Margaret Mead. It was wonderful. Anthropology was indeed an enticing proposition, but had our history teacher taken him aside and told him with similar forcefulness that he sensed in Stephen a craving to get stuck into the study of medieval Europe, and consequently presented him with a copy of *The Waning of the Middle Ages*, Stephen could in all likelihood have been persuaded that medieval history would prove an immensely rewarding area of study, just as, had our English teacher sent him home with extravagant praise ringing in his ears and a copy of *Seven Types of Ambiguity* in his pocket, he could have decided that three years of his life might fruitfully be devoted to the reading of English literature. But the voice of Miss Anscombe was the first to be heard (and probably would have prevailed in a hypothetical three-way shoot-out anyway), and so Stephen gratefully borrowed books from her and did not confess that the supposed brilliance of his essay on Saharan oases, like the brilliance of his writing about the Inuit, was largely attributable to certain books he'd found in his local library, which had seemed to be safely obscure because nobody had ever borrowed them. On the other hand, although he knew it wasn't true that the way people lived their lives was what principally interested him (nothing principally interested him), he did find the books he borrowed from Miss Anscombe challenging in a way that few other books had been, and he continued to get high marks from her, even for essays that made little use of unacknowledged sources. And so he became, for three years, an anthropologist.

(Before we lose sight of Miss Anscombe I should record she liked me, if not as much as she liked Stephen, and perhaps a little too much on account of what another teacher was pleased to call my 'pluck'. It was the example of Miss Anscombe that led me to answer, when asked what I intended to do with my life, that I'd like to be a teacher, an ambition that was maintained until the age of fifteen or so, when it became apparent that any livelihood involving intensive face-to-face work wasn't going to be the right one for me. Even when I was affecting to be satisfied with the prospect of doing paperwork for my brother while pursuing a course of autodidacticism (and this is in fact what happened – I was a clerk for Charlie until Stephen found copy-editing work for me, through his boyfriend of the time), Miss Anscombe endeavoured to persuade me that I too should go to university. My parents were of the same opinion, and I did go so far as to visit Celia one weekend. Most of her friends were very pleasant to me, but a shade too strenuously so. House-mates strolled into the kitchen and – finding me there – strolled straight back out again. It was unbearable: the lovely girls taking the sun on the grass below the library; the students passing, some with a glance for the boys, some with a glance for the girls, all with a glance to the right, where I cringed at Celia's side.)

Stephen's university years were not a thorough success. Required now to devote himself to a single subject, he was frequently bored. He was intimidated by students who, having been to public school, were wholly at ease from the very first day: Jeremy's father would collect him in a Bentley at the end of term; another had actually been to Samoa; another called a tutor by his first name, as though they were cousins. Some of his contemporaries were so smart they could read their Lévi-Strauss in the original. Seminars were like revivalist meetings, with everyone spouting paraphrases of *Orientalism*. Stephen himself spouted paraphrases of *Orientalism*. He thought it was the most amazing book he'd ever read, and he agreed with every word of it. Unfortunately he found that, while he was reading them, he agreed with every word of almost every book he read, even those that took issue with books by which he'd previously been similarly convinced. After a year he'd come to think that, although he could read as quickly as anyone and memorise facts with ease, he didn't have a thought in his head – not a real one, a thought he could call his own. His essays weren't expressions of his thinking: they were collages from which the seams had been adroitly erased. He was a fraud, except in the area of his emotional life, where at last he was fully and genuinely himself. It was for the boyfriends, and so as not to disappoint his parents (to whom he could never admit the slightest self-doubt) that

Stephen stayed the distance – and for the films. Discovering a passion for cinema, and finding that he absorbed film credits as readily as any other type of data, Stephen became the secretary of the film society at the end of his first year. Before long it had become in effect a one-man enterprise, with Stephen planning each term's screenings, doing most of the administrative work, and writing a programme note for every film. These notes began as little more than a list of credits but soon grew into mini-essays, and he took such pleasure in writing them that he began to wonder if he might have happened upon something for which he had a true talent, something that might even in some way become a means of earning a living. The re-evaluation was accelerated when one of his tutors, having read his programme notes for *Tokyo Story*, remarked that it was the best thing he'd written all term, which was a little dismaying, because Stephen had been putting a lot of effort into his course work – i.e. producing text-collages of ever greater complexity. But as exams approached he was obliged to reduce his extra-curricular activities, and his confidence suffered a setback when, after the final screening under his regime, he was approached by a second-year history student who introduced himself as 'something of a film buff' before pointing out a serious error in Stephen's notes for *Rome, Open City*. He proceeded to air several criticisms of the piece that had been handed out prior to the showing of *The Magnificent Ambersons*. Before the term was over the pugnacious historian had taken over Stephen's role at the film society, and though one or two people told Stephen that the programme notes were now as dull as train timetables, the image of himself as the *Guardian*'s future film reviewer had been destroyed. (The love of cinema has never waned, however. And it was at a cinema that he met Oliver, his spouse in all but name. A screening of Syberberg's *Hitler: A Film from Germany* at the National Film Theatre was what brought them together. When the lights went up they were the only two customers left in their seats.)

During the immediate post-university years, while waiting for his life-path to make itself visible, he took a variety of temporary jobs. He fitted kitchens with a friend of his father's, who soon had to let cack-handed Stephen go; he was briefly a bicycle courier (his ability to memorise the London A-Z was an advantage; his lack of courage in the face of London traffic was not); for a while he was a proof-reader; he was a sub-editor and film reviewer for a short-lived magazine; he was a courier again (collision with parked car; he'd been experimenting with contact lenses, at the suggestion of boyfriend who'd had to tell him that the whole geek-chic thing wasn't working for him any longer); he worked in the bookshop of the ICA; and then he got a job in the Horniman Museum, which is where a new passion possessed him. Surrounded by musical instruments from every cranny of the planet, he found himself being lured down a dozen different paths at once. Every month brought a new excitement: *zydeco, merengue, degung, qawwali*. He'd turn up at our house with a carrier bag full of music: 'You have just got to listen to this,' he would say, putting on a disc with such urgency it was as if he thought the thing might crumble in his hands if not heard immediately.

(Here is perhaps the place to mention that Stephen's promiscuous taste in music changed my brother's life. Having dropped by to see the parents on an evening when Stephen happened to be with me, Charlie heard an intriguing voice emanating from my room. He knocked, walked in and asked Stephen (standing by the door, in his customary posture of immobile ecstasy): 'Who on earth is that?' And thus, with a recording of Bill Monroe, was spontaneously born Charlie's love of the folk music of the United States. The relationship between Charlie and Stephen was transformed too. This relationship had improved in recent years, partly because they didn't encounter each other very often, now that Charlie was no longer living at home, but partly – as Charlie saw it – because Stephen himself had improved greatly: he was less ostentatious in his cleverness now (Charlie's view was that Celia had brought out the worst in him, but Stephen's new self-restraint was more the result of what he perceived to be his failures as a student than of the absence of Celia as cheerleader); he was less prone to affectations of otherworldliness (Stephen had indeed from time to time overplayed the thought-distracted persona, just as Charlie sometimes played up the stolidity); and he less frequently emitted the whiff of a person who believed himself to be spiritually superior to the rank and file money-grubbers of the world. Prior to the evening of Bill Monroe they had for some time been civil with each other, and once or twice had managed to conduct conversations without the aid of an intermediary. They could not, however, have been described as friends, not until the revelation of Bill Monroe.)

Let us complete the CV of Stephen Siviter. He stayed at the Horniman until he knew the museum so well he could have drawn a plan of the whole place from memory, marking every single stuffed bird and monkey skeleton, every hurdy-gurdy, *shamisen* and *nagaswaram*. Once the Horniman was exhausted, it was time to move on. An interlude of false moves followed: he reviewed films for a website (his last piece: 'Man Overbored' – on *Titanic*), reviewed CDs for a world music magazine (it went bust within a year), and worked in a number of shops – a bookshop, a charity shop, another bookshop, an outlet for Italian furniture where his monthly cheque wouldn't have bought him a half-share in any of the sofas he was selling. The sale of an unconscionably expensive dining table turned out to be a pivotal event. We needn't go into the details: suffice it to say that a fleeting relationship with the buyer of the table led to a job in a private gallery – owned by a friend of the buyer of the table – that specialised in Japanese and Chinese antiques, and this job led to a lowly position at the Victoria and Albert Museum, where Stephen embarked upon another burst of intensive self-education, which brought about his appointment to a considerably less lowly position at the V & A, which in turn led to a better-paid and more stimulating job at the Wallace Collection, whence he progressed to his current post at the Burrell Collection, where the nine thousand artefacts (tapestries, alabasters, stained glass, furniture, silver, table glass, paintings (Degas, Cézanne, Renoir . . .), Islamic art, items from ancient China, Egypt, Greece, Rome . . .) should keep him interested for a few more years. He's a happy man; the happiest man I know.

Janina would rather I didn't spend all day in here, typing away. 'What are you writing?' she asks, as if this activity were as peculiar as building a canoe out of matchsticks. I'm writing my memoirs, I tell her – the highs, the lows, the women I have known. She gives me a short smile and blinks three or four times, as though waiting for a noise to cease so she can resume our conversation. 'OK,' she says, 'but why stay up here? You can bring the laptop outside.'

'But I like my room,' I tell her.

'I'm glad you like it, but—'

'I know. It's not good for me.'

'It's not,' she agrees, then belatedly gets the point. 'OK,' she says. 'I get the message. I'll back off.'

An hour later, Ellen reports that Janina has been rigging up a screen on one side of the terrace, so it couldn't be more private.

'I'm on a roll,' I tell her. 'What shall I tell you?'

'Whatever you like,' she says. 'Something about yourself.'

I do a search for Dr Finnegan. It takes five minutes to find him – there he is, giving a lecture at King's College. He's retired now, and age has withered him. I don't recognise him, but it must be the same man; the CV fits.

Of Dr Finnegan I retain little more than the impression of a very tall man and a white coat, unbuttoned, over a scratchy-looking, peat-coloured waistcoat. I see also a beaky nose, and a ring that has a large green stone set into it. I'd only ever seen such rings on women's hands before. To the side of his desk, on the wall, hung a picture of a man with bright orange muscles instead of skin. The floor was covered with shiny lino, like the corridor outside, but the chairs on which my mother and I were sitting had a bright blue rug underneath them. My mother, when recalling Dr Finnegan, would invariably mention first the grey-green eyes and the way his hair was swept backwards off his forehead and temples in a style that was almost but not quite unruly. She imagined that he regarded himself as distinguished-looking. He'd pause after her questions and do a quick frown, as though her words needed to be translated into something cleverer before he could understand them, then he'd reply in the soothing murmur of a man talking a distraught woman into putting the gun down.

We were shown into the room and told that Dr Finnegan would be with us shortly. Ten minutes later he arrived, flinging back the door as if he were the busiest man in the world. He was followed by a dark-skinned nurse who took me by the hand and led me into an adjoining room, where I drank a glass of orange squash and read a comic. This I remember.

So: enter Dr Finnegan, the tails of his white coat flapping like the wings of the angel of the Annunciation. ('Hail, thou that art not so highly favoured.') 'There are Lisch nodules,' he explained, once the child was out of the way. An incomprehensible photograph was presented, ostensibly for clarification. 'In themselves they are nothing to be alarmed about. However, in combination with the macules—'

'Macules?'

'The spots.'

'Oh.'

'The café-au-lait macules and the Lisch nodules, taken together, are not good.'

'They're not?'

'No, I'm sorry to say. They're not good. Together, they are indicative of neurofibromatosis. The lump on Daniel's neck, Mrs Brennan, is a dermal neurofibroma.'

Hearing the name of her son's condition, my mother cast in her mind what manner of salutation this was. How, she wondered, could this be?

'Well,' proceeded Dr Finnegan, easing back in his chair, surrendering space to the enormous question that had now arisen between them, 'there are two possibilities. The first, of course, is that Daniel's condition is hereditary. In other words, that he has inherited it from yourself or from your husband.'

'But—' my mother began, and Dr Finnegan smiled and nodded, inviting her to articulate the thought, banal though it would inevitably be. 'But that's not possible. We haven't had these spots—'

'Macules.'

'These macules, or anything. If we had, we'd have . . . well, we'd—'

'But it is possible, Mrs Brennan. This is the most unpredictable of disorders. Often no signs are visible to the naked eye. None whatsoever. You might go through your entire life unaware that you were carrying it. You might have nothing more than these tiny imperfections in the eye. It can happen.'

'Oh God,' my mother sighed.

Dr Finnegan waited for her to uncover her face before he continued. 'The alternative,' he said, 'is that we're looking at a spontaneous mutation.' A pause, and then the plain person's version: 'Your son could well be the first in the family to have it.'

The word 'mutation' had concussed my mother: for a few moments her mind was populated with vague ideas of monsters, laboratories, panic-stricken scientists. When her thoughts regained coherence, she did not find Dr Finnegan's explanation persuasive. The notion that a disorder of such severity (and the fearsome name of the disease, plus Finnegan's frigid and fearsome manner, were proofs enough of its severity) might have arisen spontaneously within her son's body sounded as improbable as the proposition that I'd been infected by gamma rays from the Crab Nebula. Immediately convinced that she had unwittingly blighted her offspring (perhaps all three of them – 'no signs to the naked eye,' the doctor had said), she had been pierced by a shaft of guilt, and though Dr Finnegan's assurances had some palliative effect ('It's very far from uncommon, Mrs Brennan: almost half of the patients I've seen have had no family history'), the wound was still painful, and she was to suffer acutely until it had been established that I was indeed the solitary freak of the family. (Even then her guilt was transfigured rather than eradicated: she still felt obscurely that she was to blame for not contracting the disease herself, as if the faulty chromosome had been some sort of spore floating above the Brennan family, and she rather than her son should rightly have been the one to catch it.) 'There's no doubt that this is what it is?' she asked.

'None,' replied the doctor, in a tone of adamantine certainty, with a thin gloss of sympathy applied.

Head bowed like the handmaid of the Lord, my mother submitted to our fate.

'Fear not,' Dr Finnegan only now instructed her – or words to that effect. 'This is not as rare as you might imagine. Many people have it and get through life unhindered. Daniel's condition may progress no further than it has already.'

'The lump will go?'

'Of its own accord, no. But we can make it go away. Excision would be straightforward.'

'It won't grow back? You said it's unpredictable.'

'That is correct,' Dr Finnegan confirmed, bringing together delicately the fingertips of his raised hands before touching the hands lightly to his lips.

'So more could appear. It could stay the same or it could get worse.'

'That is possible, yes.'

'He's young. He has one now, so it must be likely he's going to get more.'

'There is no way of telling.'

So now the anguish of guilt was compounded by the anguish of uncertainty. It might have been better if she had been told that her son's body would continue to produce excrescences in riotous profusion, that his face would end up resembling a coral reef and his torso a monstrous root of ginger. Possibilities and probabilities tended to make my mother uneasy; she liked situations in which the variables were minimal. (Thus, whereas some girls might have found Charles Brennan – my father – a little deficient in spark and vim, in the eyes of Sylvia Wilkins – my mother – this manifestly steady young man was far more attractive than any flashy charmer. Celia might have been created specifically to drive her to the brink of madness.)

'But as I say,' Dr Finnegan went on, 'for many people it does not have a significantly detrimental impact upon their day-to-day lives. None at all, quite often.'

'For some it does, though,' my mother would have responded, lured by the glint of gloom.

'For some it does. Yes.'

'So what could happen? At worst.'

'Various things could happen, Mrs Brennan, but I think at this stage what we—'

'I want to know the possibilities.'

Dr Finnegan duly told her that we might expect further neurofibromas to develop. 'Nearly all adults with this disorder have dermal neurofibromas,' he explained. 'The lesions tend to appear, when they appear, from puberty.'

'So it will get worse. If you're talking about nearly all adults, that's a safe prediction.'

'Yes. But many neurofibromas are minor blemishes. And in many instances we can deal with them easily.'

'You can cut them out.'

'Yes.'

'And what else can go wrong?'

Reluctantly Dr Finnegan tallied the manifold complications, with the emphasis on infrequency wherever appropriate. Hyperpigmentation and hypertrichosis were mentioned, as were long bone dysplasia, scoliosis and optic gliomas. 'Reduction or loss of visual field,' he explained, then added the good news: 'Nearly all optic gliomas appear in the first four years of life, so we can be confident that Daniel is in the clear.'

'What else?' my mother persisted.

'A small percentage will develop facial plexiform neurofibromas. Some of these – a very small minority – may undergo malignant change.'

'How small a percentage? How small a small minority?' Dr Finnegan gave her the figures, which were indubitably small. My mother reverted to the question of the neurofibromas: he'd said that many could be dealt with quite easily – this implied that some could not. She wanted to know about these.

Dr Finnegan impressed upon her that by far the commonest complication of her son's condition was a degree of mental impairment, typically manifested as difficulties with visuospatial orientation, attention span and short-term memory. 'This is not an issue with Daniel, is it?' he encouraged her. 'Never had difficulties at school, has he?' My mother having agreed that this was so, I was brought back into the presence of Dr Finnegan. 'We'll monitor the situation,' he said, rising from his seat. 'But please, try not to worry. Neither of you should worry.' At the door he shook my hand. I remember that. His watch had a black face and lime-green hands.

Years later, my mother would say that her appointment with the horrible Dr Finnegan was the worst hour of her life. It wasn't the worst of mine. She relayed to me, as we hurried along the shiny, tangy corridors of the hospital, the essence of what the doctor had told her: in one or two percent of cases like mine, the illness may give rise to cosmetic problems. Those were good odds, I thought, and cosmetic problems sounded trivial – they were the sort of things that make-up could take care of. And I had quite enjoyed my visit: it was rather gratifying to be of such interest to these important medical people, and the nurse had been very nice to me too – she was from India, and had a lovely soft voice.

My mother and I walked to a bus stop not far from the hospital. We stood side by side, gazing down the road, and as the bus came into view she took a small, lace-fringed handkerchief from her handbag. Dust had been blown into her eye, she said, and I remember looking at the pavement and seeing quantities of grey dust swirling about, like a scaled-down sandstorm. The bus came to a halt and drove away without us; my mother hugged me strongly then we went to a café, where she bought me a large ice-cream in a glass. I remember this as well, and catching a glimpse of her looking at me as if I'd been away from home for months and might be going away again soon.

I don't know when I first noticed that my mother was subject to episodes of anxiety and heaviness of spirit, but some time before the consultation with Dr Finnegan I had come to suspect that I had an explanation for these troughs. Between my parents there was very rarely any show of discord, and so, with marital difficulties excluded as the cause, it seemed probable that the children were to blame. Looking after three offspring (and a husband whose contribution to the manual labour of the household rarely extended beyond an occasional turn with the tea-towel) was enough to rub the shine off any woman (as Celia, from the age of twelve or so, often pointed out to obtuse Charlie), and of course the burden must have been heavier when two of those offspring (after years of getting along just fine) were regularly in conflict. (In the years before the illness emerged I was the easy one, my mother would tell me. Post-diagnosis, I soon was not.) Photographs of our mother as a young woman gave support to this analysis. There she is on the pier at Margate, with a couple of friends from the typing pool, waving her arms above her head and laughing so wildly that she doesn't look like herself. Crossed-eyed, she sticks out her tongue as she paints the fence of the house in which Charlie was born. She runs down a grassy hill with her skirt tucked into her knickers. Sitting on a rock, wearing a polka-dotted sundress, she tilts her head back and gives the camera a joyful smile, a smile such as I cannot recall ever seeing, except in this and a couple of other pictures. There's a similar smile, with a hint of exhaustion about the eyes, in a photo of her holding new-born Charlie, and then the other kids arrive and the face becomes more strained with each year.

'That's what happens: women get knackered,' Celia informed her brothers, in a precocious show of gender solidarity. Charlie couldn't see that a woman's lot was terribly arduous, and was never convinced that the photographs of our worn-out mother proved anything. On this latter point he was right, but it was not until after she had died that this became apparent. Walking back from the cemetery on a Sunday afternoon, our father reassured Celia (it was the week of his birthday; Celia had come back for a few days) that he had a wealth of memories to keep him going. He had been fortunate to have had so happy a marriage, he told her. (Only to Celia would he ever have said this, though it was understood that Celia was permitted to pass on to her brothers as much as she saw fit to.) He knew of very few marriages that had been as solid as theirs, he went on, and Celia prepared herself to receive her father's habitual commiseration for her lack of success in the search for the right man. Instead, he remarked that the marriage of Sylvia's parents (and only to Celia was our mother ever referred to by her name – to the boys she was always 'your mother') had also been strong, and then there was a pause, a long pause, and Celia could tell, from a glance he gave her, that he had never spoken to her about whatever he was now on the point of telling her. She took his arm to lead him across the road. 'But you know,' he began, 'there was always a shadow. Her father. It all goes back to him.' In the half-hour that followed, Celia's understanding of her family was altered so markedly it was as if, she said, some of the pictures in the photo albums had suddenly changed from black and white to colour.

The maternal grandparents – Jim and Iris – were the ones we children preferred. When we went to their house we were let loose in the back room with a pile of games and scrap paper and coloured pens, and a pitcher of ginger beer and a plate of biscuits to keep us going until tea-time; at the house of Grandpa Stanley and Grandma Emily, on the other hand, we were confined to a corner of the room in which the grown-ups were talking (left unsupervised, we might have rearranged the cushions or pushed up the thermostat a degree or two), and were fed sandwiches that contained salmon paste spread to a depth of one molecule. Stanley and Emily made us conscious that we were being assessed according to timeless and stringent standards of behaviour (obedience and gratitude being the primary virtues), whereas Jim and

Iris seemed to like us for who we were. Grandpa Jim had remarkably soft hands that he would press against our cheeks
when we arrived, and he talked to us as if everything we said
was of interest. For myself and Charlie he'd make wooden
swords and boats, and for Celia he'd make doll-beds and
other items of miniature furniture. But when we turned up at
their house, we never knew if we would be seeing him. He'd
had to go out, Grandma Iris would apologise (she never explained where he'd had to go), but then one afternoon Celia
went to the upstairs toilet and heard a creak of springs from
the bedroom, and as soon as we were back home she told
me and Charlie what she'd heard. After that we were given
the truth: that Grandpa Jim suffered from headaches called
migraines, and these were sometimes so bad that he had to
stay in bed, in the dark, and not talk to anyone. That was the
story, and there was never any reason to question it.

Sylvia had told the same story to Charles Brennan, after
they had been courting for several weeks and he still had not
set eyes on his girlfriend's father. Charles and Sylvia had met
on the steps of the cinema, where they had gone to see *The
Ladykillers* – Charles alone, Sylvia with her mother. Leaving
the cinema, Mrs Wilkins tripped, toppling her daughter
as she fell, and it was Charles who came to the rescue, using a pristine handkerchief to bandage the wound on Mrs
Wilkins' shin. The next week, seeing Sylvia across the street,
he crossed to ask after her mother. The week after that, he
appeared in the shop in which she worked, and as she was
assisting him to select a scarf for his mother's birthday (a
birthday that was still four months off – not that she knew
this) he admitted that it was not coincidental that he'd chosen
this particular shop for his purchase. (He didn't yet confess
that he'd followed her all the way to the shop after their last

conversation.) His embarrassment at his own boldness was immediately appealing, as had been his solicitude towards her mother. The fact that – as she soon discovered – he'd been to France and Italy gave him a kind of glamour as well, but what made her realise how unusual he was, what above all else made her fall in love with him was his extraordinary patience. (Charles, for his part, would tell his daughter that he had known he was in love right away, when Sylvia had smiled at him on the steps of the cinema.)

Any other man, in the early weeks of courting, would have demanded to know why, all of a sudden, his sweetheart had to stay at home to look after her mother every night until some unspecified point in the future, and would not have been content to be told that it was a family problem which had nothing to do with the way she felt about him, and that one day she'd be able to explain exactly what was going on. Yet Charles did accept it, and when at last she did explain – that her father sometimes fell into the doldrums and found it impossible to speak to anyone except her mother, and that when this happened her mother had a very great need of her company – the delicacy of his sympathy made her cry, and within a month she had said she would marry him. The doldrums, as she always called her father's bad times, came upon him in the winter usually, but sometimes in summer too, as abruptly as a light being switched off; sometimes the darkness would last for no more than a few days at a time, but sometimes it would go on for weeks, and they would begin to think that, this time, there'd be no end to it. At his worst he would take to his bed, talking to no one, not even his wife. He had been like this since he was a child (he was an intelligent pupil, but his teachers didn't know what to do with a boy who could get a mark of eighty percent in a test, and only twenty percent in the same subject the following month; he left school as soon as he could), and when things became serious with Iris he had told her the truth about his affliction. Other girls had been unable to bear his moods, but Iris had succeeded (albeit not without crises along the way) in adapting to the wild climate of Jim's mind: she ensured that they made the most of the good spells, and when the darkness descended on him she would leave him alone, because this was all she could do for him. She would make up a bed for herself in the back room, and take him his meals (he might be barely capable of filling a glass of water), for which sometimes she would not receive as much as a word of thanks. During the terrible periods, when Jim could not work (he was an electrician, and poking a screwdriver into a socket is not something you want to be doing on days when you're having problems distinguishing left from right), she did the odd bit of temping. When her husband emerged again, she managed to resume their life as if the hiatus had merely been a suspension of normality.

For Sylvia, however, her father's depressions came to pervade the atmosphere of every day, not just the days when he was not himself and her mother was in need of her company nearly as much as her mother was needed by her father. Even when he was back with them, and she was expected to carry on as doughtily as her mother, she could not rid herself of her awareness that everything was precarious. At any moment, as an ordinary person might sneeze, her father could simply break. Each day was like tiptoeing across a fraying rope bridge that she knew might fall apart before she reached the other side. And sometimes her father would experience spasms of happiness that were almost as difficult for her to bear as his bouts of gloom: more than once he grabbed her without warning and squeezed her so hard that she'd felt her chest crackle; and there was a day on holiday that she could never forget, when she saw her father, as still as a statue, staring into a rock pool, and she couldn't bring herself to approach him, not knowing if he had plunged into misery or floated off into a trance of joy.

Sylvia too, in the early years with Charles, had occasional bouts of uncontainable happiness (he remembered in particular a twirling dance under oak trees, on a sunny day in Wales), some of them so acute that once or twice she worried that she might after all be a bit mad, like her father – but to Charles it was obvious that, more than anything else, it was relief at being freed from her life at home that accounted for these outbursts of skittishness, outbursts which became less frequent as a new and stable life replaced the old. (And as these brief interludes of radiance dwindled, she became subject to attacks of guilt at having left her mother to cope with her father alone.) So, to sum up, life with her parents had made Sylvia an adult at an age when other girls were still playing with skipping ropes – and an adult who, wherever she looked, saw fragility and impermanence before anything else.

Ellen says she's not happy about reading what I've written about my mother. 'I feel like I'm intruding,' she says. 'There are things here your parents wouldn't have wanted strangers to know.'

'You're not a stranger,' I tell her.

'To your parents I am,' she answers.

I point out that I'm merely reminiscing about my parents, as people do. The only difference is that talking isn't easy, so I'm writing it down.

'I know,' says Ellen, 'but somehow that makes a difference.'

'Why?' I ask her.

She doesn't know, but it does.

'Think of it as my diary,' I suggest. 'If I'm happy for you to read it, what's the problem?'

She's concerned that Charlie might not be pleased if he knew that she'd been told about things that his parents and grandparents had wanted to keep private. 'I'm not a stranger, OK, but I'm an employee, not family. There are boundaries,' she says.

So I ask Charlie to take a look. He has no objections, of course, but he has no recollection of being lectured by little Celia on the hardships of motherhood. Neither does he think the sandwiches of Stanley and Emily were quite as grim as I make out. He has a memory of Emily presenting us with a huge bowl of peaches or cherries; this rings no bells with me.

Charlie digs out some photos and Ellen brings them to me. Charlie can't put his hand on the one of my mother sticking her tongue out, but the others are here: Margate pier, running down the hill, sitting on the rock in her polka-dot dress, holding fresh Charlie. There are several of baby Charles and the subsequent infants; it's been many years since I've seen most of them. Ellen turns the pages slowly, as if fearful that the next spread will be the one to trigger an avalanche of sadness. 'Is this all right?' she asks, after the polka-dot snap, which is indeed the toughest.

I wake up: I'm on a lounger on the terrace, and while I've been asleep Ellen has moved the screen to keep the shade on me. She's on the phone, talking to Roy. Janina's at work. Closing the phone, Ellen looks at me as if she thinks I've overheard something that requires explanation, and then she begins to talk. She talks for nearly an hour.

In telling Charlie that she had separated from her husband, Ellen was perhaps slightly misleading in her choice of tense. Only when she came here did she leave the house in which she and Roy had been living for five years, initially as man and wife, latterly as largely autonomous co-occupants.

They'd been having problems for such a long time, says Ellen, that they were in effect already living apart when Roy revealed, a few months ago, that he'd been involved with another woman. It had begun early last year, when his workmate Max suggested that, instead of going for their customary Wednesday evening pint together, they could, for a laugh, drop in on the speed-dating session that was going on in a room above the bar. Since his wife had walked out on him, two years ago, Max had not once enjoyed the pleasures of female company. He was desperate, but not as desperate, says Ellen, as a woman would have to be to settle for an evening with Max, who smokes thirty a day, is somewhere in the region of thirty percent above his optimum body weight (if the fish and chip shop closed down he'd starve to death), and is infrequently sober after 7 p.m. (Roy is the Wednesday night boozing partner – there's a different one for each night of the week), and is in possession of less than a quarter of his hair, which he's dyed darker than a squaddie's boots. And he's a boring little sod as well. He builds model aeroplanes and spends every weekend flying them.

So Roy accompanied Max to the speed-dating event, where it would seem that Max took a fancy to Margaret the big-boobed sunbed-basted leg-waxer and fingernail technician, who responded by taking a fancy to his friend. The standard procedure at events like this, or so Ellen gathers from what she's heard, is for the women to stay in their seats while the men (invariably the larger contingent) circle the room, taking turns to blather on about themselves and their various misfortunes, most of which are to be attributed to the women they've had the bad luck to encounter. Roy – she'll say this much for him – is more a listener than a talker when you first meet him, so perhaps he stood out from the crowd in that respect. And of course he would have looked good alongside deadbeat Max. Anybody would. So Margaret and Roy hit it off, and things moved rapidly. On Sundays, when Roy was believed to be fishing (a routine observed throughout his marriage – Ellen even went along occasionally, and was never sure which was worse: staring at the water and waiting for something to happen; or watching the hideous fish gasping for air on the bank), he was in fact with Margaret. On Fridays, when he was supposed to be in the pub with whichever of his colleagues was in the mood for an after-work round or five, he was in the pub for no more than an hour, then he was with Margaret. Though he was coming home late, Ellen didn't suspect anything. She heard him crashing about in his room, and thought he was drunk, that's all. There wasn't a clue in the way he talked to her – he was the same old miserable Roy, until one day he was noticeably glummer than usual. Sitting at the kitchen table with a plate of something that had come out of a can, he was stirring his food as if waiting to be asked what was the matter, so she asked him, and he told her he'd met Margaret, that it hadn't been anything serious, and now it was over. He looked so sorry for himself, she wanted to punch him. 'I've been an idiot,' he told her, with a look that said he knew she couldn't forgive him right now but if he kept this expression on his face for long enough then maybe she would at least start to.

He told her everything, or what he said was everything. 'You must hate me,' he said, looking at his plate of can-contents as if it were a dollop of poison and that was all he deserved. She couldn't bring herself to speak to him.

Roy has had a great deal of practice at feeling sorry for himself, and is now very good at it. One of his favourite laments, first heard by Ellen a couple of weeks after they were married (she talks as if Roy came out of his shell as soon as the wedding was over, and was a far nicer person with the shell on) is that he didn't listen to his father when he was a kid. 'You're a bright boy,' his father would tell him, 'but you need to work harder.' His father wanted him to stay at school and get the most out of his education, but there was always something better than homework to do and Roy didn't get on with the teachers, so he was out of school at the first opportunity. He should learn a proper trade, his father told him. His father was a plumber. As long as people have bowels they'll need plumbers and plumbers earn decent money if they're any good, his father always said, but young Roy couldn't be bothered with an apprenticeship, and shoving his arm into a pipe full of crap never appealed much. He knew what he wanted to be: a long-distance lorry driver, like Uncle Terry, his father's younger brother. His father wasn't very close to his brother: Terry had been a handful as a boy, had later done time after helping himself to a vanload of jeans, and had developed into a severely sub-standard husband and father. Terry acknowledged that Trevor – Roy's father – had grounds for holding a grudge or two against him (as a kid, for example, he'd sold Trev's bike and pretended it had been stolen), but had no difficulty in persuading the boy Roy that the fundamental

problem with his dad was that he simply didn't understand
the call of the road. Driving had been the making of Terry: being on his own gave him time to think (about what, however,
was never precisely specified), and it was great to have a job
in which you drove your office all over the place. Trevor still
lived within ten miles of the estate they'd grown up on; he'd
been to the Algarve once or twice, and that was about it. Terry,
on the other hand, had been everywhere: he'd driven through
the Alps more times than he could remember; he'd eaten great
food on Spanish beaches; he'd seen forests in Germany, lakes
in Switzerland, topless hitchhikers in the south of France.
From time to time Uncle Terry would turn up and take Roy
for a ride in his lorry – it was best when they went out at night,
because Terry would turn all the lights on at once, so they were
driving into this wide corridor of light, with the engine making a noise that made him feel unstoppable. Occasionally the
cousins, Tom and Colin, would come along too, and Roy had
the feeling that he got along with Uncle Terry better than his
sons did. His parents pointed out that the surly cousins were
probably not best pleased that their father was away from
home so much, just as Aunt Louise's tendency to be a bit of a
moaner might have something to do with her having to cope
at home on her own so often, but more important to young
Roy was the affinity he had with his uncle, to whose faults he
remained blind until the day Terry failed to come home, having decided to start a new life with a woman in Birmingham
in whose bed, it was revealed, Terry had for a long time been
in the habit of recuperating from the rigours of the road.

By then Roy had become a long-distance driver and had
acquired a wife, Lauren. The marriage didn't last long: Lauren
couldn't cope with the absences and (as Roy tells it) the lower
than anticipated earnings. Not long after Lauren had fled, Roy

was driving on the M3 when he fainted. He was unconscious for no more than a second or two, but the next thing he knew he was bearing down on a queue of cars and it was only by slewing across the road that he avoided shunting them. He came to rest within a yard of an open-top Saab, whose driver was so stricken with terror that her fingers had to be prised off the steering wheel. Tests followed; nothing was found, but he was kept off the road for a few months, as a precaution. A couple of years later, on a sweltering day somewhere to the south of Lyon, he blacked out completely, moments after bringing his lorry to a halt. A form of epilepsy was suspected, and his licence was revoked for five years, during which period he held down a desk job with a haulage company. Shortly before he was due to be allowed back behind the wheel of a truck, Roy keeled over at his desk, and that was the definitive end of his dream of a life on the motorways. He's now a pen-pusher for a different haulier, a job that makes him stir-crazy. The world, as Ellen says, is stuffed with people who hate what they have to do for a living, but with Roy it's as if he's been singled out for unfair treatment. His first marriage broke up because he was on the road too much, and his second broke up because he wasn't on the road at all – therefore, he can't win. That's the way he sees it, says Ellen. He carries on, she says, 'like he's an astronaut being forced to work in MacDonald's.'

Back to the main story. In the weeks following the revelation of the dalliance with Margaret, penitent Roy was often to be found in the kitchen, wearing his Death Row face. Evenings with Max were suspended; most Fridays he stayed away from the pub; some Sundays, even, he stayed at home. He thought they should have another go at making it work, he told her, as if everything had been absolutely fine until he'd made this one silly mistake, whereas in reality they'd slowly ground to a standstill a long time ago. When he'd told her about Margaret it was like turning off the life-support machine on someone who was never going to come round again. 'I know you must hate me,' he kept saying, but she didn't hate him, she says. If anything, she was almost pleased that he'd done something to give them a push, otherwise God knows how long they'd have carried on as they were, living together only because they were too worn out by each other to make the effort to move out.

With reluctance Ellen takes the laptop and reads what I've written. Five seconds later she's frowning. 'I didn't mislead anyone,' she tells me, then the face settles into an expression of mild disgruntlement. The eyes move quickly, simply to get it finished as soon as possible, but after a minute or so an approximation to a smile appears, at the description of Margaret. 'Not exactly what I said, but it's her all right,' she says. She doesn't remember saying that much about Roy in Terry's lorry, and the idea of the life-support machine definitely didn't come from her, but it's what she meant all right. I promise her that I won't write anything about her that I wouldn't be happy for her to read.

When I ask, she says firmly that she and Roy are never going to get back together, yet there's a hint of over-emphasis in her insistence that Roy is deluding himself if he thinks there's any chance of reconciliation. 'It's pathetic,' she says, and I detect an exasperation with herself at being unable to rid herself of sympathy for him. 'He thinks he's the King of the Road, but the fact is he hardly knows how to make a slice of toast. A few weeks I've been gone, and it's like he's been stuck on a desert island. He looks terrible,' she says, then winces at what she's just said.

In the course of a routine scan of the terrain I spy an old man who resembles very closely the old man I saw before, in the Land Rover, in the rain. He's standing at a gate, beside a tractor, and seems to be involved in an altercation with the driver – the driver of the Land Rover, I'm almost certain. The faces are not perfectly legible from this range, but the gestures are clear: the driver's arm goes sideways in a hurling motion several times; in reply, the walking stick is flourished with some vigour. The old man appears to be in mid-sentence when the tractor is driven off; he takes a swipe at the adjacent vegetation and sets off down the lane. I keep the lens trained on him as he tacks slowly from verge to verge, muttering all the way. The muttering is garnished with some snarling, directed at an imagined nuisance to his left. He's about fifty yards away, nearing the house of the Mercedes, when an object in the gutter appears to seize his attention. He stoops; his free hand dangles above the tarmac, squeezing at the air. Having straightened as much as he can, he stirs the ground with the ferrule of the stick. Considering the problem, he scowls at the empty street, and is so immersed in perplexity that he doesn't hear the young woman who's cycling at speed down the lane he's just descended until she's past him. Too late he calls out to her – or perhaps she hears and, knowing who he is, decides not to stop. He remains at his post for at least five minutes, hunched in vulture-like vigilance over this portion of gutter, then help at last arrives: a car pulls out of the drive of the third house from where he's standing, and he waves his stick at it as if he's been adrift on a raft for a month and is seizing his last chance of rescue. The driver gets out of the car and, thinking something is seriously amiss, trots over to him. Directed by the stabbing of the stick, she bends to pick an item off the tarmac. She places it in the proffered hand, seeming to receive nothing more than a nod for the prompt performance of this civic duty. Smiling to herself, she returns to the car. The moment she leaves his side the old man takes a handkerchief from his pocket and starts polishing; that done, he turns the thing over and over on his palm, grimacing, disgusted by its failure to turn out to be anything better than a coin.

Ambroise Paré on the thirteen causes of monsters: 'The first is the glory of God; the second, his wrath; the third, too great a volume of semen; the fourth, too small a volume; the fifth, imagination; the sixth, constriction of the womb; the seventh, the inappropriate sitting position of the pregnant mother, who remains seated too long with her thighs crossed or pressed against her belly; the eighth, by a fall or blows struck against the belly of the pregnant mother; the ninth, hereditary or accidental illness; the tenth, by the decay or corruption of the semen; the eleventh, by the mingling of semen; the twelfth, by the scheming of vagrant beggars; the thirteenth, by demons.'

The walk proves to be too ambitious: the gradient is more arduous than it appears from up here. Instead, I veer down the lane that leads to The Meadows – this, I learn from the billboard on the junction, is to be the name of the prestige development that is rising a short distance beyond the scope of my window. The name is emblazoned in an extravagant cursive script above an image of life as it shall be in this enclave of architectural easy listening. A computer-generated couple (he in blue polo shirt and fawn slacks; she in golden sun-dress), strolling on the smooth and lustrous pavement, are waving to another couple (he in red polo shirt and fawn slacks; she (approximately Asian, lest we jump to the wrong conclusion as to what the term 'exclusive' means in this context) in white sun-dress), who are taking the air on the slender balcony that fronts the upper storey of their spacious and highly desirable property. Four or five computer-generated executive cars are parked on a road that gleams like an avenue of lacquer. At the moment the road is a track of mud and gravel, not the easiest terrain to negotiate in the dark, and I'm about to turn back when there's an owl's cry from somewhere ahead – a peculiarly forthright cry, like a sound effect. (Aluminium clouds scudding across face of moon; cripple lost in contemplation of the interstellar vacancies: cue owl.) I aim the torch, and the beam strikes the timbers of an unfinished roof, producing a clatter of wings to the left of where I'm pointing. I rake the air with the light, sensing that the bird is flying towards the trees, but I can't hit it. On the way back, however, I strike lucky. Hearing a disturbance in the grass beside the road, I halt and wait. Something is foraging along the ditch, twenty or thirty feet ahead, sniffing as it goes, then the sound of brushed grass stops, and there's a patch of motion in the gloom directly in front of me. On with the torch, and it's a direct hit: a hefty badger waddling down the road, exactly in the centre, as if steering by the white lines.

Janina on the phone to Freddie, very displeased. 'It takes less than an hour,' she repeats; one would think she was talking to a builder who'd let her down yet again, rather than to her son. Ellen reports that Janina told her that Freddie was having to work all hours at the moment, and Ellen could see that she was embarrassed at having to make excuses for him. 'What do you know about the boys?' I ask her. She's been told what they do for a living, but not much more.

Ellen is convinced that Janina has something on her mind – other than the monster in the attic, that is. What has given rise to this suspicion? 'I just have this feeling that there's something going on. She'll talk to me about you, but there's something else, I think.'

'And what does she have to say about me?'

'Well, for one thing she thinks you think she's a Stepford Wife. You and Celia.'

'That's not what I think,' I tell her.

'That's what I told her.'

'And what did she say?'

'"Maybe it isn't, maybe it is."' Then she adds, as though refusing to back down: 'I like her a lot.'

By the time Peter and Freddie reached school age they were remarkably mature and attractive children: imaginative, considerate, humorous, attentive, polite, et cetera, et cetera. They were, everyone agreed, a credit to their parents. Chiefly, it must be said, they were a credit to their mother, who had assumed full-time responsibility for their upbringing (no nannies for these boys, and she regarded nurseries as little better than battery farms for small hooligans), while Charlie assumed responsibility for earning the requisite cash, a function he performed so conscientiously that from Monday to Friday his sons barely saw him. It must be made clear that this deeply conventional arrangement was not dictated by any aversion on Charlie's part to the mess and tedium of parenthood. Far from it: no man was ever keener to sterilise teats and liquidise bananas, but his opportunities to partici-pate in these joyous chores were necessarily confined to the weekends, because the infancy of the boys coincided with the rockiest episode in the history of the business that our grandfather had founded. This was the period in which Charlie rescued the Brennan family enterprise and set it on the path to becoming what it is today, and Janina ensured that his boys grew up fully aware that their father, though for several years a somewhat peripheral presence, was every bit as devoted to them as she was. And, conversely, the boys from a young age understood that their mother's devo-tion, though absolute and freely given and a source of the profoundest pleasure, nonetheless entailed a great deal of work, which was not to be regarded as a less valuable or less demanding form of labour than the salaried work of men. Inculcated with a deep respect for work in all its aspects, the Brennan boys were never idle, and no teacher ever had to tell them to keep quiet and pay attention. For Peter and Freddie, teachers ranked just below parents in the hierarchy of estimable adults.

Their Aunt Celia, of course, was a teacher, and their mother often impressed upon them what a difficult job she had, teaching adults to speak English, which was a very hard language to learn if you weren't born into it. Aunt Celia, however, was a special case. She lived in a foreign country – or rather, she lived in one country one year and a different country the next, which was even more exciting. It was never clear why Auntie Celia had moved from Italy to Spain and then to Portugal. The boys assumed that her job must be very important if she was being asked all the time to travel from one part of the world to another. When she came to visit, she brought an air of holiday with her. Her skin was always several shades darker than their father's, and she wore interesting clothes: multicoloured shawls and heavy plastic bangles and big earrings, like an actress. She had seen so many things and had so many stories to tell, and whenever she came to London she brought them terrific presents, like the box of crystals from the Italian cave and the little black bull that pawed the ground with its hooves. Nearly all the aunts of their friends were married, whereas Auntie Celia had a boyfriend – not just one boyfriend but different boyfriends, which was confusing because Auntie Celia was the same age as their mother, but this just made Auntie Celia even more mysterious. And when Auntie Celia came back to London to live, it was wholly in keeping with her image that the new boyfriend was not a man who worked in an office – he was an artist, sort of, and was going to be famous.

When Celia came back from Lisbon the boys were six and seven years old; when she departed they were nine and ten. This period – Celia's last sojourn in London – might be seen as the Golden Age of our generation of the Brennan family. Charlie had by now turned the company around; from Monday to Friday he was still out of the house for ten hours each day, but it was no longer necessary for him to spend whole evenings at work, and alarming letters from the bank were a thing of the past. The intra-familial relationships were at their best: Celia, charmed by the boys, had nothing but praise for Janina's talents as a mother, and for Charlie's unexpected creativity in devising ways of keeping his sons entertained, no matter what the cost to his personal dignity; Janina and Charlie, having been impressed by Celia's tenderness with the infant Peter and the frequency with which, unprompted, she had volunteered to lend a hand, particularly in the months before and after Freddie was born (hence disappointment when Celia went through with her decision to leave), were even more touched by the warmth of the affection that grew between aunt and nephews (hence more acute disappointment when Celia re-emigrated), while never making the mistake that so many others had made, of bemoaning Celia's childless condition. It was clear to them that aunthood was as close to motherhood as Celia wished to get, certainly for the time being, possibly for ever.

The family circle was completed by myself. I had by now been re-integrated into the world of Peter and Freddie, having spent some time on the sidelines. Peter had been introduced to me soon after he was born, and I saw him regularly in the first year of his life. Whenever Charlie and Janina visited the parents and myself, Peter came too. But with Freddie's arrival things changed. For a while it was simply too tricky for Janina to get out of the house: the practicalities of caring for one neonate plus a highly active one-year old would have been enough to tether her to the home, even without the complications of Charlie's schedule. So it was necessary for the grandparents – with whom I resided – to travel to see the boys, which they were perfectly happy to do.

After six months or so, however, Freddie had become the ideal baby, sleeping through the night, rarely crying, eating well, et cetera, and Janina had achieved a steady routine. Charlie was still working the hours of a junior doctor, but nonetheless it would have been possible for them all to stay for a night at the weekend: beds could easily have been rigged up for everyone. But when Janina and Charlie eventually came over again, they left the boys in the care of a babysitter for a couple of hours. They'd all managed to take a week's holiday in Switzerland without any apparent problems, but a five-mile excursion within Greater London was an insurmountably complex operation, it appeared. There was a second visit from Charlie and Janina, minus offspring. On this occasion Charlie, with excruciating tact, confirmed that my supposition was correct. Exposing the very tiny Peter, sparingly, to the bizarre form of his uncle had not been contentious, given the rudimentary state of his cognitive apparatus, but he was now a considerably more sophisticated little entity – he was acquiring a sense of the abnormal, but was of course far too young to understand what he was seeing. 'I think we have to wait until he's a bit older,' said Charlie, meaning that this was what Janina thought. She was quite right: I might have terrified the child. And so, pending the ripening of the nephews' faculties of comprehension, I stayed out of their sight.

It became known to them that there was an uncle, and that this uncle wasn't well. The question of where this uncle lived was fudged until the evasion became unsustainable. 'Why don't we ever see him?' Peter began to ask. The truth was broached; a picture was shown to Peter, who reacted more or less as Janina had expected he would. He had nightmares. Then one day he asked to see the picture again. He put it on the table and stared at it for five minutes without looking up, as if someone had bet him that he couldn't do it. 'I want to see him,' he announced. He may have been only six years old, but Peter knew his own mind.

(And at this point let's note that one of the cardinal rules of Janina's method of mothering was that there was never to be any baby-talk in the house, because baby-talk was a hindrance to the child's development. Dogs were dogs, not doggies. Cats were cats, never pussy cats. That neither of her children ever threw a tantrum was directly attributable, she was convinced, to their having been treated as rational beings from the outset.)

The reintroduction to Peter was arranged. He was brought into my room by his mother – she had her hands on his shoulders, to brace him against the shock. 'Do come in,' I said to him, in as mellifluous a voice as I could muster, and Peter obediently took two steps forward and looked at his mother, fearful that she might leave him there. 'How are you?' I asked, and Peter squeaked: 'I'm fine.' I invited him to sit down; there were chairs, but Peter sat down on the spot where he was standing. Janina squatted beside him and directed his attention to the big new television in the corner. 'We could watch something later,' I suggested. I asked him what his favourite programmes were, but he couldn't remember. He looked to his mother again. I thanked him for coming to see me and said that I hoped he'd visit again, which he did, a month or so later, and this time he stepped into the room alone. We watched cartoons; I concentrated on the screen, giving him time to study the uncle's face unobserved. 'Does it hurt?' he asked, and when I told him that it didn't he replied, very seriously: 'That's good.'

On his second visit, he came in carrying some drawings he'd done, of Batman and Spiderman. On his fourth or fifth visit, he brought Freddie in. That didn't go well. Emerging from the lee of his brother, Freddie instantly stepped back, pulling at Peter's hand, as if I were an animal on a chain and he was afraid they were standing too close. 'Yes' and 'No' were I think the only words that Freddie uttered in the five minutes he was in my presence. In the following months, Freddie on occasion joined me and Peter for half an hour of Bugs Bunny, but he was never to be as comfortable with me as his brother had become within a mere month.

Both boys, as I say, loved Celia, but Freddie's attachment to her was especially intense. Auntie Celia was a bit bonkers and always ready for a spot of rough and tumble (not one of his mother's strong suits), and could also be pretty and ladylike. And Celia, though she would never admit it, had a particular fondness for the softer lad; Peter, at times, was a somewhat unnerving boy. You might come across Peter in the garden, staring open-mouthed at the antics of a starling, as if it were a stray from the rainforests of the Amazon. Often, while the family was watching TV, Peter would go into a reverie, with his eyes trained for minutes at a time on a place an inch or two above the screen. Death seemed to be on his mind more often than was normal in one so young. The folklore of the family has preserved the day on which, aged three, Peter insisted that they should cross the road before they reached the cemetery, because he knew that cemeteries were where people died, so if you didn't want to die you had to keep clear of them. His questions about death and infinity were never answered satisfactorily by his parents. Aged six he was seized by a fear of being buried alive, a fear that grew to be a terror that kept him awake night after night, trembling as if in a fever, and led to sessions with a child psychologist who concluded, correctly, that he was being bullied at school. (Exemplary though they were in the eyes of teachers and other elders, neither Peter nor Freddie was immediately popular with their classmates; gung-ho Freddie's standing soon improved,

but sport-loathing Peter's entourage was never extensive.)
Peter was an unusual boy, and I became very fond of him.
I remember him coming up to my room one afternoon in
spring. Holding one hand cupped over the other he crept
towards me, saying nothing, smiling as if he were about to
reveal something incredible. He raised his hands to my face
and parted the thumbs slightly, so I could peer into the cav-
ity of his palms and see in there the insect he'd just caught.
'This creature,' he murmured, 'is alive for only one day,'
and as he peered at the captured insect his frown suggested
that his mind had been occupied by an idea that was impossible to grasp in its entirety and therefore thrilling. For his
tenth birthday he was given the telescope; they set it up in
the garden of my parents' house, and I remember Peter's
expression when he stood back from the eyepiece to let
Freddie take a look: it was a smile of astonishment, which
then took on an abstracted quality, as if he were hearing in
his head a succession of questions that he couldn't answer
but which he knew had to be answered.

This may be the fancifulness of hindsight. But I can hear
in my head, as clearly as a recording, Peter telling me 'Light
is less ductile than gold', as if he'd made the discovery that
morning, and as if the very word 'ductile' was a treasure of
adult knowledge. This was followed by a pause, in which
it became evident that the uncle was failing to appreciate
the enormous repercussions of this announcement, and
then there came an explication – with the aid of diagrams
– of how it could be proved, very simply, that there were
parallel universes, in which Peter and I existed, but in many
different forms. 'You see?' he shouted, jabbing his pencil
through the paper. He would have been thirteen or fourteen.
I didn't see. None of the family saw. His grandmother,

listening to his news about black holes and whole galaxies rushing away at unimaginable speeds, would smile and try not to look appalled; his grandfather, no less bemused, found it easier to adopt a demeanour of fascination, which wasn't wholly a pretence; his parents, startled and proud, strove to make some sense of it all, but almost none of it made sense, and it was saddening, a little, that their boy was so quickly disappearing into a world that was beyond them. (And with each month it was becoming clearer that the Brennan commercial dynasty would be coming to an end with Charlie. Neither son underestimated his father's talents; neither ever expressed, except in infancy, any interest in following in his footsteps.) Even his brother was often baffled – and Freddie was smart and scientific, albeit in a more pragmatic way. Mechanisms and systems were Freddie's speciality; quasi-philosophical speculation he was happy to leave to his brother. (On Peter's weblog, should you wish, you can read some of his thoughts on quantum gravity – *If the deep structure of spacetime is that of a causal set . . .* The text hereafter is off-limits to the layperson.) Whereas Peter came to regard his visits to the uncle as an opportunity to instruct and confuse, Freddie was more a chap for computer-based entertainment and technological advice. (I should say that, even through the turbulent years of adolescence, both boys came to see me quite frequently – once a month in Peter's case, rather less in Freddie's. Freddie never came without Peter.)

In the summer of his second year at university Freddie took a barely paid job at a company that developed computer games. He took along a neat little programme that he'd written, and a full-time job was quickly offered. Freddie reasoned that there wasn't much point going back to university to sweat over exams just to get a degree that was only of use as a way into a job of the type that was now his for the taking, so he quit university, to his parents' dismay. This dismay quickly evaporated with Freddie's rapid promotion. One day, says Freddie, he's going to be earning a packet – and living in the States. Making a packet is not one of Peter's priorities, and neither has he ever shared his brother's obsession with hi-tech make-believe. But Peter is fond of his brother and wants him to have a rewarding life, so if Freddie finds pleasure (and profit) in crashing virtual cars and slaughtering virtual stormtroopers and falling off virtual snowboards, so be it.

Charlie and Janina have always been commendably even-handed with their sons. Observing the family together, one would never observe anything that might lead one to suspect that either parent in any way favoured one boy over the other. With Charlie, I believe, there is no underlying preference. The paternal love, now that the boys are adults, has perhaps a stronger element of self-distancing than the maternal; it approximates more closely to admiration. For Janina, I think, the situation is different. I wouldn't say that she loves the elder son any less than she loves the younger, but Freddie inhabits the same world as she does; he gets a kick out of many of the things she gets a kick out of, and their dislikes often overlap as well. (Hot weather and folk music, notably – more on the latter later, perhaps.) Freddie likes tennis; Janina likes tennis; Peter – whose hand-eye co-ordination was once compared by a games master to that of a blindfolded drunk – has an aversion to all ball games. Janina enjoys skiing, and is proficient at it; Freddie took to skiing like a sparrow to the air; Peter regards ski-resorts as a heinous form of landscape abuse. (The family's customary holiday destination – Munich and environs – might be regarded as unusual, but it was chosen partly as somewhere that might appeal to the increasingly divergent temperaments of the siblings, and proved to be an excellent choice. One day they'd go skiing (or hiking, depending on the season), the next day they'd do the greatest science museum in the world. This was the template: hike/ski – Deutsches Museum – hike/ski – Deutsches Museum. Freddie liked the museum too, but not three times in a single week, so Janina would take him elsewhere while husband and number one son returned to the never-ending galleries of scientific knowledge. Pale Janina's intolerance of intense sunlight made summertime in the Mediterranean inadvisable. They did risk a week in Cyprus once, where she spent most of the week indoors.) Other instances of the deep congruency of Janina and Freddie could be adduced, but for now suffice it to say that they have been well attuned to each other for a considerable time, which is why Janina is particularly aggrieved by Freddie's failure to visit us. She's worried too about some aspects of his lifestyle, having noticed at Christmas that he had developed a new nose-rubbing mannerism.

The nasal fidgeting was something I noticed myself when Freddie last visited me. I hadn't seen him for a long time and it struck me that he was strangely twitchy. But he was on good form, and very happy with his latest girlfriend, the lovely Valerie. A month or so before I saw him he'd taken Valerie down to meet the folks. He'd told them a little about Valerie Johnson – that she was a layout designer for a magazine, that she was gorgeous and intelligent, that he'd met her at a club in Covent Garden – but he hadn't explicitly told them that Valerie's parents were from Trinidad, and although his mother on saying goodbye had given Valerie a protracted hug (a blessing conferred on few girlfriends at first meeting), there was nonetheless a perceptible self-consciousness to the evening, especially in the conduct of his mother, who was distinctly quieter than usual, as if afraid she might violate some unknown protocol that should be observed with a black person. There's no way that his parents are in any way racist, Freddie insisted – it was a new experience for them, that's all. I think this is genuinely what he believes, and he may well be right, but Celia might take a somewhat different line, having several years ago, when staying overnight with Charlie and Janina in London, been taken aback by a remark made by Janina in response to a salvo of high-volume reggae from the sound system of a car that had stopped outside, a remark which Celia relates as juxtaposing the crudity (or, as some would put it, warmth and spontaneity) of African and African-derived cultures with the more sophisticated creativity of civilisations nurtured in the beneficent mildness of temperate zones. Celia believes she has also discerned that Janina has a particularly strong aversion to those recordings in her husband's collection in which the performers are not white, and reports that she once felt compelled to point out to her sister-in-law that in the final analysis we are all Africans – which prompted the rebuke: 'Don't be silly.' And Celia is also convinced that for Janina one of the many attractions of this corner of England is its population's un-Londonlike homogeneity of pigmentation.

But however awkward the introduction of Valerie might have been, there are several other reasons for Freddie's apparent reluctance to come down here. He is a very busy lad – it's a competitive business that he's involved in, and mere nine-to-fivers soon go to the wall. Valerie is very busy too – the magazine is doing well, and deadlines are deadlines. Their weekends, when there's no work to be done, are packed with action. Furthermore, there's the fact that Freddie thinks this corner of England is (and here I quote him exactly) 'the land of the unburied dead.' (Peter, on the other hand, thinks it's OK. Almost everywhere is OK with Peter – his immediate environment has never been of overwhelming importance to him. A room with a door and a desk is all that Peter needs.) And of course there is one other factor to consider: the sight of me makes Freddie feel a little queasy.

In order to enhance the commercial potential of my memoirs, I explain to Charlie, I may have to exaggerate a little: I was kept in a cage and fed on fish-heads for ten years, that sort of thing. I have a title: *Is There Life Before Death?* 'I'm sure it'll do well,' says Charlie. Pause. Then: 'But seriously, is that what you're doing?' The dominant tone is one of encouragement, but there's a small measure of unease in the mix. 'No,' I tell him. 'I'm just keeping myself entertained. Whistling in the dark.'

Celia is due in forty-eight hours, ETA 6 p.m., but she will certainly be late, as Janina tells Ellen, making the sister-in-law's unpunctuality sound like a personal slight. I explain to Ellen that Celia believes that she's doomed to be unpunctual. Mishaps happen to her in a way they don't happen to other people: keys suddenly, at the worst possible moment, become jammed in the lock; traffic jams materialise around her as if her car were a magnet. She was once late in joining a group of friends because of a signal failure on the Swiss rail network. How many times does that happen? It's fate.

A morning in eighteenth-century pastoral mode: washes of pale yellow light on the grass; sheep perched on the tips of forty-foot shadows; a lethargic stampede of clouds; thin dressing of mist about the trees. From the shadows of the houses I guess it's approximately 6.20. I check the clock: it's 6.23. I have become a country boy already; the sun is my chronometer. The day disappoints, however. By noon the sky has decayed to the colour of exhausted denim, and that's how it stays throughout the afternoon.

3

'I'm sorry. Sorry sorry sorry,' Celia begins, with an eye-roll of self-exasperation. The intention had been to take the train down, but her friend Christine had insisted that she borrow her car – the lesser of the household's vehicles (a two-year-old Audi), but still more luxurious than anything Celia has been driving recently. So Celia readily acquiesced to the proposal and took the opportunity to stop somewhere along the way, or more or less along the way, to see some garden that's open to the public for one week of the year only. And, having seen the garden, she took a shortcut that turned out not to be a shortcut because a road was being dug up and she had to take a detour which worked out longer than the original route would have been. One of the tyres looked soggy as well, so she stopped to put some air in it, but the pump at the garage where she noticed the problem wasn't working properly, and she had to find another one, and so on and so on. Bemused by the volume and pace of the performance, Ellen can do nothing but smile. Celia is already getting on her nerves.

The occasion calls for something special, says Charlie, who has decanted a couple of dusty bottles; with no satirical intent, I think, Celia copies him in raising her glass to peer through the wine before tasting it. 'Sensational,' is her judgement, and Charlie accepts the compliment with a faux-smug nod. This get-together, says Celia, is the most exciting evening she's had for ages. She explains to Ellen that she's teaching English to groups of businesspeople, and most days she isn't out of the school before ten o'clock, so her social life is in tatters. One of her pupils, Mr Orlandi, who is something fairly big in radiators and lives with his wife and four teenaged children in an apartment across the street from his mother, had let it be known that he'd not be averse to some after-hours activity, but hanky-panky with Mr Orlandi is not her idea of fun. 'Holding on to the last shreds of self-respect,' she says, smiling at Janina, whose laugh doesn't spread to her eyes. Mr Mascarucci has phoned his brother from Tunisia, promising to come back soon, she informs us; Mr Mascarucci, she explains to Ellen, ruined her previous place of employment by siphoning the school's cash into bank accounts as yet untraced; 'the effing finance director – can you believe it?' A wince-smile from Janina.

Under questioning from Celia, Ellen summarises her employment record in the fewest words compatible with politeness; ditto her personal history – Roy's name is not mentioned. Janina shares a few items of local news, with emphasis on the asylum-seekers issue; Celia, providing the Italian angle, talks about the gypsies in Florence (no mention of her sweeper), then excuses herself – she needs a fag. 'Trying to give up,' she tells Ellen. 'Tried nicotine gum, nicotine patches, hypnosis, acupuncture, yoga, alcohol. Last year I tried willpower. Three days that lasted. Hopeless,' she says, with a shrug for Janina.

I take her arm and we go out into the garden. 'So, how are things?' I ask her. Lips compressed, she considers how frank an assessment of her current situation she should give, then answers: 'Broke. Well, not exactly broke. Next to nothing in the way of liquid assets. Day-to-day revenue unhealthy. And I don't know what I'm doing. Middle-aged, semi-employed and semi-skint,' she sings and she smacks her thigh, marvelling at her achievement of such comprehensive failure. She may have to think about coming back to England, she says, as if this would be tantamount to giving up on life. Before that, however, she's going to try starting her own school, probably with Elisabetta, possibly with another friend who might be able to stump up some cash. They've found premises near the university: good-sized rooms, in need of refurbishment, but perfectly located. 'Snag is, start-up costs. Deficiency of funds on my side,' she laments, hands upturned, as though inviting a downpour of money. Even if she empties her account, and Elisabetta is on board, and the unnamed third party as well, she's still going to be a few thousand quid short. She's going to have to have a word with Charlie. 'Perhaps he'd be interested?' she suggests. 'Could earn a nice return on his investment. He wouldn't notice it, would he? Ten grand. He can afford it. Fifteen, tops. He'd hardly miss it,' she says, but already the credibility of the plan is beginning to dwindle. 'What do you think? Not a hope, is there?' she asks, as Janina announces that coffee is ready.

Developments with the step-sweeper. Two days ago Celia took him the list she'd promised. It was briefly encouraging that he remembered who she was: as she came up the steps he stopped what he was doing and raised a hand to her. 'How are you?' he asked her, grinning. She knew this was going to be a tricky encounter, however, when he pulled from his pocket – as if it were an abusive letter he suspected her of having sent – the tissue on which she'd previously written the names for him.

'I'm fine, thank you,' she replied.

His brisk nod quite clearly said that it didn't surprise him to learn that she was fine. He came immediately to the point: 'These are no good,' he told her, opening out the tissue to display her list. 'All of these I try and they are all not good. This one' – pointing to the map she had sketched – 'is not here.'

Celia apologised for the inaccuracy of her drawing, though she knew the restaurant in question was still in business, in the street she'd named. 'You didn't find it?' she asked.

'All are no good,' he said, stuffing the tissue back into his pocket. He folded his arms and regarded her in fierce and doleful accusation.

At this point, Celia admits, she was tempted to get away promptly. The reason she didn't, or so she says, is that it seemed possible he might clout her with the broom if she tried to retreat. 'I have some more,' she said, passing the second list to him, plus a map from the tourist office, on which she'd highlighted the relevant streets. He took it sullenly. 'I know it's difficult,' she said to him, while he scanned the new list. She heard herself: a duchess commiserating with a peasant at the failure of the harvest.

'This is why I ask you,' he responded, as if he believed her to be – or had believed her to be – as influential as the head of a masonic lodge. He worked through the names, checking each against the map, and when he was done he folded each piece of paper neatly, unzipped his jacket (the same jacket as before) and posted them into the inner pocket. He glanced at her, and the brevity of the glance seemed to signify that they both knew that this was a waste of his time, but then he reached into another pocket and took out the envelope, from which the photograph was again removed. 'Ilinca,' he said, putting a finger to the woman's face. The fingernail was the colour of urine, tipped with a thick arc of black. 'Mircea. Constantin,' he said, touching the children. 'Petru,' he named himself, jabbing a thumb onto his chest with such force that a tiny boom came off the breastbone. 'Your name?' he demanded.

'Meredith', Celia found herself replying. She has long-standing friends who are unaware that this is her middle name.

'Meredit,' he repeated.

'Meredith.'

'Petru.' The exchange of names felt like a contractual transaction. 'Next week you have more names,' he said, and it had the intonation of a statement rather than a question.

Celia told him, more apologetically than she had intended, that next week she would be in England.

'OK. In England,' he said, nodding, and for a second or two he smiled and looked steadily at her, with a gaze of stupid and judgemental certainty. Giving the broom-head a kick to set it moving, he resumed his sweeping.

Having stopped herself from protesting that what she'd said was true, Celia wished him good luck and put a couple of coins in the tin. 'Thank you,' he muttered, grasping the broom to his side in what might have been a mock salute.

'Bloody typical,' says C. 'Got myself obligated to a loon.' She's standing by the telescope, but only now does she appear to notice it. 'What's with the equipment?' she asks, and I point to Peter's bird book.

As she's leafing through it I ask her if she can remember the morning we saw the hoopoe in Devon. 'Vaguely,' she answers, turning the pages. I remind her of some salient details: the early hour, the saturated grass. 'I remember a bird, but I couldn't tell you what it was,' she says, not looking up from the book, then she says she'd better go downstairs and be sociable.

The hoopoe. It was very early: I wiped the water off the windowpane and saw the sky tinged with yellow at the top of the valley. Celia and I were in the same room; I woke her up and we walked down the slope, leaving long black footprints in the tin-coloured dew. The sea was grey and silent, and the trees were motionless. We crossed a field that had some cows in it; from a hundred yards off we could hear the grass being ripped in their jaws. The track down to the beach went across a golf course. The smooth damp sand in one of the bunkers was irresistible: we stopped to draw in it with sticks, and it was then that we saw the bird to the side of the flag – peach and cinnamon, with black and white markings on its back and dashes of black on its crest, probing the turf with its thin arc of a beak.

Ellen and I are in the garden when Celia emerges from the house, carrying a pair of well-worn hiking boots. She's going to have to take herself off for a while. She hopes we will understand.

When Celia has gone, Ellen says that she wouldn't have thought of her as a hiker.

'You don't like her, do you?' I ask, and Ellen replies that she doesn't know her so she can't possibly not like her.

'She has a good hairdresser,' she says, 'and she knows what suits her.' Ellen is greatly taken with the grey cashmere top.

'OK, but you don't like her.'

'That's not true,' she says. Eventually she tells me that there was a woman who worked in Roy's office once, who – as Roy put it – never dipped her headlights. That's what she feels about Celia, sort of; but she likes her. Janina, apparently, says that Celia should be on TV. I point out that there are several ways of taking this, but Ellen assures me that it was meant nicely.

'Celia's taken a liking to you,' I tell her. 'But don't get carried away. Celia usually takes a liking to people when she meets them. This was one of her big problems.' I explain that she tends to arrive at an opinion within thirty seconds of meeting someone, and to stick to that opinion way past the point at which the evidence proves she's wrong. And she's often wrong.

'Thanks very much,' says Ellen.

'Don't mention it,' say I.

Voices raised last night and high tension in the air this morning: Janina and Celia staying out of each other's way as much as possible. Celia goes for a walk immediately after breakfast. I ask Ellen if she has any idea what's going on; she says not.

Celia reappears at noon, and comes up to my room after showering. Things started to go wrong during the news, she reports. George Bush appeared, uttered the word 'freedom', and Celia – she admits – jumped up on her soapbox. It was an outrage, she said, that these people carry on as if words can be made to mean whatever they want them to mean, and that the British public seems happy to let the lies wash over them. Charlie asked if she really meant to suggest that the world would be a better place if Saddam Hussein were still around, to which Celia replied that only an idiot couldn't comprehend what was wrong with the US government paying their cronies billions of dollars to rebuild what the US government had destroyed using weapons supplied by other cronies at vast profit, all in the interests of future vast profits. Whereupon Janina joined in, incredulous that these wretched people weren't more grateful that the Americans are prepared to spend billions and billions of dollars on a country whose population kept trying to kill them. That's where the shouting started.

Before going to bed, Celia apologised to Charlie for losing her temper. (Janina had already withdrawn, with the air of a woman who expected to be receiving expressions of regret in the morning.) She was on edge at the moment, she told him. Her situation was a bit worse than she'd let on – well, more than a bit: quite a lot. But rather than linger on her woes, she moved on quickly to the good news about the Celia Brennan Language Institute. She did her best to make it sound like a sure-fire money-spinner. 'What happened to the money from the will?' asked Charlie. She told him she'd sunk it into the flat, most of it. Charlie went through the motions of pondering, before announcing that he was not at this moment in time inclined to favour the idea of a loan, on principle. 'What principle would that be?' Celia inquired. Answer: 'The principle that I'm not a bank.' Charlie expects to have rows with Celia every time he sees her. The rows don't bother him, because he knows he's in the right. But he cannot pardon her rudeness to his wife.

This morning Celia apologised again, at length. Charlie's response was that he hasn't yet mentioned it to Janina, but that, as far as he's concerned, a loan of some sort might not be totally out of the question (i.e. she can forget about fifteen thousand or anything near it). But he would need to see some figures, he informed her – as if he is indeed a bank and she's Mrs Random Fuckwit who's just dropped in off the street. She impressed upon him that she would sell the flat to pay him back if things went pear-shaped – to which Charlie rejoined that he didn't want to be in any way responsible for her losing the roof over her head. Celia thinks that the stuff about the business plan is a red herring: she could come up with figures that would satisfy the International Monetary Fund but Charlie still wouldn't be happy, because the figures themselves aren't really the problem – the problem is that the figures are hers.

An hour later, Charlie's view – Celia's latest outburst is conclusive proof that she's getting crankier as she gets older. Details missing from Celia's version of events are now provided. For instance, demanding of Janina, in reaction to a perfectly reasonable observation on the situation in Iraq: 'What the fuck are you talking about?' Another instance: telling Janina that her opinions were 'utter bullshit.' Janina thinks Celia is having a severe midlife crisis and needs help. She could suggest the name of a good man she knows, a therapist who's the husband of the woman who runs her yoga group, but she's afraid that Celia in her present state might bite her head off for suggesting it. This is true. Celia in any state would bite her head off for suggesting it, because Celia knows that in Janina's world it's only the inadequate who have need of a therapist.

The hypothetical language school, in Charlie's opinion, is a crack-brained notion, but he wasn't going to say as much to Celia, not bluntly, not when there's a risk of her chucking the crockery out of the window. He asked for a look at the business plan, but – as you'd expect – there is no business plan, just some very optimistic guesswork. He proposed that it would be useful to draw one up; Celia took offence at this (she clearly wanted to take much more offence than she permitted herself, but prudence for once got the upper hand), but he can't imagine why she should think he'd be ready to get out the chequebook when she hasn't yet done even the most rudimentary sums. The thing hasn't a chance, that's Charlie's line, and he also very much doubts that she's as hard-up as she's making out – she's in work, she has her own flat in a nice part of town, she's not buying her clothes from the flea market, she's obviously eating well, therefore there's no crisis. Celia has had some bad luck, but she should just get over it and forget about this ludicrous get-rich-slowly scheme.

With Charlie and Janina out for the evening, Celia does the catering. 'Put your feet up, girl,' she orders Ellen, placing a glass of wine in her hand. It's a Morellino di Scansano from Charlie's cellar, but the rest of the ingredients have been bought by Celia, from an Italian delicatessen recommended by Janina. 'And I have to say, it is very good,' she concedes, laying out the provisions. Last out of the bags is a cake – a squat cylinder of moist dark sponge, topped with thick shavings of top-grade chocolate in four different hues. 'A thousand calories per spoonful, but what the fuck, eh?' she says to Ellen.

She's knocked together some figures for Charlie, whose interim judgement is that they strike him as 'naive'. 'So it's back to the drawing board to make Big Brother happy. But stuff it. This wine is very agreeable, isn't it? I'll say this much for him, the boy knows his grapes.' She asks Ellen if she's been down into the cellar. It seems that this is going to be the prelude to another variation on the theme of anal-retentive Charlie, but she doesn't make too much of Charlie's rage for order (the bottles arranged rigorously by region and date; the climate controlled to the finest gradations of temperature and humidity) and pays him the compliment of contrasting him with others in Charlie's wine crew. One of them, Celia tells Ellen, goes through this ludicrous rigmarole whenever he withdraws a super-special vintage from the cellar: he brings it up one step at a time, raising the bottle by one step every twenty-four hours, supposedly so as not to spoil it by hauling it too quickly into a higher temperature. This can't be true, says Ellen, but Celia assures her that Charlie is incapable of inventing something as daft as this.

Not until we reach the cake course does Celia give voice to a complaint: Charlie never forgets anything she's done wrong, or that he thinks she's done wrong. And he has this compulsion to revisit her offences, apropos of absolutely nothing. This morning, in the kitchen, she pushed her hair back from her face and uncovered the scar on her hairline, which was enough to set him off. Seeing the scar, he started talking about the night she'd come home drunk from a party with Dan and had contrived to throw up all over the kitchen floor and then to skid on her own vomit and go head-first into the cooker. 'He knows I remember it,' Celia tells Ellen. 'It goes without saying that I remember it. But he just loves to remind me of what a klutz I've been.'

Ellen states that she thinks Charlie is a nice man. 'He can be,' says Celia, then pauses to consider what she's just said. 'Yes,' she decides, 'he's a decent chap. Very decent. And he genuinely wants me to be happy. But as long as that means being happy like Charlie. As head of the family – and he's a man who believes that families should have a head – it's his responsibility to save me, cost-effectively. But Janina thinks he shouldn't bother. I'm not quite to her taste, as you may have gathered.'

'And vice versa,' I have to point out, and within a minute Celia has informed us that Janina, having had the household contents revalued for insurance purposes, was shocked by the premium she was quoted this morning. '"Really, I was appalled,"' says Celia, placing a hand to her heart, fingers delicately arched to suggest the perfectly manicured fingers of the sister-in-law. 'The earrings, Dan – you'll never guess what they turn out to be worth.' These earrings, she explains to Ellen, were items that our mother had always intended to bequeath to Janina, though no one other than Janina ever heard her say anything of the sort. 'Our father's will, that's what it's all about,' she says, chucking back another glass. 'Having done so much to help Mr Brennan in his last months, she and Charlie ended up getting the same share as me. Which was grossly unfair, of course, because I'd done nothing except gallivant about in Italy. The injustice rankles, believe me.'

I tell Ellen this isn't true.

'Yes it is,' says Celia.

Soon after, Ellen thanks Celia for a lovely meal, declines coffee, and says she must get to bed. At Celia's instigation there is a hug.

'Did I go on too much?' asks Celia, once the door has closed.

'Yes,' I answer.

'I must try harder. But God, she gets on my wick. I'm trying, I really am. I've been with her to the shops. I've admired the great new washing machine. I've admired the new curtains in the bedroom. Sorry, that should be "the master bedroom". I mean –"master bedroom", for God's sake. Nobody talks like that, except estate agents. Do they?'

It's midnight; she looks tired. 'You should be in bed,' I tell her.

'In a bit,' she replies. Making herself a coffee with the state-of-the-art Italian machine, she says: 'I'll show you something.' This is intended to appear as a sudden inspiration, but it's obvious that whatever she's going to show me has been on her mind for a while. She beckons me to follow her to Charlie's study, where she goes to the computer and takes us to www.matttaussig.com. In the New Work section we see pieces from a collection entitled *Boundary*, currently on show at a gallery in Antwerp. Celia clicks on a small picture of a fence and it enlarges to the dimensions of the whole screen. The steel fence runs down one side of the photograph, with branches protruding through the bars at intervals; to the left a gum-scarred pavement stretches away. 'They're absolutely huge. Taller than me,' Celia explains, opening another image. 'He's doing well,' she says, returning to the home page. 'London, Antwerp, group shows in Los Angeles, Berlin, Milan,' she reads. At the bottom of the page we're told that Matt Taussig lives in London with his wife Vanessa and son Lothar. Celia shuts down the computer. For a moment she stares at the dead screen, then we go back to the living room.

We watch a wildlife documentary. The blowhole of the Sperm Whale, we are told, is set slightly to the left of the top of the head, which gives its blow a characteristic tilt. The Fin Whale is unique among the larger whales in having clearly asymmetrical colouration: the left jaw is dark whereas the right jaw is white or light grey. The white markings on the pectoral fins of the Humpback Whale are unique to each individual. I knew none of this.

Turning off the television, she says: 'I really do think he was the one, you know?'

'Who?' I ask, knowing what comes next.

'Matt.'

'Arse.'

'It's becoming clearer with every passing year. Matt was the one,' she says, breezily nostalgic.

'You don't believe that.'

'I do, Dan, I do,' she says, with regret that this should be so.

'You don't.'

'The one that got away.'

'Cobblers.'

'No, it's true,' she sighs cheerfully.

Ellen doesn't approve of the way Celia talked about her brother, and didn't much care for the way she talked about Janina either. 'They are my hosts,' she says, 'and I like them both as well. She shouldn't do it.' She rips the sheets from the bed as though snatching them from Celia's grip. I tell her that I'll make sure the offence is not repeated. 'No, don't say anything,' says Ellen. 'I'm just saying I wish she wouldn't, that's all.' The chores are completed in record time. She's on her way out, bearing the dirties, when I call her back to take a look at the screen.

'What do you think of this, El?' I ask, showing her Matt's photo of the back of a warehouse. Amid the pieces of broken glass and scraps of squashed cardboard there's a flattened

Coke can. 'This is the same size as a real-life can,' I explain. 'And the ticket stuck to the ground right next to it – you can actually read what's printed on it.'

Ellen doesn't see the point. 'I see old cans every day of my life,' she points out. 'I don't need a photo to show me what they're like.'

I tell her that the picture is by one of Celia's ex-boyfriends.

'Really?' she says, as if I've told her that the Bishop of Aachen wears green silk socks in bed.

Charlie's full name is Charles Philip Brennan. For a brief period, somewhere around the age of twelve or thirteen, he affected (on the cover of school exercise books, pencil cases, record sleeves and so forth) the title Charles P. Brennan, thereby distinguishing himself from the senior Charles Brennan – our father, Charles Bernard Brennan. The P, Celia liked to tell her friends, stood for Photocopy. Right from the start, Charlie's face bore the unmistakeable stamp of his father (whereas Celia was a perfect hybrid, and I – after a little over a decade of being something like a twenty percent maternal to eighty percent paternal mixture – grew to be wholly my own man), but the resemblance was more than a mere matter of the disposition of the features. His expressions and mannerisms (the smile that didn't quite take hold of the whole mouth; the arched left eyebrow; sitting with his hands on his belly, fingers interwoven), his general manner of addressing his surroundings (the air of cautious observation; the sustained silences) – these were all, well before he started school, uncannily like those of Charles the elder. To those who loved him, he possessed a gravitas in advance of his years; to those who didn't, he was a rather heavy and dull little chap.

It soon became evident that there was a deep affinity between father and son. Young Charlie was never much of a reader, but there was one certain way to persuade him to persevere with his book, and that was to place him in the vicinity of the armchair in which his father was sitting: cross-legged on the floor, he would quietly mouth the words to himself for as long as his father was occupied with his paperwork. Their tastes were congruent: Laurel and Hardy films (unamusing to the rest of the family) they found hilarious; *Steptoe and Son* – which made Celia want to shoot the TV, or herself, and rarely eked from our mother anything more than a smile – was a favourite; ditto *Up Pompeii*. At weekends, if his friends weren't playing football, Charlie would often take his homework to his father's desk in the back room, deriving comfort and encouragement from the air of commerce that the ledgers exuded. And in the management of money the younger Charles Brennan was of the same mind as the elder, just as Charles the elder was proud to say that he took his essential values from his father, Stanley Charles Brennan, a man who is on record as having said repeatedly that he would have eaten stale bread for a week, and fed stale bread to his family too, rather than borrow a halfpenny from anyone. (Stiff as a portrait on a banknote, his skin as smooth and pale as alabaster, this exemplar of fiscal rectitude confronted you as you stood at our father's desk; alongside, in a separate frame, was his wife Emily, wearing a hat that looked like a crushed cardboard carton, and slightly cross-eyed too – from the undernourishment of the Stale Bread Diet, according to Celia.) Our father's often-repeated tale about the man to whom he once foolishly extended credit (a mistake never to be repeated), overriding his misgivings about this customer's character (in a nutshell, there was simply too much blather about him; it has been pointed out by Celia that the man was Irish, and that plain prejudice plays a rather more significant role in this parable than Charlie is prepared to acknowledge), was absorbed by his eldest child in much the same way as other children absorb the lesson of Little Red Riding Hood. 'Read people as carefully as you'd read a contract,' our father urged, and Charlie listened. He is still proud of the fact that, as a mere beginner in the firm (he was just twenty), he sniffed that there was something wrong about a builder who wore a very expensive watch: the man appeared in the papers a couple of years later, having been sent down at the Crown Court for living off immoral earnings.

Anyway – young Charlie's pocket money (stowed in a small wooden box like a scaled-down treasure chest) was invariably a fuller fund than the accounts of his siblings (it's impossible to recall what he spent the money on, other than the occasional LP), and it was to be expected that when he learned that Celia had loaned a few pounds to Christine (whose favoured brand of make-up was too expensive for the miserly allowance she received from her parents), affronted Charlie would take the opportunity to caution her: 'Neither a borrower nor a lender be.' This was something of a catch-phrase ('The only bloody line of Shakespeare he knows,' said Celia, 'and he doesn't even know it's Shakespeare'), and yet, finding herself somewhat short of cash (for a skirt in the January sales?) and needing an instant solution to the crisis, Celia did once, in an impulse of need, appeal to Charlie, who handed over the requested amount without hesitation, but not without delivering to his sister a homily on the virtues of thrift and self-sufficiency (despite the meagreness of his out-goings, Charlie had for a long time been doing a paper round five mornings per week – partly in the hope that he might pedal away some of the excess weight), a speech so patronising that Celia told him (after the money had been pocketed) that if he ever spoke to her like that again she would shove his money-box somewhere that would make riding his bike a very uncomfortable procedure. This was the last time prior to the present, I believe, that Celia asked Charlie for financial assistance.

Celia has always been prone to fads, says Charlie, and with little prompting he will list a selection of them: the Bob Dylan fad (circa seventeen years of age, deciding she loves Bob Dylan, she buys three of his albums in one batch; is forced within months to acknowledge that Bob's voice is about as lovely as an unoiled bike chain; never listens to Bob again); the jogging fad (buys expensive trainers and slinky kit; joins club; decides that joggers are as tedious as bridge-players and her knees aren't designed for this type of punishment anyway); yoga (she's fundamentally ill-suited to the philosophies of the East and a low-velocity lifestyle); emigrating to India/a Greek Island/Japan . . . he could reel off a dozen inside a minute. The school, says Charlie, is just the latest of Celia's whimsical schemes and will fade as quickly as all the others. He wishes she'd grow up and sort herself out, but what can he do? She doesn't want advice from him, just money, but it's advice she needs. Celia is a terrific teacher, he's sure of that, but she hasn't a clue when it comes to finance and she'd be bored witless by the day-to-day slog of running a business. She simply has not got what it takes to do this kind of thing, and deep down she knows she hasn't, because otherwise she'd do what anyone else would do if they thought they had a viable commercial proposition, and that's go to a bank.

In essence, my brother's grand narrative of the adult lives of himself and his sister is as follows: he labours morning, noon and night to make a success of the business and to support his wife and sons; Celia fritters away her years at university, flibbertigibbets around Europe for years, and now earns her money (such as it is) by chatting away to a miscellany of Italians – an undemanding activity that leaves her with plentiful hours of leisure in which to conduct a succession of more or less unsatisfactory affairs. The caricature of himself is an accurate one. Charlie has worked hard, and the Brennan business was indeed in trouble until he took it in hand and – perceiving that it was impossible to compete with the DIY warehouses when it came to flogging the cheap stuff – persuaded his father (with assistance from Janina, whose taste was to prove infallibly attuned to emerging trends in the world of middle-class domesticity) that they should move upmarket and offer the public such high-grade materials as Breton limestone, Turkish travertine, and Italian ceramics in any colour you could think of. When his sons babbled on about what an amazing thing the internet was going to be, Charlie took note, with the result that Brennan Tile & Stone had a website that was markedly superior to the competition's, and had an employee answering queries by email at a time when others were still using postcards. Turnover increased steadily during the time that Charlie was working alongside his father, and rose even more steeply once Charlie alone was in charge. On his gravestone, says Celia, they'll carve his name, dates and forty-year sales graph.

'That makes your brother sound stodgy, but he's not stodgy at all,' says Ellen. 'He's a gentleman,' she says, and she doesn't see what's so bad about being successful. What's more, there's a twinkle to him when he's with Janina, which is nice to see. (This, I'm pretty sure, is the first time anyone has used the word 'twinkle' in connection with Charlie.) Furthermore, Ellen tells me, I'm a terrible snob about Janina. So what, if she buys a dozen different magazines each week? Everybody reads magazines. And some of the magazines that Janina buys are really beautiful.

'I'm not a snob,' I answer. 'That's not the right word.'

'Yes it is,' she insists.

'No. I'm a sick and twisted gentleman.'

'That you are,' she says, scooping me off the mattress.

On the doorstep Celia puts her arms around Ellen and gives her an embrace, which Ellen reciprocates with a fine simulacrum of warmth. Tears from Celia. From the window I watch as she piles her bags into the car, while Charlie kicks the soggy tyre and shakes his head. He smiles and passes her a handkerchief for her eyes; they have a long hug, with Charlie gently patting her back. Then it's Janina's turn. Looking her squarely in the face and holding her by the wrists, Celia says something at which Janina shrugs, before giving her a delicate kiss on the cheek – just one cheek.

An hour later, Charlie has gone to the garage and the three of us are sitting in the garden. Ellen compliments Janina on the garden, and Janina tells her that the garden was one of the main reasons they moved here. She'd always wanted a proper garden, she says. The London house had just a scrap of grass and a border the size of an ironing board. Charles would have been content to stay there forever, but moving to this place was Charles's way of paying her back, because she'd stayed at home all those years, with the boys, living in a city she didn't much like any more. It wasn't easy for Charles. She loved being away from the noise and the dirt, but it took Charles a while to get used to the quietness of it. And of course the commuting wasn't easy either. She was aware that Celia thought Charles was an old-fashioned man and a bit of chauvinist, but Celia was wrong. 'How many men would have done what he's done for me?' she says. 'How many men really understand that a woman is working when she's at home? Not many.'

'You're right,' says Ellen.

'In many ways, Charles is more of a feminist than his sister,' says Janina. Then she adds: 'But he has great affection for her. He really does.'

'I can see that,' says Ellen, and Janina smiles gratefully.

4

To Charlie's way of thinking much of Celia's adult life could be described as nothing but one damned episode after another, and this in itself is something he finds problematic. As an adult, thinks Charlie, one has an obligation to achieve a greater life-coherence than Celia has managed. Herewith a précis of Celia's incoherent life to date, commencing with her leaving home to go to university (the first in the family). She had decided to read politics, because – as she herself put it (provoked by pompous Charlie) – she intended 'to study the real world'. Both elements of this phrase are significant: the act of studying in itself elevated her above Charlie on the scale of human endeavour (Charlie was an all-accepting dullard; she would accept nothing until she had tested it); and the decision to make 'the real world' the object of those studies gave her a greater integrity than certain airy-fairy contemporaries, for whom the songs of Leonard Cohen were as tough a challenge as they could handle. Charlie's view was that Celia chose politics because she thought she could bluff her way through it merely by watching the news, and he found it hilarious when she came home for the first

Christmas with a thousand pages of Karl Marx to read before the new term began. Our mother, convinced that it was simply not possible to write a thousand pages on anything without repeating yourself a great deal, thought it must be possible to skip about eighty percent of *Das Kapital*; that would be like trying to skip through a sheep-dip filled with glue, said Celia, before giving up after fifty pages. (There was a boy in her seminar group who was certain to finish it within a week – he could tell her all she needed to know.) Our father, worried that she might be turning into a student activist, was in something of a quandary: dismayed by her lack of application (he'd hoped, arguing against Charlie's scepticism, that university would inculcate a greater capacity for self-discipline), but relieved that the founding father of communism only bored her to distraction.

Boredom was to be a recurrent problem during the ensuing three years, from which she emerged with a poor degree and no enthusiasm for heavy-duty political participation. Disenchantment with her coevals played a part in this conversion. She had a comprehensively limp liaison, for example, with the aforementioned book-devouring bright boy in her seminar group (every weekend another demonstration to attend; every trip to the corner shop another struggle with the ethics of high-capitalist consumerism) and an ill-considered dalliance with a faux-prole pretty boy who now works for the Conservative party, to the surprise of very few. After these and other disappointments with student politicos, she developed a penchant for tunnel-visioned big-brains of a more scientific cast of mind. (It was notable, however, that none of these deep thinkers occupied the ugly end of the spectrum.) Unfortunately, most of these boys were too immersed in their subjects to bother themselves overly with the needs of Celia, and so they gave way to a sequence of more or less handsome boys of a vaguely neo-Romantic tendency (the English Literature department was fertile territory), whose general attitude to the short- and medium-term future (it's too soon to worry about money; let's get some living done now, while we're equipped to enjoy it) came to be her own. Most durable of this squad was Louis, who by his final year (the year of his affair with Celia) was marching to the beat of a drum that none but he could hear, attending only lectures that had nothing to do with his courses, submitting a couple of pages of aphoristic jottings (he'd recently discovered Nietzsche) in lieu of a dissertation on *King Lear*, et cetera, et cetera. He possessed a fine library of poetry (a tribute to his shoplifting skills), and was an inveterate composer of verses. A sonnet sequence dedicated to Celia was found in her room at home by her mother, who declared that it was sheer pornography (the parts of it that were comprehensible, that is); Charlie's angle was that Louis had espoused poetry because his brain was so scrambled by dope that he couldn't rise to the logical connections of prose. Three months after he and Celia had decided that their world-views were not, after all, entirely compatible (an incident in which he pitched face-first into a plate of curry seems to have been pivotal), Louis embarked on a spiritual quest to northern India, accompanied by Melanie, a fey and floaty-skirted first-year philosopher with an untameable mane of russet hair, preternaturally assertive breasts and a perpetual expression of semi-vacant astonishment in her huge indigo eyes. Though Melanie returned within the month, Louis was now lost to all his erstwhile friends. Celia came across his mother once, on Oxford Street; Louis was by then living in northern Thailand, and had changed his name to something

Celia made no attempt to remember. His mother gave the impression that she held Celia in some way responsible for her son's decline into para-Buddhistical lunacy.

Long before she went to university it had become clear that Celia would never have any interest in the family business. After she had graduated it became clear that she had no interest in undertaking anything that her parents or older brother might term a career. Political engagement was henceforth to be limited to voting in every election in which she was eligible to participate, a donation of a steady percentage of her income to various Third World charities, and a few protest marches. (But no marches after Lisbon, where, running from the cops, she received a clout on the cranium from a baton; the consequences were half a dozen stitches, brief experimentation with a Jean Seberg crop, and a briefer fling with Cristiano, the dishy doctor.) 'You have absolutely no idea what to make of yourself, do you?' Charlie once accused her. She didn't think of herself as a self-assembly kit, she replied. As for her future, all she knew for certain was that she couldn't bear to stay in a country run by the vicious, money-grubbing, life-denying, self-serving cabal of free-market zealots for whom her brother had unaccountably voted. In addition, she positively wanted to travel. (Charlie, by contrast, was a devotee of anti-travel, having a penchant for resorts with swimming pools and tennis courts and perimeter fences and a tour rep constantly on hand, to ease any social interaction with the natives. His honeymoon was spent in a five-star compound in the Bahamas, which was technically abroad but with the quotient of foreignness reduced to nil, or near enough (and unlimited tennis coaching included in the package, plus as-much-as-you-can-eat buffet breakfasts and lunch). 'Having a wonderful time,' Janina wrote, underlining the word in red, and on the front of the card she or Charlie had scored an X across one of the hotel windows, though God knows why they supposed we might want to know behind which of the fifty or so identical windows of this top-bracket dormitory block they had been frolicking.) Celia also knew that she wanted, for as long as possible, to live and work among people who were intelligent and vital and youthful. (Charlie, as far as Celia was concerned, had leapt from adolescence to middle age in a single bound.) And so, having no need of an income above what was necessary for the maintenance of a bedsit and a moderately sociable existence, Celia thought she'd have a go at teaching English as a foreign language. It did not take her long to get herself hired by a school in Barcelona, on a one-year contract.

Led to believe that another contract would be offered at the year's end, she went into the job at full throttle: studying for a diploma, attending Spanish lessons two nights a week, plus lessons in Catalan at weekends. Though her room was a trek from the school and the ill-fitting windows made it so cold in winter that she could barely afford to keep it heated to a tolerable temperature, she loved the city and would have stayed there, given the chance, but when the year was up her employers regretfully informed her that they would have to let her go (money was found for a replacement – at a beginner's salary), and so, as an interim measure, she came back to London to teach and gather more qualifications. In London, after a year, a better contract was on offer, but by then she was pining for the sun and better food and livelier people, and was profoundly antipathetic to English men, in the wake of a sequence of deadbeats that culminated with Patrick Fontenoy.

(Let's get him out of the way now. She met Fontenoy at a party. He was skulking in the garden, letting his moody charisma do its work. Prison-cut hair, with a neat scar athwart the crown; eyes like olives in glycerine; broad-shouldered but lean; jeans on the verge of disintegration, paired with a classy belt – a philosopher-assassin kind of image. The day before the party he'd put in his last performance as a deranged Spanish prince in a pub-theatre production of some minor Jacobean tragedy. His rent was being paid, however, by a TV advert in which he appeared as a yogurt-fuelled grand prix driver. Celia was much taken by Fontenoy's combination of self-mockery and saturnine seriousness, and by the cold-eyed stare with which he silenced the dandified idiot who shrieked at them: 'Forgive me for asking, but are you two fucking?' A few weeks later she went to Canterbury to see him in an adaptation of a Kafka story; he was 'unbelievable', she told me. His finest moment followed: a surprise trip to Morocco for a long weekend. That he'd recently borrowed a couple of hundred quid from her was of no concern – there was a TV role in the offing, in a big period-drama production. It was a small part, but enough to settle his debts, and his agent was confident that major roles were just around the corner. Celia was also certain that Fontenoy's breakthrough was imminent, and this was a source of some anxiety: once his name was made, would he still want to be hanging around with a language teacher? Celia kept him 'grounded', he reassured her. She was his 'anchor', he liked to tell her, but might there come a time when an anchor was merely an encumbrance?

Patrick Fontenoy did not become famous. His turn as the sinister factotum of a dissolute Regency buck did attract the attention of a casting director, thanks to whom he landed a part in a low-budget movie, playing the sinister English boyfriend of a kidnapped heiress. This led to an appearance as a sinister lawyer in a low-budget British gangland film, after which he reached what turned out to be the zenith of his fame, in an American sci-fi thriller that was released only on video: he impersonated a sinister Russian scientist who turned out to be a robot. 'He gets killed by a blood-sucking blancmange in the third reel,' wrote Celia, who had long since been cast aside in favour of an Irish actress, fifteen years Fontenoy's senior, who had played the pious aunt of said Regency buck. This was a blow which she had not seen coming, as Patrick had seemed to find this woman as irksome as she had. Celia encountered her at a post-production party, and described her as a hefty specimen with the smug half-smile and drowsy eyes of a mature yet highly sexual woman who had learned to look with indulgence upon the foibles of the inexperienced. A week or so after the party, Patrick sent Celia a note. He hated himself, he told her, but he really didn't know who he was right now, and needed to take some time to find out. (The time he took out, she discovered, was a fortnight in Galway with the worldly-wise middle-aged fatso.) 'You might not know who you are,' Celia replied, 'but I can tell you what you are,' and she told him, at considerable length. I met him once: he had insisted on being introduced to the mutant brother and I had succumbed to Celia's pleading. I recall him examining my room with spurious deliberation and respect, as if it were some sort of art installation, and subjecting me to much guff about the 'little mind' being absorbed into the 'great mind' of creation, by which I think it was intended that I should know that Fontenoy had considered deeply the subject of suffering. 'What do you think?' Celia asked me. 'Never trust a man who wears a necklace,' I replied, and she barely spoke to me for a month. Enough.)

After Fontenoy's desertion she applied herself to securing another post in Barcelona, which was duly found. This time, though she enjoyed the city as much as she had done before, the school itself was less than satisfactory (a martinet at the helm; staff resigning every month; classes too large) and the latter stage of the second Barcelona sojourn was soured by a libidinous landlord who insisted on collecting the rent every fortnight in person, bearing gifts of steadily increasing desirability (extra-virgin olive oil; a bottle of Rioja; two bottles; a case; two tickets for a European game at the Camp Nou), progressing from amusement through incomprehension to indignation at her resistance. In the end he evicted her to make way for a young woman who was purportedly his god-daughter. The offer of better-paid employment soon took her to Cyprus for a brief interlude (too many Brits, and nothing to do except lie on the beach), then to Athens (another mistake: air you could chew, heat that liquefied her brain, monotonous food, tough language), whence she transferred herself to Turin, which revealed itself to be not quite Italy as she recalled it from the family holidays: an attractive city in parts, but it could almost have been England when the rain came off the mountains, and the natives were a different breed from the expansive and highly tactile extroverts who seemed, in her memory, to have populated every picturesque cranny of the regions she had visited as a girl. Almost everyone was friendly, and the students were the most appealing she had ever taught, but half a year passed before any colleagues invited her to visit them at home, and at weekends she often spoke to nobody but shop assistants. As acutely as in Spain, she was conscious that she could never be anything other than a spectator here, and, perhaps dulled by the isolation, she struggled with the language ('if anyone tells you Italian is easy, you can be certain they don't speak it'). Nonetheless, as a spectator she liked much of what she saw in Italy, so from Turin she migrated south to Bologna, where the climate was more to her liking, the city more pleasing to the eye and the colleagues more congenial. She shared a flat with Maria, a teacher at the same school, who had been born and raised in Calabria and can be glimpsed for an instant (aged four) in the background of a scene in Pasolini's *The Gospel According to St Matthew*. Maria was a good friend (and has remained a friend ever since), and the Bologna experience was generally good, being blotted only by the incident of Mr Cipolla, which happened at the beginning.

The pungently unattractive Mr Cipolla (an administrator at the school; late forties; thinning bouffant, with blatant colourant usage; pillow-belly; over-applied and noxious aftershave; fascist in all but name) one morning, alone in the lift with Celia, reached for the top-floor button at the same time as she did, and allowed a finger to graze against her hand with unmistakeable meaning, an advance that Celia ignored, as she ignored the next one (a summons to his office to receive item of information that could have been transmitted by phone in five seconds; compliment on new shoes), and the one after that (cigarette lighter proffered with absurd lingering gaze). Maria explained that the attentions of Mr Cipolla were a rite of passage for any female employee, and that sooner or later the perpetually jealous Mrs Cipolla would be making an appearance, because although Mr Cipolla – to her knowledge – had never succeeded in seducing anyone other than his weird wife, he evidently made a habit of tormenting the poor woman by regularly letting drop the name of the latest object of his horrible affections. And lo, very soon afterwards, Celia was confronted on her doorstep by a woman fitting Maria's description of Mrs Cipolla (deep red lipstick applied a centimetre too widely; hair held in place with huge silver combs; face of a boxer), who told her – with a violent faceward jabbing of the fingers – to stay away from her Sergio, then stormed off before Celia could work out how to say in Italian that nothing could give her greater pleasure. Incorrigible Sergio tried his luck again, inviting her to join him and some friends for a drive to Rimini on Sunday. Again Mrs Cipolla appeared outside the apartment (this time she was waiting when Celia came home): 'I'm warning you. Keep away or there'll be trouble.' To Celia's insistence that she had not the slightest interest in her husband Mrs Cipolla laughed (or yelped – her laugh was the sound you'd make if you trapped your finger in a door), as though the very idea that any woman could fail to feel a flutter for her Sergio were utterly preposterous. 'My wife is obsessed with you,' Mr Cipolla informed Celia one morning in an empty classroom, his face (a saggy assemblage at the best of times) express-ing the sadness of his wife's unreasonable behaviour and of his hopeless love for Celia. When next she came face to face with Mrs Cipolla, Celia seized the initiative and said to her, before the wretched woman could open her mouth: 'Leave me alone, and tell your husband to leave me alone as well.' Speechless, Mrs Cipolla clutched at her head as if to assure herself that it hadn't cracked under the pressure of her anger, before withdrawing with an insult. Thereafter, Mr Cipolla kept his distance from Celia (in the lift he'd stand as far from her as possible), and life was extremely enjoyable until Maria had to go back home, to look after her ailing mother.

Bologna minus Maria palled surprisingly, and when a friend from her days in Athens contacted her from Madrid, enthusing about the city and the school in which she was working, Celia was soon on her way once again. Madrid too was good, though the former friend had changed in ways that were not conducive to the continuation of the friendship

– she had acquired, for one thing, a predilection for recounting, in company, incidents from their time in Athens that often did not reflect well on Celia, and which Celia rarely recalled as having happened quite as related. The nightlife was of course wonderful, yet Madrid did not have quite the same kind of buzz as Barcelona, and on the other hand it had more buzz than Celia could cope with: she was already beginning to feel too old to keep pace with her colleagues, and she still remembers vividly her first intimation of middle age, at the age of just 28, at 3 a.m. on a hot July midweek night, in an alley behind a Madrid club, as friends conferred about where to go next, just a few hours before they'd be starting work. And an argument involving half a dozen sixty-ish men in a bar near Plaza del Sol – an overheated exchange with much roaring and table-pounding; perhaps a show intended for the entertainment of themselves and their audience, but with explosions of what seemed to be genuine rage – made her think (and acknowledge that such thoughts had been lurking under the surface for some time) that she would never be on quite the same wavelength as people who could whip themselves up into such a passion in a disagreement over a football match that had happened thirty years previously. So now it was farewell to the heart of Spain and hello to the heart of Portugal.

Ask Celia what she thought of Lisbon and she'll say it was fine. The men were a little on the short side, *fado* was the most tedious music on earth, and she pretty soon reached a point where she never wanted to see another platter of shellfish as long as she lived – but Lisbon was fine. She never tired of the sight of the river. The Port Wine Institute was fun. There was some nice countryside nearby. But Lisbon was rarely exciting, and from time to time she saw herself not as a woman who had taken a stand against inertia, but as someone who was merely drifting. She worried that she was losing her nerve. Her brain was too full of Spanish and Italian and fragments of Greek to make room for Portuguese, and she was mugged one night (a black eye, because she wouldn't relinquish the bag; most of a week's wages gone; photos of boyfriend (name momentarily unavailable) thrown into the Tagus, along with her keys). And of course there was the clobbering from the cop. As soon as a decent stretch of free time became available, she took a trip to Genoa to visit Maria and her husband (Moreno the marine engineer, whom she had met – he was on holiday – not long after her mother had died) and the recently arrived baby Marta. The week was delightful in all respects but one: several times a day Maria would implore Celia not to deprive herself of the joys of marriage and motherhood, and refused to believe Celia (who could, Maria had often pointed out, have any man she wanted) when she said that her unwedded and childless condition was less a matter of choice than of chance. 'No, I think you're afraid,' said Maria. And: 'You would be a beautiful mother. I always thought so. Always.' (This was not true: Celia could recall the subject cropping up just once, when a now-haggard colleague came into school with her yowling newborn, and Maria's reaction had been even more emphatic than her own. 'No, no, no!' she wailed, as they walked home. 'We will wait. We will wait for ever.') Maria's ceaseless proclamation of the blessings of maternity created some strain, but temporarily; at the next visit the advocacy was less intense, and within a few years she had entirely ceased striving to win her over, perhaps concluding – seeing Celia so gentle with the girls (Cecilia, Celia's god-daughter, was born a year after Marta) – that still-single Celia really wasn't unmarried by choice, and was fated, as some very attractive women mysteriously are, to remain alone. Celia left Genoa, after that first visit, more convinced than ever that the obligations and anxieties of motherhood were to be avoided, a conviction from which she has hardly ever wavered.

Intermittently pining for Bologna, for her former life with unmarried Maria, Celia persevered in Lisbon, but she was reaching thirty with just a few hundred pounds in the bank, and lacking true attachment to the place in which she was living. (The lack of true attachment to any particular man was not problematic, it should be noted.) Back to London she came again, where she was soon earning a decent salary and leading a life that was not without its delights even before her involvement with Matt, and yet – prior to Matt – there were days when the sprawl and gloom of London revived a longing for Bologna that she now knew was a longing for the city itself rather than for a life that had gone forever. And though this yearning ceased for the duration of the affair with Matt, she came to feel that the idea of Italy was constantly present in the depths of her mind, like a slow, strong current in steady motion underneath the incidental activity of the waves. Thus, when things with Matt worked out as they did, and she found herself again on her own, it was – as Celia described it – like being adrift on a boat at night, and when you wake up in the morning, after hours of worrying over what you would do when daylight came, you find you've been carried close to the shore, but not the shore from which you'd departed.

To Italy, then, but not to Bologna (no jobs at her former school, where Cipolla was now in charge): first to Lucca (confirmation almost at once that she's in the right country for her; somewhat slower acceptance that demure Lucca isn't the right spot); then on to Pisa (getting closer: swarms

of students a good thing, but problematic aura of provinci-
ality); then to Florence, and an immediate sense that final
landfall has been made. And now, at last, we're only one step
away from the present. (Antonio. The Lisbon boyfriend was
called Antonio. He'd once had a trial for Benfica, he said, but
his friends laughed when she reported what he'd told her.)

When living in Lucca and Pisa she'd made forays to
Florence with a frequency that increased as it came to seem
inevitable that she would move there, and long before the
right job was found she had selected the quarter in which she
would be living (in the vicinity of the flea market), where,
thanks to Elisabetta, a tiny flat was quickly found, only to be
vacated a few months later in favour of her current address,
two blocks away.

Elisabetta – let's do Elisabetta while we're at it. Elisabetta is
Elisabetta Cecchetti, née Voltolina. A proficient linguist (MA in
linguistics from University College London; fluent in English,
Spanish and French; capable in German), she was contemplating an academic career when she met, at a tedious dinner
in a villa outside Prato, the beguilingly unusual Simone, who,
though trained as an archaeologist, and still fascinated by
certain aspects of the subject (their first holiday together, in
Cairo, would be spent mostly in museums), was now a director of a textile factory in the city, a change of career that had
come about through one of the factory's former bosses, a family acquaintance, who, upon hearing that ancient textiles were
something of an obsession of Simone's, had informed him that
his own son, Gino – who was then starting out in the business
– would like to meet him, having developed an interest in
the early history of the industry. Simone and Gino met, and

got on well. Introduced to creative young fabric technicians and crazy clothes designers and a seductive industrial chemist called Carla, Simone found himself drawn to the world of textile production and accepted a temporary placement at Gino's factory, a placement which evolved at great speed into a profession, as Simone gave proof not only of a superb eye and a sure grasp of the technologies of fabric manufacture, but also of mercantile skills previously unsuspected by anyone, himself included. He had recently returned from a mission to Tokyo (where his understanding of Japanese business etiquette and his knowledge of Japanese fashion – he appeared to have committed to memory every garment ever created by Rei Kawakubo, Issey Miyake and Yohji Yamamoto – had proved invaluable) when Elisabetta (not long back from London; doing bits and pieces of translation work while she pondered her next move) met him. Marriage followed within a matter of months, and two children within as many years. Elisabetta stayed at home until the younger child had started school, taking on as many translations as she could manage (about three times as much work as any normal multilingual woman could have found time for, says Celia) and somehow finding time to formulate her own methodology for teaching a second language to adults, a methodology she introduced, with excellent results, at the institution of which she was the director of studies at the time she interviewed Celia. (The institution from which Mr Mascarucci, finance director, would one day abscond.)

Elisabetta took to Celia strongly on first sight, and vice versa. It was in September that Celia began work in Florence, and by Christmas she'd been to the home of the golden couple several times. Home was a vast apartment near the Trìnita bridge, furnished in impeccable taste: sleek and modern, but not pretentiously so. A decade Celia's senior but an exact contemporary to the casual eye, thanks to expensive and subtly applied cosmetics (brands obtainable from outlets known only to the cognoscenti) and an assiduous exercise regimen, Elisabetta is a woman who is not merely successful in everything she does, but successful without any manifestation of effort – a quality which Celia, lacking it, admires hugely. Elisabetta possesses (persuasive photographic evidence has been produced) an unostentatious elegance and sharp-edged beauty. She is graceful and urbane, and, though her life is exactly as she would want it to be, she never appears complacent. She's grateful for the good fortune that has brought her a husband who's intelligent and desirable and faithful (to the best of her knowledge), and two talented and loving children: Alessandra (architect) and Gianni (metallurgist). And though money will never be a problem in the Cecchetti household, one has the impression that she would take in her stride any downturn in the family fortunes, being the daughter of a librarian and an archivist of limited means, who throughout her childhood had impressed upon her the worthlessness of pecuniary (as opposed to spiritual) wealth, illustrating its transience and moral taint with frequent invocation of the case of some tenuously related individual by the name of Massimiliano, once the owner of a construction company, who had devoted his youth and middle years to the accumulation of money by means that at best were barely legal (becoming in the process a man so unpleasant that other crooks were his only companions; no woman would go near him, except women with no self-respect), only to lose it all when one of his buildings fell down and his firm went bust, leaving him as poor and lonely and bitter as an ogre in a folk tale.

It should be noted in passing that Charlie, citing Celia's adoration of the style-goddess Elisabetta, has long maintained that there is a fundamental contradiction in his sister's world-view: she belittles him as a capitalist lackey, but has a penchant for the trappings of the good life, as long they come with a veneer of creativity.

'I had hoped for a more enthusiastic response,' I tell Ellen. 'Best part of three days, that lot took me.'

'How would Celia feel if she knew I was reading this?' she says.

'She wouldn't mind.'

'I think she'd be embarrassed.'

'And I know she wouldn't.'

'Have you told her that you're doing this?'

'No need. There's nothing here she wouldn't tell you herself.'

'Well, it's one thing for her to tell me; it's something else for you to tell me. There are things here she might prefer to forget about. We've all done things we'd like to forget.'

'Speak for yourself, missus.'

A hundred yards beyond a flattened rabbit (macerated and pressed into the tarmac so thoroughly that one plump paw and an upraised ear are the only unequivocally rabbitty features of the fur-pat) the torch beam catches a beige hummock on the verge: a deer, young. A foreleg, snapped between knee and hoof, is angled the wrong way, but otherwise it presents a profile which is more or less that of the live animal standing. Evidently it has been placed on the grass with care. The tongue, blood-spotted, is touching the grass lightly, as if to taste it; the eye towards us, wide open, is steel-coloured. Insects are chewing at the lips and eyelids, trotting up the tongue and onward to the interior. Activity can also be detected in the under-tail region and within the fur of the flank: here and there, individual hairs vibrate. In the gravel at the edge of the road lies a moist pink pile of skull-contents, and here a company of bugs is hard at work. I select a single scavenger and track it for a minute with the torch, as it sprints back and forth across the slick little mound, stopping every few seconds to carve itself a portion of meat, apparently oblivious to the light that's burning above it. It is so pleasant and so healthy to set oneself down in solitude, face to face with eternal things.

From the back bedroom we are afforded a view of the older part of town. Not a greatly uplifting prospect, but today it's looking as good as it can. The russet expanses of undulating clay tile are weakly pleasing. A thin skim of cirrostratus to the south gives some form to the sky. The church spire's weathervane twitches an inch or two in the breeze every now and then. In the middle distance, chaffinches are firing themselves in and out of an oak. Down in the garden, Janina works her way along the flowerbed, fork in hand, imposing order on the vegetable matter. The only other visible human activity is taking place in one of the gardens that backs onto the opposite side of the stream: a girl, seven or eight years old I'd guess, in red dress and with a red band in her hair, is running round the perimeter of the lawn, arms outstretched. Another girl joins her and they whirl in the centre of the lawn, making their hems fly. They spin together, eyes shut, until they fall. Lying side by side, hands joined, they drum their feet on the grass. I have them both gathered in the circle of glass when Ellen, on her way upstairs, comes upon me.

'How did you get that down here?' she asks.

'Sheer willpower,' I answer.

'What's to see?'

I tell her I'm watching the kids in the garden, and step back to invite her to take a look.

'Lovely, aren't they?' I remark.

Ellen takes a look. 'Yes,' she agrees, uneasily.

I assume a lyrical mood. To a child, I muse, the garden is a tumult of colours, not an arrangement of things with names.

'I suppose,' says Ellen.

'No notion of categories,' I maunder. 'No ideas about who they are.'

'Pardon?'

'I was wondering who they are. Haven't seen them before.'

'Neither have I,' Ellen replies. 'I'm going to sit in the garden for a few minutes,' she says, 'unless you need me.'

'No,' I tell her, taking hold of the eyepiece. 'I'm fine.'

'Come down with me,' she cajoles.

'In a while.'

'It's nice and warm outside.'

'It's nice and warm inside,' I point out, but the tease has gone far enough and a few seconds later I'm following her.

I scuttle from the pergola to the shade of the tree, and thence to the cover of the bushes at the far end of the garden. The girls are inaudible. Ellen, having pegged the day's laundry to the line, joins Janina at the shrubs; I assume she's reporting on me. Applying the secateurs with a surgeon's delicacy, Janina makes no visible response, other than the slightest of nods, but as she hands a cutting to Ellen she looks over at me. I adopt what I hope is a wistful posture, but I can't be sure I've got it right. Janina resumes her labours, frowning intermittently.

'You're bothered, aren't you?' I say to her later.

'About what?' she asks, though she knows.

'The kids. The girls.'

'No, I'm not,' she insists. 'I don't like the idea of you hauling that thing downstairs on your own, that's all.' I pretend to believe her. 'When are you going to write something more for me to read?' she asks.

'I don't know,' I answer. 'The Muse is fickle.'

Janina leaving to play tennis – the squeak of her new tennis shoes on the wooden floor sets me off. I must set aside time to write about it: the quality of quietness in a hospital at night; the occasional groan, the occasional sigh, above the low soft chorus of breathing; the squeak of shoes, as the nurses walk from bed to bed, checking on us; the muffled flurry of an emergency at the end of the ward. The gorgeous nurses, and the one who didn't like me. I could tell she thought I was a big-head. This was a relief, because most people felt obliged to like me. To this nurse, though, I was the same as any other big-head. What was her name? Karen? Kerry? And the students: the ones who touched me as though prodding a bear through the bars of a cage; the ones for whom I seemed to be little more than a teaching aid; the ones who looked as though they might faint. The doctor who couldn't disguise how delighted he was to have come across such a remarkable case. My skin was 'spectacular', he said, as though congratulating me on growing it. But I liked him; he talked to me as to a collaborator on a special medical project. He was called —? This information appears not to be available to me. Janina's legs are remarkably lissom.

It hadn't been possible for Christine to talk to Celia properly before, but now Jack has gone away and it turns out that Christine is in need of advice. Christine regards Celia as a woman of superior life-knowledge, a misperception traceable to their years at primary school, when Celia could be relied upon to avert punishment for nearly all misdemeanours through a mixture of charm and highly inventive lying, and to repel the attentions of undesirable boys with an aplomb to which those oafs could find no riposte. Most of the boys were undesirable, but Jack was one who was not. Christine and Celia and Jack became a trio at around the age of ten, and remained a trio even after their dispersal to different secondary schools. Upon reaching the hinterland of puberty, the girls wasted no time in acquiring boyfriends – a succession of boyfriends, of whom Jack was never one. Nevertheless, whatever the girls' other commitments might have been, the trio spent at least part of most weekends together, and so it continued for three years or so, then the gatherings became less regular and the girls became a pair, with Jack as an increasingly distant satellite. This change was attributable chiefly to Jack's attachment to Katrina, a highly intelligent and immensely unrelaxed girl who didn't much care for rowdy Celia and her pretty but tongue-tied little sidekick. (Sound and Vision, as she nicknamed them.) Katrina followed Jack to university, where her drunken liaison with the comically masculine captain of the rugby team promptly put paid to their relationship. At home for the summer, broken-hearted Jack took solace from Christine, who was herself in shock after being ditched by a boyfriend who had more or less informed her – in response to her admitting that she'd found *I, Robot* so boring she'd stopped reading it after a day – that perhaps they weren't quite on the same intellectual level and he needed to be with a girl who was a bit more comfortable with advanced abstract thought. (He did have the good grace, though, to send her a letter the following week, to soften the blow. He hoped that, when they had both recovered from their dissappointment (sic) at what had happened, they could still be friends. Christine never spoke to him again.)

Within the year Christine and Jack were married, and they've stayed married for more than twenty years. She's a picture-framer, operating from a tiny shop in Dulwich; he runs a firm that makes instruments for chemical laboratories. They live well. They take a minimum of two holidays per year, not counting the odd spontaneous city break; they live in a capacious house with an immodest garden; they have a highly personable son, who is about to leave home for art college. Christine has a life that many women would envy, and many do. She knows this. Yet Christine has increasingly become prey to the suspicion that – notwithstanding the plentiful vacations, which have taken them to Madagascar, the Yukon, Venezuela, Laos and many other wonderful places (with copious film footage to prove it) – she hasn't really lived. She still, she supposes, loves Jack, but she's begun to wonder lately if it's true to say any more that she wants him. Imagining a scene in which she (for the purposes of this scenario unattached and unaware of Jack's existence) is at a party where she meets Jack (similarly innocent of her), she can't be sure that she'd pick him out – or vice versa, for that matter. (Well, Celia points out, if you had no memory of

Jack and Jack had no memory of you, Jack wouldn't be Jack and you wouldn't be you, so the whole idea is bloody daft, isn't it? This is taken by Christine as hair-splitting rather than a dash of cool good sense: 'You know what I mean, C. I need you to be supportive here.') Or it feels too often as if their life together has become – if such a thing is possible – just too damned harmonious. She sometimes thinks of herself and Jack as two different colours that have been blended so thoroughly that they've become one perfectly even tone. (Yes, but who did the blending? And what about the amazed discovery, post-Katrina, that she and Jack had been soulmates all along?) A bit of friction and spark is what Christine yearns for, once in a while, and she knows that Celia is the only friend she can say this to, because Celia is the only one who won't think she's gone mad. Recently she's found herself attracted to one of her customers, a man of about fifty, not especially good-looking but well preserved and well dressed, and very intelligent. Over the last year or so he's brought her half a dozen posters to be framed – posters for art exhibitions, mostly French. He's Scottish, from near Oban, and that's about all she knows about him, except that he teaches at Goldsmiths, has been divorced twice and has a son called Jules who lives with his mother in Wales. His name is Douglas. He always wears a luminously white shirt, and he has this amazing deep blue coat that looks like it must have cost a fortune, but his car is a duffed-up old Peugeot. Christine and Douglas have been for a coffee, once or twice, that's all. Nothing will come of it, but she's tempted, and is feeling as guilty as she would do if she'd given in. Jack hasn't the faintest idea that anything is wrong; he's entirely happy, or so it appears, and assumes that so is she. Perhaps nothing is wrong – there's just something else in sight, perhaps on offer, that would be different from what she has with Jack. What Christine wants is for Celia to talk her out of it, but she also wants complications. She wants intermittent tumult rather than a slow easy slide into old age. 'What a laugh, eh?' says Celia. 'She thinks she'd like to be me. Well, if she wants to swap, I'm game. Jack's OK. I could learn to love the walk-in wardrobe.'

Other women just get on with it and have affairs left, right and centre, moans Christine, so why on earth can't she? What's the matter with her, for God's sake? Why is she so fucking timid? The implication is that if only Christine could bring herself to cast off the burden of her conscience – as Celia and cohorts of other irresponsible good-timers have so easily managed to do – her life would be so much easier. Celia's opinion, speaking as a woman who has given adultery a go (she made it sound like a lifestyle choice, akin to sampling a new brand of coffee, but Christine seemed to miss the irony), is that Christine shouldn't do it: at best she'll get a few orgasms out of it; at worst (and worst is by far the more probable outcome) the bouts of sex will pall, and she'll pay for them by making herself and Jack (and maybe the boyfriend too) extremely unhappy. This wasn't the advice that Christine had intended to elicit. Nodding and gazing into her glass, she stoically contemplated the joyless labour of self-denial that lay ahead. Celia has decided that a year is too short an interval between visits to Christine.

I show the Christine pages to Ellen. 'Daniel,' she says, 'I don't dislike Celia. You don't have to convince me.' I'm not trying to convince her of anything, I say – I'm just reporting what's going on, and filling in a bit of background. 'This

woman sounds like a nightmare,' she says, 'but you're telling me things about her that her own husband doesn't know,
and that's not right. I shouldn't know. I don't want to know.'
She's rather annoyed; I undertake to give more thought to
questions of confidentiality in future.

An afternoon amid Eugène Atget's photographs of Paris. In
front of the church of Saint-Médard, a blurry horse appears
to be the only living thing; but look carefully: there, by the
railings – a black-caped phantom. Another picture: light
flares at the end of passage Montesquieu as if an angel might
be about to step out of it. More: a dead man looks at me
through the reflections on the half-glazed door of *L'Homme
Armé*, rue des Archives; two dead women, each occupying
her own pane of glass, gaze at me through the door of *À la
Biche*, rue Geoffroy-Saint-Hilaire. And here's a rarity, a full-
length person in focus – a mustachioed man in slipper-like
shoes, selling lampshades on rue Lepic. (Might his wife, I
wonder, upon seeing this, have said to him: 'That's not
a good picture. It's not you, Gustave. It doesn't look like
you at all.' Now he is no longer a likeness of anyone – he
is perfectly what he is, the pedlar of lampshades in the
photograph entitled *Marchand d'abat-jour, rue Lepic, 1900*.)
Walking along rue Saint-Dénis, window-shopping in the
Galerie Vivienne, strolling on rue du Petit-Pont, people have
rubbed themselves out, leaving smudges of smoke in their
stead. And on a day in 1907, outside a shop in rue Chérubini,
to the left of a group of transparent people, stands a man
in a long apron, with his cuffs rolled up; and there he is
again – on the corner of rue Chérubini and rue Sainte-Anne.
It's the same face and body, without a doubt. It's a shock to

recognise him, as if the figure has crossed from one page to the other to prove that he was alive.

E: Why do you like these pictures so much?

D: They get me out of the house.

E: Seriously. Why do you like them? I want to know.

D: I was being serious.

E: Please don't talk to me as if I'm stupid.

D: Any news of Roy?

E: Did you hear what I said?

D: Yes. I'm sorry. I don't think you're stupid. Any news of Roy?

E: No, Daniel, there is no news of Roy. Roy is a waste of space and effort. The situation is unchanged.

It's possible that, as the thickets of middle age begin to envelop her, Celia is coming to see her unattached state (previously a badge of integrity) as a condition that now has more negatives than positives. The idea, however, that Matt Taussig was the soulmate whom she, by neglecting to make clear how she felt about him, allowed to slip by, is a rewriting of history. She didn't let him go: he ditched her, for Vanessa Koskinen – Vanessa of the website, mother of Lothar – and the ditching was not caused by any failure on Celia's part other than her failure to be Vanessa Koskinen.

Vanessa was not short of a few dollars (father a director of big-budget TV commercials; mother a TV producer), and was a fairly smart young woman (degree in Film Studies), but the exterior surfaces of semi-Finnish semi-American Vanessa were what made her stand out. Slim and well-toned as a dancer, with deep-set almond-shaped cornflower-blue eyes and a sulky mouth, she made you feel, when you looked at her, as if you'd walked into a glass door. She did not affect to be unaware of her impact: when meeting a man for the first time, she had a way of withholding herself a little during the preliminary exchanges, as if to give him some time to master his confusion, to adjust to the flawless face and figure. In Matt's studio she shed her clothes as if she'd happened, alone, upon a secret tropical beach. At the sight of the unselfconsciously nude Vanessa, Celia experienced no more than a tweak of envy (the girl was a different species – you wouldn't envy a gazelle, would you?), and the merest touch of jealousy (Vanessa was just a 'breathing statue', Matt assured her; she was vapid; and there was a boyfriend, wealthy, to whom she was engaged). But less than six months later Matt told Celia, as he boxed up some prints for a show in Paris, that he thought it would be best if he went to Paris on his own, even though the flights and hotel had already been booked. This was a great surprise to Celia. But hadn't she once said, Matt reminded her, that she'd want their relationship to end with a fall of the blade rather than a slow fading away? She might well have said that, but they were nowhere near fading away, she said, to which Matt replied that he felt they were settling into a routine, by which he seemed to mean that they now watched television together from time to time, instead of fucking each other to the brink of cardiac failure at every opportunity.

It was from Matt's sister that she learned what had really happened. Once a month Celia and Ursula used to meet in the West End for a drink at whichever designer bar Ursula had discovered in the intervening weeks, and when Ursula rang to say that she'd only just heard that her idiot brother had broken

with Celia and to ask if she still wanted to get together, Celia
– who had always enjoyed accompanying supercool Ursula to
places she'd never have had the nerve to go into alone – readily
decided that there was no good reason not to. So they met in a
bar where purple and turquoise and scarlet Perspex prevailed,
and on the second cocktail Ursula let slip that Matt had recently received a black eye from Vanessa's ex-fiancé: 'The least
he deserved,' she said, at which point she realised that Celia
was not aware of the full extent of Matt's idiocy. 'The thing
about Matt,' said the beautiful Ursula, 'is that he makes a fetish
of beauty. It's always been his weakness. It'll mess up his life
and it'll mess up his work.' This analysis was of some consolation to Celia, and before long it had become possible for her to
think of blandly gorgeous Vanessa as nothing more than the
emblem of Matt's pitiable enthralment to pleasing exteriors.
She soon convinced herself that the fire had indeed started to
go out, and that sooner rather than later she would have ended
it herself. 'I'm not sure Matt can handle a real woman anyway,'
Ursula flattered her. (They continued to see each other, until
Celia's final departure for Italy.) 'Is there anything more to be
said about shapely young women with no clothes on?' Ursula
would ask, and Celia would agree that there was not. Matt's
latest pictures were deplored. 'They are very tasteful, very
accomplished, and very uninteresting,' Ursula would drawl,
which may or may not have been what she thought.

It's possible, nonetheless, that Celia feels a nostalgia – an
ever-deepening nostalgia – for her time with Matt Taussig.

The affair began when she was back in London, not long
after she had started to teach the language teachers at the
school in Covent Garden. Celia had finished work early,
and after searching for two hours she'd at last found the
right present – a blouse – for Janina's birthday. She was

on her way home when she saw a photograph in a gallery window. It was the presentation of the photograph (placed on its own against a black background, secured by tiny clips to two vertical wires) rather than the picture itself that had caught her attention, but the image – three city streets, converging symmetrically at the camera – proved interesting. Shops lined both sides of all three streets, and the doors of some were open; the shadows indicated strong sunlight; in one of the streets a scooter was parked; three bikes leaned against a wall; and in the entire scene there was not a single person.

Inside, two dozen photos were on show. All had been taken in daylight, in central London, and every street in every picture was deserted. The flank of an office building occupied the side of one photo, and Celia checked each window: nobody was to be seen at any of them. Standing as close as she could, she searched in phone boxes, in the shadows, in the far distance, but she couldn't find anyone. Four or five people were going round the exhibition; one of them – she looked like an art student: twentyish; waistcoat over an untucked white shirt; frayed camouflage trousers; khaki canvas bag over her shoulder – was peering at a picture of Northumberland Avenue, as Celia examined the adjacent vista of Threadneedle Street. The student looked at her, perplexed, and remarked: 'Has he rubbed them out?'

'I can't see where they would have been,' Celia replied. 'Can you?'

'We could ask him,' said the student, pointing towards the end of the gallery, where a pink-haired leather-jacketed woman of about fifty-five was talking loudly to a tall man of Celia's age. Celia and the student sidled closer to them. Receiving a smile from Matt, the student signalled that she'd like a word with him, and took up a position a couple of paces behind the woman, arms crossed as if waiting in a queue at the bank. Celia, struggling with an urge to leave, tried to concentrate on a picture of Waterloo Bridge.

Here perhaps is the place to offer a description of Matt Taussig, because his appearance was not irrelevant to Celia's confusion. He was tall, and altitude has always been regarded as a good thing by Celia. Her catalogue of lovers also suggests a strong preference for the dark-haired – to my knowledge no blonds other than Stefano have ever made the grade. The Lisbon footballing boyfriend was another anomaly, in being both a sub-six-footer and sporty, as Celia's taste has for many years inclined towards the artier varieties of masculinity (e.g. the undergraduate poet; Fontenoy; Stefano (to whom we must find time to return)). As Charlie has more than once observed, tall and dark are somewhat banal predilections for a self-styled enemy of convention; one could also argue that Celia has generally adhered to a similarly orthodox line when it come to the issue of handsomeness. 'Handsome', however, was not the right word for Matt Taussig. Most of the time, in fact, he was unequivocally not good-looking. At certain moments, on the other hand, he would suddenly become extraordinarily attractive, just as at other moments he would suddenly become quite strikingly not so. The nose – broken twice before he'd reached fifteen – was not a noble thing; the cheekbones, prominent and high, might have worked better in a different context, but in combination with his heavy brow they severely limited the space available to the lovely green eyes; and the mouth (though it proved to be superb kissing equipment) was too wide for the head, which flared outward at a jaw that, while sharply modelled, would also have benefited from being narrower and shorter. In other words, Matt Taussig's face was unlike any Celia had ever seen before, and the English language did not have the right word for his alluringly strange unhandsomeness; Italian did, however, as she was later to learn – he was *brutto-bello*. The attire didn't detract from the attractiveness – jeans (Levi 501s – nothing pretentious), plain white shirt, and what looked like an expensive jacket, cut from a remarkably fluid and deep blue material – and neither did his way of dealing with the garrulous pink-haired woman: he seemed courteous and modest (the self-deprecating shrug, however, would come to be seen as a mannerism: Matt was not uncomfortable with compliments), and he brought their conversation to an end with a handshake, in a manner that seemed to leave his admirer – though she'd have gone on talking until nightfall, given the chance – well satisfied with the attention she'd been granted.

The student stepped forward, beckoning Celia to follow, and said: 'I think we're going to ask what everybody asks.'

'OK,' replied Matt, squinting at her as if to read the text of the question in her eyes. 'Well, the answer is: what you see is what was there.'

'No tricks?'

'None,' he confirmed. Even the pitch of his voice – light, with an underlying deep vibration in the throat – was uncommon. Celia, fearful that she'd say something inane if she tried to join in, let the student do the talking.

'So you're there at dawn?'

'There for sun-up, plus Sundays and Bank Holidays. Sit and wait and hope it works out. Sometimes you're lucky, sometimes you're not. More often you're not. Usually I have to go back.' Only now was there a reciprocated look between himself and Celia. 'That one was a pig,' he said, pointing to a shot of Ludgate Hill in orange light. 'Seven sessions. People start work at ludicrous hours. You wouldn't believe it. Cleaners going in and out at dawn. Suits getting out of taxis. Terrifying.'

Conscious that she was at risk of presenting too beguiled a face, Celia gave her attention to the picture of Ludgate Hill, and found, as she looked at the image of the eventless street, that another image was emanating from it: the image of the dedicated artist, alone in the cold morning, waiting for the single instant that would make real the picture that he'd seen in his imagination.

'I'd love to see it looking like that,' the student comment-ed. 'I'll have to try it one day.'

And then Celia said, to the student: 'But we wouldn't see it like that, would we? Only the camera sees it like that: all at once and everything in focus. This isn't real. It's more than real. In a way. Well, what I'm trying to say . . . ' And so Celia was gabbling when a woman emerged from the gallery of-fice, holding a phone, and called Matt over.

'Two minutes, OK?' said Matt, interrupting Celia with a gesture that seemed to signify that he'd like her to continue, but when he came back he said he was going for a coffee, a quick one, because he had to be somewhere in an hour. The student said she had to leave. 'What about you?' Matt asked Celia, as if he'd been interested in the student and now felt obliged to invite her friend. Celia said she had twenty minutes to spare; in fact she had the whole evening.

She didn't come away from the chat in the café thinking that a relationship might be beginning. 'Is photography a particular interest?' Matt asked her. Her answer was incoher-ent and embarrassing. He asked where she worked; she told him more than he needed to know. He wanted to know what she'd thought of Barcelona – it was his sister's favourite city, he said. There was a bluntness to the questions, as if they had been forced into each other's company. Other than that he had three siblings and taught adult education classes (he had a class this evening), the only things she learned about Matt in that half-hour were that he'd been taking photographs ever since his parents dragged him into a Walker Evans exhibition at the age of ten, and that for his fifteenth birthday his parents had given him a second-hand Leica, which he still used.

Several days later, having scanned the window of a camera shop by the British Museum, Celia understood that the second-hand Leica was a further indication (with the expensive-looking jacket, and the precise and accentless diction) of an upbringing that was several grades more privileged than her own. (The privilege, Charlie maintains, was an inseparable part of Matt's aura.) And Matt's background was indeed unlike Celia's. His father, Martin (son of a surgeon who had removed his family from Bamberg to London in the spring of 1934), was a lawyer, specialising in shipping law ('an inexcusably lucrative racket', to quote Matt, who loved his parents dearly but would have been happier, Celia claimed, with less wealth in his immediate environment – hence the evening classes, when parental subsidy would have been his for the asking); his mother, Veronica (daughter of a professor of medieval history (the father) and a lecturer in the same subject (the mother – formerly a pupil of the father)), was one of the country's pre-eminent Assyriologists. ('Martin, Veronica,' said Matt, introducing Celia to his parents; they had always been Martin and Veronica to their children.) The Taussig progeny had all grown up to be high-flyers (except – at the time Celia knew him – Matt): Christian (eldest brother) worked in Brussels, advising on the formulation of European agricultural policy; Emeric was a cardiologist in Paris; and Ursula ran her own design studio, specialising in hi-tech furniture.

The collective personality of the Taussigs was apparent the moment one stepped into their house. An unexceptional (if larger than average) Victorian dwelling on the outside, it had been completely refashioned within: the staircase was steel and glass, with lights in the treaders; the living room had casts of ancient carvings under spotlights, and no fewer then three sofas – vast red rectilinear items from Italy; the dining table (designed by Ursula) was twelve feet long and had a resin top that looked like a slab of obsidian. Prototypes of Ursula's chairs were strewn about the house, positioned as carefully as sculptures in the corners of rooms and the angles of landings; most of them functioned better as sculptures than as chairs, Ursula commented, as though passing judgement on the work of someone she didn't like. Photographs by Matt were displayed in various places, including one (in an alcove on the first-floor landing, where any guest would be certain to see it) that showed a sleek, long-legged and naked girl sitting on a rock, laughing, with limpet shells on her nipples and a triangle of seaweed in her lap: this was Ursula, aged sixteen.

On the second floor of the Taussig house, in the alcove corresponding to the one in which sea-nymph Ursula could be admired, hung another photograph: a wavy-haired blond girl in a gauzy dress, screaming into the angle of a high stone wall. 'Matt drives all his girlfriends bonkers,' his father told Celia, as if being Matt's girlfriend were a post akin to being his personal assistant. The screaming girl, he explained, was Ulla, Matt's 'grand passion' for a year, and something of a star of student drama productions; Matt had spent a lot of his time in Oxford hanging round with actressy types, and most of the rest of his time in the darkroom, which is why he'd ended up with such a lousy degree. Martin was not surprised to find that Celia didn't know about Matt's less than dazzling academic career: not because Matt was in any way ashamed of it (the hours in the darkroom had been a good education, after all), but because Matt had always been the secretive one – it had taken him months to get round to telling them, for example, that this particular photograph had won a prize. From her tour of the house with Martin, Celia learned as much about Matt's past as she had learned from Matt himself, perhaps more. In the course of a year Matt revealed to Celia less of his biography than some of her lovers had revealed in a week, and for Celia – one of whose life-principles was that an affair was dead the day you felt you knew everything about each other – this was, on the whole, another point in Matt's favour.

We must get back to Matt and Celia in the café. By the time Matt got up from the table and announced that he had to get a move on (looking at his watch in a way that suggested she had delayed him), Celia was convinced that he'd suggested going for a coffee only because he'd been interested in the cute young student. As for what he now thought of Celia, she had no idea. He'd given her a lot of eye contact, but it had felt more like being interrogated than being seduced. Not once had he smiled at her.

On the last day of the exhibition she went to the gallery after work; she did not go in the expectation of finding Matt there, and was not sure if she wanted him to be there. Matt was there. They talked for five minutes, then he walked with her to the door. Out on the pavement he kissed her, as if he'd been waiting to kiss her for hours and only at this instant had the chance arisen. A minute later he was gone – he had friends to meet. He wrote his address on a card, and the very next evening she went to his flat, where, of course, he took a photograph of her. It was the way he looked at her that made Celia's brain go haywire. It wasn't, she said, as if he were looking into her heart, into the depths of her soul. ('None of that crap. It wasn't like: "Let me see who you really are."') He put her on a stool, in front of a screen of white paper, and then he stood beside the camera and just looked at her, from a distance, as if her face were an immensely complex object and he didn't quite know what to make of it. He seemed to be able to ignore the fact that she was looking at him; she knew she was being regarded by someone who did not see things in the way that most people saw them, and this was what was so exciting.

Matt, then, was a distinctive man, and Celia's relationship with him lasted longer than any of her other affairs, before or since. 'Passion lasts ten weeks' – that was another of Celia's maxims, but Matt was the exception. Yet Matt Taussig was never, at the time, 'the one'. The very idea that anyone could be 'the one' for anybody was an absurdity, thought Celia. In the immediately post-Matt period she often reiterated the principle: love is not a matter of finding your missing half. But Charlie, true soulmate of Janina, believes that Celia has now, belatedly, been converted to the creed of unique affinity, and that her conversion has come about primarily as a consequence of her betrayal by Mauro, a setback which prompted her to at last give some thought to what has happened in her life and why it has happened. It's possible that Charlie is right. Certainly, Matt was never referred to as 'the one' before Mauro's misdemeanour. When Celia said to me 'I really do think he was the one,' it sounded plausible. But merely plausible is what it was, like a rendition of an idea that has been rehearsed many times. So is it only a story that she's telling herself, a story she might in time succeed in making true? Having been humiliated by Mauro, increasingly aware of the passing of the years, is she rewriting herself and Matt Taussig (a significant person, I don't doubt), in order that her life might have a peak from which to descend? It's possible. I don't know. We must have more on Mauro.

'Look, Ellen,' I tell her, 'you don't have to read it if you don't want to. It's not a condition of your contract.' She says she enjoys it, most of the time, but the stuff about Celia and Matt is 'too much'. She doesn't want to read any more about Celia's sex life. 'But there's no sex in it,' I point out. 'Just a passing mention.'

'I think sex is overrated anyway,' she says, and doesn't appear to be joking.

I tell her that I agree completely.

The manufacture of micromosaics is an extremely labour-intensive process. Stage one: a layer of plaster is laid in a stone base or a tray of copper. Onto this plaster the picture is traced. Following the lines of the drawing, the artist removes a small section of plaster, then fills the excavation with a mastic that dries very slowly. The micromosaics are composed of glass threads so fine that as many as five thousand are needed to fill a single square inch. One at a time, these tiny glass threads are pressed vertically into the mastic, and when the picture has been assembled it undergoes a triple polishing, first with a hard stone, then with emery, then with lead. The chief workshop for micromosaics was the Vatican studio, which was established principally in order to address the problem of the decay of the paintings in Saint Peter's. By the 1620s, a mere two decades after their completion, these paintings had become so badly damaged by damp that replacing them with pictures of glass appeared to be the only way of preserving the church's decoration. A little over a century later, the work was finished. Employing a stock of almost 30,000 tints of glass, the Vatican's micromosaicists created their facsimiles with such skill that few visitors to St Peter's are aware that the images above their heads are not painted.

Ellen examines my trainers and discovers on the sole of one of them a pellet of clay that I had failed to remove. 'What have you been up to, Daniel?' she asks, having put two and two together. I confess. 'But what if something happens to you?' she says. 'What happens if you take a tumble?'

That isn't going to happen, I tell her. I move very slowly; I take Charlie's umbrella as a walking stick; I take a torch; nothing's going to happen to me.

'I'd be happier if you'd let me come with you,' she says.

I answer that I appreciate her concern, but I like to go out in the dead of night, and she wouldn't thank me for waking her up at 2 a.m. She says I should take a phone with me; I point out that, not being mobile, I don't have a mobile phone. She proposes that I should take hers; she could leave it on the kitchen table at night, so I could pick it up if I decided to go out. 'The keypad is too fiddly for these fingers,' I counter.

Within the hour Janina arrives to have words with me about my misbehaviour. 'It's so dangerous,' she says. 'Can't you understand why Ellen is concerned?'

It would be quite funny, I suggest, if I were to topple into a trench and the builders found me lying there in the morning. Whatever would they make of that?

'Danny, it's not a game,' says Janina, hardening the voice. She tells me that she's going to get one of those alarm buttons that frail old folk wear around their necks. This, I tell her, would not be a sound investment; I'll take Ellen's phone with me if I ever again feel the urge to do something silly.

Later, I accuse Ellen of being an informer.

'That isn't fair,' she says. 'I'm here to look after you.'

'And a very fine job you're doing,' I tell her. I add that I'm going to write about Dr Goffman for her, and there will be nothing to offend in it.

Doctors I Have Known, Part 2.

An afternoon in early summer – June, I think. I see Dr Goffman in wide-legged linen trousers, and sandals with beaded roundels above the toes. We each had a tumbler of water. A window was open: at one point she leaned over to close it, so we could hear each other speak over the traffic. I was telling her about the things that had happened to me since I'd last seen her, such as they were. There would not have been much to tell: another book or two proof-read; perhaps something to report from the world of Celia, who had embarked upon Barcelona Part II. The foxes of the South Circular had been the high point of the intervening period, albeit not as high a point as I made them out to be, for the benefit of Doctor G. I put considerable effort into maximising the charm of the scene. Picture them: a vixen and two cubs, tripping across the road in single file, circling to inspect a cardboard box in the gutter, before returning the way they'd come, again in single file, with one cub-length of space between each animal. The foxes in themselves were not of interest to Dr Goffman, but she allowed me to run on. She told me she'd had a fox in her garden a few days back, sunning itself on the grass in the middle of the afternoon. 'They've become fearless, haven't they?' she said. 'People, traffic – they're not bothered by any of it.' Well, I told her, there wasn't much traffic about, and here Dr Goffman favoured me with one of her frowns. With Dr Goffman – deeply trained, as she was, to maintain composure in the face of deviousness, obscenity and florid irrationality – a frown was merely a minor and fleeting and very fetching corrugation of the brow.

'It was four o'clock. I have a taste for night-time,' I said. I wanted Dr Goffman to understand that a lawn in daylight is a sight most ordinary, whereas a zone of damp grass singled out for attention under streetlights has a lushness that makes you stop and wonder. I would have her see that a long straight empty road, lamplit in the rain, a tunnel of bright grainy air under the blackness of the sky, is a thing that can lift the heart; that even the dreariest street can acquire an aura of the sublime at night, like a cemetery in which you are the only one alive. 'Night-time makes you think,' I told her.

'And what does it make you think, Daniel?' she asked, in a cadence I can still hear – a tone of professionalised tenderness, an exquisite equipoise of the genuine and the fake.

'A car stops at traffic lights at some ungodly hour, and you take a look at the driver: it's a young woman laughing to herself, mad with happiness. And you wonder what the story is. Where has she been? Where is she going? Why at this hour? A week ago I saw two men trading punches in a front garden, lethargically, as if they were under water. A tonic to the imagination, it was. I recommend it,' I replied, taking a sip of water, aping suavity.

(Other things seen in the dead of night but not disclosed to Dr G, for obvious reasons: two lovers under a tree, their coupled bodies – blanched by the moonlight – looking from a distance like nothing so much as a monstrous maggot wriggling on the grass; a couple going at it in a ground-floor room (lights off but curtains wide open), on a table placed so close to the window that it seemed inconceivable that the possibility of being observed was not an element of the thrill.)

'It would be difficult to fit into my schedule,' said Dr G.

'Ah, well,' I commiserated. 'Not a problem for me. Snooze by day, work and stroll by night.'

'So you're doing your work at night?'

'Sometimes.'

'How often is sometimes? In the past fortnight, let's say, how many times have you been outdoors in the middle of the night?'

'Three. Four.'

A note is made. 'What would you say if I were to suggest that this might not be an altogether healthy state of affairs?'

'I'd point out that I'm not altogether healthy.'

The last two sentences are recalled precisely; also recalled is the pause of Dr Goffman, a pause which generally presaged a nugget of doctorly profundity. 'To be fully who you are, to realise your fullest potential, you need society,' she opined, or words to that effect.

'What about monks and nuns? Are you saying they're all barking up the wrong tree? If so, I have to say I think you're being rather unfair to some very dedicated and remarkable people.'

'They have a vocation, Daniel. You're not a monk.'

'But you take my point?'

'We have a problem, you and I, that we need to tackle together. I need you to work with me. We must examine the psychological and social factors that are at work here.' (All direct quotes; not necessarily from this conversation.)

'Are you trying to say that if I buck my ideas up the lumps will fall off?'

'No, Daniel, I'm not trying to say that. You know I'm not saying that.'

'A man thinking is always alone.'

'Please, Daniel, don't play games.' (A frequent request.) 'Do you like coming here?' (She removes the glasses, a sign that little of the appointed time remains. My God, Dr Goffman, you're lovely.)

'Coming here? You mean do I like the process of getting to this office?'

'Obviously that isn't what I was asking. What I meant was: are these conversations of help to you?'

'Oh yes. Very much so.'

'Do you mean that?'

'Most definitely.'

'Good.'

The word 'good' did nice things to the shape of Dr Goffman's mouth. I can see that shape almost as clearly as if I had a photograph of her, and I can hear her voice saying 'Daniel' too.

It was Dr Goffman who made me start writing. 'Don't let a day go by without writing a page,' she advised me, and I did as I was told. I enjoyed it, even if what I was doing wasn't quite what Dr Goffman had wanted. Her idea was that by writing I would take control of my life. ('Take control' was one of her catchphrases.) Writing would stop me thinking of myself as a victim. 'You have access to unique experiences,' she told me. 'Make use of them.' Writing would help me to make sense of my life, she suggested. But my life already made perfect sense: genetic damage had given me an incurable and increasingly repulsive illness. Nothing could be clearer. I had no interest in writing a self-help manual for myself. Dr Goffman said that this wasn't quite what she was saying – 'Just write, and see where it leads you.'

So I wrote my observations, and Dr Goffman was disappointed in me. 'I need to see more of you here,' she said to him. I pointed out that all these sentences had been written by me, therefore I was what she was seeing. These pages were full of me. This was being evasive, said Doctor G – a regular accusation. 'What are you thinking?' she kept on asking. 'What are you really thinking? Write it.' One day she remarked that we are all in some way wounded. 'Some more than others, doc,' I thought. But what I said, when Dr Goffman asked me what I was thinking at that moment, was: 'I was wondering what you'd look like with your top off.' And that was in effect the end of the road for Dr Goffman and me.

Ellen's only comment: she once had a crush on a doctor, when she was in hospital to have her appendix removed. He was an Indian chap, with long and silky eyelashes. Ellen sits with me while I search the internet for Dr Goffman. It takes a minute to find a nice picture of her, taken last year. Dr G is well into her fifties now, but she's still a very nice-looking woman: smooth face, clear blue eyes, thick grey hair cut in a stylish lopsided bob. I gaze at the picture for a long time. 'Hildi, Hildi, Hildi,' I exhale, moonstruck.

The thought of Dr Goffman lingers, and perhaps contributes to the afternoon's little incident, at shower time. We have a new sponge, bought by Janina. Saturated and soaped, it's as soft as a ball of water. It feels extremely nice – so nice, in fact, that as Ellen is swabbing my back an erection appears, the first for God knows how many months. 'Insurrection of the unemployed,' I remark. Ellen peers over my shoulder and says: 'I'll leave you for a minute or two,' as if a friend has just joined me and she's leaving us to gossip for a while.

Celia the schoolgirl, a very popular classmate, was often invited to parties, and on occasion the invitation was extended to the younger brother, who might not have been the most photogenic or exciting of boys, but had a bookish air that, for certain girls, made him more palatable than many of his more ebullient male contemporaries. But I was never a sociable character. I tended to react adversely to anything that smacked of charity, and I was always quick to scent the whiff of charity in a generous gesture. Therefore I declined nearly all such invitations. For reasons that are no longer clear to me, however, I did decide to tag along with Celia on the occasion of Madeleine Firle's sixteenth birthday. I suspect that I had turned down so many opportunities to socialise that I felt under some obligation to display more willingness to engage, and Madeleine Firle's party would have been a less unenticing proposition than most, because Madeleine had been to our house two or three times, as an auxiliary member of Celia's entourage, and I'd quite liked her. She was a stocky young woman with no breasts, big vase-shaped calves (Irish dancing was her thing) and a peculiar pudding-bowl haircut that made her look like a medieval pageboy. She was also rather earnest – some would have said ponderous. Celia once asserted, on the basis of nothing more than an overheard conversation on the subject of, I think, the Amazon rainforest, that myself and Madeleine were kindred spirits. We were certainly alike in our lack of allure in the eyes of the opposite gender. It was assumed by several of her classmates that Madeleine was not a boy's girl. 'Which I'm not,' she once told me. 'Boys are idiots. I'm waiting for the men.'

This party followed a familiar pattern: I located the shadowiest corner; Celia kept me company for a while, then went off to dance. I found myself, inevitably, in conversation with Madeleine. Half-hidden in the folds of the dining-room curtains, we discussed at some length the plight of the great whales. Wildlife and ecology were Madeleine's other two passions. A few years later she would appear on a BBC news report, decrying the fur trade while being dragged towards a police van, having deposited a litre of scarlet gloss paint on the shoulders of some fashion editor; in the same week, her girlfriend fire-bombed a guinea-pig farm. Now, I was flattered that of all the people at the party I was one of the tiny minority – and probably the only boy other than Stephen – with whom Madeleine thought it possible to conduct such a conversation. And the conversation was informative: Madeleine knew her stuff. I admired her grasp of the economics of the Japanese and Norwegian whaling industries, and of the cultural niceties of those two nations. Nonetheless, I was troubled by a hankering for stimulation of a different kind, such as was happening in various parts of the house as Madeleine and I sat talking in the gloom of the dining room. Boys and girls were locked face-to-face in our vicinity. On every step of the staircase, kissing and groping was in progress. Even high-minded Madeleine felt the need for something less virtuous than whale-talk. The sound of Donna Summer came through the wall. 'Sorry,' said Madeleine, 'but I just have to dance to this one.'

I stayed in the dining room until I had finished my beer and the one that Madeleine had abandoned. Celia appeared in the doorway, to check that I was all right. I assured her that I was. This was true: I was nearly drunk. I raided the kitchen for another beer and returned to my post. Every couple of minutes someone would peer in. 'OK Dan?' they'd ask, and I'd reply with a thumbs-up. Celia and her boyfriend came in, and we chatted for a while. I told her I'd be going home soon. 'Stay a bit longer,' she said; she brought me one last beer before being dragged off to dance. At ten o'clock I picked my way up the stairs to retrieve my coat from Madeleine's bedroom. The coat was in my hand when the door closed and the room went dark.

Within seconds a hand was on my waist, and sliding southwards. The hand, I discovered when the deed was almost done, belonged to a girl called Kate Sanderling. One could say that Kate Sanderling had something of a reputation. Parties often ended with Kate vomiting into the bushes. Before that, Kate would be seen snogging a minimum of three different boys. She was famed as the most voracious snogger in the class, and by this I mean not just that she accumulated a high tally, but that she went at it as if the aim of the exercise were to dislocate the snoggee's jaw. But I did not get snogged by Kate Sanderling. Far from it – the face was turned away as the hand did its work. This work was done so briskly, it barely qualified as an erotic experience – a drain being unblocked is what came to mind. 'All smooth and shipshape down below,' she said, wiping her fingers on a coat, and that was the only thing she said while she was with me. The following week, on the way home from school, Celia overheard – as was almost certainly the intention – friends of Kate Sanderling talking about the party. Someone had bet her two quid that she couldn't do what she'd done. Exactly what Kate had done wasn't perfectly clear to Celia, but the gist was clear enough. That evening I told her what had happened, and the next morning she went up to Kate Sanderling as she was walking down the steps to assembly and, without any preamble, whacked her soundly in the mouth, which gave me some gratification, even if it did result in the wider circulation of the story of the hand-job in Madeleine Firle's bedroom.

This was my second sexual experience in the presence of a third party. The first can be dealt with more briefly. It was a Saturday afternoon in November or December, a couple of years after the diagnosis. I had been caught in a downpour that had gone through my clothes by the time I reached the front door. I hurried to my room, and as I passed the bathroom Celia called out: 'Who's that?' She was in the bath, immersed in thick suds that were spilling over the sides. A long soak had become one of her great pleasures, but she could never take as long as she liked when other people were at home. I stood in the doorway, shivering, as Celia brushed bubbles from her face. 'Come and warm up,' she said, closing her eyes. My father was at work, my mother had gone into town, Charlie was at a friend's house. I undressed and climbed into the bath, and Celia drew her legs up to make room for me. My feet rested on hers. At this time, new growths were beginning to appear on my arms. 'Let's see,' said Celia, leaning forward, and as she moved the bubbles slid down from her throat, slipping so far that a nipple showed pink through the thin white foam. 'There's not enough room,' I said, putting my hands on the sides of the bath to haul myself out. 'Close your eyes again,' I told her, and she did, but she opened them again right away. 'And hello to you,' she said, in the drawl of a young woman who has seen everything, to the thing that had emerged from the bubbles.

Herewith we conclude the account of the public appearances of my organ of generation. There are no others to record.

At ease in my chestnut bower, daydreaming in the mild breeze and the soft surf-sound of the leaves et cetera et cetera, when Janina comes over and asks if she might join me for a minute or two. Evidently we are to have a significant conversation. Today she's culling the slugs – 'creeping dog poo' she calls them, with a quick dilation of the nostrils, as if a stink comes to her nose at the very thought of them. We discuss the difficulties of maintaining a healthy garden, and then we have two or three minutes of substanceless chat before she comes out with the news: she has been speaking to her mother. She squints into the upper branches, as if in defiance of someone who is trying to make her weep. Her mother phoned last night, and told her that her father's mind is going. 'Charles thinks I must go,' she says, 'and I think he is right.' The tears have been stemmed at source. The ruefulness in her voice is that of a woman conceding that she has been outmanoeuvred. Little more information is volunteered. 'I thought you should know,' she says, applying fingertips to my shoulder. She returns to the massacre of the slugs.

A fuller account from Charlie. It turns out that Janina's mother wrote to her back in November, telling her that her father was becoming confused. 'Some mornings he does not know where he is when he wakes up,' she wrote. Charlie thought a call was required, but Janina preferred to reply by post: she spent a whole evening composing her letter, which she did not show him. Weeks passed before the next letter arrived, but the tone was more urgent. Her father was getting worse, and he had asked after her. It was terrible: he'd walk out of a room and come to a stop right away, having no idea what he'd been intending to do. 'You must come. You must,' the letter ended. That night Janina spoke to her mother for more than an hour – or rather, she was on the phone for more than an hour. Charlie retired to the kitchen, but was close enough to hear that Janina wasn't doing much of the talking. When she rejoined him, she was mildly dazed. 'I've just been having a conversation with a very old woman,' she said. She'd been told that her father was talking about her every day; that morning he'd suddenly called out her name, as if he'd just heard the door open and thought it might be Janina coming home. 'Well,' Janina said to her mother, 'you told him where I am, presumably. If he wants to speak to me he can pick up the phone.' He couldn't do that, her mother replied. 'Why "couldn't"?' asked Janina. 'Are you telling me he can't talk? Physically can't talk? He can't form sentences?' No, things hadn't reached that stage, not yet, not quite. 'It's too difficult for him. He couldn't say what he needs to say,' her mother explained. If he needs to speak to me that badly, thought Janina, he can manage a minute on the phone. 'Let me speak to him. Put him on,' she said, but the prevarication continued: her father was taking a nap. 'He sleeps a lot,' her mother said, with a crack in the voice. 'Well, wake him up,' Janina suggested, but her mother refused to disturb him. So Janina in turn refused to carry on: 'Tell him I'm ready to listen, as soon as he's ready to talk.' A few weeks later, her mother rang. 'He can't speak to you. He just can't,' she said, then she came to the heart of the matter: 'He's ashamed.' This knocked Janina off-balance for a moment or two. It was strange, she remarked, that this should be the first she'd heard of his feeling ashamed. Allowing, for the sake of argument, that this remorse was making it impossible for him to speak to her, it was odd that he'd never stirred himself to put pen to paper. No satisfactory answer was given to this point. 'Come for me, Janina. Come for my sake,' her mother responded. Janina impressed upon her that there was no question of booking a flight if she hadn't exchanged as much as one syllable with her supposedly shamefaced father beforehand. Only now did her mother give in. She shuffled away from the phone; there was much fussing and huffing in the background; at last her father spoke. 'I'm sick,' he told her. 'I get so tired.' He sounded sick. His voice was tremulous and there was a thin squeak to his breathing. He seemed to have difficulty in understanding or hearing much of what she said. 'What medication are you taking?' Janina asked. After a pause the answer came, in a wheeze: 'I don't know.' Janina was experiencing no upswelling of sympathy. 'You must know,' she said. 'The tablets are yellow,' he answered. It was too pathetic to be true, and on the subject of his shame there was not a word. 'I have to go now,' he said, after less than five minutes. 'Give it to me, Karol, give it to me,' her mother was coaxing, as though to a simpleton. Janina stood firm – if he was so sorry, she told her mother, he could say he was. This provoked a sorrowing rebuke: 'I wish you were kinder.' Whereupon Janina brought the exchange to a close.

Some weeks passed before the next communication. Janina's mother phoned to report a further decline. The police had brought her father home that afternoon; he'd been found wandering the streets a dozen blocks away. If her mother was to be believed, he was spending hours on end with his Polish dictionary, desperately trying to prevent it all from slipping away. Again it wasn't possible for him to come to the phone: he was sleeping, of course. 'Then why not call me when he's awake?' asked Janina. 'You know, I'm sorry the way things worked out,' her mother told her, which was some sort of progress, enough for Janina to answer, when her mother pleaded 'Will you come?', that she'd think about it, but wouldn't be coming until she had some proof that her father did actually want to see her and had some awareness that he might have been at least in part to blame for the way things had worked out. During the next conversation she spoke briefly to him. He managed to bring himself to utter more or less the same words as his wife: 'I'm sorry things worked out bad.' This was far from adequate, but Janina knew that she was beaten. 'I'm going to book a flight next week,' she said. 'That would be nice,' he responded, as if she were talking about hopping on a bus.

Last night Janina rang to let her mother know when she would be arriving. 'Thank you, Janina, thank you,' her mother said, as if she were speaking to someone grand. This show of deference upset her as much as the rants about ingratitude used to do, says Charlie.

All this has been going on, and I knew nothing of it. 'Janina didn't want me to bother you with it,' says Charlie.

Ellen, it turns out, knows that Janina will be taking a trip to Canada, but little more than that. 'Did you get on with your parents?' Janina asked her this morning. 'Mine always drove me crazy,' she said, then dropped the subject.

The old man of the farm is loitering near the house. 'Oh God, him,' says Ellen, when I point him out. A few weeks ago he accosted her in the street, wanting help to cross the road. Straight away he started complaining about the idiot politicians who'd banned fox hunting, and droning on about how city folk don't understand the countryside. She was wondering why this old codger might think she wanted to hear his views about foxes when he suddenly switched tack and asked how 'the lodger' was. 'Staying for long, is he?' he asked. Ellen didn't like his tone: 'It was like he thought I owed him an explanation.' He has nasty little eyes as well, like a ferret. Ellen let him know, as politely as possible, that she didn't think it was any of his business. 'You the cleaner?' he asked, and Ellen said: 'That's right,' just to be done with him. His name is Ridley.

In 1920 Janina's paternal grandparents emigrated from a village in the vicinity of Rogalin, initially to New Jersey, then onward to Toronto, where their sons, Adam and Karol, were born. Adam was to die of pneumonia at the age of six; Karol, not quite three years old when his sibling died, would often swear to his daughter that not a day went by without his feeling the pain of his older brother's absence – sometimes, says Janina, he would even force out a corroborating tear. The boys' father, Pawel, was a cobbler, an occupation into which his one surviving son followed him for a while. However, Karol found it demeaning to spend his days repairing other people's filthy footwear, and so – being a dextrous, quick-witted and enterprising lad – almost as soon as he reached the age of independence he set himself up as a repairer of radios and phonographs and electrical goods in general, an enterprise that gave him the opportunity not merely to put the agility of his fingers to better use but also to develop an expertise that was truly modern and would earn him more respect from his customers than had been accorded to his father. What it didn't earn him, ever, was a substantial income: indeed, in later years his revenue would often decline almost to the point of non-existence. Karol attributed these periods of penury chiefly to the public's ignorant preference for the cheap and disposable (his late father's footwear now being the epitome of the sort of well-made objects which today's people held in contempt), an analysis which his daughter learned never to contradict, even though she knew that other factors were more pertinent, such as her father's habit of not completing work by the promised date, and his acquisition of a tremor that eventually made it impossible for him to manipulate a soldering iron with the requisite accuracy.

For a couple of decades, however, things were not bad. Karol was diligent and reliable, and the throughput of customers was fairly constant, if never overwhelming. He was moderately content. He earned enough for a single man who lived in a two-room apartment and had no vices. However, in order to sustain himself he had to spend most of each day, and most of most evenings, in his workshop, with the result that his social life was limited. He'd had no serious romance, in fact, before the middle of his fourth decade, when he married Mary – 'his one true love', as he was liable to declare, in company, taking his wife's hand and pressing it to his heart. More than ten years his junior, Mary worked as a typist in an insurance office two doors down the street from Karol's shop. She had been employed there for more than a year before she and Karol spoke to each other. Before that, they would acknowledge each other with a wave, but the sharply trimmed red beard and the crown of wiry red hair made him slightly frightening, and his face often gave the impression that he was on his way to or from an argument. But one evening, having worked late, she stepped out into the snow at exactly the same moment as Karol, whereupon she found herself walking alongside him, and discovering that she had allowed herself to be misled by his demeanour, because in fact he was a very interesting man. He loved the snow so much, he said. He loved the soft shapes it made, and the look of the city when it was all white and black. Coldness, he thought, kept the mind in good condition. Hot weather made the brain misfire, whereas the cold kept the circuits clean and running smoothly. He had 'snow in the blood', he told her.

And Mary in turn, though they walked only four or five blocks together, told him things about herself that made him want to know more: that she was born in the depths of Saskatchewan, for example, and had known from an early age that she was in the wrong place. Life – real, full-blown life – was going on elsewhere, in the cities, she'd come to feel, and by the time she left school she was determined she was not going to become a farmer's wife like her mother and her older sister – which was not to say that her sister wasn't perfectly happy to live in a place where the horizon was a day's ride away, and sometimes had not a single body in front of it. (The sister, Jane, remained on her farm all her life and was always happy, as far as Mary could tell; Jane visited her in Toronto just once, for a week, and spent the entire time with a headachy look about her eyes, as if the chaos of the city were something she had to bear, without complaint, for the sake of her sibling.) So Mary had come to Toronto, and her only regret was that she could not afford to visit her parents as often as she would like. (Janina was hardly to know her grandparents. Karol's parents died within a month of each other, when she was still an infant. The maternal grandparents she met half a dozen times before the age of ten: she remembers them hazily as an amiable and silent old couple, both of them shod in men's shoes; they cooked side by side in a kitchen that was huge and had bare wooden floors and smelled of vinegar; the whole house groaned when it was windy and creaked at night.) 'Our families are very stretched,' Karol remarked as they parted, as if to say that a meaningful affinity had been revealed.

One thing led quickly to another. Mary was soon describing Karol to her workmates (and to Karol himself, giving him great pleasure) as a romantic and a thinker. On their first date he talked about the exploration of space, and how humans would be living on Mars in the next hundred years, but most of all he spoke about the homeland he had never seen (and would see only once, aged sixty-seven – a pilgrimage of which Janina knows nothing more than was related on a single postcard from Krakow). Throughout his life, Karol liked to present himself as a man in exile. To his daughter it seemed that he was reading *Fire in the Steppe* and *The Teutonic Knights* in perpetual rotation. (Janina was obliged to read them too – this is the source, she explains, of her unshakeable antipathy to novels.) Chopin was the official composer of the household and bison grass vodka the official drink of the household's head. There was a print of the Black Madonna in the bedroom, and when John Paul II was elected pope you'd have thought it was a favourite uncle who'd got the job. (Karol's faith had been tested to the brink of destruction by his experiences in the war: thrown overboard when a torpedo struck, he had seen his closest friend drown just out of reach, and heard the screams of the men who had been locked into the burning engine room and left to die there; he had seen things so terrible they could never be described, he said – and he never attempted to describe them. Immediately after the war he had believed, at best, in a God who was not quite as vigilant a proprietor as he had been brought up to imagine, but in time his faith flowered anew, as strong as before. Marriage and fatherhood had opened his eyes again, he told Mary, who took to accompanying him to church on Sundays, though Janina – who was forced to come along as a child, before absenting herself as a teenager – was convinced that her mother's attendance was prompted primarily by the belief that life would be a good deal worse for her if she didn't comply.) When Gierek was removed from office Karol celebrated mightily, but also lamented (as though he had no family to consider) that he was now too old and too foreign to return (as he put it) to Poland. When martial law was imposed, he punched the radio. A few months later, his daughter left for London, thereby furnishing further proof of the unaccountable hostility of Fate. (It was never quite clear to Janina how this regularly invoked concept was to be squared with a faith in the all-loving, all-seeing and all-powerful deity.) Other men had been allotted children who honoured them; Karol had been given a monster of ingratitude.

Saying goodnight on a freezing November evening, Charlie asked Janina, for the first time, why she had left Canada. Her reply, as she buttoned his coat against the wind, was that it was simply too cold there for too much of the time. She had no snow in her blood, she said. (Later, she'd tell him that she'd once said the same thing to her father, and he had reacted with the fury of a man ridiculed in front of friends, though nobody else was present.) The following week she told Charlie that she'd wanted to live in London because in London you had people like Elvis

Costello and The Clash and Adam Ant, and you'd not find many boys like those in Toronto. (Celia's consternation upon discovering Janina's copy of *London Calling* buried in the midst of Shania Twain and Simply Red was that of a palaeontologist unearthing the bones of a bird amidst ammonites and fossilised worms. And if you were to see a photo of Janina circa 1979, you too would instantly be inclined to categorise her as an Eagles or Supertramp type of girl. Shown such a picture (Janina at an ice rink: tight pink sweater, white jeans, hair as bouncy as a cheerleader's), Celia remarked on the notable absence of safety pins or any other kind of punkish paraphernalia. To which unembarrassed Janina replied, with surprising and (as Celia admitted) admirable aplomb: 'Exactly. That's my point.') Also, she explained to Charlie, Canada was just too big: she liked the idea of living in a place where you didn't have to take a plane to reach the edge. (Janina made the most of dwelling on a narrow island. For half a year she lived in a tatty bedsit above a newsagent's shop, cooking meals that cost no more than a pound to put together (a skill learned from her mother), never staying for more than one drink when she went out with the girls from the office, limiting cinema evenings to one per month, putting aside a sizeable portion of her wages so that, when work finished on Friday night, she could take a coach or train to a town she hadn't yet visited, where she would explore the streets as assiduously as a cartographer. She'd seen more of England in six months, said Charlie, than he'd seen in his whole life.) Then, in reply to his asking her a question about her parents (at this point he knew only that they existed, and where), she confessed (it was more of a plain statement than a confession) that she didn't care for her father and mother very much. (They were crossing Hungerford Bridge, and were going to spend the night together for the first time. Not that Charlie knew this as they walked across the bridge; it's possible, however, that Janina had decided how the evening was to end, and that the statement about her relationship with her parents was the one last important disclosure she had to make before she could take him to bed.) 'By "not care for them" I mean "don't like",' said Janina, not with any animosity, but rather as if her only concern were to remove any ambiguity from what she had said. And when she said, 'That's one other reason I'm here,' it did not seem to Charlie that they had now at last reached the ultimate truth, the one essential fact which only now could Janina bring herself to reveal – no, it seemed rather that her dislike of her parents was, as she said, merely one additional factor to be considered, a factor no more or less significant than the terrible winters and the impossible dimensions of the territory.

(Whereas some people, Charlie was already aware, might find Janina a little too cool, to him this coolness was crucial to her allure. In public she conducted herself as if every gesture were being judged for its economy and sureness. She knew precisely what she was going to say before she spoke. She was never hurried, never visibly disconcerted. Janina, in short, was more composed than any young woman Charlie had ever met, and yet she kissed him as if she wanted to weld herself to him. ('She's a tiger,' Charlie later confided, eyes widening in gleeful alarm as he poured one last drink for each of us. This would have been a week or two before their wedding. 'She's fantastic, I tell you,' he said, passing a glass to me, and he looked me in the eye, to elicit a promise that I would always know that this was a fact, no matter what anyone else might say – and by 'anyone else' we mean primarily Celia, whose misgivings about Janina ('The North Pole' she called her – not in Charlie's presence, of course) he foresaw hardening into antipathy, and vice versa.)

Over the morning-after breakfast, Charlie returned to the subject that Janina had abruptly closed on the bridge, when she'd declared that they should talk about his parents instead, because the senior Brennans were more interesting. Her mother, Janina now told Charlie, loved her husband 'for all his faults' and was dismayed (to put it mildly) that her daughter could not find it in her heart to forgive him his imperfections, because the truth of the matter was that he loved them both very much and was wearing himself out to support them, and he had a sadness in his heart that he could never get rid of. He could never get rid of it, according to Janina, because he could never stop thinking about himself and the better life he believed was owed to him. Vast self-pity was one of the many paternal imperfections now enumerated by Janina, entirely without emotion. 'When he's sober he gets angry at the slightest thing; he's even nastier when he's drunk; he's drunk a lot of the time, because he drinks vodka like water,' she recited, and she might have been saying: 'His hair is red; he is left-handed, he is five-foot-six.' Charlie learned that Karol had often, after a glass or three, struck his wife. When Janina was a girl, he used to slap her too, because she had a bad attitude to school, or a bad attitude to her mother, or – above all – a bad attitude to him. At around the time of her fourteenth birthday she cut her hair short with the kitchen scissors and he screamed at her that she'd made herself look like a homosexual boy, and when she responded with a comment he didn't like he smacked her across the face so hard that his wedding ring cut the bridge of her nose. 'You won't ever hit me again,' she told him (he did, though), then she locked herself in her room; he punched the door so hard that his knuckles left four little hollows in the wood. 'You are not my daughter,' he would bellow at her; the accusation, she thinks, was first used when she refused to continue to struggle through the second-hand Polish textbooks he brought home for her. (Nowadays she can comprehend little more than some rhymes that her father had recited to her at bedtime when she was small – the same five or six verses, repeated over and over and over again.) Her mother did nothing to stop him. His rages, she'd have her daughter believe, were the eruptions of a mind as restless and troubled as a poet's; he was powerless to prevent them, and the anguish they caused him was as great as theirs. There were, it's true, sessions of extravagant weeping and bouts of extra church attendance, which his wife took as evidence of deep contrition, and Janina saw as play-acting and self-indulgence. Janina herself, her mother told her, was partly to blame, because she was always goading him. 'One of us has to stand up to him,' Janina retorted, for which she was banished to her room for the rest of the day. It was ridiculous: her mother was a hefty woman and her father was just a little runt – she could have flattened him with one blow, and if she'd done that, right at the beginning, the first time he raised his hand to her, their lives might have been completely different.

In the eighteen months between leaving Canada and meeting Charlie, Janina had spoken to her parents just once and written to them three or four times. They did not come to the wedding: a card arrived, in which her mother had written a message of just four words: 'We wish you happiness'. It did not accord with Charlie's notion of the rightful order of things that he and his parents-in-law had never set eyes on each other, even if Mr and Mrs Kasprzyk were as difficult as Janina portrayed them, as he was of course sure they were. In sending them a selection of wedding photos with their Christmas card (Janina vetoed a message expressing regret that they had not been able to attend), Charlie was hoping to create the conditions for a rapprochement. The immediate response was not very positive, but Charlie chose to take encouragement from the fact that they had signed the card 'Karol' and 'Mary' rather than 'Mother and Father', and had appended the line: 'Thanking you for the photographs.' Charlie was in favour of sending best wishes to the parents on their birthdays – they did, after all, acknowledge Janina's. Pointing out that a mere acknowledgement of the anniversary was all it was, Janina refused to tell Charlie when their birthdays were. Before long, however, Charlie had an undeniable occasion for resuming contact. He dispatched a brief letter and a single picture, bearing on the reverse the following text: 'Peter James Brennan, born 7.09 a.m., July 1st 1985, 7lbs 8oz.' A fortnight later a parcel of baby clothes was delivered; on the inner wrapper Mary had written: 'We send you congratulations and we hope that we will see Peter one day.'

The perpetual round of cooking, shopping, washing and sleeping in two-hour instalments (Peter the future whizz-kid was not an easy baby) seemed to have no detrimental effect on Janina. On the contrary: whereas Charlie (though absolved of responsibility for household chores) looked as if he were in need of a blood transfusion, Janina was effulgent with well-being. She was, in Celia's opinion, changed very much for the better – and Janina, in return, believed that aunthood had effected something of a transformation in her surprisingly supportive sister-in-law. Judging that, in her fog of maternal contentment, Janina might be less than absolutely hostile to the idea, Charlie suggested that perhaps they might, one day, introduce their son to his Canadian grandparents. 'Maybe,' said Janina, as if humouring an impossible whimsicality, along the lines of: 'Perhaps one day we'll live in a castle beside an Italian lake.' He took it upon himself, on Mary's birthday (Janina had softened enough to reveal the date), to send her a letter, giving news of the infant, with pictures enclosed. Eventually a card came back: the boy looked lovely and very much resembled Karol, Mary wrote. (He didn't resemble Karol in the slightest, said Janina.) Though Janina's name was nowhere in the message, this was nonetheless an advance, and Charlie persisted with his quiet campaign, reviving the notion of a visit to Canada once every two or three months, but never pressing the point. Further exchanges of cards occurred, sporadically; more clothes arrived for Peter (high quality, Janina conceded). On September 9th 1986, at 1.01 p.m., Frederick Charles Brennan was born. A parcel of clothes was received; the card exchange intensified; Charlie began to make plans for the expedition to Toronto. When he suggested that he could of course take the boys and Janina could stay in London if she really couldn't bear the idea of coming, he knew, from the way she said 'I suppose so,' that sooner or later he was going to prevail. 'Just think about it,' he said, and left it at that. They flew to Toronto a few months before Peter's second birthday. If they'd delayed any longer they'd have had to pay full price for three seats, and Janina wasn't having that.

A husk of a man – that was Charlie's description of Karol Kasprzyk. The eyelids made a particularly strong impression: the upper lids drooped like waterlogged awnings, and the lower sagged so much that they had turned halfway over, showing a thick red crescent of wet flesh. His hair, grey

and thin and long, had been dyed a hazelnut colour, streak-
ily; his cardigan would have accommodated an extra twelve
inches of girth. Just as Janina had said, he held himself like
a man who was proud of the dignity with which he was
facing perpetual adversity. When Charlie shook his hand, it
was like taking hold of a leather glove stuffed with broken
chopsticks. His wife – twice her husband's width – had clear
grey eyes which frequently blazed adoration in the direction
of her husband, but also suggested to Charlie, once or twice,
the image of a prisoner in whom the hope of release has not
yet been wholly extinguished. They sat around the table in
the kitchen, to eat a cake that Mary had baked in their honour and drink extremely strong coffee from heavy old mugs.
Taking Freddie from his father, Mary manoeuvred the child
stiffly on her lap, like a doll, and smiled at her daughter as
if accepting an unspoken apology. Most of the talking was
done by Mary, and for most of the time it was Charlie she
was talking to. 'So you are in business,' she said, in a way
that implied that no guest could be more welcome than a
businessman. She questioned him on the subject of the family firm as thoroughly as a bank manager assessing the risk
of a loan, while Janina picked at the band of plastic that ran
around the edge of the custard-coloured table, and her father
squinted at Charlie, taking the measure of the man who had
accepted the challenge of his daughter. When the world of
domestic tiling could be made to yield no more conversa-
tional material, Karol smiled broadly, evidently satisfied with
what he'd observed. Two small tumblers were filled to the
brim with bison grass vodka. 'The Rogalin Oaks?' ingratiating Charlie enquired, raising his glass in the direction of the
faded picture above the door, and Karol, immensely pleased
by his son-in-law, confirmed that this was correct, and gave

the oaks the sort of look one might give the photograph of a close and senior relative who had been decorated for bravery. Before they left, Karol showed Charlie the bedroom that had been Janina's; it was as tidy as a long-unoccupied hotel room, exactly as it had been on the day that Janina left. Her father shook Charlie's hand as they stood in the middle of the room and said solemnly: 'I hope she will respect you.' Janina had stayed at the kitchen table; Charlie could hear only Mrs Kasprzyk, babbling at the boys.

They were in Toronto for a week. A nice city, Charlie thought: well-run, manageable, with friendly people. As informative and as detached as a veteran tour guide, Janina took him wherever he wanted to go. There were moments when it seemed as if she might believe that the maintenance of her current life depended on her complete resistance to the temptations of reminiscence. One afternoon, at Charlie's insistence, she met up with a woman – Robin – who had been her best friend when they were teenagers. 'How was she?' asked Charlie. 'She's well,' said Janina. 'She's fine. It's been five years. We've changed.' There has been no subsequent mention of Robin.

At lunchtime on the penultimate day, the family reconvened at a restaurant. The children were fractious, Karol drank a full bottle of wine in less than an hour, and Mary told a tortuous story about her sister and her five delightful children. 'Mom,' said Janina, 'the kids were not delightful. They were wild. You always said you came away screaming.' Mary shook her head and, in replying to her daughter, placed a hand on Charlie's arm: 'No, dear. That's not right. I didn't say that.' When the meal was over Janina and her parents stood facing each other in the street for half a minute, before hugging like politicians putting on a show for the cameras. Somewhere over the Atlantic, Janina kissed Charlie and kissed the boys and said: 'Never again.' And though the exchanges of cards at Christmas and on birthdays continued, as did the gifts for the grandsons, the messages inside the cards soon dwindled to single sentences, and two decades have passed since Janina and her parents were last in the same room.

E: Doesn't it occur to you that you're making things complicated for me? I see Janina every day and this makes it really awkward.

D: There's nothing here to make you think badly of her.

E: That's not the point, is it? You're telling me things that she didn't even tell Charles at first, so she wouldn't want you to be telling me, would she?

D: But people talk about other people. That's all I'm doing. Except I'm writing it instead of saying it.

E: If you were saying it, I'd ask you to stop.

D: But without this you won't understand. I'm helping you to know Janina better.

E: I know enough. I don't need to know anything about Janina's father to know that I like her.

D: OK. I thought you'd be interested.

E: I am interested. I like a gossip as much as the next woman. But that's not what I'm saying.

D: This isn't gossip. It's the bigger picture.

E: Whatever you want to call it. The fact is, I know Janina as well as I need to know her and as well as she wants me to know her.

D: [deflated, with pathos] Point taken. I'll be more discreet in future.

E: Is that a promise?
D: Maybe. No.

Ellen has had a rancorous conversation with Roy, and has stayed up late, watching TV. I wander into the living room, to announce that I'll be going for a stroll in about an hour, and she's welcome to accompany me.

A semi-clear night; the moon in its last quarter; air mild. We creep up the lane, arm in arm; after half an hour we move into the stink of the deer. A dash of torchlight suffices to locate the animal exactly. Nothing much is left of it now: a backbone, a skull, ribs, some fur that looks like a dirty old towel that's been chucked over the bones. Ellen, retreating, wonders why it is that babies don't seem to find any smells disgusting; I must find out why this is. Hamming it up, I crouch over the remains to rake it with the torch, like a policeman at the scene of the crime. A thought-bubble hangs over Ellen's head: 'This is morbid.'

By way of counterbalance, I insist that we stop on the way home, to observe in silence the beauties of our environment. Mighty convolutions of Prussian blue cloud traipse across the moon; the distant hills are vast heaps of dimly luminous ash. We venture further than I've gone before, and pass a pond that gleams like a pool of mercury. Something small shoves its way through the grass behind us; wings clack; we hear a clock strike two o'clock – the nearest house is fifty yards away. Ellen, looking up, shivers. She remembers being a kid, lying in bed after her parents had gone to sleep, looking at the stars through a chink in the curtains, and understanding that we're nothing more than specks of dust. 'But we have to forget it, don't we?' she says.

Janina, clearly a woman under some stress, comes up to ask me if I might turn the music down, as she needs to get an early night. Leaving, she asks: 'Don't you get bored with it? Always the same music every day.'

I point out that it is not always the same music. 'More than five hundred sonatas here,' I tell her, whacking the CD box.

'Yes, but they all sound the same,' says Janina. She turns to Ellen. 'Do you like it? I don't know how you can bear it.'

Ellen answers that she hardly hears it any more. 'We moved house when I was six or seven,' she says, 'and I thought I'd never get used to the noise of the traffic. But after a few months I didn't notice it. It's like that.'

'But do you find it interesting?' Janina asks her.

'Sometimes,' says Ellen. 'But I can't say it moves me at all.'

I have to intervene. 'Nor me,' I tell them. 'That's not the point. It's not meant to move you. That's why I like it. It's just music. It doesn't mean something else. It doesn't mean anything.'

My guardians look at me, united in scepticism. 'That doesn't make sense,' says Ellen.

Consider the blackbird singing in the garden, I suggest. 'What does that mean? It means nothing, but it's beautiful. It gives pleasure.'

'It means something to the blackbird, presumably,' says Ellen. If I could, I'd kiss her.

Cheered by a call from Stephen – he'll be with us soon. Uplift of mood so conspicuous that Ellen remarks on it. 'The only true friend I've ever had,' I tell her, with a tragic moan, hands crossed over the heart, buckling under the weight of sadness. Straightening as best I can, I add: 'Until you came along, that is.'

'Don't tease, Daniel,' she says.

'I ain't teasin',' I answer. This reply requires an expression (a Brando-ish smoulder is what I have in mind) that the face cannot manage. It would also be better if the mouth could manage the appropriate accent.

I find myself considering the guest list for the funeral: family; Stephen; and who else? Dr Goffman? Zoë, if she can be found? (Zoë and Janina – a combination with potential.) And then Marion comes to mind. I haven't thought about her for a long time, and haven't heard a word from her in years.

Ellen, after I've told her that I'm going to write about a new character for her, says she had a friend with whom she was so close that she was one of the woman's bridesmaids; after she got married, Ellen used to ring her once every month or so, but before long the traffic was all one-way, and within three years they were no longer in touch, even though they lived only thirty miles apart. Says Ellen: 'That's what it's like with a lot of people: if they don't see your face every day, you cease to exist.'

Marion McMordie was the daughter of a woman called Evelyn McMordie, to whom we must apportion some of the blame for my love of Scarlatti. Evelyn McMordie was a solicitor, and she worked for a practice that operated from a building near Waterloo station. I walked past it once, with Marion. From the street one saw only a pale blue ante-room, occupied by four black leather chairs and a fearsomely elegant receptionist, who was seated at a sparsely furnished glass and steel desk (appointments book; phone; one flower in a slender vase). One glance at the receptionist, with her minimalist work station and finely tooled haircut, and you knew that this was an office in which the machinery of the law ran smoothly and expensively. Mrs McMordie herself cultivated a style that looked the part: the jackets were well-cut and invariably black or dark grey, the slacks severely pressed and of matching hue, the brief-case rectilinear and aluminium-trimmed. The wristwatch – a slim and austere Longines – spoke of fussless efficiency and high income. She worked hard: during the week there was rarely an evening when she didn't put in an extra two or three hours.

And yet, though Mrs McMordie was an industrious and determined and extremely professional woman, she could also give the appearance of being oddly distracted: a smil-ing vagueness would often come into her eyes, as though she'd suddenly been struck by a pleasant sense of déjà vu, or was receiving sympathetic advice from a voice that only she could hear. I attributed these moments of self-detachment chiefly to the fact that, though she was no more than forty years old when I first met her, she had been a widow for almost five years. Both Marion and her mother were of a deeply unfrivolous cast of mind (there was no TV in the house – proof of their profound aversion to triviality), and I soon came to understand that a permanent seriousness had taken hold with the death of Mr McMordie. Marion very rarely referred to her father, and he was invoked with such tenderness, on those rare occasions, as to make it plain that the enduring pain of bereavement was the reason for her silence. 'He died a week before Christmas,' she told me, explaining why she never looked forward to the end of the year. (I assumed, from the word 'died', that he'd been ill – it was many months before I learned that he'd been hit by a motorbike on Regent Street.) There was another factor to Mrs McMordie's episodes of serene detachment, which was her faith. This, like her daughter's, was intense but unostentatious: I never saw a Bible in the house, nor any crucifix or Christian trinkets, and indeed I was greatly surprised when Marion told me, as we walked back from school one Friday, that her mother was going on a retreat the following week, and that this was an annual event, during which Marion would be left to the care of Aunt Joan and Uncle Gordon. Moments later, Marion asked me: 'Do you believe, Daniel?' I told her that I didn't, which she accepted with absolute neutrality, then stated 'I do,' quietly, but in such a way as to imply that her faith was a philosophical position at which she'd arrived after a great deal of thought. I knew Marion well for more than three years (her mother removed her to a private school, whereupon a slow but inexorable separation from me commenced), and in all that time she never attempted to convince me of the error of my world view. Her mother, too, was silent on the matter – with one exception. 'I'll pray for you, Daniel,' she said to me, a day or two before departing on retreat. (My skin had been especially active that year. And here let me record that although Mrs McMordie never touched me, I never felt that she regarded with me with revulsion.)

Marion as a child had been touched by death, and I as a child had been maimed by a genetic mutation at chromosome 17q11.2. This was perhaps the basis of our friendship. To young Marion had been revealed an eternal verity: in the midst of life we are in death. I, likewise, had been brought by disease to a wisdom that many fail to achieve in a lifetime. I knew what was important in life and what was not (having slightly fewer opportunities than your average boy to be diverted by the things that aren't important, but are nonetheless a lot of fun). I understood the superficiality of externalities, the foolishness of vanity. I knew the truth of my essential self, of the soul that cannot be touched by the decay of the body. I knew that one of the foundations of a valid life is truth to oneself, and I was always true to myself. (Marion did actually say this to me, some time after she'd started at the upper-crust school, and a certain hauteur had begun to colour her style. It would have been nice, I replied, to have had the opportunity of trying to be someone other than Danny the grotesque.) And of course I knew who my real friends were. I recall this being stated with an undertone of satisfaction in her own dependable virtue, but Marion was unquestionably a genuine friend. My outbreaks of rage she absorbed without complaint, many times. Whereas Charlie during this period (and Celia too, for that matter) would tend to take the line that things weren't as bad as I felt them to be, Marion understood that attempts at persuasion were futile. The solace of the confessional was what Marion provided, and an assurance of constancy. The hours that we spent together were generally spent in companionable silence, and I found few things more pleasurable. Often after school and sometimes at weekends (though on the weekends Marion customarily benefited from her mother's unwavering attention), we'd hurry to her house (from the age of twelve the capable Marion was entrusted with the run of the place) and install ourselves on the huge sofa of the back room, foot to foot, to read for an hour or two. (Marion never shied from contact.)

I cannot recall a single argument between us. Nonetheless, whenever Marion took it upon herself to remind me of what she perceived to be my sterling qualities of character, I would find myself wishing that she'd shut up, for two reasons: firstly, she was talking nonsense; secondly, and more to the point, she would enumerate these qualities with a directness that was intended to betoken that what she was saying was a matter of objective fact rather than merely personal approbation, but which reinforced one fact above all – that this was a friendship built from more spiritual material than the average adolescent boy-girl bond. This was the cause of some anguish, intermittently, because I quickly came to regard Marion as a very attractive girl. Others, I know, found her too solemn, too solid of limb, too heavy of jaw. To me, though, her aura of self-composure and competence was powerfully sexy. Her relationship with her mother – sealed by the death of Mr McMordie, it had a greater density than any other mother-daughter relationship I knew of – was attractive to me. She had alluring handwriting, as fluid and strong as a printed script. Her hands were beautiful, with extraordinarily long fingers that turned upwards very slightly at the tip. (Her mother had remarkable but unlovely hands: thin, tinged with violet and traversed by jutting veins, they looked twenty years older than her face. However, when I picture Mrs McMordie what I see first is a morpho-blue silk scarf which I saw her wearing only once; it struck me as emblematic of an exuberance that was otherwise submerged – and of course might not have existed.) Marion had a way of tucking a stray lock of hair behind her ear that stirred in me an almost unsuppressible tactile impulse. In summer she'd leave the top two buttons of her blouse unfastened, revealing a small portion of breast-slope – a convexity so modest that perhaps only I could have been so excited by it. Most exciting of all, though, was Marion practising the piano. Her teacher told her that she would improve if only she could learn to relax: she was too busy worrying about playing the right notes to let the music sing. She had to be less pedantic, he'd tell her, and he'd make her play the same few bars over and over again until they'd become musical enough to please him – which sometimes they never did. Often she wasn't certain that she understood what the problem was, because the performances that the teacher praised sounded to her much the same as the performances he had judged to be unacceptable. This, she supposed, simply went to show that fundamentally she wasn't musical.

'You're sure?' she'd ask, every time I asked her to play something for me. Regarding her as a far better pianist than she believed herself to be, I was beguiled by her modesty. Half a dozen times in succession she'd run through the same Bach prelude, apologising for the misfingerings and hesitancies. The mistakes did not diminish my pleasure – on the contrary, I loved her doggedness, her refusal to be deterred by failure. And I loved the sight of her playing: the way she scowled at the score, as if incredulous at what was being asked of her; the hands rising and falling as if immersed in thick oil; the mouth opened slightly in a silent gasp. That Marion had not considered the possibility that she might have been the object of my desire was proved by the confession of her feelings for a boy called Roger Hartleberry, a dull athletic swot who routinely bore away a tranche of prizes at the end of the school year. Sanctified and invested with wisdom by my burgeoning hideousness ('I will praise you because you are fearfully and wonder-fully made,' as the psalm almost has it), I could be told things that Marion would disclose to nobody else – that she was worried about her mother's use of sleeping tablets, for example, or that she'd been having dreams in which she murdered a particular classmate. 'I think I might be in love,' she told me, and I, the eunuch confidant, replied, as though exactitude in the definition of Marion's emotional condition were my only concern: 'But you're not sure?' She was surprised to find herself admired by the boy; this, in other circumstances, I might have found endearing. 'No, I'm not sure,' said Marion. I knew that with Marion there was no question that this would be a passing crush. She and Roger Hartleberry were still together five years later, when I last spoke to her.

I have lost sight of Mrs McMordie and Scarlatti. I'll be brief. It was a Saturday afternoon, August, nearing the end of the school holiday. Marion and I were outside, reading in the hammocks that were a major attraction of the McMordie garden. Rain commenced abruptly. I dashed indoors; Marion for some reason delayed, and received so thorough a dousing that she had to go upstairs to change. Piano music was playing in the living room. I stood by the closed door, as close as I could. I was amazed by what I heard: a jubilant flow of small and brightly ringing notes, inhuman in their rapidity and clarity. For a minute or two the effusion continued, then there was a short period of silence before Mrs McMordie, having noticed that a downpour was in progress, called out through the window: 'Marion? Daniel?' I knocked and went in. She had turned the record over, and the music had started again. I asked her what it was, and in reply she passed the LP sleeve to me. Watched by Mrs McMordie I read the sleeve notes, then I handed it back. 'Stay, if you'd like,' she said, gesturing to an armchair, and the gesture, coming from her, had the force of a substantial compliment, and I stayed to listen to the whole second side with Mrs McMordie, even after Marion had come back downstairs. That Christmas, Mrs McMordie bought me a copy of the LP. It's now so worn that it sounds like a rhino chewing a bale of cellophane.

Have almost finished with the McMordies when – sitting at the table on the terrace – a remarkable pain appears: it seems to strike at the spine and set it ringing; shock waves of pain peal through the body, from hip to throat. I cannot prevent a gasp from coming out, and Janina, taking the sun on the lawn, turns to me. She hurries over. 'What can I do?' she asks; there are tears in her eyes. 'What's happening?' She seizes me by the shoulders. 'Well,' I say, 'there is a great big fucking pain.' Her eyes, terrified, are just three or four inches from mine. 'Where?' she cries. 'What kind of pain? Tell me.' With clawed hands I make gestures that encompass the entire torso. The waves soon subside; I tell her that there's no point in trying to describe the sensation. I can't describe it. A pain cannot be described. 'What's a cup of coffee taste like?' I ask. She takes the remark as you'd take an utterance from a man who's delirious, and curls her fingers over my wrist; an unprecedented intimacy, and an arresting sight – her long pale fingers look as if they are grasping something on the sea-bed. Her hand is cool, and an exquisite object; she's leaning over me in such a way that I glimpse the skin – buttermilk-coloured, tight, unmarked – that covers her breastbone. In other circumstances I'd have had half a mind to get excited. 'That helps,' I tell her. 'I'm not joking. That helps.' I tell her she's lovely; I actually say it – 'You're lovely.' Behind her smile she is clenching her teeth, which are also perfect.

Charlie has an email from Celia. She's sent him some more figures, but the sums are completely mad, he says. At the table there's a lot of talk about Celia. 'She's a very good teacher,' says Charlie, four times at least. And because she's such a good teacher it shouldn't be much of a problem for her to find a good job, he opines. Janina agrees, naturally, and adds that Celia's problem is that she's still too emotional about things. 'She needs to settle down,' I concur. Janina takes this at face value and says I'm right: what Celia needs is to find a good man and settle down. 'Easier said than done,' says Ellen; supportive smile from Janina. 'The basic problem,' states Charlie, 'is that she's living in the wrong country.' She's too trusting and too naive, he says. She needs to be in a place where people say what they mean and mean what they say. Living in Italy, she's always going to have people taking advantage of her, he says. He mentions Mauro. 'Say no more,' says Janina, raising her eyes to heaven. 'We refer to him as the duplicitous prick,' I tell Ellen. 'Though, as Celia has pointed out, that's a contradiction in terms.' Janina and Charlie gather the plates. 'That kid with the ponies, he's got a lot to answer for,' he mutters, departing. A questioning look from Ellen. 'Tell you later,' I whisper.

Celia knows she is living in 'the wrong country', and that's the point: she likes living in a place where she doesn't quite belong. Of course, she doesn't quite belong in England, but that's not the same kind of misfitting: in England the distance between herself and her surroundings is a measure of disenchantment. And in Spain the perceived mismatch of world-view and temperament between Celia and the natives proved to be too great. The situation in Italy is not the same: there the fit is comfortably loose, or sometimes lightly chafing. The degree of separation, to put it another way, is enough to permit a pleasurable clarity of observation. Whereas in Spain she was watching the game from the sidelines, in Italy she's playing it. Yet she is still the foreign player, and always will be.

(In the early years of what has turned out to be her career, Celia's appetite for being out of place was somewhat stronger than it is now. Indeed, she once entertained the idea of working in Japan, after a term of teaching a group of especially amiable Japanese students – none more amiable than the ingenuous, garrulous and ever-gleeful Kachiko. 'Come to Tokyo. Every day you see something you not understand,' said Kachiko, for whom nothing was better for the soul than a dose of strong bafflement, such as London provided for her on a daily basis. Making her case, Kachiko showed Celia pictures of a sign-choked Tokyo street and translated the scene for her. She brought to class the comics sent by her half-sister Yuko, and taught Celia the magical phrase of Creamy Mami: *Pam-Pululu Pim-Pululu Pam Pim Pam*. A recurrent subject of conversation was Kachiko's father. Celia thought her own father had worked too hard at times, but he was Mr Sloth compared to Mr Inoue, who was at his desk by eight, rarely left it before ten, and slept four nights per week in a rented cubicle in the neighbourhood of the office. The hours of sedentary misery were alleviated by bouts of self-annihilation in backstreet drinking dens with his colleagues from Research and Development, sessions which might end with Mr Inoue and his team on their backs, shoe-to-shoe in a star formation – the Busby Berkeley salarymen. Kachiko proved beyond question that every day in Tokyo would be extremely weird for a Londoner. But there was, Celia decided, such a thing as too damned weird. What is one to make of a country in which a luxury car is branded the *Cedric*? What is one to make of a place where, after a janitor has been sacked for closing the school gates on the stroke of the hour and thereby crushing a child to death, scores of parents petition the school, protesting that the man has been punished unfairly for simply doing his job? Celia never went to Japan.)

It makes Celia furious that around ninety percent of the women on Italian TV are fabulous specimens with great legs, superb chests and hair as glossy as a mink's pelt, and that every prime-time programme, whether it be a games show or football analysis, seems to require the presence of an attractive young woman with no discernible function other than to be decorative. She shakes her head in disbelief at the shopping channels, with their delirious women screaming about the wonders of the latest buttock-firming apparatus, and bald blokes in shiny suits shouting 'Buy my carpets! Buy my jewellery, for God's sake!' hour after hour after hour. She can't resolve the contradictions of a country where spontaneous generosity is as likely to be encountered as petty deviousness; where a predilection for emetically sentimental ballads accompanies a disconcertingly hard-headed approach to interpersonal relationships (friends summarily discarded, to be barely acknowledged when they pass on the streets); where veneration for tradition competes with an infatuation with the latest technology, however low the standard of manufacture (the toilet in Elisabetta's apartment wouldn't look out of place on the Acropolis, but it doesn't flush properly; her brother-in-law's Ferrari is as fragile as a newborn giraffe); where sophistication and the maintenance of *la bella figura* are of primary importance, while the television programmes are the most infantile and demeaning in the world; where there's a church on every corner yet religion often seems a form of social decoration, albeit a form of decoration that's essential to life – 'It's like the wallpaper is holding the house up,' Celia wrote from Rome. She'll never make sense of Italy, but that's the attraction, or a major part of it, which is something Charlie will never understand, she says. But he does understand it, to an extent. He can understand how one might find it interesting for a while, for the duration of a holiday; he just doesn't understand how an English person – an English woman, especially – could live there.

And now to the subject in hand: what can be recalled of the kid with the ponies, the lad with whom Celia's infatuation with Italy supposedly began? Gianfranco was his name. He was fourteen years old, a year older than Celia, with a fetchingly piratical proto-moustache and goatee. Every afternoon he took tourists pony-trekking from the farm that his family ran, which was about half a mile from the house we'd rented for that summer's holiday. We walked across a field of poppies to get to it, and our mother made us wait with her until Gianfranco and Celia and four or five other youngsters had ridden out of sight, up the flank of the valley. It was hard to watch them, the hills were so bright under the sun. Other than the poppies, everything was the colour of khaki that had been boiled for days. Charlie's hair looked as if he'd just stepped out of a shower, and the ground crackled when we walked. Later in the week, Celia was allowed to go down to the farm on her own. We were to reconvene at the house between five and six, but at six o'clock there was no sign of Celia. Eventually she appeared on the path above the house: her red T-shirt was visible from a long way off. The sight of the blanched field and the spot of red moving down it, with a spot of azure alongside, is still clear, as is the sight of the azure spot taking its own path, leaving Celia to walk alone (her hand blithely swatting the air around her face) into the glare of her mother, who was standing in the doorway, arms crossed, wristwatch prominently on display. Charlie, in the kitchen with his father when the miscreant was escorted to her room by our mother, heard a long argument through the bedroom door: there had been such confrontations before, but this one was the fiercest yet. 'Leave her be,' our mother ordered us, coming into the kitchen, then nothing more was said about Celia until Charlie was instructed to tell her that food would be served in five minutes. During the meal, she spoke to Charlie, very politely ('Could you pass me the water, please?'), and to nobody else. Neither parent, in turn, spoke to her.

The next day was a heavy-duty session of sightseeing in Pisa. Sulky Celia, three steps to the rear, was vehemently bored. A few days later, realising that non-compliance was a self-defeating policy, she forced herself (the effort was perceptible) into resuming her participation in the daily outings and was rewarded, after protracted discussions between the parents, with permission to go riding again, albeit with Charlie as chaperon – an unnecessary precaution, in the event, because Gianfranco that day was in charge not just of two Brennans but also of an extended Dutch family who seemed barely to know which end of the horse should be pointing forwards, so he was too busy to give much attention to Celia. Weeks later a postcard arrived from Italy. Charlie, passing her room, seeing her holding the card, asked her if she was OK; she, in tears, told him to piss off – for which she apologised, after a delay of approximately a week.

If asked about Gianfranco, Celia will say that she can picture only a blue football shirt, heroic dark hair, the demi-beard, and eyelashes like a pony – that's all that remains of him. The afternoon she had come down the hill looking dishevelled, there had been one little kiss, a light but lovely collision of the lips, that's all. Gianfranco had talked to her about horses and his family, but they didn't talk much because they couldn't understand each other very well; most of the time they had just lain in the hot dry grass, bare arm close to bare arm, taking the sun. This proximity and languor had been delight enough for her, though part of the delight had been her anticipation of a day to come, a day that never came, when things would change between them.

Celia's afternoon with Gianfranco was something to be held apart from the family. Even if Charlie hadn't been Charlie she wouldn't have talked to her older brother about him; and Charlie being Charlie it would have been inevitable – even if he'd sworn not to – that at some point he would not have been able to resist making fun of her, because Charlie was incapable of understanding what she was feeling. Chronologically he was four years ahead of her; in terms of emotional development, however, gauche and chubby Charlie was lagging far behind. He wouldn't have known what to do with a girl if she'd handed one to him in a paper bag. One afternoon during that holiday they were strolling through Lucca when a resplendent young woman – thick black hair; Sophia Loren mouth; rear end of outrageous curvatures – went past them on a bike, and Celia jabbed Charlie in the ribs, whispering: 'Look at that one.' And Charlie's reaction? 'Very nice,' as if passing comment on the bike.

By contrast, Charlie was nearly wetting himself with excitement, as Celia tells it, when we arrived at the marble quarries. 'It was like a kid discovering that Santa's grotto is real after all,' says Celia, imitating her brother's wonderment at the sheer cliffs of snowy stone. For Celia it was a cruelly boring jaunt, but she attended uncomplainingly, as her penance for the imagined misdemeanour with Gianfranco. Similarly she submitted in silence to the tedious and revolting spectacle of the Chapel of the Princes in Florence. A room made of solidified vomit, Celia called it, but Charlie was in ecstasy, dumbfounded by that ice-slick floor of multicoloured rock. Putting a finger to the inlays of golden and steel-blue and straw-yellow stone, he named them: *Breccia Lavante* and *Breccia Pernice*; *Rosso Pistello* and *Rosso Atlantide*; *Rosso Orbico*; *Rosso Lavante*. The names were pleasing to pronounce, and Charlie took great pleasure in uttering them, despite corrections of his thick-tongued diction from Celia. As Celia saw it, his enjoyment of the hideous chapel confirmed that Charlie had the mind of a trainspotter. So obsessed was he with the naming of things that he couldn't see how ghastly they were. But Celia was wrong: the material itself, not its label, was what fascinated Charlie. 'This,' he said, patting a grey column in the nave of a church, 'is *pietra serena*,' and he stood back to marvel at it as if it were a beautiful tree that had risen through the pavement. Somewhere else – a chilly, pale and high-ceilinged room in which only he and I lingered – we crouched to take a closer look at a tiny figure of a golden saint, set on a seat of lapis lazuli. The saint swooned between miniature columns of glassy purple stone; behind him rose stone steps the colour of mixed butter and blood. 'Disgusting isn't it?' Charlie commented. And then: 'But amazing, no?'

A digression beckons. In many ways, as has been noted, Charlie is very much the son of his father. And for both of them the experience of Italy was something that addressed the essence of who they felt themselves to be. A crucial distinction is to be made, however. Whereas Charlie at the Carrara quarries can be seen as a young man gazing happily down the long straight road of his future life, for his father the discovery of Italy had brought about the discovery of something within himself, and the awakening of an ambition that could never be fulfilled.

When the senior Charles Brennan's national service was completed, it was understood by his father that he would shortly begin working for the family firm, a service to which it was expected (as one expects the sun to rise tomorrow) that he would devote the entirety of his active years. (As with the younger Charles, there was no demurral – not the faintest inclination to demur, as yet.) Assured of his son's lifelong commitment, and confident of his son's ability, Stanley Brennan granted Charles special dispensation to take a brief break between the army and the office, and an allowance to pay for a modest trip abroad – though this was more of a loan than an allowance, as it was offered on the understanding that Charles, on his return, would for a period be working for a minimal salary.

I first heard of my father's trip to Italy when I was nine or ten years old. Looking through an album of photographs with my mother, for some reason I now asked for the name of a man I'd seen many times before (at the end of the back row of a company of young men in baggy suits; my father was next to the face in question) but had previously regarded as belonging to the shadowy pre-history of our parents, a mysterious time-place to which we children were admitted only by invitation, and in which we rarely had much interest anyway. The face was that of Bill Cowdrey, my father's closest friend during his national service. They were not congruent characters. Bill was garrulous, quick-tempered, quick-witted, and did things with a somewhat showy panache (reversing his truck at speed, one-handed, with barely a glance at the mirrors; playing the tenor sax as blithely as whistling), and yet taciturn Charles soon came to like the cut of Bill's jib. He amused him more than anyone he had met before. (It's a possibility – once raised by my mother – that a residual affection for Bill Cowdrey was a factor in his leniency towards Celia's transgressions.) And, after a slightly longer delay, Bill in turn came to appreciate the unflamboyant qualities of Charles. A consummate skiver, Bill was adept at minimising the discomforts and inconveniences of barracks life, but his sloppiness often landed him in trouble – and would have done so many more times had it not been for Charles Brennan's skill with the blanco and polish, and his overdeveloped sense of comradeship.

Whereas Charles asserted the moral value of hard work, Bill lacked all aptitude for toil; he had simply been born without it, he said, as some people are born without a limb; if something didn't come easily to Bill, it was never going to come to him. There was an appropriateness, then, to the circumstances in which Charles and Bill set off on their foreign escapade: the former financed by an advance against future labour, the latter funded by two pieces of extraordinary good fortune. The first of these was that a cantankerous old woman known to Bill's father as Aunt Dolly (she was only a neighbour), who had survived a direct hit on her house during the Blitz (she was found in the back garden, beneath an upturned bath-tub), had died a month after Bill's call-up, having tripped over one of her cats and plummeted down the stairs; in her will Dolly left most of her estate (which was of a decent quantity: her husband, an actuary, who had predeceased her by more than thirty years, had made some astute investments shortly before his sudden stroke, and Dolly had barely touched the money) to the members of the fire crew who had rescued her from underneath the bath-tub, and much of the remnant to Bill's father, for no better reason – as far as he could see – than that, as a boy, for a year or two after the premature death of Dolly's husband, he had done her shopping for her on a regular basis. The second piece of luck: a few months before Bill's demob, his mother was informed that a remote relative – so remote that she hadn't the faintest recollection of ever having met the woman – had passed away and bequeathed to her a box of old coins by which, apparently, Bill's mother had been entranced as a child. This box contained a rarity in very good condition, which fetched a large sum at auction a matter of days before Bill came home. A portion of these twin windfalls was diverted into Bill's pocket, in order that he might see a bit of the world before turning his mind to the question of gainful employment. (His father, an engineer turned senior manager at Rolls-Royce, saw that it would be folly to hurry his son; he esteemed precision in all things, said Bill, and it was his conviction that the blueprint must be finalised before you begin making a life for yourself.)

As to which area of the world Bill might choose as the ground for his self-preparation, there was never much doubt.

His father had a weakness for Italians, a weakness attributable in part to his mother's enthusiasm for Verdi (she had wanted to be an opera singer, but her parents – joy-resistant Baptists – regarded a career on the stage as being but an iota less reprehensible than prostitution) and in part to his admiration for Italian automotive engineering. Close to his father's office there was a food shop run by a man from Palermo, who, whenever Bill's father dropped in on his way back from work, would sometimes slip into his hand a small gift for the boy: a pastry or some licorice sweets or sometimes a postcard of somewhere in Sicily. (Always Sicily: 'I am not an Italian. I am a Sicilian,' the man insisted, fiercely jovial; Bill didn't understand what was meant by this distinction, but it enhanced the mystique of the island.) The cards were pinned above Bill's bed: Etna in full spate (with hand-coloured plumes of smoke); mosaic peacocks; a donkey-drawn cart loaded high with grapes; a wilderness that looked more like Africa than Italy; a row of mummified bodies hanging on a wall, all wearing suits, with eyes like leather buttons. One of these cards – a stupendous girl sitting on the base of a wellhead – was produced from Bill's wallet and displayed to Charles, on the evening on which he disclosed his obsession with Sicily. It was the one place that he absolutely had to see before he surrendered to a life of drudgery, he said. There followed, at idle moments, invocations of a land of sun-blasted olive groves and blue seas and buxom nut-brown girls – visions so attractive that when demob at last arrived there was no need for any discussion as to what they might do with their allotted free time and cash. Within a fortnight of ditching the uniforms Bill and Charles were on the ferry.

They didn't reach the blessed isle. Even had Bill not been diverted in Milan, they might not have reached Sicily, because before they had reached the Italian border his insistence (having resources somewhat deeper than his friend's) on paying for the odd night in a decent hotel or a proper meal (they weren't yet halfway through France when Bill decided that these would be required every day) had depleted the kitty considerably more quickly then had been estimated. Then Bill went and fell in love in Milan. They were sitting in a café, making their coffees last an hour, when Bill, hearing high-spirited laughter, looked up to see two young women at a nearby table, one of whom – the more demure of the pair, laughing with a hand to her mouth (lovely fingers; no rings) – was without question the most astonishing creature he had ever seen outside of a cinema. Mustering as much suavity as could be managed in his state of smittenness, he nodded to her, and observed in response what he took to be an encouraging glance. Never a chap to hesitate, Bill sauntered over to the girls' table, where, through the use of mime-work and a self-mocking medley of English, risible French and worse Italian, he succeeded in ingratiating himself with Rita and her sister Anna. Charles, beckoned over by his friend, did his best to make himself agreeable, but he found his inarticulacy an insurmountable barrier to enjoyment (faced with young women who looked as good as this pair, he would have been inarticulate even had they been English), and soon withdrew. By the evening Bill was a man in the grip of a passion that had obliterated all thoughts of the purpose of their expedition. He wanted Charles to hang around with him in Milan. They could make a foursome – he'd got the impression that Anna might not be averse to a bit of fun with Charles. How he'd got this impression was unclear, but even assuming that Anna's apparent indifference had been a mere guise, Charles would not have been in the slightest bit interested in having fun with a young woman he knew he would never see again once he'd left Milan.

(As Bill was to tell Charles's fiancée, Charles was the straightest bloke he'd ever met. This on the whole was a good thing. Charles was the one man he knew he could rely on in an emergency: once, going completely against character, Charles had even forged a Warrant Officer's signature on a 36-hour pass, so Bill could have a long weekend with a girlfriend. But sometimes, as was the case with Anna, Charles was too bloody straight for his own good. My mother was told this story within a couple of hours of making Bill's acquaintance, shortly after she and Charles had become engaged. She wasn't greatly bothered by the idea that her husband-to-be might once have been tempted into dallying with a pretty Italian girl, but she didn't much appreciate the clear implication that she was a far less exciting proposition than the Italian girl had been, and neither was she charmed by Bill's inability to get through ten minutes without recourse to bad language. The tale of the forged signature likewise reflected well on Charles (it surprised her that he'd been capable of the subterfuge, but the incident just went to show how high a value her Charles placed on friendship – even if this friend wasn't likeable now, having failed to grow up as Charles had grown up), but the smacking of the lips at the mention of the girlfriend did not charm her (whereas Charles's embarrassment at the story was very endearing). All in all, even though much of his swearing was intended to emphasise the absolute decency of Charles, she didn't warm to Bill: he was a boaster as well, and he spoke rudely to his wife (who did not remain his wife for much longer – Bill, they were soon to discover, had another woman). After that evening, they saw Bill infrequently. Although she'd made an effort to be courteous, and had said nothing to Charles about how she felt about his friend, Charles nevertheless understood the situation, and was himself cooling towards his one-time best friend, as he would later admit. In 1963, by now divorced for a second time and bored to insanity by his job in car insurance, Bill emigrated to Australia, where he became a boat-repairer, married a much younger woman, had six children and built himself a large house by the beach. For a couple of years he and Charles corresponded, then two successive letters from London received no reply and Charles was happy to let it lapse.)

So, Bill remained in Milan to woo the splendid Rita while Charles went on alone to Venice, where, though the weather turned wet and frigid, he passed every day in a stupor of delight. The canals were picturesque, of course, but what thrilled him was to be in a city where almost every square inch of land had been built on. Venice was the apotheosis of stone and brick. Swaddled in every item of clothing he had brought with him, he chugged up and down the Grand Canal, marvelling at the palaces that rose shoulder to shoulder from the water. He gazed at wooden ceilings that had the shape of upturned boats, at staircases wide enough to drive a car up, at ancient pavements of kaleidoscopic stone. More than any other building it was San Giorgio Maggiore that stirred him. (This is the word he used: 'stirred' – uttered as if the experience had caused an unprecedented turbulence of mind.) For much of one afternoon he sat in the nave of the great white church, uplifted not by any apprehension of the presence of the Almighty (God had been expelled from the Brennan household: like Janina's father in the later war, his father had undergone a reverse conversion, but his had proved to be irreversible; two good friends, calling to him

across a wall when a shell struck, had in an instant, in a gey-
ser of red mud, disappeared from the face of the earth), but
by the perfected order of space and light, by the sensation
of being in some way changed, if only temporarily, by the
exactitude of this man-made place. By the time he left Venice
to rejoin his companion he knew that in an ideal world he
would have been an architect. And he knew that there was
no possibility of his ever becoming an architect: the idea was
a fantasy, and my father had little tolerance for fantasies,
even his own. This imaginary career was mentioned to his
fiancée once or twice, as something that had momentarily
seemed appealing, one among many whims of his youth.
Thus she was startled by the forthrightness with which – the
idea having lain dormant for more than a decade and a half –
he declared (this is some time around Christmas; neighbours
have joined us for drinks; I'm eleven years old, perhaps):
'The one thing I always wanted to be was an architect.' For
the children this was an arresting announcement: to none of
us would the notion have occurred that our father should
ever have wanted to be anything other than what he was. He
was as fully and necessarily himself as a tree is itself.

(Bill – to finish him off – had failed to get what he wanted
from Rita, chiefly (so he told Charles immediately upon
his return to Milan) because she never ventured out of her
family's apartment without Anna in tow. Had Charles stuck
with him, things would certainly have gone differently, because Charles could have taken care of Anna, leaving Bill to
focus the full force of his charisma on her sister. Reunited at
around five in the afternoon, the friends had a falling-out at
eight, after too much wine. In the morning, killjoy and wast-
rel went their separate ways: Charles caught a train north;
Bill struck south, determined to cure his hangover from Rita

by the only method that was guaranteed to succeed: another dose of the same. In Rome he was duly re-smitten: at the Trevi Fountain he met a young lady named Clio who was very nearly the equal in looks of the Milanese tease. The flirtation ended when – having been informed by Bill that he would have to think about getting back to England soon and couldn't afford to pay for a meal for both of them that evening – she threw the brooch he'd bought her (in fact removed from an unguarded coat on a park bench) into the river, with a sneer so magnificent he didn't know whether to applaud or protest.)

And now, when I think of the holiday of the pony-boy and Charlie enthralled at Carrara, what I see is a painted chapel. My mother is keeping me entertained by pointing out the marginal details (the boy falling out of the window, the monkey on the camel's back, the blue angel above the trees); Celia, holding a leaflet, is making sense of the scene for Charlie. The disintegration of my face has begun: growths have appeared in the nasal area, a couple elsewhere. A guard sits on a folding wooden chair, reading a newspaper, which is lowered a few times, to permit a surreptitious inspection.

And it occurs to me that Charlie's love of wine is yet another area in which we must acknowledge the paramount importance of paternal influence, and that our father would trace his own penchant for fine vintages to a moment in Treviso, where he changed trains on his way back to rejoin Bill. Having some time to kill before the next Milan-bound service, he wandered into the centre of the town and stopped at a café, where he ordered a roll and a glass of *rosso*. He sat at a table in the window. Across the street, workmen were putting a roof on a bomb-damaged building. For some reason – uncharacteristically – he lost track of the time. Perhaps he was unsettled by the ambivalence he now felt at the thought of rejoining his friend; perhaps he was conscious of some loss of enthusiasm for the future that awaited him. It was a fine day, cloudless and cold, and maybe he was prompted – consciously or not – to make the most of what would be the last occasion on which he would sit alone, on a pleasant day in a pleasant Italian café, watching people going about their business. He called for a second glass, whereupon the barman, seeming to have taken a liking to him, said, 'You have this' and poured a measure from a different, and by implication more expensive, bottle. Across the street, the arm of a crane swivelled through the perfect light-blue sky. He sipped, and it was the most wonderful taste he had ever experienced, a taste he could never describe. He should have asked the barman what it was, but there were other people at the bar now and he would have been embarrassed to ask in front of them, and then the barman went out and a different man took over, someone much older and less approachable, so he never found out what it was he had drunk. As he used to tell it, our father's enthusiasm for wine began as a search for a bottle that would match the taste of Treviso. He sampled many that were similar and many that were marvellous. None, though, was ever the same. It took him a while to realise that the search was futile.

Charlie digs around in the family archive and finds, in a wallet of our father's old photos, the monochrome group shot of the baggy-suited young men. I show it to Ellen, pointing out my father and Bill Cowdrey, next to him. Leaning over

Ellen's shoulder, Charlie says: 'No, that's not Bill – that one's Bill.' He's indicating the man beside the one I know is Bill Cowdrey, and he's adamant that he's right. He empties the wallet, searching for a corroborating picture of Bill. There's no picture of Bill, nor of the man Charlie thinks is Bill. There are seventeen photographs of our father as a young man, none of them labelled; in five of them he's with other young-sters, male and female, well-dressed and self-conscious, as if in rehearsal for middle age. Neither Charlie nor I have any idea who most of these young people might be, though Charlie is fairly sure that the young woman in the cardigan, with the corrugated hair, was a cousin. And then we find, lying in the bottom of the box, in its own sleeve of thin paper, the snap of Uncle Neville, standing in the jungle with a rifle in one hand and floppy hat in the other. 'Haven't seen this for a while,' says Charlie; he studies it for a couple of min-utes, before slipping it back into the box.

Uncle Neville, my father's older brother, was a soldier – one of the very few professions their father regarded as an ac-ceptable alternative to running the family business. Neville spent a long time in Malaya, where he was wounded and received some sort of medal. As a young man, our father had looked up to Neville – revered him, or so Charlie gathered. But then, when Charlie was eight years old, Neville did something terrible, and our father never had anything to do with him again. None of us knows what it was that Neville did. For a time the story our mother told us was that he'd gone to live on the other side of the world and they'd lost contact with him. Charlie suspected this wasn't true, and later it was admitted that there had been a big argument. It bothered Charlie very much that there was this lost member of the family, but he learned not to persist with his questions. 'He's washed his hands of us and we've washed our hands of him. That's all you need to know,' our father once told him, and his eyes were furious – so furious that Charlie has not forgotten the look of them to this day. He can also remember, dimly, a day when Uncle Neville came to visit. It was a sunny day and Uncle Neville and his wife and sons arrived in a huge black Citroën that Uncle Neville allowed him to sit in, so he could pretend to be driving. In the garden, his uncle sat him on his lap and showed him the bullethole in his arm. That's all Charlie can remember of Uncle Neville, and of his wife – Aunt Clare – there's nothing left but the memory of her amazingly thin shins, and a flowery dress that Charlie could see through when she stood against the sunlight. The two boys, Alexander and Philip, are almost completely forgotten, except that Charlie thinks that the elder, Alexander, had a very peculiar haircut, like a tight-fitting hairy helmet. Charlie has done a few internet searches for Uncle Neville, but there's no trace of him. Even Freddie has had a go, and he can't find him.

5

Stephen has been renovated in the eight months since we last met: the teeth have been whitened at great expense, and he's switched his custom to a new hairdresser, London-trained – not cheap, says Stephen, but you could easily pay more for a mediocre meal. A wing of grey is spreading above each ear, which augments the dash of the hairstyle. The roll-neck top – midnight blue, merino wool – impresses Janina, who is first in the queue to greet him; a double kiss from her, and a compliment on the aftershave, which she identifies correctly as a Guerlain concoction. Ellen next: 'Very pleased to meet you,' he says, shaking her hand; Ellen charmed by the light gallantry. 'Danny,' he calls; 'Mr Siveter,' I reply; he throws his arms out wide and I walk into them, to press my head to his chest. Ellen touched and embarrassed.

The atmosphere around the table is light and good-humoured. Janina in a vivacious mood – flirtatious, even. Much approval of Stephen's wardrobe, and teasing of Charlie's. 'Just look at his shoes,' she says to Stephen, pointing at hubbie's feet as he goes to fetch a bottle from the kitchen. Charlie is wearing a battered old pair of suede loafers, whereas

Amtrak Guest Rewards®.
Free travel fast.
Enroll at AmtrakGuestRewards.com

Forgot to provide your
Amtrak Guest Rewards number?
Submit a Missing Point Request to receive
credit at AmtrakGuestRewards.com/Retro

Amtrak is a registered service
mark of the National Railroad
Passenger Corporation.

Reservation
Cancellation Code

Passenger Receipt

Riders **AMTRAK** Baggage

Name of Passenger
UTIZER/BARRY MR

From
NEW YORK PENN,NY
To
WASHINGTON,DC
Carrier Train Date
2V 2253 11SEP11

Accom Space/Car
K

EXPRSS BSNESS

Form of Payment
AX232.00 1093
Rail Fare
$232.00
Accom Charge
$.00
Fare Plans
Total
$232.00

KOAE
Ticket Number No. of
2511127573099 01 01
Date of Issue Reservation #
08SEP11 250C56

PASSENGER RECEIPT

Stephen's shoes are beautifully cared-for brogues, in ox-blood leather. 'Appalling,' Stephen sympathises. 'Comfort before all things,' says mellow Charlie, taking a bow. 'You must take my husband shopping. He won't let me help him,' Janina tells Stephen, taking his hand. I slide my trainers out from under the table: 'You can tell a lot about a chap from his footwear,' I mutter to Ellen.

In the garden, Stephen philosophises. Why is it, he wonders, that we can happily contemplate the time that preceded us but not the time that will follow us? Logically the two extents of time are identical, in that they are immeasurable and we are absent from both, so why should the latter disturb us? Perhaps it's because we are not in fact entirely absent from the former? The year 1860 passed without me, but I know it as the year in which Garibaldi's army won the battles of Calatafimi and Milazzo and Volturno, in which Abraham Lincoln was elected president of the USA and South Carolina seceded from the Union, in which Chekhov and Albéniz and Mahler and J.M. Barrie and Paderewski and Billie the Kid were born, and Schopenhauer died. So the past is not a void as the future is a void. Next year I shall not be here, and I can never know anything of it. I am deprived of it entirely, yet it is so close to me. Is this an aspect of the answer? More thought needed, we agree. Might delegate the thinking to Stephen.

Stephen just happens to have a DVD of *Werckmeister Harmonies* in his bag. As soon as Charlie and Janina have retired for the night, we put it on. Ellen lasts less than an hour: it's the most boring thing she's seen in her entire life, she says. 'But a dose of boredom is good for the soul,' says Stephen. 'It clears the brain,' he tells her. 'Not this brain it doesn't,' says Ellen, reaching for Janina's stack of magazines. A few minutes later, after an exchange of glances with Ellen, he proposes that we put it on pause and go for a walk. Evidently there has been some collusion between them. I tell him it's a bit too early for me, but Stephen is insistent. He has to leave early in the morning, so it's now or never.

Stephen is on my right hand, Ellen on the left. It's like our cinema formation, he tells her: Stephen on the right side, Celia on the left, tickets bought in advance, get to our seats before anyone else, get out the instant the credits start to roll, straight into a taxi. At this point a car comes down the lane, and I almost fall over, twisting away from the lights.

Moon minimal, clouds sparse, stars profuse. It would be a good idea, Ellen suggests, if streetlights were shut off at midnight, or if we had a special day or two when all the streetlights are shut down, so we townies could all have a chance to see what the night is really like. Stephen says that on some of the Scottish islands, before they had electricity, they used oil from seabirds to light their houses, and that the stormy petrel was so oily a bird that all that had to be done to make a lamp was to take a dead petrel and shove a wick down its gullet.

We see no wildlife. Despondent, I feel as if I weigh thirty stone.

'I'll be back,' says Stephen, grasping my hand, like a Roman swearing an oath. When he returns, will I be able to talk to him? At the gate, he has a conversation with Ellen. 'What was that all about?' I ask her. 'What do you think? she replies, and we change the subject.

6

A pleasant afternoon. Charlie has fashioned a canopy from an old tent and rigged it up at the end of the garden, by the bushes. Through a gap in the leaves I can see the stream; a heron comes and goes; no kingfishers. One person sighted in three hours; Ellen proposes that we walk to the water one afternoon – she's taken a stroll along the banks and it's really lovely, she says. There are plenty of places to take cover, she assures me. 'Not in a million years,' I answer. Her mobile rings – it's Roy, wanting to see her. She's too busy, she says, and gives me a wink. I read and doze, and at one point, as I'm closing down, I see Zoë's face: it's a shock, an image so precise it makes me realise how far my memory of her has decayed. When I think about Zoë nowadays, what do I see, usually? Glimpses, as if into a room through an almost-closed door. Mostly, words are what come to mind: descriptions of her, stories about her, propositions. She could almost be someone I've only read about.

I look at the Tat2 website: rear-view of a pink-haired woman, who has a meteor on the nape of her neck. It may be Zoë; it may not be.

During the first decade of disfigurement, my father would from time to time take me aside for a pep-talk. It was understood that these words of encouragement were spoken on behalf of both himself and my mother, who never said anything to me that I might have taken as criticism, but who occasionally betrayed – by a doleful glance or some other momentary motion – a forlorn wish that I might find it in myself to take life more robustly. (When my father urged me to get out into the world and face it down, he was of course acting partly from concern for the well-being of his wife, whose anguish at my condition might have been to a degree diminished if I could have ceased sulking in my cell.) One of these paternal homilies took as its inspiration the wounded servicemen of the two World Wars. Many of these soldiers had suffered the most terrible injuries and subsequently been obliged to endure operations that were barely less agonising than their wounds. Hundreds and hundreds of these men were in a considerably worse state than I was in, and yet they were able to confront the world. They'd been dealt a very bad hand in life, but they just got on with making the best of it. There was no point in worrying about what other people were thinking, my father would say. If we worried about that all the time we'd never get anything done. I should simply ignore them, he urged me. Determined to emulate the heroic wounded, I conducted some research. In Westminster Library I found photos of heads so misshapen they appeared to have been pounded with a sledgehammer. Glass eyes stared out of faces that had been burned as flat as a drum skin. I looked at men who might have been stitched together from lumps of assorted corpses. It was inconceivable that anyone could survive such injuries, and inconceivable that, having survived, they could show themselves in the world. I owed them a greater resolve than I had so far shown.

Sometimes I managed to carry on as if I had successfully achieved an indifference to being observed. My father, watching me march along the street with the purposefulness of a boy with a point to prove, was proud of me. Charlie too was pleased. My brother's stance on the question of my life in public was a modified version of my father's. Ignoring the attentions of bypassers was, he understood, hard enough now, but in future, if the condition were to continue to flourish, it would be all but impossible. A different strategy was desirable: 'If they stare, you stare back.' That was Charlie's advice. 'Throw it back at them. If they can't take it, it's their problem.' I had to do this, not solely for my own sake, but for the good of society as a whole. Through my refusal to meekly accept their attention, I would oblige people to rethink their attitudes. This new strategy, Charlie acknowledged, might at first be difficult, more difficult perhaps than the strategy of indifference, but in time it would become easier. I tried it. I tried to return curiosity with curiosity. Charlie was fifty percent correct – I found it difficult at first. But it never did become easier. In fact, it quickly became impossible. Afraid of provoking more of a reaction than I could cope with (in Dulwich park I returned a look; 'What the fuck's the matter with you?' the starer demanded), I preferred – in the periods when I was feeling bold – the approach recommended by my father. I would charge about the city at weekends as if I'd enclosed my eyes in blinkers. Ploughing a path through the crowds, I could convince myself, for an hour or two, that these people were focused on their destinations as intently as I was on mine. But I could never make the illusion last long. Exhausted by the effort of it, I'd allow my gaze to snag on the gaze of someone whose face I had sensed turning in my direction, and soon I'd once again be conscious of every passing glance. My father told me that I shouldn't concern myself with what these people were thinking, and I wasn't much concerned. (I knew what they were thinking – they were thinking what I'd be thinking in their position: 'Christ, look at that!') It was the simple act of looking that was the essence of the problem, the awareness of perpetual surveillance, the friction of being seen. When you look at the world you project yourself into it, you possess it, you subject it to your vision, to your mind. But I was an object, not a subject. I glanced at a face and I saw my appearance reflected back at me. Most people are fundamentally decent, decent Charlie would tell me, and I had no reason to take issue with him, but the squirm of sympathy could be as intolerable as the flinch of disgust. And I did provoke some extravagant reactions: the girl who yelped after colliding with me in a department store; the young woman who came across me in an alleyway off Oxford Street, and froze as if she thought I might murder her; or the woman who, in Kensington Gardens, put her hands over her child's eyes, and departed at speed, whimpering.

To minimise the hazards of venturing outdoors I required company. Fixing my attention on a companion made it easier to disregard the attentions of others, and this companion, more often than not, was of course Celia. With Celia I went to many an event or exhibition that I could not have attended alone. Seeing me hesitate on the threshold of a busy room, she would hook an arm to steer me through the crowd. 'Just pretend we're famous,' I remember her saying as she dragged me along, and 'We're not going to be bullied by the stupid.' But my sister espoused a more militant version of Charlie's philosophy, that the starers should be made to pay, and there was always the risk, despite my telling her that her counter-offensives didn't make things any easier for me, that she would take it upon herself to fight back as my proxy. Sometimes her retaliation was mild: a scowl; an eyebrow raised questioningly; a shame-inducing smile. Occasionally, however, she couldn't control herself, and she'd turn on the gawper in a fury. 'You want to know what's up?' she'd yell. 'They're cutaneous neurofibromas. Wanna touch?' Or: 'It's an autosomal genetic disorder. Shall I write it down for you, fuckwit?'

After Celia had gone to university I didn't often go up into town – once a month, perhaps, and nearly always with Stephen. When Stephen left home the excursions became rarer. The experience of being among so many people had by then become almost unbearable – not solely because of my aversion to being seen (though this had certainly deepened), but because of the din and the crush of it too. I was well on the way to becoming a hermit of the suburbs. But I remember very clearly a later evening, an autumn evening during the year between Barcelona Part I and Barcelona Part II. Celia, Stephen and I had been to a cinema in the West End, and we'd climbed into a taxi on Shaftesbury Avenue, taxis now being the only form of public transport that I could bear. Somewhere near Trafalgar Square we were trapped in traffic, on a pedestrian crossing. People were massing on the pavement on both sides of us, and Celia was looking steadily at the cluster on my side. The affair with Fontenoy had recently disintegrated, so she was in a thoughtful mood. 'Look at them,' she said, in a wistful tone that was very unusual for Celia. 'Who knows what's going on there?' Randomly she pointed out half a dozen faces in the crowd, and tallied their imaginary woes: 'That one's going home to drink herself unconscious; that one is so bored with her life she can barely move; that boy's broken-hearted;

that man hasn't seen his family for a year; that woman has lost a husband.' If we knew what everyone around us was feeling we'd go mad, she said. 'Marks of weakness, marks of woe,' murmured Stephen, and when I surveyed that morass of faces they did indeed seem burdened, every one of them. But as I looked at that huge group of individuals, every one of whom seemed oblivious of everyone around them, a different thought presented itself: that in all likelihood this moment was of no significance to any of them, and that experiences that mean nothing, that have no weight, are more important to a good life than any of them realised.

But let's finish on a note of amusement. On the staircase of a subterranean West End cinema Stephen is hailed by someone he'd worked with a year or so earlier. I am well swaddled in my customary gear – voluminous scarf, long coat, dark glasses, the big floppy beret brought back from the Basque country by Stephen. I step out of the way, to lurk beside the drinks machine. Nodding in my direction, Stephen explains that his shy companion is Doctor Bleb, a scholar from Brno, visiting to assist with a forthcoming show at the V&A. Doctor Bleb is a shy man, and very self-conscious about his defective English, but a brilliant figure in his field. 'He's forgotten more about Renaissance majolica than I'll ever know,' Stephen informs his erstwhile colleague, his voice grave with respect.

'What do you think of this, El?' I ask her. On the screen we have a picture of a woman's chest: not her breasts, but the area above, covered with a tattoo of a wide necklace of seaweed. 'A chest plate, they call it,' I tell her. She thinks it looks horrible. 'You ain't seen nothing yet,' I announce, scrolling down the page for pictures of the woman's back. Every square inch is covered with tattoos: a bear, a fox, a snake and a leopard peer through swirls of leaves and vines. Pointing to a capuchin monkey, I tell her that two months ago this was an empty space, the last one. 'She'll regret it when she's older,' says Ellen. 'Her name is Trix,' I go on, 'and these are messages from the tattoo-loving public.' *Love your ink. U R soooooooo cool*, writes Billee. Pause, to maximise the impact of revelation: 'That's me. I'm Billee.' Ellen perplexed, but makes no comment. Another couple of clicks and there I am again, taking issue with some halfwit's opinion of the last James Bond film: *LOL OMFG that is so hilarious*, remarks BBBitch. Elsewhere, Blebby commends a girl's glove-puppet video for an Eminem track: *Your so amazing*. Barbz is greatly impressed by a sculpture constructed from magnets: *Shit man that fucken thing is aliiiive*. Bozza finds he cannot agree with DaYak's point of view on Tony Blair: *You take the cake of ignorence*. It's a game I play every now and then, I explain. Frowning deeply, Ellen reads a few more postings before giving up in dismay. 'It's like dogs barking,' she says.

Celia took me to Matt's place half a dozen times – this was the final flourish of my extra-domiciliary social life. Perhaps Matt invited me primarily in the hope that one day I'd agree to be photographed. Perhaps not – but it was the high possibility of being regarded as a potential subject that had made me even more uncomfortable about meeting Matt than I'd been about meeting Celia's previous boyfriends. (I had always been conscious (with no good reason, Celia insisted) that the boyfriends were being introduced to me as some sort of trial of their character: if they balked at the sight of the brother, they were not made of the right stuff. One was so keen to get his hand up Celia's skirt that he feigned finding me as engrossing a conversationalist as Gore Vidal; another, however, looked as though he'd swallowed a pint of cod liver oil a few seconds before being led into my room.) 'If Matt suggests it,' Celia had said, 'all you have to do is say No and that'll be the end of it.' This was disingenuous, as she knew that he'd suggest it sooner or later ('He's always looking; he sees a picture wherever he looks,' she'd said in the first flush of admiration), and whether or not Matt would try to persuade me to face the lens was beside the point – the prospect of simply being observed by a professional observer was unappealing in itself. Also, from what Celia had told me about him, I'd imagined Matt as a man somewhat in thrall to his own mystique, and in this respect I was of a similar mind to Charlie, who was predisposed to be suspicious of any boyfriend of Celia's, and had initially pictured the latest one as the preening golden boy of what sounded like a family of insufferable preeners. But Charlie met Matt several weeks before I did, and reported that, though he took himself a bit too seriously (Celia's view is that Charlie, had he been introduced to Michelangelo, would have concluded that Mr Buonarroti took himself too seriously), Matt was an interesting chap, and Janina thought so too. (Matt, by the way, took a snap of Janina that has remained one of Charlie's favourites; he likes it because it reveals, if you look carefully, a vulnerability that people tend not to see; Janina hates it because it makes her look so old.)

Of course Matt asked how I'd feel about being photographed (not right away – on the third or fourth visit), to which the answer was that I'd rather take a bath in toxic waste, but saying No wasn't quite the end of it. A portrait, he assured me, wasn't what he had in mind. 'Can I show you something?' he asked (though Matt had no doubt that what he was doing was of merit, he did not presume that everyone must find it of interest), before going into the next room to fetch a batch of photographs, all of them large, in vivid colour and very crisply focused. I can recite the images from memory: a water glass mottled with water-stains and greasy fingerprints; a fur of dust on a wooden surface; a scar (Vanessa's appendectomy scar, I later learned) like a trench in a bank of pale clay; a crumb of pottery magnified to the dimensions of a breeze-block; the nub of an amputated finger, which at first glance I mistook for a tree stump.

The idea for the series had come to him, he explained, one morning on Ludgate Hill. He was waiting for the street to clear when he became mesmerised by the paving stone on which he'd set the tripod. In the centre of the slab there was the oily impression of a boot sole, and around the boot-print were the flattened remnants of perhaps fifty pieces of chewing-gum. The gum blobs made shapes as intricate as a slide of cells seen under a microscope, and that's what suggested the new direction. 'But I'm not sure where I'm going with it,' he said (he was going nowhere, it would seem – none of the close-ups appears on his website), and at this moment Celia came into the room and exchanged with Matt a look which proved to me that she had known he would raise the subject this evening. So his idea, I put it to him, would be to exhibit a portion of my skin alongside, say, the finger-stump, maybe with a caption: *Can You Guess What This Is?* (A cat's tongue magnified one hundred times? A floor of young stalagmites? A ruminant's stomach lining?) 'I don't have an idea in mind,' he replied, which could not have been true. He was at pains to impress upon me that his interest was not in any way prurient, which I would never have thought it was. 'I'll think about it,' I said, in the face of his earnestness, but I never did. 'I'm sorry, but I can't,' I told him the next time we met. 'That's fine. I understand,' he said, and this – to his credit – was the last word that was said on the matter.

On the evening in question we were eating, the three of us, when the phone rang and it was Zoë, saying she'd like to drop in to pick up the pictures of herself and Trix in about half an hour. Matt tried to dissuade her, but it wasn't possible to put her off: tomorrow the band was going to Southampton and then on to Cornwall and she'd really like to have the pictures before she went. She was in the area anyway, and she'd just come to the door and be gone in ten seconds. Considerably less than half an hour later the doorbell rang. 'Be right back,' Matt said, but I was halfway drunk by now and in any case I'd been intrigued by Celia's description of Zoë as a girl she couldn't readily describe – 'semi-feral' and 'guileless' would have to suffice. I'd also seen a photo of Zoë's pert and huge-eyed face, a very enticing picture in which she appeared to have just been told something about a friend that was funny, shocking and intriguing. (Perhaps, as well, I acted from the suspicion that there might not be many more evenings at Matt's, and thought that I should therefore make the most of it. I thought I had detected a cooling – extremely slight – in Matt's manner towards Celia, but I wasn't sure. Another point in Matt's favour was that he had always seemed to take care not to make a great show of his affection for Celia in my presence. This I took to be indicative of a sensitivity to the inappropriateness of advertising the pleasures of coupledom to the eunuch sibling.) In conclusion: I was the one who told Matt to let Zoë come in. 'I can hide in the bathroom,' I said.

There was a slight delay before she entered the room, which was to be explained – I told myself – by the necessity of her receiving a briefing as to what awaited her at the table. Certainly her entrance was that of someone who was seeing what she had expected to see. 'Hi C. Hi Daniel,' she called from the door. She smiled at me as if my face were an outfit I'd put on for the evening, and she approved of it. 'Sorry for crashing in,' she said, but Celia was already getting a glass for her, which was all right with me. The sight of Zoë was a delight: she was tiny, as Celia had said (many twelve-year-olds are taller), and was wearing heavy black boots that came halfway up her shins, with a short red kilt and a black T-shirt over a long-sleeved black fishnet top; her hair was dyed fuchsia, and rose three or four inches perpendicularly from the crown of her head, with spirals of paler fuchsia over the ears. Invited to sit down, she kicked off her boots at the doorway and walked over to the table with bouncy steps, as though crossing hot sand. She sat cross-legged on the chair as casually as she might have done at home, but her mouth tightened nervously as she lifted the glass.

On her nearer arm, through the mesh of the fishnet, I could make out a shape. A question formed, and in the next instant it barged out into speech: 'Could I see that?'

Caught off-guard by the abruptness of my remark, she turned to me, and this time – unprepared – her eyes betrayed an instant of something akin to vertigo.

'The tattoo,' I said, with a nod at the arm.

'Oh, right,' she said. 'Yeah. Sure. Right. Of course. Be my guest.'

She rolled up the sleeve, revealing a little blue and crimson dragon on a bed of clouds, and placed her arm on the table. 'It's Chinese,' she answered. Her hand trembled a little. Only later did I realise that Zoë's nervousness was almost constant; whenever she spoke, her fingers shivered as if wired to a battery.

'It's fantastic,' I told her.

'I found it in a book.'

'Really nice.'

'Thank you,' she said, with a smile that made me hear the pulse in my head. Answering a question from Celia, she turned towards her without moving her arm. She sipped her wine, apparently content for me to study her arm for as long as I wished.

I looked closely. Small segments of skin between the clouds and the dragon's wings had been left uninked; it was difficult not to touch them. 'Must have taken a while,' I said.

'Hours and hours,' said Zoë. 'But you ought to see Trix's. We're talking Sistine Chapel.'

I had already seen some of Trix's tattoos, but I said nothing as Matt passed the package of prints across the table. Zoë took one out. 'Get that,' she said, grinning amazedly as she handed me a photograph of a Gorgon's head in a tornado of serpents.

This was what had brought Matt and Zoë and Trix together: Trix was standing beside him, going through the racks in a record shop in Soho (this was shortly after the epiphany of the Ludgate Hill pavement), and he'd become transfixed by the snakes on her bicep.

'She thought he was a perv,' Zoë told me. 'But she's a vain cow, so she said OK, as long as I could come along.' She took another picture out of the envelope and slotted it gently into my hand. 'There's loads more,' she said, then she asked Matt, with a slight tilt of the head towards me, to signify that she was speaking on behalf of both of us: 'Any more we can see? Done the colour ones yet?'

A movement of one of Matt's eyebrows formed the first stroke of a frown.

'Go on, Matt,' urged Zoë, with the familiarity of a friend, rather than of someone who had spent no more than an afternoon in his studio. 'What you worried about? Trix isn't going to mind, is she?'

'Yes, but—'

'Not happy with them? That it?'

'Well—'

'Please, Matty,' she pleaded, applying a winsome simper.

Matt extended an arm in the direction of the room he used as his studio. 'Over by the window,' he said.

'Love you,' said Zoë, jumping up. She hooked a hand under my elbow; I felt her fingertips through the sleeve. 'Let's go, Danny.'

Overlapping prints, dozens of them, covered the top of the plan chest below the window. Zoë began to turn them over quickly, setting aside blow-ups of wood-grain, paving stones and tarmac. Vanessa's scar brought a pause, as did a huge fried egg in a pan (the egg-white like wet marble with a fringe of amber curlicues; the grease around it gleaming). 'Trix,' she said, passing a picture in which huge arm-hairs sprouted from blue-tinted skin like rushes from a bed of blue silt.

(Trix, Zoë told me later, had always had a taste for pain. At school (where her name was Patricia Yeatman) she'd excelled at cross-country running; she got such a buzz out of feeling her lungs rip that she'd cross the line just seconds short of blacking out. Sometimes she'd take off her shoes and socks to walk up the path of gravel at a friend's house. A good pain made her feel more alive than anything else did; pain was delicious. But that's not why she went under the gun. The pain of the gun was nice, but it wasn't big. It was a stroll up an English hill, when what she wanted was the Himalayas. (For Zoë, on the other hand, the pain was a major disincentive: that's why she'd limited herself, so far, to the dragon and a couple of other miniatures.) An expanse of white flesh, as far as Trix was concerned, was a canvas in need of paint – it was as simple as that. Some people thought she was punishing herself with the needle, that she was deliberately disfiguring herself. That wasn't it. Trix was the daughter of affectionate, patient and well-heeled parents, who may have been bemused by their daughter's lifestyle, and couldn't pretend to be happy about her mania for body decoration, but they had never so much as raised their voices at her, and would even have come to see the band play if they could have done so without causing embarrassment all round. If Trix had any problem with self-esteem, said Zoë, it was that she had too much of it – that's why she was the lead singer, lead guitarist and main songwriter.)

After the blue-silt arm came a nipple as wide as a dinner plate. 'Not Trix,' stated Zoë. 'Not me either. Maybe Celia?' She extracted a photograph of a sunburst tattoo, another of a lizard on a hip, both Trix. At a picture of a carnation on a plump convexity of flesh she announced: 'That's my arse.' (Said with a wondering pride, as a young mother might say, watching her daughter win a race at the school sports day: 'That's my girl.') The carnation, she explained, was her first tattoo, so it was in a place where her parents couldn't see it, not that they'd have been bothered. It wasn't very good, she thought, so one day she might have some new ones put around it. She pointed out where the inking was messy; perfectly unabashed, she might have been showing me a picture of her thumb. Next was the lizard again – 'European Fire Salamander, actually,' she said, mock-proud of her exactitude – and then the picture that Matt had taken right afterwards, which had come about because Trix had taken her kit off for the salamander shot and she'd told Matt he might as well take a pop at the dolphin while he was at it. Arching its back on the swell of a muscle, the dolphin pushed its snout towards a crease of skin, and at the edge of the frame one could see a little bit more of Trix – a small bulge of goose-bumped flesh, and a frill of darker skin, like the skirt of a snail. 'It was no problem,' Zoë assured me. 'Celia was there all the time. She's brilliant, your sister, isn't she?' (Half naked, splayed on the table, Trix – Celia reported – had chatted away throughout the session, as if she were having her toenails painted.) And Matt was brilliant too, said Zoë. A girl she knew had answered an ad from a company looking for models for a fashion shoot, but it turned out to be just a bunch of sleazy old tossers – all gold-rimmed bifocals, comb-overs and signet rings – who expected her to parade up and down, starkers, in a room above a pub in Deptford. But Matt wasn't sleazy at all and he was really interested in what the tattoos were all about. From one look at Matt's pictures she knew that he understood what it meant to be an outsider. (And here there was a significant sideways glance, at which was born my suspicion that her reason for calling at Matt's on this particular evening was not the ostensible one. She'd known I'd be there.) 'This one's Celia,' said Zoë, showing me a photo of the underside of Celia's left foot, as if making a gift that she was confident would be received with pleasure. (I had recognised the foot at once, from the triangular scar on the heel, created by a broken bottle in the sand at Porthchapel.) 'You're very close you two, aren't you? C told me,' she said, with a nuance of curiosity.

This is where I said: 'Are you here because you wanted to get a look?'

'A look at what? At these?' Tears had started into her eyes instantly and she half-turned away, glaring at the floor.

'At me.'

'No I didn't,' she answered in a wavering whisper. 'Is that what you think?'

'It occurred to me.'

'This was the only night I could get here. I wasn't going to come in,' she said. Jutting her lower lip, she gave me a slighted glance that was plausible and winsome, then started to leaf through the rest of the prints. (Many months later she owned up: 'I did want to meet you. But not to take a look. That wasn't it.') She smacked at a tear on her cheek, as if swatting at a mosquito. I apologised. 'It's OK,' she said, dragging an arm across her face. We were in the room for another ten minutes or so, waiting for the redness to go from her eyes. The empty streets, we agreed, were more interesting than the close-ups. Soon after we had rejoined Matt and Celia (a brow-downturn of wry enquiry from Celia as I followed Zoë out of the studio), Zoë announced that she had to be going. 'Nice talking to you,' she said to me, in the tone of a remark made to conclude a disagreement that had almost expired, then at the door she added that the band might be playing down in Forest Hill and would I mind if she dropped in to say hello, on the way to the gig? Two months later, with barely an hour's forewarning, she came to the house for the first time.

She brought some beer and a tape of the band. Gunnr – that's what the band was called. Track One (*Graveheart*) sounded as if the guitarists and drummer and vocalist had recorded their tracks in different places; the singer shrieked as though bawling from a tenth-storey window. The second track was less arduous: there was some evidence that the musicians had at least been in the same room simultaneously, and the vocalist (a different one) sounded more like a girl trying to get the attention of a friend on the other side of a busy street. 'That's me,' said Zoë, glancing at me in a way that suggested that the music was intended as a serious-minded provocation, and that sooner or later I might understand it. She roamed around the room, touching the computer, TV, video, books, CDs, phone, as if compiling an inventory. She wished she could live like this, she said, and perhaps she thought she meant it. 'People are rubbish, ninety-nine percent of them,' she said, and high on her list of rubbish people she would place her parents. Her father was a fucking shitbag arsehole: that's all there was to say about him. On the subject of her mother she was little more expansive: 'a slob' (watching TV in her nightdress – the same one week after week, till you could smell the thing three streets away), 'bone idle' (she'd never held a job for more than two months), 'a dope-head' (dope, for Zoë, was the drug for people who were happy just to sit on their big fat arses all day long), 'an ignorant bitch' (far from being impressed if Zoë ever received half-decent marks at school, her mother reacted as if praise of her daughter were a criticism of herself; books, she thought, were for people who had no life). When Zoë had her tongue pierced (she was fourteen) her mother pretended not to have noticed and didn't say a thing. And when Zoë left home her parents didn't even ask where she was going. It was just like checking out of a hostel, she said, and she never saw them again. She didn't hate them. Hating anybody was a waste of time – her parents didn't exist for her any more, and she didn't exist for them.

In the space of eighteen months Zoë came to our house a dozen times or so. Usually she brought a video (she had a penchant for sci-fi & Italian horror movies), or a tape borrowed from one of the girls in the band, whose boyfriend worked on nature programmes and had an amazing collection of sounds – warring chimpanzees, howler monkeys screeching like a man under torture, a bird imitating the whirr of a camera's motorwind. On one occasion she brought a tape she'd made after a gig, in a pub: a boy was chatting her up, and was so pissed he hadn't noticed that the recorder was on. *Snyznem, Zoë. Sluvlynem. Tis. Sluvlynem. Sbootfulnem. Nyurrabootfulgirl . . . Ummamushishn musself. Yam. Ummamushishn. Drumsh. Ummadrumma . . . Yoonme, wodyazay? . . . Cmere. Cmere babe. Cmere.* [Glass breaks.] *Fakit. Fak. Fakfakfak.* [Zoë speaks, inaudibly]. *Duznmarra. Znuffin. Cmere. Gwon, cmere. Cmon. Wozfunny? Wozzofunny? Cmere baby. Cmere. Oooh babybabybaby.*

She rode a bike that had no lights. Having no lights, she reckoned, was safer for a girl after dark – people walking on the pavement couldn't see her so easily, so no creep was going to jump out from behind a tree, which is what had happened to someone she knew. The world was full of creeps, Zoë was convinced, having by the age of twenty encountered a greater number of unsavoury men than most women come across in a lifetime. But the creators of the slasher necrophiliac movies she brought on a couple of occasions – all male, all with a pre-dilection for naked girls in conditions of extreme peril – were not creeps. They were visionaries and poets of the camera, who saw the human soul for what it was: a pit of black desire, to quote a Zoë-penned line from a Gunnr song.

My mother, taking Zoë's jacket at the door on her second or third visit (a nice piece of leather like that had to go on a hanger), glimpsed (having already heard about) a por-tion of the dragon on her forearm, and remarked upon it, whereupon Zoë pulled up the sleeve to show the entire tableau. Inclined to like Zoë for the simple reason that Zoë

had become a visitor (this just about outweighed the various irregularities of which my mother was by then aware,
the chief of which were that she had no job, had no proper
home, was a bit mad-looking, and had taken her clothes off
to be photographed, albeit by Celia's boyfriend), my mother
commented: 'That's very . . . bold.'

'Thank you, Mrs Brennan,' Zoë replied, as freshly as a
schoolgirl responding to a compliment on her fetching new
haircut. 'And there's this as well,' she said, yanking her
top and bra-strap off her shoulder to expose Saturn and its
moons.

I saw a tremor of panic on my mother's face, at the possibility that the stripping wasn't going to stop here. 'But
doesn't it hurt, when they do it?' she asked.

'Oh yes,' said Zoë, sighing.

My mother was not sure what to make of this, nor indeed
of Zoë in general. 'She seems a very nice girl,' she remarked,
after Zoë's other arm had acquired a rose bloom and drop-
lets of blood, 'but I don't understand why she has to do that
to herself. Does she think it looks nice?' It was a shame, she
thought, because Zoë was a perky little thing, and she liked
her – and not solely because she was the only person (other
than Stephen) who visited me with any regularity. (My father
recognised that Zoë was a kind-natured girl. He had little
more to say about her than that, but it was plain that there
was nothing in her way of life of which he could approve.)

The next time Zoë called, my mother kissed her: a peck on
one cheek, which was the cause of some embarrassment and
pleasure (embarrassment at the pleasure, in part), and also a
twinge of anxiety – detectable in a momentary widening of
the eyes and a floorward glance – that the gesture might signify an overestimation of the depth of the relationship (which

it did), and was furthermore a request (almost a demand) that she should remain loyal to me. My mother, it's almost certain, had got it into her head that sexual activity was at last taking place in her son's bedroom. This notion was not based on the observation of any intimate non-verbal communications passing between myself and Zoë – there were no such communications to be observed. Rather, I believe that the reasoning was that a girl who'd vandalised her skin with pictures of dragons and bleeding flowers clearly had an eccentric angle on the issue of body image, and that her presence in my room for a whole evening and God knows how many hours of the night (usually the parents were asleep when Zoë left) did strongly suggest that some form of sexual congress was occurring, given that it was impossible to imagine what the bookworm and the wacky elfin rock-chick could find to talk about for so long. It was of course less than ideal that Daniel's girlfriend should be quite so young, but on the other hand my mother knew that less than ideal was the best the misshapen son could hope for – and the very fact of this problematic full-blown relationship was further proof that this strange girl was fundamentally a good little person. But in fact no sex was taking place, though the exposure of the additions to the tiny solar system on Zoë's shoulder was not without an erotic charge, for one of us at least. Talk was all that was happening, and less of that with each visit.

Once I told her about Stephan Bibrowski, otherwise known as Lionel the Lion-Man, whose mother – so P.T. Barnum would have had the punters believe – had seen her husband savaged by a lion while Stephan was in her womb, thereby suffering the shock that transformed her foetus into a monster. Half-lion and half-human he may have been, but Lionel was popular with women, I informed Zoë, so hypertrichosis might have been a better career option for me. This was taken as a joke, but a later remark about the sexual liaisons with which the literature on dwarfism abounded (perverse and exploitative liaisons, but liaisons nonetheless) made her uncomfortable. In our early days she had told me, as confident in her analysis as any professional therapist, that she liked me because, as she put it: 'You don't need anybody.' This line was never heard again after the remark about fornicating dwarves, and there was no uncovering of new tattoos in the last six of our eighteenth months, though I knew they existed. And one evening (this would have been not long before the last visit), while we were watching a film about alien abductions, I confessed to Zoë that from time to time I had wondered what sex felt like. (She had been frank with me, earlier that evening, about her feelings for more than one boy, and for Trix. Thus I felt frankness on my part would not be out of place.) 'It feels great,' she said. 'I'm sure it does,' I answered, 'but that doesn't tell me anything.' For a few moments she thought, then she said: 'I can't tell you, Danny. It's like nothing else. Sex is like sex,' she said, and I wanted to kiss her for that, just to kiss her on the cheek.

It was not long after Celia and Matt had gone awry, and Celia had gone back to Italy, that I had what turned out to be my final visit from Zoë. On her way to a boyfriend down in Croydon, she arrived on a semi-derelict Vespa that she'd borrowed from one of the squatters. We watched a programme about film stunts that had backfired: safety nets missed, misjudged explosions, head-on smashes at not quite the intended speed. She left early, around eleven, saying she'd be back soon, the week after next maybe. My parents would be away then, I told her, so we could watch a film on the big new TV they'd bought. (They were going to France, visiting

places my father had last seen on his grand demob tour with
Bill Cowdrey.) 'Sure,' she said, and I knew immediately that
she wouldn't come, that she didn't want to be alone in the
house with me. The excuse, when she rang, was that she'd
split with her boyfriend and wasn't feeling too good. Then
she was moving to another squat on the other side of London,
but she'd be in touch soon, which she was, but now she was
in a bad way and needed to sort her head out. And so it went,
the intervals between calls getting longer, each of us pretending that the excuses weren't excuses, until in the end there
was nothing to say. It was impossible to make my life sound
interesting. 'What did you do today, Danny?' she'd ask. And
I'd tell her: 'This morning I read the proofs of a book about
Bismarck. In the afternoon I read a different book. Also I listened to two sonatas by Scarlatti. I have looked out of the
window and I have watched TV too. Tomorrow I shall do
something very similar.'

It's past midnight when Ellen returns from her tête-à-tête with
Roy, but she's positively breezy when she comes in. 'What
you watching?' she asks. I'm watching *Chinatown*. 'Went
better than expected?' I ask. 'Beyond belief,' she answers.
'Mind if I join you?' Revelations are afoot, clearly. There's a
flush around the eyes, indicative of alcohol consumed. 'Tell
me tell me tell me El,' I sing, pausing the DVD, and she does
tell me.

The neutral territory chosen for the rendezvous was a new
tapas bar, recommended by one of Roy's pals. The man must
have lost his sense of taste, says Ellen, because the food was
criminal: lumps of sausage as tough as chunks of old tennis
balls, and *patatas bravas* that seemed to have been made by

dicing a bag of oven-ready chips and dousing the pieces in tomato ketchup. It's called *Pablo's* – hence pictures of Picasso all over the walls. The music – too loud – was a mix of flamenco and Ricky Martin. Fibreglass wine barrel segments were embedded in the walls; above Ellen's table hung a swag of plastic garlic. Into this scene, ten minutes late, walked Roy, wearing a horrible brown suit and a wide, shiny and garish tie (sky-blue and lemon-yellow stripes). Had it been brand new, the suit would have been vile enough, but what made it especially unacceptable was that Roy had worn it on one of their first dates, and even then it wasn't new. Years ago, however, its awfulness had been endearing, in a way. Here was a man, Ellen had thought, who needed someone to take charge of him. He'd bought the suit in a sale, he told her. The man in the shop had convinced him that it looked good. (Roy had the dress sense of a blind man, and was highly susceptible to persuasion from anyone who appeared to have a modicum of expertise in such matters. If the man in the shop had told him he looked good in purple satin flares he would have bought them.) The suit had never been fashionable; now it looked like something from a museum. Worse still, he was nowhere near the right size for it any more: the waistband cut a deep groove into his belly, and he couldn't have buttoned up the jacket if he'd had every molecule of air sucked out of his lungs.

Why in God's name, Ellen asked herself, had he decided this evening to resurrect an outfit that should have been consigned to the bin years ago? Perhaps it had been the first thing that came to hand, or he was hoping that the sight of it might rekindle memories of happier times. (He'd never known that the sight of it had always been unpleasant to her, despite the fact that, whenever he'd proposed wearing it for an evening out, she'd usually steered him towards an alternative ensemble.) Or perhaps he wanted to show her that, while he was capable of making a bit of an effort to impress (the tie was new), he was so helpless without her that couldn't muster something smarter than this exhausted old suit. This was the most convincing explanation: the desperate garment was saying that its wearer was in need of her care – and her cash.

The sufferings of Roy's wallet were a leitmotif of the evening, introduced during the overture: no sooner had they sat down than he proposed that they should split the expenses of the evening. 'Hope you don't mind, love,' he apologised. ('You never heard anyone say "love" and sound so bloody sorry for themselves,' says Ellen. And when Roy asked how things were going with the sick bloke, you'd have thought the sick bloke was the fancy-man for whom she'd left him.) Later, irritated by Roy's complaining about how much a builder had quoted him for repairing a lintel, Ellen observed that she couldn't help noticing that he hadn't yet been forced to pawn the car (an overpowered Subaru that does about one mile to the gallon and costs a fortune to insure; it's a 'driver's car', says Roy, meaning that its priceless qualities must remain incomprehensible to the likes of non-driving Ellen), so he still had some way to slide before hitting skid row. Roy's response was to contemplate ruefully the precious vehicle, which he'd parked directly opposite the restaurant, under a street-lamp, so he could keep an eye on it while they were eating. Grinding his cigarette into the ashtray, he muttered that the car was just about his only pleasure nowadays.

'Apart from a drink every now and again,' Ellen pointed out.

Roy inspected the glass of wine in his hand, considering whether or not it could be classified as a pleasure. 'Not drinking much nowadays,' he replied. (By the end of the evening he'd downed ninety percent of the bottle of Rioja (cost shared fifty-fifty, however), plus a whisky before the meal and a brandy afterwards.)

'And don't forget the fags,' said Ellen.

Roy grimly studied the evidence of the ash tray. He needed to cut down, he admitted.

'And the fishing,' she reminded him.

'Haven't been out for weeks,' murmured Roy, with a slow shake of the head, bewildered by how heavily his spirit had been crushed.

'That bad, eh?' Ellen commiserated. It was all she could do to prevent herself from laughing. 'Nothing from Mags, then?' she enquired. She'd never called her Mags before; she found the nasty syllable peculiarly satisfying.

'Of course not,' said Roy. He did another slow head-shake, and his eyes were full of bitter self-reproach. 'She's history,' he stated. When the waitress brought him his brandy he thanked her with the excessive courtesy of a man who has been severely chastened. 'I'm in with a chance of a job,' he told Ellen. 'Gatwick. Better money. Good money,' he said.

Ellen had intended to talk about money. They needed to start talking about selling the house, she was going to tell him, but it probably wasn't a good idea to start on the subject after Roy had sunk the best part of a bottle.

When the coffees came, Roy gave his cup a long and thoughtful stir. About twenty times the spoon went round the cup. Clearly Ellen was expected to ask him what was on his mind, but she wasn't in the mood for any more of Roy's thoughts. Determined to tease the question out of her, Roy introduced a hint of a smile, directed at the cup. This also failed to achieve a result. Ellen remarked on the odd taste of the coffee. 'Seems fine to me,' said Roy. He resumed the stirring; he frowned lightly. 'You're going to wear that bloody spoon out,' said Ellen. He gave her a sad and soft smile, a smile that spoke of regret and at the same time was intended to project something of the appeal he had once possessed, but in fact looked like the sort of smile he might give a young barmaid after six pints. 'Maybe we could go away for a weekend together, you and me?' he suggested. 'Little place out in the countryside. A walk and a talk, you know. That's all.' Ellen pointed out that she was needed at the house, and anyway she could see the countryside perfectly well from her window. 'No rush,' said Roy, showing his palms like a salesman easing a customer towards the close of the deal. 'I know you've got commitments. I understand that. I can wait. I have to wait. Whenever you want. Months from now. I don't mind. Whenever. But what do you say? Just as an idea. What do you think?' Propping his face in his hands, he looked steadily at her.

Such was the depth of his delusion that, despite everything she'd been through with him, despite all the nonsense of this evening, Ellen almost felt sorry for him – almost, but not quite, because behind the tenderness he'd put onto his face she could still see an aggrieved hostility, like a brick wall seen through a curtain of gauze. 'Sorry, Roy,' she answered. 'There's not a chance.' She waved for the bill.

'Just think about it.'

'No need to think about it,' she said. 'I'm going home.'

'No you're not going home.'

She was fishing about in her handbag when he said this, and she heard the words as a threat. Glancing up, though, she saw a face pumped full of pathos.

'You're not going home,' Roy elucidated. 'You're not living at home. I'm living at home. That house isn't your home.'

'It'll do for the time being.'

'And then what?'

'Then I don't know.'

Roy drained the last drops of his brandy. He looked at her as if her last utterance had been enigmatic, and as he looked at her he seemed to be hearing a voice that was advising him not to push his luck, to accept this as a position from which future negotiations could proceed. 'I know this is what I deserve,' he said meekly.

'Yes, it is,' she told him.

'I can't argue with you.'

'Glad to hear it.'

'I'll give you a lift,' he said, putting the tip on the edge of table and making sure that the waitress saw how generous he was being.

'I'll walk,' said Ellen.

'I'll give you a lift,' Roy repeated, with the quiet insistence of a man who was content to have achieved what he'd set out to achieve. He nipped in front of her to open the restaurant door; at the car he opened the passenger's side first.

'I'm walking,' said Ellen.

'Come on,' he wheedled. 'Let me drive you back.'

'I'm walking.'

'Why?'

'One: it's a nice night. Two: it's not far. Three: you're ratted.' (By the end of the evening, the flame of his lighter was no longer hitting the end of his cigarette on the first attempt.) And, she might have added: 'Four: I'm not getting myself locked into a confined space with you when I know you'll turn nasty.'

Roy remonstrated: he was not ratted; he'd been taking it slowly and had drunk lots of water. 'Come on,' he pleaded. 'I don't want you to walk.'

'I'm walking.'

He tried a change of tack: the streets weren't safe at night for a woman on her own, he said, demonstrating a hitherto unsuspected awareness of the female perspective on life.

'Damned sight safer out here than in there,' countered Ellen, and she started to walk away. 'I'm tired. I'm going,' she said, at which point he ran up to her and grabbed her by the arm, so strongly she could feel the pressure of every finger.

'Please,' he said. 'Please, Ellen. Come on. I'll drive slowly.'

'Let go,' she ordered. He released her arm and held both hands up, as though to show to a policeman that he wasn't carrying a weapon. 'You want to wipe the slate clean?' she asked him.

Suspecting that this was a trick question, Roy hesitated before answering: 'That'd be good, but I know it's not possible. I know that.'

'No, Roy, it's not possible.' She was addressing him as if he were a child in a remedial class, but she was so angry now, after he'd clutched her arm, that she didn't care if he felt insulted. 'But we can do the next best thing.'

'What's that?'

'For a start: you go that way and I'll go this way. Then, in a few days' time, we talk about selling the house. That's what we should have done tonight. We'll do it soon. Then we'll sell the house. And then we'll never bother each other again.'

Second by second his temper was rising. 'Look—' he began, jabbing a finger.

'No,' she interrupted, 'you look.' But there was nothing more she wanted to say to him, so all she said was: 'Just fuck off, Roy.' She was surprised to hear herself swear, but not as surprised as he was. The way he looked at her was wonderful – it was as if he couldn't fathom out how those words could have come out of that mouth. It was like a man baffled by a talking shop-window dummy. She walked away quickly, so quickly that Roy's last contribution to the debate was not perfectly audible. That he was furious, though, was plain from the way he revved the car before performing a turn that made the tyres screech.

It's amazing how quickly things change, Ellen muses. By the time they'd finished the food, she says, she was asking herself what she'd ever seen in her husband. The reason Roy is so keen to get back together, she knows, is that the debacle with Margaret has made him think that podgy old Ellen might be the best he can hope for at his age.

'No,' I protest, but she's firm in her view of what's going on, and apparently sincere when she says that she can't condemn him for it.

'Because isn't that what people do? It's what I did,' she says. 'I made do with the best that was on offer. And there wasn't a lot on offer. Nothing at all, to be honest. There was never a queue at my front door. Still, I should have been pickier. Sometimes it's better to miss the boat.'

'And it was an experience, being married,' I suggest.

'I suppose,' she says. We watch another half-hour of *Chinatown*, then she goes to bed.

7

Janina departs. 'I'll still be here when you get back,' I say, and she gives me a stern look: 'Yes, you will,' she says, as if my dying would be an egregious betrayal of her trust. She has left instructions and lists of phone numbers for Ellen that cover every eventuality from a blocked sink to the collapse of the roof. She's left her a debit card for the shopping, but on no account is she to think that she's obliged to cook for Charles: 'That was never part of the agreement. He can take care of himself,' she says. But Ellen is cooking for me anyway, and poor Charles is at work for twelve hours a day if you count the travelling, so of course she cooks for him. The first evening: she attempts a recipe from one of Janina's books – a Moroccan dish. An hour is spent planning it and an hour cooking it, but it doesn't quite go right. 'Controversial,' I remark, after a mouthful of sugary meat. Charlie tells her that his brother has never had any manners. The food is delicious, he assures her, but even Charlie can't quite clear his plate. Back to pasta tomorrow, Ellen tells us.

Arriving home, Charlie finds the parcel that the postman delivered this morning. He's so keen to get it open he doesn't even take his coat off. It's a boxed set of CDs entitled Goodbye Babylon, and it really is a box – a cedarwood box, with a couple of balls of cotton packed around the CDs. 'Living, Stirring, Sacred Songs, Odes and Anthems', its says on the cover of the booklet. 'That's the next few evenings taken care of,' Charlie announces, bearing the box into the living room. He explains to Ellen that he can't listen to his hardcore stuff if Janina is in the vicinity, because it drives her round the bend. 'I see her point,' says Ellen, after Charlie has played us a random track: the Charles Butts Sacred Harp Singers, recorded on August 3 1928, bawling something called 'Murillo's Lesson'. Ellen looks as if she's got toothache. 'Fantastic, isn't it?' says Charlie, and he really does mean it, as Ellen says to me later, bemused. She could hardly make out a word of what they were singing, if you could call it singing, and when she could make out the words she wasn't any the wiser. 'Sounds like a singalong at the deaf school,' I tell Charlie. But CD 6 looks promising – a collection of sermons, including 'The Black Camel of Death', 'That White Mule of Sin', 'Death May Be Your Santa Claus' and 'Black Diamond Express to Hell'. We listen to a selection. 'Death winked at your mother three times before you was born,' the Reverend J. M. Gates reminds us.

Ellen and I read together in the living room for an hour, in silence, like a long-married couple. Ellen is sitting on the other side of the room, with a stash of Janina's magazines. Tranquillised by drugs and sunlight, I fall asleep on the sofa. Am woken by Ellen, shaking me. 'What on earth did you do that for?' I shout. 'I was skiing.'

'I'm sorry,' she says. She's short of breath and her eyes are wet. 'I thought you—' she begins.

'Patience, girl.'

'Don't, Daniel,' she says.

In the bedroom of teenaged Charlie there were two large laminated maps of Britain, the sort of maps you might find displayed in a school classroom. One showed the geological sub-structure of the land, while on the other were marked the larger towns and the prominent features of the terrain. For three or four years these maps were pinned to the wall, side by side. The former remained in pristine condition, but the latter was extensively modified by Charlie, who applied to it scores of small yellow stickers, each bearing a number inscribed in black ink with a very fine nib. These stickers marked the location of quarries, and the numbers corresponded to entries in a card-index file, in which Charlie made note of the type of stone that was cut from each of the identified locations, along with summaries of whatever additional information he had managed to find: the volume of material removed annually, for example, or the longevity of the quarry, or notable buildings in which the stone had been used (Beer Stone: Exeter Cathedral, St Paul's, Westminster Abbey, Tower of London, Hampton Court, Windsor Castle), or some technical data (Aberllefenni slate: weathering – excellent; resistance to pollution – excellent; resistance to delamination – excellent; colour retention – excellent; porosity – nil). Under his bed he kept cardboard trays of stone samples (numbered, naturally), some the size of bathroom tiles, others no larger than dice. Most of these scraps were obtained by his father, but several were garnered by enterprising young Charlie, who between the ages of ten and fourteen (or thereabouts) was in correspondence with dozens of stone-cutting companies from Portland to Sullom.

One might reasonably conclude that young Charlie's maps and documentation were indicative of his appetite for order and completeness. It is Janina's belief that this enduring appetite lies at the root of her husband's success as a businessman – no rival can match his knowledge of the suppliers and their products, and none offers so thorough a customer service. Furthermore, she believes that commerce alone cannot satisfy this appetite, and that this is the major reason for his obsession with the acquisition of recordings of terrible folk music. (In passing we might note that Janina thinks all the Brennan men have the mentality of collectors: Charlie has his music; I have my books; Freddie has his computer games; and Peter crams his head with information that nobody else in the family can begin to understand.) It's true that the acquisition of recordings might sometimes seem to be more important to Charlie than listening to them, and that his expenditure on CDs is immoderate. Go into the loft and you'll find racks and racks of them, and most, as Charlie knows, will never be played again.

Let us have an example of Charlie's assiduousness as a collector. Stephen recommends volume two of Alan Lomax's *Southern Journey* (*Ballads and Breakdowns – Songs from the Southern Mountains*), and Charlie duly buys it. He likes it very much. One track in particular – 'Fly Around My Blue-Eyed Girl' – he plays so often that you'd think (says Janina) it was some kind of coded key to the meaning of life instead of just some toothless yokel hammering the hell out of a busted piano. The next step is to buy volume one of *Southern Journey* (*Voices from the American South*), and volume three (*Highway*

Mississippi). Pleasure is had from both, as it is from volume four (*Brethren, We Meet Again*), and from every subsequent CD in the thirteen-disc *Southern Journey* series, but even Charlie has to admit that not every disc affords pleasure in significant quantities. Volume ten (*And Glory Shone Around – More All Day Singing From the Sacred Harp*), for example, is a record to which he has never returned, having had his fill of the 1959 United Sacred Harp Musical Convention in Fyffe, Alabama, with volume nine (*Harp of a Thousand Strings – All Day Singing From the Sacred Harp*). And yet, even though he had known that a second instalment from the convention in Fyffe would prove to be a surfeit, it was never a possibility that he would suffer an interruption in the series.

There's no doubting, then, that Charlie has a mania for completeness. And there's no doubting either that he has a passion for the collected objects as objects. As Celia has more than once remarked (and Charlie has never demurred), this passion has an element of fetishism. He relishes the lustre of obscurity that radiates from a recording of some long-dead backwoods farmer sawing away at a fiddle in an Appalachian shack. When he unwraps a new CD, he partakes of the labour that the shiny little disc embodies – the effort, say, of hauling equipment heavier than two grown men up and down the hills of Mississippi, to get on record the sound of an ancient blind man who has never in his life played in public. Whenever Charlie takes delivery of a package from a New York record store, his expression is precisely that of young Charlie opening a box from Bavaria and lifting from its bed of cotton wool a polished slice of Jura limestone with a perfect little ammonite embedded in its centre.

(Charlie's fascination with stone may have lost some of its ardency with the passing of the years, but arcane recordings are not the only artefacts that can fascinate him. Items manufactured to the highest standards can similarly inspire – Janina's kitchen implements, for instance. Ask him to show you one of her Tojiro Senkou knives. 'The blade has more than sixty layers of steel,' he'll tell you, and he'll angle it under the mini-spotlights, so you can appreciate the Damascene effect. 'It's called *kasumi-nagashi* or "floating mist",' he might say, turning the blade over and over in the light, entranced by the misty grain of the steel. Janina, on the other hand, will say that a Japanese wonder-knife is not a work of domestic-industrial art but simply an instrument. She's not – she'll insist – a collector of high-end kitchenware, not in the way that Charlie is a collector of CDs. The new German coffee machine, the French copper pans, the Italian gadget that'll whisk the rind off any citrus fruit in three seconds flat – these and the multifarious other pieces of restaurant-grade equipment are all functional devices that perform their function better than any other devices you can buy, nothing more and nothing less. And yet, I'd say, there was a hint of the sacerdotal in the way Janina handled a newly acquired knife and passed it over to Celia, so she could experience for herself the perfect balance of it. This was during Celia's last spell in London, when Janina had come to think, for a while, that carefully rationed exposures to the satisfactions of domesticity might rescue Celia from her rudderless life. Celia took the knife and went through the motions of testing the blade on the air. 'It really nestles in your hand, doesn't it? Somehow it seems to weigh nothing,' suggested Janina, like a mother letting her daughter hold an expensive violin, in the hope that the feel of it would be a more effective way of persuading the child to take music lessons than nagging would.)

To resume: Janina has an understanding of what drives Charlie, in common with so many men, to collect and organise (it goes without saying that the CD archive is rigorously ordered; Charlie's system observes a triple hierarchy: region – genre – artist), and she can understand how one might find the folk music of America an absorbing subject, in the abstract. It's interesting that there were families in which not one person could read or write but everyone could play the banjo. It's interesting – laudable, even – that people went to such lengths to tape their playing. Actually listening to it, however, is an entirely different matter. It is beyond her comprehension that her husband can derive the enjoyment he claims to derive from a churchful of worshippers screaming hymns to the accompaniment of a piano that hasn't seen a tuner in twenty years, or the screeching of a fiddle that sounds like a hundred fingernails scrabbling at a blackboard. Her ears are attuned to music that's performed professionally and recorded to the highest standards, and she can't retrain them to accept the catterwauling of amateurs, any more than she could force her skin to tolerate the scratch of hessian.

Janina tends to characterise Charlie's music as an oddball hobby, his loveable streak of eccentricity, but at times, I think, she's envious of it. One afternoon at their house in London, for instance, she and I passed the door of the living room and glimpsed Charlie, slumped in his favourite armchair, aghast at the voices of the Louvin Brothers. 'Having one of his moments,' she remarked. The smile and accompanying shake of the head were for his incorrigibility, but there was something else in her face, for an instant, that said she wished she could share the experience that Charlie was having at this minute – more than that: she was saddened that there was no equivalent in her life to what his music is for Charlie. This is not to say that Janina suffers from a sense of being unfulfilled – far from it. She loves Charlie and their sons. The garden is a delight: she gains a deep gratification from it, as she does from what she creates in the kitchen. But these things do not take her out of herself in the way that Charlie is transported by his music, if only for a minute or two, and I am certain that there are times when she wishes this were not so. And I am certain, furthermore, that Janina would be a shade happier if Celia – who otherwise is more or less incapable of seeing the world as her brother sees it – weren't a little more closely attuned to Charlie's obsession than Janina will ever be.

It is not the case that Celia likes the stuff that Charlie likes – in fact, she generally finds the fiddlers and banjoists as much of an ordeal as Janina does. But it's when Charlie says to Celia 'Just listen to this for a minute' and, sliding a CD into the player, urges her to take the chair on which the speakers are trained, that Celia is most vividly returned to the time when she and Charlie were as fond of each other as one could reasonably expect a young girl and her four-years-older brother to be. Seeing Charlie so enthusiastic, she is changed briefly into someone who resembles closely a former self, and it's an intensely pleasurable thing for her, she says. It feels more like a self-contained little enclave of anachronistic time than a memory of a time in which they were closer to each other than they are now, and when it's finished she rarely feels any regret for what has gone. It doesn't matter that it's unlikely that she'll be able to partake of his enthusiasm for whatever it is he wants her to hear – their musical tastes were never similar. Whenever, as a pre-teen girl, she wandered into Charlie's room to ask him about the LP he'd just bought, it was in the expectation of hearing something grim – Popol Vuh, perhaps, or Amon Düül II. She'd take the bean-bag and Charlie would lie on the bed and close his eyes while a twenty-minute free-for-all meandered nowhere. They wouldn't talk, and she'd usually tiptoe away long before Side One was over, but Celia never felt a stronger attachment to her brother than when she was sitting in his room, listening to the portentous maunderings of a band of German hippies, because this was a special favour that he was granting her (Charlie preferred to listen alone, with the lights off), and her very inability to understand the appeal of these excruciating albums imparted to the quiet and generally unmysterious Charlie an aura (albeit a thin and temporary aura) of the enigmatic.

(This aura soon evaporated for ever. Having assumed that progressive rock was one of those things that suddenly would make sense when she reached a certain age, Celia found instead that it became more irritating. Charlie, she saw, was simply in error in liking this crap. Charlie himself arrived at a similar opinion not much later, and by the time Janina arrived on the scene his record collection had been completely purged of the pretentious. Not a single Tangerine Dream LP was allowed to remain for old time's sake; unimpeachable classic rock now ruled the shelves. His discovery of American folk music might therefore be seen as a kind of recidivism.)

Talking to Janina on the phone this evening, Charlie raises his voice in a way that suggests she's standing in a call box – this is not a good sign. Brevity of conversation supports this analysis. And the fact that he can't give her a call, but has to wait for her to ring, further indicates some tension in the situation. 'How's it going?' I ask him, and he says it's going OK, all things considered. 'Never going to be plain sailing, though, was it?' he adds. Ellen knows no more than I do.

A packet arrives. 'Another one,' says Ellen, shaking her head as if at a manifestation of gluttony. It's a book on the moon landings. 'Not the sort of thing I'd have thought you'd be interested in,' she says. This irritates; my reply is patronising, inexcusably. 'Everything is interesting,' I say to her. I think I might sometimes have spoken to my mother this way. Ellen flinches. Later, by way of penance, I watch *An Officer and a Gentleman* with her. Manage to fall asleep promptly; when I wake up she's not there and the TV has been turned off.

At about three o'clock it starts to rain; by four the sky is plum-coloured from pole to pole and the rain is making the windows hum. The gutters can't cope with all the water: the clattering on the terrace is so loud I have to turn the radio up high to hear it properly. I put on Charlie's cagoule and grab his golfing umbrella. 'Coming, El?' I enquire, when she comes into the kitchen. She's surprised, pleased, and (taking note of the downpour) appalled. Janina's wellingtons are too tight; she makes do with Charlie's. Arm in arm, we clump and squelch to the gate. Visibility is almost zero; the rain is coming down like one of those deluges you see in films, where there's obviously a gang with fire hoses standing just out of shot. We're the only people out of doors.

The long grass twitches in the rain and the stream is so battered and brown it looks more like wood than like water. The noise under the umbrella becomes intolerable; I hobble out from under it, and move away until all I can hear is the seething of the stream. On the opposite bank there's a willow, quivering, and within the foliage there's a heron, standing on a tongue of silt. Only when I reach the lip of the bank, no more than twenty feet away, does it take flight. Ellen, unaware of its presence until now, emits a strange little wail of surprise.

I watch the bird disappear into the murk. After it has gone there is nothing to see except the rain, but I stay where I am for a few minutes more, looking towards where the hills would normally be.

'What are you thinking?' asks Ellen.

'Nothing,' I tell her, which I think is true. I was listening to the sound of the rain. 'What about you?' She says she was thinking that the heron was such a spectacular bird that it didn't seem quite right that it lived in England.

The horizon is starting to reappear, and within a few minutes there's a crack of light underneath the clouds. 'Time to go,' I declare. With every step, bubbles appear around my lace-holes. I make her hurry when we come to the road. 'I need to lose some weight,' she says; I call her a nice big lump of a woman. Within half an hour I'm asleep in an armchair. I'm sleeping too much. Before I nod off, Ellen tells me that when she was seven or eight she and her parents went for a picnic one afternoon, by a river. As she was watching some ducklings pass by, the edge of the riverbank collapsed, depositing her in a bed of thick grey sludge. She tried to clamber out, but every step was like lifting a manhole cover with her foot. Her shoes were pulled off; she sank to her knees in the slime. Her father jumped down to pull her out, but he began to sink too, and for a moment there appeared on his face a look of alarm which in an instant changed the way she thought of her father – never before had she seen him in a situation in which he did not know what to do. And ever since that day, she says, she's been nervous of going close to the edge of rivers and streams. Sometimes, the mere sight of a certain grey-brown colour is enough to give her a funny turn. Janina has a coat that's almost that colour.

Celia calls with good news: Petru has a job, mowing grass in the grounds of an unspecified hotel in the vicinity of Florence. I put two and two together and she admits that Mauro is one of the people – many people – she rang on behalf of her step-sweeper, but denies that Mauro is Petru's employer. 'It's a friend of a friend of a friend of a friend,' she says. 'You know how it works here.' Well, I have an idea, but I know my sister better than I know how things work in Italy, and I know she's not telling the truth. Mauro is back on the scene, and I wouldn't be at all surprised to learn that sex is occurring. And now it's obvious: the anonymous potential backer of Celia's hypothetical school – that must have been Mauro too. 'You're being evasive,' I tell her; she says, evasively, that she wants to speak to Charlie. She's given up on the idea of starting her own school, having finally realised she's not cut out for capitalism. Charlie reports her surrender with no more than a hint of smugness.

It is curious, some might say, that Celia should regard Charlie's value system as being irredeemably besmirched by its emphasis on the accumulation of material goods, and yet be so attracted to a man who appears to be more thoroughly devoted to material self-enrichment than her brother. Charlie has his music, whereas Mauro Pascolato has no artistic leanings, unless one is using the adjective in the broadest sense and allows the development of expensively equipped holiday accommodation to be classified as a species of aesthetic activity. 'The Armani barbarian' Celia once nicknamed him. The first part of the description is accurate: soft jackets from Armani are his favourite upper-body garments, usually navy blue, teamed with a white shirt (no tie), navy blue or sand-toned trousers (the unconscionably expensive belt is a crucial detail), and shoes from Loake or equivalent long-pedigree English footwear manufacturer. As for the other element of the epithet, it's true that, left to his own devices, Mauro would never set foot in an art gallery or museum, and would rather eat chalk than sit through a single scene of an opera. His preference is for life unmediated, yet Mauro is no barbarian: he is a smooth man, more gourmet than gourmand. He does nothing to excess, but appreciates all things that make a body buzz: fine food, fine cars (last time we heard he was driving a vintage Maserati), fine clothes, holidays in exotic locations, the company of women. The last of these pleasures is, according to some, of paramount importance to Mauro.

Though on the cusp of fifty when Celia met him, he has never been married. Elisabetta, giving Celia some background to the man, paused after disclosing this fact, before proceeding to make her meaning explicit. For Celia, however, Mauro's sustained avoidance of matrimony was not in itself to be taken as evidence of suspect character – on the contrary, she was inclined to take it as a sign that this was a man who said Yes to life. People who were not well disposed towards Mauro (and there were several of these, Elisabetta intimated) might describe him as something of a playboy – a 'little playboy'. Big playboys pick up models and starlets in Milan and Paris and New York; Mauro picked up his women wherever he could find them. 'They could be anybody,' said Elisabetta, raising her eyes skyward. Last summer he'd had a fling with some girl who worked on the perfume counter at La Primavera. 'She wasn't good-looking, she wasn't clever. So who knows why?' wondered Elisabetta, with an expression that said she couldn't bring herself to think too closely about the basis of the shop girl's attraction. 'He likes them young?' Celia suggsted – but no, this wasn't the case. From the perfume girl he had moved on, more or less directly, to a German woman who might even have been older than him (she certainly looked it); she lived in Vicchio, where she'd been making ugly pottery for the last twenty years. 'They could be anybody,' Elisabetta repeated. There was perhaps a portion of warning in this, but Elisabetta would have found it almost impossible to imagine that her friend could have any interest in man who, for all his undeniable (if facile) charm, was a classic case of arrested development. She respected Celia as a woman who could never, merely for the sake of company or sex, tolerate a man who was not up to the mark.

In fact, Celia had enjoyed several evanescent relationships with men who, in one way or another, were very much not up to the mark, but she had revealed to Elisabetta only those affairs that she knew would not have a detrimental effect on Elisabetta's estimation of her. (Elisabetta was never to know about the dalliance with Mauro – who, intuiting that Elisabetta was not an admirer (she saw him as being just one rung up the social scale from a bricklayer, he said), was quite happy to comply with Celia's request that they keep their relationship a secret.) To Elisabetta's knowledge, the roll-call of Celia's romantic involvements in the previous two years featured only two liaisons: the first with a man from the Feltrinelli bookshop, who was one day going to write the definitive study of Freemasonry in Italy (a project of which no more than five hundred words materialised in the months that Celia was with him); and the second with an employee of the science museum, whose unhappiness at the gulf between what he had become and what he had once dreamed of becoming (if not quite a second Enrico Fermi, then at least a professor), grew steadily more oppressive until it achieved an unbearable weight in the immediate aftermath of his fortieth birthday, an event which was about as much fun as a funeral. These were serious relationships with serious people, which had foundered because – as far as Elisabetta could see – the men had failed to keep Celia mentally engaged. If two intelligent individuals such as these could be found wanting, a gadfly such as Mauro would bore her from the outset, thought Elisabetta.

But the man from the bookshop and the man from the museum hadn't failed to stimulate Celia's mind. Every week, right up to the end of each affair, she had learned things from them. The problem had been that, though each was gentle and affectionate and in his own way interesting, they had allowed themselves to become torpid. One had, by his own admission, more or less given up; the other simply hadn't got round to admitting that he had given up. From the sound of him, Mauro was not a torpid individual. It might be that he was indeed the slave of an undiscriminating libido, but the variety of his lovers was in itself no proof of this. She knew nothing about the girl from the perfume counter, and would not dismiss her automatically as just another drone of the retail hive. She knew nothing of the middle-aged German potter, but it might be counted to the favour of a man who could still attract young secretaries that he should choose to have an affair with a woman to whose sexual allure many other men in his position (charming, with money) might have been blind. The brute statistics of one's bedroom activities, as she knew from her own experience, were not in themselves sufficient proof of sexual incontinence.

Elisabetta's debriefing was delivered in advance of a party given in a villa near Fiesole, by a relative of Mr Mascarucci, whose family had once had some sort of business dealings with Mauro. Sitting with her friend in a quiet corner of the garden, Elisabetta pointed out the notorious ladies' man. He stood in profile to them, and profile was not his best angle, what with the doughy midriff and the lack of definition in the chin area. He had rolled up his sleeves, revealing deeply tanned arms and a watch with a thick gold bracelet; his hair, thinned to a few strands on top, was glued to his scalp with oil. He looked, thought Celia, like someone you might see in the background of a casino scene in a James Bond film. The two middle-aged women to whom he was talking, though, seemed to be finding his conversation delightful. On the other hand, as Celia noted when she surveyed the garden, almost everybody seemed to be having a delightful conversation. (Whereas she and Elisabetta had sought each other out, having escaped from the tedium of, respectively, a retired optometrist and a dolt who knew more about recent developments in the science of road-traffic management than any other man in Tuscany.) Elisabetta was borne away by the host to meet someone who had just arrived; soon after, Celia met Mauro. In taking a glass of prosecco from the huge rustic table on which the food and drink had been arrayed, Celia snagged the hem of her dress on the leg of a similarly rough-hewn chair. No sooner had she felt the tug than Mauro was there, detaching the fabric from the splinter so quickly and so precisely that not the slightest rip was suffered. The gallant intervention was more than impressively swift and skilful: it was executed with perfect impersonality, as if the dress had been merely a decorative banner hanging on a pole. Damage prevented, Mauro gave her a perfunctory little smile and turned to resume the conversation from which he'd been distracted by her mishap – a mishap he could have observed only, of course, if he'd had his eye on her, as Celia later realised.

'He'll be back,' Elisabetta predicted, but he wasn't. Several times, in the course of the evening, Celia and Mauro crossed paths, and he acknowledged her with a nod that was no more than courteous. It was past midnight and she had decided it was time to go home when, taking her leave of yet another stupefyingly unfascinating man (an earnest believer in the wisdom of the Tarot), she turned to find herself face to face with Mauro, who was in retreat from a man whom he was promising to call the next day. Stepping aside to let her pass, he gave her a look that was wry and weary, and seemed to say that he'd had enough of socialising for one night, almost. '*Buona notte,*' said Celia. 'Good night,' replied Mauro. Then Celia said 'Thank you'; and Mauro said 'For what?'; and then they were talking.

They talked, in English, for half an hour or so, chiefly about Celia's work and her experience of living in Italy. He found out that she had lived in Bologna; they talked about restaurants in Bologna – his favourite was a place she'd never heard of, somewhere out in the suburbs. A promising young chef would shortly be opening a restaurant in Florence, Mauro informed her, and for a second she thought that he was preparing an invitation to go there with him, but the subject was immediately discarded. He wanted to know more about what she thought of Florence, how she'd come to be here, et cetera, et cetera. As soon as she had answered one of his questions he had another ready, but his curiosity seemed genuine and disinterested; his gaze, though steadily direct, was cool. Conscious of having ceded control of the conversation, Celia tried to divert it onto the topic of Mauro's business. 'That's not interesting,' he said, and steered them straight back to Celia's profession. A friend of his, a software engineer, had a name for a particular kind of technical Italian verbiage – 'smokeware'. With this word, delivered deadpan, in a voice that could have been formed in an English public school, and with eyes that widened in a way that was suggestive of a sardonic sense of humour, she had an intimation of the efficacy of Mauro's charm. She complimented him on the excellence of his English, and felt a twitch of annoyance for having done so, as if she'd broken a promise to herself. For many years, he said, he'd been a devotee (the very noun he used) of the BBC World Service. 'Crewe Alexandra' he intoned, by way of demonstration of his best BBC delivery. At this point Celia became aware that Elisabetta was standing by the table, waving her car keys at her enquiringly. 'You must go,' said Mauro, with no shade of disappointment. 'It was nice to meet you,' he said. 'Ditto,' answered Celia. 'Ditto,' Mauro repeated, as if this were an amusing new word to learn. She took the offered hand: the skin was remarkably soft, and his handshake was not an act of self-assertion. Neither did he maintain the contact for too long, or treat her hand like an object of extraordinary delicacy, as men on the make so often did.

'He knows where you work? He'll call, just wait,' said Elisabetta. He didn't call, and Celia didn't wait. From time to time she remembered with amusement 'Crewe

Alexandra', but not often. One or two men were on her mind, and Mauro was not one of them. Then, three or four months after the gathering in the villa, she and Elisabetta were invited to a party to mark the opening of Mauro's latest venture: a holiday complex of which he was the part-owner, comprising apartments, a spa, a fitness centre, a restaurant, a nine-hole golf course and a multitude of other leisure facilities, constructed on the site of a long-abandoned farm up in the Mugello. On arrival she spotted him at once, chatting to a bunch of well-groomed senior citizens beside the outdoor pool. He glanced her way and raised a hand, as you might acknowledge someone you didn't feel any great desire or need to talk to. After giving a speech from the steps of the restaurant, he went into the building, and during the next hour or so she glimpsed him twice: laughing uproariously with one of the senior citizens, and looking rather solemn as he strolled across the lawn beside a tall and shockingly beautiful young woman who was perhaps half his age. Fireworks were lit, and as an immense silver chrysanthemum lit up the hills suddenly Mauro was at her shoulder, as though to resume a conversation that had been interrupted only a few minutes earlier. 'Last year I was at a fiesta in Spain,' he said, 'and there was a man running about with fireworks on his body. All over his body. A suit of fireworks, and he was running through the crowd with flames everywhere. Crazy people, like you say. I like crazy people.' Celia, having no recollection of having said anything about crazy Spaniards, had to be reminded that she'd told him, in the garden of the villa, about seeing men jumping from one moving car to another, after Barcelona had beaten Real Madrid. It became apparent, in the next few minutes, that Mauro had remembered everything she'd told him about herself, about her family, her job, the places she'd lived.

'So this is my business,' he said, with a gesture that was not immodest, as if inviting her opinion not of something that he had played a part in bringing into existence, but rather of a place where he just happened to work. 'It's impressive,' said Celia, though she'd never contemplate staying in a place like this, which perhaps – judging by his momentary quarter-grin – Mauro understood. The farm had been going to ruin for a long time, he told her. An old man lived alone here for years, barely managing to grow enough to live on. Where the swimming pool was – that had been a vegetable garden, so overgrown that it was impossible to walk across it. In the farmhouse, one of the rooms downstairs was a metre deep in garlic, and they'd found a mummified kitten under straw in one of the bedrooms. Every roof and floor had to be rebuilt, but the stone walls were sound, mostly, and there was plenty of land. 'And of course the big thing, the biggest thing,' Mauro declared, offering her the panorama, 'is where it is. It is here.'

With a deep satisfaction, he surveyed the darkening hills. 'You have been here before, in this area?' he asked. Celia confessed that she had not. Mauro nodded, as if she had confirmed what he had suspected. If a gunman ran amok in a Chianti village tonight and sprayed the piazza with bullets, he said, he'd hit more British people and Germans and Dutch than Italians. 'But here it is different. Here he could hit some Florentines, maybe. Otherwise, people who live here.' After a pause to admire the landscape, Celia commented that if the gunman were to wait until next month he might hit some tourists who were staying here. Mauro looked at her; it was impossible to tell if offence had been taken until he replied, as though answering an observation of great weight: 'Yes, it is a difficult problem. We want people to see that this is beautiful. But people come, and they make it less beautiful. It is a conundrum.' It was all a matter of balance, he told her. Balance had to be the guiding principle – a balance of the natural and the fabricated, of the old and the new. (One can read more about the importance of the concept of balance to Mauro's enterprise on its website. *The philosophy addresses the whole person – mind, body and soul. Recognising the physical, the mental and the spiritual, it works towards their equilibrium. A philosophy of balance; between exercise and relaxation; between conventional* [sic] *and innovation*.) There was an element of sales-talk here, but the promotional material was not overdone, and when Mauro, surveying the hills, repeated that the issue was complicated, his expression of thoughtfulness was more than plausible. 'We want to make money, of course. We are in business,' he stated. 'But we don't want things to change too much. Things must not change too much. We have to be respectful. We make a mark, but it must be a small mark.'

Months later, recalling this little speech, she found it hard to believe that she hadn't found it bogus. Had it been delivered inside the building, to an audience of twenty, perhaps she would have done, but out on the terrace, in the warm dusk, under a sky thickly veined with gold and indigo, she heard it differently. Below the terrace a slope of grass descended to a stand of chestnut trees. The trees screened a small pool: 'for looking, not for swimming,' Mauro explained. 'It is special, isn't it?' he said, as if he knew that some people wouldn't be able to see that it was, but was certain that Celia would not be one of them. She nodded. Mauro, gratified, nodded back, and for a minute they leaned on the balustrade, a yard or so apart, not talking, just looking at the hills. Violet shadows were filling the slopes; scraps of mist or smoke hung in the hollows; the lights of isolated houses were like the lights of fishing boats on the sea. Pointing to a small cluster in the distance, Mauro told her: 'I was born there.' His grandmother and grandfather still lived in the village; they were both in their nineties and had never been further than Florence. Did the English language, Mauro asked, have an equivalent to the word *campanilismo*? Celia thought not: 'We have parochialism instead,' she said. 'That is because we are a young country,' said Mauro, and they talked about this idea for a while, until Mauro, looking at his watch, said that there were some people he had to be nice to.

They walked together back towards the main building, and by the pool they came upon the beautiful tall girl. Mauro introduced her to Celia: 'Laura, my niece.' On the other side of the pool a man beckoned to Mauro. 'I must go,' he apologised to Laura and Celia. That evening Celia was wearing a dress that Elisabetta had found for her. Made of silk (pale eau de Nil – her moonlight dress, Mauro would call it), it fell in a low soft scoop at the back, to the base of her shoulder blades. Turning away, Mauro placed – as if absent-mindedly – the tip of an index finger (cooled by the chilled wine) very lightly on her back, midway between her neck and the swag of silk, and he left it there for half a second. The contact was startling, says Celia. It was like having her Standby button pressed.

The relationship with Mauro lasted approximately five months – or, to put it another way, somewhere between twenty and forty days. Mauro had a lot of projects in progress at the same time. He was busy making his small marks all over Italy, in zones characterised by Celia as medium-wild: the Apennine foothills of eastern Umbria, the higher reaches of Marche, and so on. Almost every day he would phone her, and towards the end of the week he would ask: 'Are you free?' During this period of her life Celia was nearly always free at the weekend. Once or twice she felt that she should tell him that unfortunately she wouldn't be free, to prevent the affair from appearing too blatantly lopsided, but she never did. Sometimes they'd spend the whole weekend together; sometimes Mauro had to be elsewhere on the Saturday or the Sunday, appraising yet another investment opportunity. He didn't enquire too closely about what she might be doing in the week ahead, and she was satisfied with whatever information he might volunteer with regard to his own movements – which was generally little more than a recitation of his business diary. There was no planning in this relationship: planning was something that Mauro confined to the commercial sphere. Marriage was repellent to him, he once told her, because the heart could not be contracted. Celia was of course broadly in agreement, but nonetheless, in an ideal world, she would have preferred a slightly lower quotient of uncertainty than there was in this affair. Occasionally she'd call him early in the week to suggest an escapade for the coming weekend or the one after that. These initiatives were rarely successful, because in Mauro's line of work there was no knowing what action might, with little warning, be demanded of him in order to keep a scheme alive – there might be builders to chivvy, lawyers to consult, architects to chase. He was, however, a diligent phoner. He'd ring as often as three times in a single day: from restaurants in the middle of nowhere, from hilltops and empty village squares, and once in a while – always late at night – from his office in Florence. 'Come over,' Celia would say when he rang from the office, before she'd learned that for Mauro the office day went on until he was too tired to type his name, let alone perform sex to the required standard. By this we mean the standard that Mauro required of himself, and this was a very high standard indeed, Celia attests.

And here, as Celia herself once came close to admitting, I believe we arrive at the essence of the thing with Mauro. When she thought about it afterwards, she'd known in the moment he shook her hand at the villa party that this was a man who was tremendously good in bed. The basis of Mauro's virtuosity was neither singular equipment nor superhuman stamina: it was, rather, a matter of what one might crudely define as technique. 'Technique', however, has connotations of practice and self-conscious execution, whereas what was remarkable about Mauro was that he never seemed to be bringing into play a repertoire of arousal, but was instead ever-responsive, often to signals of which Celia herself was unaware. He was an infallible reader of her body, and the most generous and delicate of lovers ('a male lesbian,' she called him), without any of the self-regard of those boyfriends who had esteemed themselves as sensitive lovers, and displayed their sensitivity by caressing the curves of desired flesh as if moulding a body out of clay.

Let us not linger on this topic. It suffices to record that several intensely pleasurable days were spent with Mauro in a variety of bolt-holes, mostly in obscure corners of Tuscany (there are such corners, Celia assures me), but with excursions into the medium-wilds of other provinces, on those occasions when Mauro thought that the necessities of business could be dealt with swiftly, leaving enough free time to make the trip worthwhile for his lover. To the latter category belongs an unforgettable weekend in a ramshackle old inn not far from Macerata, where the bedroom commanded a view of half of central Italy and was lit up by the most amazing sunset she has ever seen, and the wizened old lady who ruled the kitchen produced a plate of truffle pasta that had Mauro inhaling the sweetly mouldy steam in a daze of contentment; the truffle, he said, was the earth's alchemy. Terrific food – generally eaten in modest backwater restaurants where the boss greeted Mauro like a member of the family – was another major pleasure of weekends with Mauro. A dose of nature was generally on the agenda too. They walked in the fragrant woods of the Casentino and gulped the cold winds of the Sibillini mountains. At daybreak they bathed in hot sulphur pools, in the open air. Mauro was a veritable emperor of the senses.

Five months after the affair had begun it ended, and it ended where it had begun. Walking back up the grassy slope from the Pool for Looking, Celia glanced up and saw, through the window of the restaurant, Mauro raising his hand from the shoulder of the young woman from the reception desk, and the young woman – seeing Celia – pulling back in a way that permitted only one interpretation. 'I made no promises,' Mauro pointed out, and this was true, in the sense that no avowals of fidelity had been made. 'I like her, I like you more,' he explained. Celia was surprised to find that she wasn't greatly upset: it was as if an enjoyable holiday had finished, that was all. Mauro saw no reason why they should not carry on seeing each other: 'I am the same person I was and you are the same person too, no?' When Celia replied that, all things considered, she would rather they stopped sleeping with each other, he accepted her decision instantly, with equanimity. Celia was disappointed rather than shocked: disappointed that Mauro should have strayed so soon, and that the denouement should be so banal. But she had known that this would not be a durable relationship. It was never possible that she would fall in love with Mauro. No pain was suffered: a punch to her pride was the only damage, and her recovery was rapid. There was a period of self-analysis, of sorts. She affected to envy Charlie the stability of what she took to be his passionless marriage (The Alliance, she called it). Life would be so much simpler if she could learn to place a higher value on companionship, but the problem was that she liked sex too much. She announced that, in order to take stock of her life, a period of celibacy was in order. This self-denying ordinance was in effect for a month or two, until Stefano came along.

We have time for Stefano, I am very glad to say. Crossing Piazza Santissima Annunziata on a Saturday afternoon, Celia was asked if she'd care to sign a petition on behalf of some environmental pressure group. The question was put to her by Stefano Agazzi, who was as many years younger than Celia as Mauro was older, and in many respects his antithesis: sartorially (severely eroded sweater; jeans that looked as if they might not survive the next wash, which was long overdue); bodily (lean as a high jumper; handsome in a somewhat Scandinavian mode; the hair hay-coloured, the eyes blue); temperamentally (perpetually worried by Big Issues; could happily subsist on a diet of water and pizza); economically (working as a waiter). In retrospect, the fling with Stefano came to seem the less comprehensible of these two short-burn romances. Undeniably the boy was good-looking, which is never a bad thing. Vanity was also a factor: it was pleasant to be pursued by so personable a young man. And she really was pursued.

As she recalls, the conversation at the makeshift table on Piazza Santissima Annunziata did not amount to much more than an exchange of platitudes on the lamentable state of the planet, but it had a remarkable effect on Stefano: two or three minutes after saying goodbye to him, she heard a running footfall and turned to see him sprinting towards her down Via Cavour. He told her how much he wanted to continue their discussion; with the humility of an autograph hunter he asked for her phone number; failing to obtain it, he said he'd be collecting signatures over at Santo Spirito the next day, so maybe if she was in the area she could say hello and, who knows, perhaps they could have a coffee? Maybe, replied Celia, at which Stefano thanked her and bowed, with hands flattened together and raised to his nose as if (as it later struck Celia) he were taking his leave of a nun. She should, she came to think, have taken this fulsome show of respect as a warning, instead of allowing herself to be flattered. In the case of Mauro, she had been the one to whom things were offered, and she had decided to take them; with Stefano the situation was reversed – he was a supplicant, and perhaps, initially, in the aftermath of Mauro, this was an element of Stefano's appeal.

Very soon, though, the lad's respect became oppressive. As Stefano let Celia know, barely five minutes after they'd sat down in the café on Piazza Santo Spirito, he didn't have much time for 'girls': they knew nothing about life. Celia was very much a woman (or, as he put it, she was 'very woman'), and he had sensed a connection with her right away – nothing as vulgar as a spark of sexual attraction, more an aura of affinity. Stefano was a very serious boy, and was extremely angry about the state of the world. Perhaps talking to him reawakened the student in Celia. He excoriated the super-rich and berated the multinationals that traded with themselves to minimise tax, paying huge fees to consultancy firms that existed only on paper, selling plastic buckets for a thousand dollars while rocket launchers were sold to criminals for next to nothing. His fury was directed at the tabletop, from which he would glance up to meet her gaze for a fraction of a second and ask: 'What do you think?' Celia made some hackneyed observations on Third World debt, to which Stefano attended as if she were releasing the precious distillate of her superior experience. What Celia thought about such matters did appear to be what interested him most; they were together for an hour, and in all that time just about the only personal information he extracted from her was that she was a language teacher. This was intriguing – a young and good-looking Italian male for whom sex did not appear to be the top priority. He was working that evening, so had to leave at six-thirty. 'Could I see you again?' he asked, as one might ask an analyst if there might be any chance of another appointment.

One afternoon in the middle of the following week they walked right across Florence, from Sant'Ambrogio to the Cascine park, then over the river to the Santo Spirito café. Walk, talk and drink coffee – that's all they did, and it seemed that Stefano was perfectly content with this. Again, they talked little about themselves: on this occasion, the city was the principal topic, and Celia had never met anyone who knew so much about Florence. He had a multitude of stories about lunatic artists, feuding merchants, maniacal priests, murderers. He confessed to often feeling sorry that he hadn't been born into Dante's world; modern life, he thought, was a disaster. At the café they once again parted: Stefano went off to his restaurant, Celia to her class. They exchanged cheek-kisses and agreed that, weather permitting, on Sunday they'd take a walk out of town, through Arcetri and Santa Margherita a Montici.

Sunday proved to a beautiful day. In the shadow-dappled lanes the conversation took an autobiographical turn, but still Celia was not sure what was happening: was this an oddly diffident courtship, or a peculiar friendship? You could have ridden a motorbike through the space that Stefano maintained between them as they walked, and there were moments when, stopping to take in the view or inspect a specimen of local flora, he seemed to forget that she was there. They returned to Florence via San Miniato al Monte, where Celia told him about the time she'd sat here with Maria, and Stefano related an incident that occurred here during the siege of Florence by the army of Charles V (1530). At the crux of this narrative he broke off in mid-sentence. 'I find you so very attractive,' he said, as if this were something he had to confess in order to be able to continue with his story about the siege of Florence, which he did, and when he reached the end of the story he leaned over and kissed her. Not since she was a schoolgirl had she been the recipient of so strange a kiss: his tongue, rigid and hesitant, was like a mouse repeatedly peeking out from a hole in the skirting board to ascertain the whereabouts of the cat. That night, nevertheless, he went from the restaurant to Celia's flat.

And here again Stefano can be seen as the converse of his predecessor. Sex for Stefano was very much about 'making love', and making love was a ritual that was not to be celebrated lightly. Sex was the embodied conjunction of souls, a revelation of essences. Seeing her naked for the first time, he reacted as though he were beholding her clad in heavenly raiment, and when he touched her it was as if he imagined the slightest pressure might bruise her innards. Now, our Celia is as capable as the next woman of appreciating a delicate dose of spiritualised eroticism, as long as it's interspersed with a fair amount of common-or-garden unsacramental fucking. And yet, though as a lover Stefano was hopeless, he was tenderly hopeless, and there was no point in trying to make him otherwise, because she could no more make him less fey in bed than she could get him to renounce his political principles. He was an extremely likeable and intelligent person. Their walks and talks for a while continued to provide enough sustenance for the relationship. (Celia did her best to minimise the sexual activity, which Stefano didn't seem to mind. Most nights they slept apart.) In her weeks with Stefano she learned a lot. She could no longer walk down certain streets in Florence without thinking of images that Stefano had put in her mind: an assassin galloping past the cathedral, a child stranded on a lump of stone in mid-river, a body carried in a torchlight procession to the church of Santa Croce.

Very soon, however, walking with Stefano had become too much of a history lesson; the silences between them grew thicker; he was too earnest, too eager, too young. Sensing, perhaps, that she might soon be gone, he took her to meet his mother. (The father worked in the airline industry and spent half his life in the air.) Meeting Mrs Agazzi had the effect of accelerating Celia's departure: it was clear within minutes that she didn't approve of her son's too-mature lover ('I'd lured her boy into my elfin grot – that's how she saw it'), and Celia for her part wasn't much taken with Signora Agazzi – a wiry, tight-mouthed little woman whose relationship with Stefano was altogether too clammy for Celia's liking.

Celia's next rendezvous with Stefano was the last. 'My mother liked you,' he remarked. 'She thinks I'm not right for you,' said Celia. He disagreed: 'She takes time to warm to new people.' (The kiss that Celia had received from Mrs Agazzi on leaving was so very far from warm, it was like being pecked by a feeble emu.) 'But I don't disagree with her,' said Celia. 'I'm not right for you.' Stefano endeavoured to demonstrate, with reference to various shared interests, that – on the contrary – she was perfectly right for him. His hands manoeuvred imaginary shapes in the air, as if he were discussing two geometrical forms which, when turned through certain angles, locked smoothly together. 'No, Stefano,' she interrupted, 'I am not right for you. You are not right for me and I am not right for you. It has been fun, and I like you very much, but we have come to the end.' Stefano had problems with the word 'fun': 'This is not about fun. Fun is for children.' Well in that case, Celia replied, attempting to lighten the mood, she was maybe both too old and too young for him. This, to Stefano, was sophistry. He returned to his demonstration of their complicated compatibility; he insisted that there was a lot more they had to talk about. 'We must meet again. Here, tomorrow,' he suggested. Celia told him that she didn't have anything more to say. 'I will be here, tomorrow, this time,' he said. Celia was not there the next day. A few weeks later, on the Santa Trìnita bridge, she saw Stefano coming towards her, talking intensely to a handsome forty-ish woman who appeared to be having some difficulty in understanding what he was saying; Celia smiled at him, and Stefano looked right through her.

The affairs with Stefano and Mauro, brief though they were, were by no means the most unsatisfactory of her Italian adventures. That distinction must be accorded to Mr Nevola, with whom we shall quickly dispense. Gianluca Nevola was her first lover (not quite *le mot juste*, in this context) after the split from photographer Matt. Disorientation in the wake of that separation might be seen as the chief explanation for this lapse. Compassion was also at work: the kindly and highly cultured Gianluca Nevola, a colleague at the school in Lucca, had lost his son three years before Celia met him, and there wasn't a single hour of the day, he told her, that he didn't think of him. A few days after his sixteenth birthday, Alessandro Nevola had been killed in a crash on the outskirts of the city. Gianluca had been driving the car. A van had suddenly pulled out of the line of traffic coming towards them, but there wasn't enough room for it to overtake and Gianluca had been forced to take evasive action; the car had flipped over and gone into a lamp-post, on Alessandro's side. Deranged by grief, Gianluca was unable to work for months, and when at last he re-emerged, he was subject to fits of rage that were unlike anything he had ever experienced. He found out that the man who had killed his son had moved to Arezzo; Gianluca tracked him down, and one day, having bought a hunting knife, he drove to the street in which the driver was now living, where he sat all afternoon, knife in hand, waiting for the man to come out of his apartment. When at last the man appeared, Gianluca was paralysed by hatred and a sense of the pointlessness of what he had been about to do; he stabbed the dashboard over and over again – which meant he had to take the car to the garage right away, because he couldn't tell his wife what he'd done. She'd have thought it pathetic, which is what he thought himself.

While Gianluca was lost in mourning and then planning his revenge, his wife was walking every weekend to the road where the crash happened, to leave flowers. Three years on, she was still observing this ritual, with barely diminished regularity. She went to church, alone, three or four times a week. Gianluca told Celia that nowadays his wife talked to the priests more than she talked to him. His wife said she didn't blame him for what had happened, but she did. He had turned the car over and Alessandro had died, whereas he had been merely scratched. Gianluca knew that, whatever she said, she thought that a better man would have sacrificed himself rather than let his son die. Some evenings Gianluca so dreaded the idea of going home that he'd stay late in the staff room, preparing the next day's lessons, annotating su-perfluously his students' work.

One night, passing a bar close to the school, Celia saw Gianluca inside and he at the same instant saw her. He was reading Ungaretti – his favourite poet, he said. She'd been warned by some of her colleagues that if you were alone with Mr Nevola for more than five minutes, he'd start talking about his son. She was alone with Mr Nevola for fifteen minutes, and he didn't talk about his son – they talked about Ungaretti and about Lucca, where both the poet and Gianluca had been born. When she left, he pressed her hand between his and thanked her; the next day, there was a volume of Ungaretti's poems on her desk, with a card from Gianluca inside, thanking her for her company. The card marked the page of '*Tu ti spezzasti*', which Celia read at her desk and liked, without knowing what it meant; it wasn't much clearer after she'd read the notes at the back of the book, where she discovered that it commemorated the writer's son, Antonietto. She and Gianluca fell into the habit, if Celia happened to have no other plans, of going for a drink after work on Wednesdays. He elucidated some of the com-plexities of Ungaretti (whose poems otherwise made little sense to her); from Ungaretti it was a natural progression to the subject of suffering and the overcoming of despair; he talked about Alessandro and his reaction to his death, and his wife's reaction – but without emotion, as if they were case studies, to be analysed alongside that of Ungaretti. They usually had the one drink and parted after less than an hour; at the end of a two-drink session he apologised for being so morose and, on leaving, kissed her hand. Next time it was the other way round: Celia kissed Gianluca's hand. He had beautiful hands – 'Pianist's hands,' she told him. 'I can't play a note,' he replied, and here a smile momentarily rejuvenated his face.

His wife, the following week, went to stay with her parents, and Gianluca and Celia, instead of going to their usual bar, went to a bar on the other side of town, near her flat, and thence to the flat itself, where the affair was feebly consummated. In the course of the next two or three months he came to the flat two or three times. There was more talking and weeping (from Gianluca) than sex, and what little sex they had was dire, because Gianluca was rendered all but impotent by guilt. The last time he slept with her, he was asleep most of the time; he was most apologetic, but wanted Celia to know that she shouldn't feel insulted – the reverse, in fact, because at home he never slept well, but with Celia he could almost forget his troubles. The following week, Celia looked out of the window of her classroom and saw Gianluca walking down the street with a woman she knew immediately was his wife. She knew Mrs Nevola was slightly younger than her husband, but she looked about twenty years older. They walked side by side, a foot apart, heads lowered, as if walking behind an invisible coffin. The next day she told Gianluca that they must stop seeing each other, even for their Wednesday drinks.

He accepted without protest: she had more sense than he did, he told her; he was glad she'd taken the decision; he thanked her for the time she'd given him. He was as courteous to her as he had ever been; nobody, observing them in conversation, would ever have suspected that anything had ever happened between them. One evening, however, Celia walked past the door of a classroom that was in darkness and, glancing into the room, saw a silhouette at the window. The silhouette changed shape and a voice spoke her name. When she turned on the lights she saw Gianluca staring at her as if she were a police officer who had come to arrest him and he was about to choose between surrendering and flinging himself through the glass. Pages of students' work were strewn about the floor. He couldn't function any more, he told her. 'I love you,' he said, as if revealing that he had terminal cancer. They went for a walk, and in the course of the walk they agreed that there was only one thing to do: Celia would look for another job. There were no further intimate conversations with Gianluca. Two months later, she left the school.

Of all Celia's affairs in Italy, I think the one with Gianluca Nevola (not his real name, by the way – we must consider the innocent wife; and the real name is less melodious) is the only one she regards as an error. So keenly did she regret it, in fact, that she didn't tell me about it until a considerable time after the event, and she asked me, furthermore, not to say anything about it to Charlie. (Previously I'd been given free rein, more or less, to pass on to big brother as much or as little information about Celia's social life as I chose. So Charlie knew something about Stefano (a.k.a. the Student Prince) while the relationship was in the process of dying, and about Mauro, whom he pictured from the outset as a sort of lower-budget Silvio Berlusconi.) Charlie and Janina still don't know any of the specific details of the Nevola business, but are aware that there has been, in Italy, an affair with a married man. Celia told them of this one evening at dinner, when, pushed beyond the limit of self-restraint by Janina's remarks concerning some adulterer who was in the news at that time, announced that she herself had been a co-committer of adultery and – leaving her own failings out of the discussion for now – she would most strongly take issue with anyone who suggested that the man in her case should be consigned to the ranks of the damned. 'I'm surprised,' was Janina's immediate response, before assuming the appearance of a woman whose face had been struck by a flash flood of Botox. Unable to bring herself to look her sister-in-law in the eye, Janina left it to Charlie to make the case for the sanctity of marriage. Celia pointed out that, if you do your research, you'll find that, in the terms of the Seventh Commandment, a married man plus an unattached woman does not equal adultery, and at this provocative irrelevance Janina re-entered the fray. 'We're not saying that we've never fancied anyone else, Celia,' she said – at which Charlie's eyes momentarily registered a small shock. 'What matters is that we would never do anything about it. That's what's important. It's all about what you do.' To which Celia countered, giving the exchange a theological spin: 'But isn't the sin in the thought as much as in the deed? And how am I to make my thoughts behave?' And here Janina employed her customary tension-reducing tactic, a retreat kitchenwards.

Some chuckles from Ellen, but of course the pleasure is not unalloyed. Problem one: too much sex. Far too much sex. Problem two: I've put her in the position of knowing more about Celia than her brother and his wife do, which simply doesn't feel right. I point out that she knows what I look like in the buff, which is a morsel of knowledge that has been withheld from Charlie and Janina. 'You are privileged in so many ways, Ellen,' I sigh. 'And I know that Celia would talk to you about things that she would never discuss with Charlie.' Ellen tells me that I've used this argument before, and though she's flattered by the compliment she's not at all sure that it's true, and even if it's true it's not really the point. I'm too tired to banter; it took three days to type the tales of Celia and her Italian paramours. Then Ellen becomes irksome, in a Goffmanesque way. I could, she insinuates, be doing something useful for the similarly afflicted if I were to write more about my own life. She seems to have in mind a heartwarming tale of the survival of the human spirit in the face of awful disease. Why, I want to know, should I feel obliged to make myself useful? That's not quite what she meant, says Ellen. I suggest that she might propose to Charlie that he write a book about his experiences, to help future retailers of high-grade flooring. That would be of far greater benefit to society, I tell her. In fact, 'fucking society' is what I say. 'Don't talk to me like that, Daniel,' she says, 'and don't shout.' I ask her if she'd ever considered a career as a primary school teacher. 'Yes,' she replies flatly, and she's out of the room before I can ask her if this is true or not.

8

A taxi delivers Janina not long after breakfast. 'It's good to be back,' she says, and that's just about all she says. With apologies for her weariness, she goes upstairs for a lie down.

At four there's a knock at the door and in steps Janina. The hair has reacquired much of its bounce; lipstick is in place. Looking around the room as if I might have carried out a few alterations to the habitat while she was away, she apologises again for having been so uncommunicative earlier: 'I was whacked – I was asleep within five minutes,' she says, eyes widening at the incredibleness of this occurrence. She comes over to the side of my chair to take a peek at what I'm reading. 'Good?' she asks, and I reply that it is. She progresses to the window, where there are some particles of dust to be removed from the latch. 'You went out for a walk with Ellen, I hear,' she says. Indeed I did. 'That's good,' she comments, encouraging me to agree. Entering into the spirit of things, I nod. Last year she saw kingfishers on that stretch of water, she tells me. That was the first time in her entire life that she'd seen kingfishers, and it took a while for her brain to process what the tiny flashes of colour were – she'd got it into her head that kingfishers were much bigger. A common misunderstanding, I believe.

'So, how did it go?' I ask. She surveys the room for a few seconds longer before turning to me and answering: 'Not great.' Her parents are getting old, and her father's health isn't good. It was nice to see the city again, but she felt like a tourist. She gives this idea some thought, and revises it: 'It didn't seem real,' she says. She looked at things she'd looked at hundreds of times when she was a girl, and it felt as if she was playing the part of that girl grown up, and feeling not a thing. 'Does that make sense?' she asks. I nod, though I'm not concentrating entirely on what's being said: Janina's manner is making more of an impression upon me than her words – she's talking to me as if she's in the habit of taking me into her confidence. Also, the perfume she's wearing now is exciting and unfamiliar, and I want to ask her what it is.

Her father, she continues, wasn't in as bad a state as her mother had led her to believe. When she arrived at the apartment her mother opened the door. Of course Janina knew that her mother would be looking much older than when she last saw her, but it was still a shock – when you haven't seen somebody for so long, it brings home to you how time is flying. From the living room came the sound of a hockey game on TV. It was very loud, so perhaps – she thought – the reason her father didn't turn round when she came into the room was that he hadn't heard her. She said hello, and he looked at her with lifeless eyes and said her name, making it sound like a question. 'This is awful,' she thought. 'He doesn't know what's going on.' But then she saw the vodka bottle, half-empty. 'And that just about set the tone,' says Janina, with a wan smile for the tawdriness of it. As far as she's concerned, her father is pretty much in the state you'd expect of a man who's well into his eighties, was never very robust, drinks too much, and has always drunk too much. He wants a reconciliation, she says, so he can feel better about himself. 'We must forgive each other,' her mother kept saying, as if wrongs had been committed equally on each side. 'I did things I shouldn't have done, things that hurt them, a lot of things, I don't deny it,' Janina goes on, 'but it wasn't equal. Not by a long way.' She does forgive her mother, she tells me. She doesn't love her, but she does forgive her. No lasting harm has been done, after all. There's a big distance between herself and her parents, but that's no disaster, is it? 'I could even tell my father that I forgive him,' she says. 'I don't like him, but what harm does it do to lie?' In this instance, none at all, I agree. 'A lot of men are jerks, and my father is one of them. That's all there is to it. With a lot of people, they can't see straight when it comes to their family. It's like different rules apply. They can't see what other people see when they look in from outside the family. But me – I see what they see. The fact he's my father doesn't make any difference. He's a jerk, I can see that. End of story.' Has Janina ever been so voluble with me? I think not.

Janina has been unburdening herself to Ellen too, I discover. Ellen was taken aback a little, she admits, by the way Janina talked about the trip. When Janina said of her father, 'I won't ever see him again,' she made it sound as if she was saying something like 'I don't think I'll go to that shop again.' The expedition was really more Charles's idea than hers, she told Ellen. Right from when they'd started going out with each other, he'd wanted her to build bridges. ('This is what I mean about you putting me in an awkward situation,' says Ellen. 'I had to pretend that I didn't already know.' I am abjectly sorry.) 'In the end, I gave in,' Janina told her. 'So we all went over, and it wasn't brilliant.' ('It wasn't easy,' says Ellen, 'having to make out that this was news. And not nice, either.' I would lash my back in penance, if only I could.) Janina joked that Charles should have been born into the mafia, because he's always had this 'blood is thicker than anything' idea. Having made the joke, she closed the subject – 'Moving on' – as if concluding point four on the agenda of a business meeting.

'I admire her,' I tell Ellen. 'And Celia admires her too. Celia really admires her determination in making a new life for herself. Problem is, it's the wrong kind of life.'

'Is that Celia talking, or you?'

'Celia.'

'Well, I think she's wrong,' says Ellen.

The Vegliot Dalmatian dialect ceased to be a living language on 10 June 1898, the day on which Tuone Udaina, its last known speaker, was killed by a land mine while attempting to clear a roadblock on the island of Veglia (present-day Krk). One year earlier the linguist Matteo Giulio Bartoli had visited Tuone Udaina in order to compile a vocabulary and grammar of the dialect. Bartoli's work was compromised by the fact that Tuone Udaina, by then at least seventy years of age, had not used the Vegliotic language for some two decades, since the death of his parents. He was, furthermore, both deaf and entirely lacking in teeth, and was thus not the most lucid of interlocutors.

Again Janina comes up to see me: two private audiences in as many days. Even by Janina's high standards, this morning's turn-out is unusually smart: pristine white linen shirt; black pencil skirt, of bespoke-standard fit; shoes that cannot have seen more than half a mile's wear. She's as crisply attired and made-up as a weather presenter. I ask about the perfume: it's a scent called Lily & Spice, new this month, bought at the airport, she informs me, proffering a wrist for inhalation. She's going to have lunch with a tutor from the college, to talk about training as a counsellor. Precisely what kind of counsellor isn't yet entirely clear – that's one of the things she needs to talk to this woman about, but she thinks it'll be practical stuff: 'debt management, marriage guidance, that sort of thing.' She made her mind up when she was away: she has to do more with her life. She's a bit worried about being twice as old as the other students, and she isn't sure she has what it takes when it comes to studying, but she reckons it's better to have a go and fail than to sit around at home wishing you'd done things when you were younger. 'If you want to do it, I'm sure you'll succeed,' I tell her. 'Thank you,' she says, as if England's greatest living curmudgeon has just praised her.

Standing at the window (no dust to expunge today), she gazes over the houses. She scans the sky. It would appear that another significant utterance is imminent, but then, distracted by something down on the road, she mutters: 'Oh, look who it is.' On the edge of the pavement stands the miserable old sod from the farm. He's stationary and bent at an angle of eighty degrees, and the walking stick is wobbling as if the end of it is being gnawed by an invisible terrier. 'Watch this,' says Janina. She's seen him pull this stunt so many times, she explains – he'll stand there, making out that he's going to topple over any moment, until someone arrives to give him a hand. 'It has to be female. I think he's seen one coming,' she says, and sure enough a woman enters the scene from the left and hurries across the road to help him out. The face and the form – she's in the region of thirty, clad in tight T-shirt and jeans – seem to please: he touches his cap and he smiles like a ventriloquist's dummy. She escorts him to the opposite shore, where it seems he needs a little more help. With trembling stick he points towards the centre of town; at half a mile per hour he shuffles out of the picture, his free hand clamped to the womanly bicep. 'If you had a camera rigged up in the High Street,' says Janina, 'you'd see that routine a dozen times a day.' He has a regular route – newsagent to chemist to bank to library. For every stage he'll hang around in the doorway, fishing for a sympathetic woman to drag him to his next stop. 'Between three-thirty and four you're guaranteed to see him dithering by the pedestrian crossing, hoping for a pretty sixth-former. Failing that,' says Janina, 'any woman up to fifty. Except me. He hates me. Which is fine, as far as I'm concerned.'

In her entire life, she says, she has met only three people to whom she has taken an instant and very strong dislike. One was a man who worked in the office she worked in when she first came to England: he stank of feet, had eyes as dead as marbles, and was always reading books about Hitler. The second was a young woman who for a few months lived across the road from herself and Charlie, not long after they married; she used to snigger for no apparent reason when you talked to her, and thought it was hilarious to wave to Charlie from her bedroom window, with her shirt unbuttoned and nothing on underneath. The third was Mr Ridley.

She first encountered him at the postbox at the end of the road. She was forwarding some letters that had arrived for the people they'd bought the house from, and as she was cramming them into the postbox she became aware that this man was standing three or four yards away, looking at her as if the box were a private amenity and she was committing a breach of some bye-law by making use of it. 'Good morning,' she said, and explained that they'd recently moved in. 'I know,' replied Ridley, 'the Anketells' place.' That was right, she confirmed. 'Nice people,' said Ridley. 'Very nice,' answered Janina. 'Down from London, aren't you?' he enquired. That was correct, she said. 'Commuting, your husband, is he?' asked Ridley. 'He works in London, yes,' she replied. 'Not working yourself, then?' Ridley went on, eyeing her up and down as if to say he knew a moneyed layabout when he saw one. In short, he made her feel about as welcome as an Albanian drug-dealer. Nonetheless, when – a week or so later – she came out of the bank to find the old man propped against the wall of the bank, quivering with the effort of remaining upright, she offered her assistance. Perhaps, receiving help from her, he might show a less hostile side of his character. He took her arm as if availing himself of some form of public transport for which he had a season ticket, and during their walk (they covered a hundred yards in what felt like an hour) he spent the entire time moaning about the schoolchildren who were thronging the street.

After that, uncharitable though it was, she took a detour whenever she saw him ahead. What she and Charlie were later told by several neighbours about Ridley and his bullying of his wife and son made her feel less uneasy about avoiding him, and the last scrap of that uneasiness was vapourised by a meeting in the local sports hall to discuss the new housing project. There, upon raising for consideration the idea that the development may have some economic benefits for the town, she was heckled from the back of the hall by a surprisingly strong-voiced Ridley, who treated the gathering to some very robust opinions on the undesirability of taking in even more outsiders.

From that day on, whenever Ridley and Janina have passed each other in the street, they've pretended not to notice each other. However, a few weeks ago she was on the High Street when she spotted our man in the middle distance, leaning against a wall, waving his stick aloft. It soon became clear that he was intent on catching her attention. When she came within close range he shambled towards her, his face contorted by what might have been intended as an ingratiating grin, but looked like the grimace of a man in the grip of neuralgia. 'I need to be over there,' he informed her, whisking his stick in the approximate direction of the bank, on the other side of the road. If that was the case, she thought, it was odd that he'd let at least two women younger and more eligible than her go past. 'How's your lodger?' asked Ridley. 'We don't have a lodger,' replied Janina. 'Not what I heard,' wheedled Ridley; a sour smirk tilted the mouth. 'Well,' she said, 'I always say it's best not to believe everything you hear, Mr Ridley.' He appeared to hear the implication of the emphasis she placed on his name – i.e., 'You may think you know something about us, but we really do know things about you.' It was time for Ridley to elicit some sympathy: he leaned heavily on the stick, lurched, gazed forlornly towards the distant door of the bank. 'A lovely day, though, isn't it?' Janina proposed, smiling skyward, and then she abandoned him, adrift on the expanse of the pavement. Since then she's always given him a full-blast smile, just for the satisfaction of seeing his expression change: he looks, she says, like a man who's bitten on a slice of lime.

She's sitting on the edge of the bed, smiling, and the angled sunlight is cutting a very comely shadow on one cheek. Above her eyebrow on that side, pollen-like flecks of powder glisten. None could deny that she's a very attractive woman. Lightly she strokes the upper surface of her thighs, like an interviewee who's beginning to think that she might have talked too much. My comment is awaited, but my mind has gone walkabout: I've been reminded of my mother and the ghastly Mrs Thomas from number 84. ('How's Daniel?' Mrs Thomas would enquire, with her grimace of sympathy. 'We haven't seen him for ages. All right, is he?' Airily my mother would reply: 'Oh yes. He's fine. Working hard,' raising a bubble of cheeriness which nobody would be so hard-hearted as to puncture.) 'Not a nice man,' is all I can think to say.

'No, not nice at all,' says Janina, and the smile intensifies momentarily. I am to understand that our relationship has attained a new intimacy. 'I must let you get on with your reading,' she says, rebuking herself for her lack of consideration. As she passes behind me, her hand alights upon my shoulder for a second.

A walk through swiftly moving mist: one moment the torch beam reaches far into the fields, then in an instant everything is shut off. The moon intermittent, and never brighter than a fleck of old newspaper. Get as far as the houses, where I have to sit down for half an hour. Saturated bricks have the colour and gleam of raw liver. Owl vociferous. Brief waft of complicated stink: silage and wet soil, with an undernote of diesel. Too tired to get upstairs; sleep on sofa.

This is worth noting: a madman by the name of Marquis Maurice d'Urre of Aubais left all of his property to the French state on condition that his corpse be placed in an armchair under a glass dome, facing the sea, in a place accessible to the general public. Furthermore, his remains were to be spotlit, in perpetuity.

'Well, it was inevitable, wasn't it?' Janina remarks at the table, of Celia's abandonment of the school project, then she and Charlie set each other off, going on about how Celia is wasting herself in Italy, and how what she needs to do is find herself a proper job in England before it's too late. With her experience, it must be possible for her to find a position with a reputable organisation. 'She'll be all right,' I say, but there's no stopping Janina, who is concerned that Celia might be leaving it too late to find someone to share her life with. I repeat, a little more firmly: 'She'll be all right.' Janina hopes that she will, but she sometimes despairs over the mess that Celia makes of things. I suggest that living in one of the most beautiful cities in the world, and being happy for much of the time, could hardly be said to be making a mess of things.

'She needs to take a good look at her circumstances and make some decisions,' says Charlie. (Subtext: 'As my wife has done.')

I suggest that our sister is fully cognisant of her circumstances.

'She can't go through the rest of her life just hoping that something will come up,' says Charlie. 'She needs to have a clear idea of where she wants to be in five years' time, and to set about making it happen. It's time to get serious.'

I venture that Celia is aware of this. 'She's not an idiot,' I tell him. 'And how do you make a plan for meeting Mr Right?' I ask of the room in general. 'It happens or it doesn't.'

Observing that I am becoming agitated, Janina concurs. 'You never know what's going to happen tomorrow, do you?' she says. 'Maybe Celia's lucky break is just around the corner.'

By way of a coda, Charlie restates his line on the intrinsic dodginess of Italian men. In conclusion: he's of the opinion that Celia would improve her chances on all fronts if she were to come home.

'I think you're right,' says Janina; Ellen is of like mind. I argue vigorously and silently, as the conversation dribbles away.

The family's introduction to Janina, which took place some four months after Charlie had met her, went as well as could have been wished. My father was favourably impressed: the new girlfriend was polite (she shook his hand as if being invested with an OBE at Buckingham Palace), her accent was very pleasing, she was easy on the eye, and – more importantly – she seemed like a steady young woman. My mother, still saddened that recently rejected Gemma was no longer around, agreed that Janina had nice manners, and seemed very fond of Charlie, and there could be no disputing that she was pretty, yet she had to admit, under questioning from her husband, that she'd found Janina almost too poised and too finished (Janina evidently had a beauty routine, whereas Gemma barely knew how to hold a mascara wand), and perhaps also – how shall we put it? – a little too forceful. After the second visit – when Janina enumerated for us the various aspects of Canada that she didn't much like (omitting her family, of course) – my mother reiterated the last of these judgements, adding that Janina wasn't quite the sort of girl she'd imagined Charlie ending up with. (It was already clear that he had indeed 'ended up' with her.) As for me, I liked her: she greeted me with a face that was only lightly clenched, and although she couldn't bring herself to plant a kiss (no blame there), she did move in for a loose hug. At the table she took care to address me as often as the rest of the team, with no more than transient distress in her gaze, perhaps visible only to me.

The talk around the table barely faltered, for which Charlie must be given most of the credit. He seemed determined to direct the conversation, and to keep it away from the subject of himself and Janina as much as possible. Once or twice, when our mother strayed into the domain of the personal and particular, I detected a trace of unease about his eyes, especially when Janina, in the course of telling the parents what she really loved about London, made reference to the fantastic fireworks on Blackheath. 'Spectacular,' Charlie concurred, with a glance at me, then he started telling Janina, at some length, about the November 5th bonfires in Lewes and the amazing torchlit parade he'd seen there a few years back. The reason for the glance, and for the diversionary waffle about Lewes, was that back in October (as our parents might have recalled, had this strand been allowed to continue) Charlie had been talking about the possibility (and it was never more than the remotest of possibilities) of my going with him and Gemma to see the Blackheath fireworks, but in the end nothing had come of it, because Charlie and Gemma, come November 5th, had been going through a wobbly spell, as he'd put it. Around the middle of that month we'd been informed such wobbles had become commonplace of late, and that this one had proved terminal; we heard of Janina shortly before Christmas. Now it appeared that Mr Charles

Foursquare had been less than wholly straight. Before he left, I accosted him outside my room, out of earshot of the parents: 'Come on Charlie, what's the story?' He clamped a hand to my mouth. 'Later,' he whispered, as if cornered by a blackmailer.

The tale of unromantic Charlie's great romantic crisis was disclosed in three or four instalments, the last of which was our boozy pre-nuptial evening (the evening of 'She's a tiger', et cetera). But before we summarise the revelations, we should give some time to Gemma Prescott, who for many years had been a central figure in Charlie's life.

They met at the age of twelve, when Gemma joined Charlie's class at school, but for a whole year she was an entirely neutral presence. The turning point, as Charlie tells it, was a game of cricket in the park. When Gemma's brother asked if he could join in, Gemma asked if she could play too, and was begrudgingly given a place in the outfield. Five minutes later the ball flew towards her, and she caught it one-handed, with a leap that Charlie has still not forgotten: the catch was remarkable (it was taken behind her head, and entailed a twist in mid-air), and the shyness with which she took the amazed acclaim of the boys was beguiling. From that day onward she and Charlie were friends, but for both of them no more than one friend among several, and it wasn't until some time after his fourteenth birthday (she was one of only three girls invited to his party) that she began to come round to our house after school, and even then it was rarely more than once a week. (Gemma led a busier social life than Charlie – she might not have been anyone's best friend, but she was a pleasant and accommodating girl, unexceptional and unexceptionable, and she antagonised nobody.) It seemed that mutual aid with the homework was the principal motive for her visits: like Charlie, Gemma was outstandingly poor at no subject and outstandingly good at none either. (Only at one thing did Gemma excel, and that was tennis. Celia reckoned this was why Gemma liked him so much – he didn't object to being thrashed by a girl.) Sometimes, on Saturday, they went up to town together. When Gemma went shopping for clothes, she often took Charlie with her, because he'd always tell her bluntly if something suited her or not. For years they were like cousins; almost like cousins of the same gender.

Charlie's first girlfriend was a girl called Carol, a scatter-brained tomboy with frizzy black hair and a penchant for dungarees. (She'd been another of the favoured trio at the fourteenth birthday party.) That relationship lasted no more than a couple of months, but slightly longer than Gemma's first liaison – it was soon clear that the boy was interested only in getting her knickers off, and quickly lost interest when it became apparent that they weren't coming off any time in the foreseeable future. (His parting shot, as she told Charlie, was that she was a nice girl but too 'uptight'; and she had legs like a footballer.) Each went through one or two desultory kissing-only romances, and with the demise of each one Gemma and Charlie carried on as before. A few months after they left school one of Charlie's friends threw a party before going off to university, and Charlie ended up reelingly drunk and in bed with a girl called Judith, a friend of the friend's sister. Thus was his virginity disposed of, and he didn't think much of it as an experience; neither, it would appear, did Judith, who did not return his call, to the relief of shamefaced Charlie.

He didn't confess to Gemma about the romp with Judith until a year had passed, by which time she was working in a kindergarten and had become involved with Ralph, the father of one of the children in her care. During this period she and Charlie didn't see each other regularly: Ralph didn't like her hanging around with another bloke, as she told Charlie when they met for a drink one evening; 'Neither do I,' quipped Charlie, surprised to find that he was in fact, now he'd come to mention it, mildly jealous of Gemma's relationship with Ralph, which was the first serious affair for either of them. He felt disloyal at not being entirely sorry when, after Gemma had returned from a holiday with Ralph and his daughter, she told him that it wasn't going well, because Ralph spent far too much time talking about his ex-wife. This is when Charlie owned up about the business with Judith. When Gemma was twenty her mother was diagnosed with cancer; she ditched Ralph, on the spot, when he declined to come with her to the hospital because hospitals always gave him the creeps. (He'd been scarred for life, it seemed, by the sight of his ailing grandmother in a ward full of moribund and emaciated old ladies.) Stalwart Charlie, it goes without saying, visited Mrs Prescott in hospital and subsequently, frequently, at home. One afternoon, after her mother had been to see her consultant and been given a good prognosis, Gemma and Charlie went to Hampton Court for the day. Walking in the garden there, she dabbed her eyes with Charlie's handkerchief, and as she gave it back to him she said: 'You know Charlie, you're the only person I can talk to.' And then she said she loved him and made him stop so she could say it again and he would understand what she meant. 'I do love you Charlie,' she said, and to Charlie it seemed that of course they loved each other.

To some observers (e.g. Celia, for whom Gemma was the dullest girl in London – 'Have you ever heard her make a single interesting remark about any subject whatsoever?') it may have appeared that Gemma and Charlie were lacking the passion one would expect of young lovers, but it was incontestable that Gemma really did come to adore Charlie. Other boys couldn't resist showing off, but Charlie never showed off, as she told his mother proudly. Charlie was kind and considerate, and he was perfectly content to be quiet if there was nothing to say. Most people can't bear to be quiet, she said; they talk just for the sake of it, but Charlie wasn't like that and neither was she. And what did Charlie see in Gemma, other than a woman who adored him? Well, she would never let him down, he could be certain of that. (The immediately pre-Gemma girlfriend, having given no warning of which he was aware, had posted a message through our letterbox: 'Can't make tonight. Or any other night. Sorry.') She was thoroughly genuine and they saw eye-to-eye on almost everything. He could not imagine arguing with her, ever, and he knew – from what he'd observed of the parents of some of his friends – that such compatibility was not common, and was not to be undervalued. There were times, it's true, when they seemed to have become becalmed, as it were, but these episodes passed; he accepted that this is what happens when you are serious about someone, that a shared life necessarily has these intervals of uneventfulness. Such was the nature of adult life.

For almost three years Charlie and Gemma were a couple. After two years they rented a flat together. It was understood that one day, when they could afford it, they'd buy a place. There would be children; two of them, most likely – certainly no more than three. (Gemma had an aunt and uncle who'd had eight kids; they were grey at forty.)

Then, late on a dismal afternoon in September, Charlie looked up from his desk in the showroom and saw a rather severe but rather handsome young woman walking towards him. She was wearing a short black and white houndstooth jacket, black knee-length skirt and very high-heeled shoes. At first sight she had the air of a dissatisfied customer, but as she came up to the desk she gave him a smile that was disarmingly apologetic. 'Do you have a minute?' she asked, sitting down before he could answer. 'I have a problem,' she said, and she smoothed her hair on one side; the cut was so shapely it looked as if she'd had it done within the past hour. From her bag she extracted half a floor tile: stone-effect ceramic, poor quality. She set the fragment, like a piece of police evidence, in the middle of the desk. 'Now,' she began, 'I bought this for my kitchen floor. Don't be worried – not from here,' she said. This was the story: she'd bought these tiles from another shop; a man (found in the phone directory) had put them down for her; at first they had looked all right, but then they started to go blotchy; she complained to the shop, but they said there was nothing wrong with the tiles; she complained to the man, who said that it was the tiles that were bad; she went back to the shop, but they wouldn't help, so now she had come here. Charlie lifted the half-tile and examined it, though there was no need to – he'd known at once what the problem was. 'Blotchy?' he asked. 'Twenty, thirty big spots. Like a disease,' replied Janina. Charlie twirled the exhibit slowly between his hands for a few seconds, eking out the interview, before explaining that the wrong type of adhesive had been used. Gravely sympathetic, he told her that, sadly, the only thing to do was rip it up and start again. Janina considered the diagnosis. 'Thank you,' she said, rising. 'You've been very helpful. I shall be back.' She retrieved the half-tile and shook Charlie's hand. She had extremely fine fingers, with long and narrow nails. 'But first I will get my money from those idiots,' she told him.

From this discussion of low-grade flooring materials and incompetent workmanship Charlie emerged unsettled – Charlie who claims that not once, in all his time with humdrum Gemma, had he experienced even the tiniest temptation to stray. Some time before this crucial day, he and Gemma had drifted into one of their regular becalmings. Usually, it took a month or thereabouts for his perspective to rectify itself, for him to recognise that the temperateness of his life was a form of contentment. All he had to do was wait, and waiting required no effort of will: as surely as the weather improves, eventually, he would again be actively grateful for what he had. Now, however, he had to instruct himself to believe that this would happen, to remind himself that it had always happened before.

The following week Janina returned, having failed to get redress from the floor-layer, who had been extremely rude to her. Charlie recommended someone reliable and helped her choose new tiles. After she'd gone, he held on to her cheque for a minute, fascinated by the name and the shapely flourish of her signature. He wondered if he would ever see her again, and almost managed to convince himself that he was glad it was unlikely. Then Janina came back to the showroom on a Saturday morning, shortly after opening; Charlie's assistant went to serve her, but she said she needed to speak to Mr Brennan. The floor had been successfully replaced, thanks to Charlie, and now she had decided to go the whole hog and have the bathroom done too. The selection took more than an hour; for the trim she chose narrow strips of cobalt blue glass, made in Italy and somewhat more expensive than her budget had allowed. 'This is mad,' she reproved herself when Charlie had totted up the bill; as she took out the chequebook Charlie risked a remark that could have been interpreted as flirtatious, and Janina gave him an ambiguous look – possibly encouraging, possibly the opposite. As if someone else had taken control of his vocal cords, out of his mouth came an offer to deliver this batch himself, one evening after work. That would be very nice of him, said Janina, with a handshake so devoid of erotic nuance that as soon as she'd left Charlie began to reconstruct every sentence he'd spoken to her, trying to persuade himself that he had not made a fool of himself, that everything he'd said would have been taken innocently. He was in turmoil. The current hiatus with Gemma was no transient phase of dullness, another shallow trough before the next shallow rise. Instead, he now knew that they had travelled their full course, that they had come all the way downstream to the motionless lower reaches and were adrift on water that was as flat as a floor all the way to the far horizon. He had never before been unhappy with Gemma, not in the sense of being conscious of unhappiness; there had been, rather, intermittent absences of pleasure. Now he was definitely unhappy, and he was shortly to become unhappier, and at the same time happier than he had ever been.

Wretched and in his own mind unfaithful (though he knew he was merely infatuated and that this infatuation would amount to nothing), Charlie raised with Gemma, the following day (it had to be done before he next saw Janina, even if nothing was going to happen when he did see her), the possibility that they had become, after all this time, very good friends, the very best of friends, but only that (thinking, despite himself, that perhaps this was all they had ever been). '"All this time"?' she echoed, uncomprehending. For Gemma a new life had begun when she and Charlie became lovers, and that was not a long time ago, by her reckoning. 'I should have said something before,' said Charlie. '"Before"?' distraught Gemma repeated. '"Before"? What do you mean, "before"? Before when? Before what?' Floundering, Charlie suggested that there must have been occasions when she had wondered if things were all right between them. 'No,' she stated. 'Never.' Charlie stared into the wall, blank-brained. 'This is nonsense. You're talking rubbish,' Gemma screamed at him (having, in the preceding three years, rarely so much as contradicted Charlie and never raised her voice). 'There's someone else, isn't there? That's it, isn't it? Tell me,' she demanded. In their early days of the post-Hampton Court stage of their relationship, Gemma had once told Charlie that if ever he were to leave her, it must be because he'd come to feel they'd outgrown each other (though such a thing was unthinkable), not because someone else was involved. To leave her for another woman – that would be too sordid, too banal, she said (she had used that word, 'banal', Charlie remembered; he remembered being touched by the strange loftiness of it), and he had told her, genuinely, that he agreed, and that it was inconceivable that either of them would do anything so shabby to the other. So when Gemma asked him if he had become involved with another woman, and to tell her the truth because she'd always much rather know the truth, however much it might hurt, Charlie told her that he wasn't involved with anyone else, salving his conscience with the thought that this statement was true, literally, even if he weren't being truthful. 'Look me in the eyes and tell me,' said Gemma, and Charlie looked her in the eyes and repeated the words. Gemma became so upset (she locked herself in the bathroom, weeping loudly; breakables were thrown) that Charlie ended up talking himself into half-believing that he had exaggerated his feelings to himself; he agreed that they should talk some more, when their heads were clearer. Gemma talked about making some changes, about finding another job.

After many more hours of talking, they reached the conclusion that Charlie was depressed for some unspecifiable reason. Time would lift him out of it, they agreed; and indeed, come Monday morning, he was less gloomy. At work, he allowed himself, as a sort of test, to take a good long look at some of the prettier girls who passed the showroom; he felt secure in enjoying, analytically, the sight of them; he was with Gemma; she was his and he was hers. He was seeing sense again. Then he drove round to Janina's flat, she opened the door to him, and it was, he said, like falling off a cliff. She was wearing a white T-shirt that could have come straight from the shop, and jeans that fitted so nicely he found it hard to make his eyes behave. 'Can I make you a coffee?' she asked; 'Thank you,' he replied, though he'd intended to stay no longer than it took to unload the car.

The coffee was real espresso, made with a complicated machine. She showed him round the flat: everything was as tasteful and orderly and well-decorated as a suite in a modern hotel – even the bathroom that she was going to refurbish. She'd been very lucky, she explained to him. Her first months in England had been a grind, but then she'd found a job with a property developer, as his secretary; it was hard work, very long hours, more a PA's job than a secretary's, but this man had made so much money on one deal that he'd given her a big bonus, enough for her to put down a deposit on this flat. 'It was amazing: he just put this envelope on my desk, full of money,' she said, before adding, as if she were concerned that he might think badly of her: 'There was nothing going on with us. Absolutely nothing.' The developer had gone to live abroad, and now she was working for a solicitor, who didn't pay so well, but it would do for the time being. 'Every penny goes here,' she said, gesturing at her living room. 'I can't live in a place that isn't how I want it.' She'd appreciate his advice on something; this involved inspecting a wall in the bathroom, which in turn involved seeing the reflection of the two of them, side by side in the mirror, which had a strange effect on Charlie, as if he'd been shown a photograph of themselves in the future, as a couple. A glass of wine was offered and accepted. Janina told him a little about herself. Everything she said made things worse – now she became a bold and determined young emigrant, with the extra allure of a complicated lineage. She was exotic and ambitious and self-sufficient, whereas homely Gemma wanted only one thing, and that was a life with Charlie. He loathed himself for making the comparison at all, let alone for being captivated by a woman who was almost a stranger to him. When Janina invited him to stay for a meal ('It'll take me twenty minutes. Very simple,' she said, and he knew that it would indeed take her just twenty minutes to put a meal together, and that it would be excellent), he said that he'd like to but he couldn't. 'OK,' said Janina. 'Maybe some other time.' There were no two ways of reading the look she gave him now. Within five minutes he had told her that he had a girlfriend, but that it was finished (which it was, in his mind, as soon as he said it). Not wanting to betray Gemma further by talking about her, he said he couldn't say more. (And perhaps he was hoping that Janina would react to his evasiveness by telling him to go away.) It had ended, he told her, but the aftermath was proving difficult; they'd known each other for a very long time. (Gemma's name was not spoken; neither did Charlie have to reveal that he lived with her.) That was enough for Janina, who would rarely ask again about the difficult ex-girlfriend. (Years later, coming across a photo of Charlie and Gemma, she smiled and handed it to him without a word, as if it were none of her business.) 'Well,' she said, 'you know where I am.'

For the first time in his life, Charlie was barely able to control himself, but he controlled himself sufficiently to delay until the following weekend the conversation in which he would explain to Gemma that his problem seemed to be a fundamental one, not a mere matter of mood. He needed time to think, he told her – time, and space. So desperate was Gemma's distress ('No, no, no' she murmured to herself, eyes closed, as if he'd died), he had to pretend that he might be back. By the start of November he had rented a room, but he continued for a while to pay his share of the bills for the flat he'd shared with Gemma. In the morning he'd sometimes find a letter from her on the doormat, describing the desert of misery she was in, pleading with him to come back. She'd ring him at work, saying they had to talk, or would appear on the street corner opposite the showroom, waiting for him to finish work. Charlie, terrified that Janina and Gemma would come face to face on the street, had to go out to her and promise he'd call round later, which he did. ('It was such a mess,' he told me, and there was something in the way he said it that made me suspect that he might have been sleeping with both of them. Why else would he have been 'terrified'? He denied it. 'But it was all tangled up,' he admitted. 'I just didn't know what to do. She went bonkers.') And one day the dreaded encounter between Charlie's two women nearly happened. Gemma was at her station on the opposite side of the road; Charlie, exasperated, was holding out for as long as he could; then Janina unexpectedly came in. Before he could think of how to handle the situation, she'd kissed him. Over her shoulder he saw Gemma cross the road. As if inspecting the display, she stood outside the window nearest to Charlie's desk. She let the tears run down her face for half a minute, then looked up to give Charlie one last, long look of heartbroken reproach. She never spoke to him after that, and there were no more letters, except for a note that listed the possessions of his that were still at the flat. One night he went to collect them. She'd crushed the stuff into half a dozen plastic bags, which she passed to him on the doorstep before closing the door, having not wasted a word on him. He wrote her a long letter, which she didn't answer. The last we heard – which was only a couple of years ago – she was living just a few hundred yards from her parents' house; she married a man who looked, or so our mother thought, remarkably like Charlie.

9

In the garden, reading, when I hear a girl's voice calling from somewhere near the stream. Two or three minutes later, a rustling in the leaves beside the shed, and then I spot a patch of red close to the ground – a T-shirt. A glimpse of a child's face – I yell, and the face vanishes. The girl calls again, and a boy's voice answers. Words indistinguishable. Garden henceforth out of bounds.

A call from Peter – he has to give a talk at a conference in London, as a last-minute substitute for a speaker who's suddenly indisposed. He'll stay with Freddie and then come down – and he'll make sure his brother comes too. I'll believe it when I see it. Janina is also doubtful: she tells me yet again how busy Freddie is at work and how much pressure he's under.

E: 'Are you in a lot of pain?'
D: 'There is pain. But not sure if there's an I in it.' (E baffled; but perhaps my speech is incomprehensible today.) 'Yes, Ellen, I am in pain.'

Famous last words: *I don't know; Keep me from the rats; I'm bored; The fog is rising; Wait a second; Tell them I said something; It's very beautiful over there; Now what?* I ask Ellen to take her pick; she declines.

Since coming back from Canada, Janina has become notably more attentive. She brings me drinks and newspapers; she plumps pillows and adjusts blinds; she puts her head round the door and asks if I'm 'disturbable', as though concerned that she might be interrupting the composition of a master-work. I wonder, to Ellen, if Janina feels she has to prove to herself that she's a good person, rather than a bad daughter. This notion, says Ellen robustly, is poppycock. (How nice to hear that word.) She doesn't accept that Janina for one moment thinks of herself in that way. Janina genuinely cares for me, she says. That may well be true, I reply, but things have changed since Janina visited her parents, wouldn't she agree?

'Yes, well . . . ' says Ellen.

'And I've changed too. You're right.'

'I just wish you weren't always cynical about her.'

'Not the right word, El.'

'I think it is.'

'No, it's not. I like her. She and Charlie have been very good to me. I know that.' And I tell her that Janina had been extremely kind to my father as well. He had found it easier to talk to Janina than to me, I tell her. Once boyhood was over, I was rarely on the same wavelength as my father – as either of my parents, for that matter. But with my father I always felt that there existed, buried, a resentment of the burden that his wife had been forced to shoulder.

'Charles doesn't think that's true,' says Ellen. It would appear that: I have already made this point to her and have forgotten it; she has passed on the observation to Charles and they have talked about it.

Unreasonably, this sets off a small flare of annoyance. 'He wouldn't know,' I tell her, and I close my eyes, feigning exhaustion. I fall asleep.

There was a period during which my mother attempted to make me into a gardener. As an occupation that combined a controlled exposure to fresh air with a modicum of engagement with the living, gardening was deemed to be of considerable therapeutic potential. Our garden was tight but sun-favoured, and my mother packed plenty of colour into it. I admired her industry and her horticultural talent, just as I admire Janina's. (Hours of assistance in the garden were what made my mother truly appreciate her daughter-in-law. 'She's so helpful. She's such a worker,' my mother would repeat, over and over again, in overcompensation for her earlier doubts about Charlie's beloved. And it was from my mother that Janina acquired much of the knowledge that has gone into making her garden the marvel that it is today.) I appreciated the vision whereby my mother could look at a plot of soil and instantly envisage the medley of flora that could be made to thrive there. I envied – albeit weakly – her ability to create and sustain an ever-changing yet ever-pleasing colloquy of flowers and foliage. Once in a while, from a wish to please her, I would set aside time to study some of my mother's gardening manuals. These studies were futile. Whereas I had no difficulty in memorising, for example, the names of the churches of Ravenna (a city I knew I would never see), I found it almost impossible to remember the names of the half-dozen varieties of common hardy annual that grew within a ten-yard radius of our back door. I had a negative aptitude for gardening and not a great deal of interest in overcoming my incompetence.

For my mother's sake I pretended to be more interested than I was, and professed to be perplexed that my brain should be so inadhesive when applied to botanical facts. To Hildi Goffman, who approved of my mother's project, I likewise confessed bafflement at my selective amnesia. Dr Goffman associated the problem with my dread of public spaces, even though I told her that I was perfectly happy to take the air in the family garden, where I risked being observed only by neighbours who were habituated to the sight of me. Despite the best efforts of the comely Dr G, I never became anything more than a part-time assistant to my mother. From time to time I would volunteer to water the flowerbeds or trim the grass. Armed with secateurs, I would occasionally perpetrate some light vandalism of the bushes.

That was more or less the extent of my father's involvement too. Understanding better than any of us the garden's therapeutic value for his wife, he was content for this to be entirely her domain. At the weekend he would take time to inspect the vegetation admiringly, and on summer Sunday evenings they might play a game of cards at a folding table outside. Otherwise, my father was rarely to be seen in the garden until he'd retired from the company – after that, he would frequently wander outside, to gaze vaguely at the vegetation, for rather longer than he'd ever gazed at it before. A bench was bought, on which, when the weather was fine, he would read the newspaper. He disliked being retired, and although he was proud of what Charlie had achieved, I think there was also a degree of humiliation in his son's having proved to be more adroit a businessman than he himself had been. Becoming an old man was another humiliation. It had always been a point of honour for him (to say nothing of thrift) to hire licensed professionals only when absolutely necessary. He replaced loose roof slates and broken panes, fitted sinks and ceiling lights, decorated the house from top to bottom. Then came the day on which he had to admit that the repairing of a high gutter was an operation that he could no longer safely perform. I remember him squinting up at the builder at work on the summit of the ladder – he looked ashamed, as if he'd created the damage that the younger man was fixing. I remember, too, the way he examined his first pair of bifocals, turning them in his hand ruefully, as if they were some sort of badge of senility. He was astonished at the speed at which the years had gone. Once, after a visit from Charlie and Janina and the boys, he said to me that as he'd watched his grandsons playing he had remembered an afternoon at a relative's house, when he was perhaps six or seven. He could no longer remember whose house it had been, but he'd vividly re-experienced being watched by his parents from an open window as he played on a path that had plump wet moss growing between the slabs, and it had occurred to him that when he looked at children and young people, and remembered what it had been like to be their age, it was like looking through a telescope, because the years of his youth seemed far nearer to him than they actually were – and, conversely, when children and young people looked at him they were looking through a telescope held the wrong way round, which made where he was, in old age, look far further away from them than he now knew it to be. In his last decade my father acquired a proclivity for sagacious pronouncements. 'There are many good things about getting older,' he said to me once, 'but getting older isn't one of them.'

My mother, on the other hand, although her body disappointed her more severely than my father's did him, took her ailments with less complaint. 'Nobody of our age is healthy,' she told me. 'We've all got something wrong.' She had many things wrong. After the birth of Charlie she'd gained a stone, and with each decade she had gained a quantity of excess material, and no diet made the slightest bit of difference. By the time she reached fifty the lower joints were defective and often sore. And at sixty came breathing problems and the chest pains – diagnosed as angina pectoris, with consequent prescription of perpetual medication. One day, returning from Christmas shopping up in town, she collapsed on the train. There was talk of a bypass operation, eventually, but a change in the drug regime proved effective in controlling the discomfort, and for eight years there were no significant events until the afternoon she emerged from the post office and went down as if every muscle in her body had failed at once, and this is how my mother's life ended, on the floor of Wardle Street post office, with people gathered around her in a circle, looking down into her face, I imagine, as though they were peering down a well-shaft, and shouting into her. Some things cannot be thought about for long.

In the last year of his life my father spent a lot of time in the garden. (Charlie was certain he wasn't going to last the year. 'Twelve percent of widowers die within twelve months of the death of the wife,' he told me, as dispassionate as an actuary, and our father, he just knew, was going to be one of that twelve percent.) He tried to maintain it in the condition in which his wife had left it, and did so, approximately. Sometimes I gave him a hand, but usually he preferred to attend to the garden alone. He preferred to be alone most of the time. For hours at a stretch he would sit on the bench, holding her old gardening gloves, which had stiffened to become crude casts of her hands. He could never bring himself to discard anything that had belonged to her – it seemed disrespectful even to be alive now that she'd gone. Remembering days from their life together was sometimes a consolation, but far more often it was not. When she'd been here and they had recalled things that they'd done together many years ago, the experiences that they recalled had become a part of their present life and so had come alive again, but now that these memories existed only in his head it was as if the past had suddenly withered away from him. Friends reminiscing about Sylvia might cheer him up for a while, but more often what he felt was that he had entered a state between being alive and being dead, and that soon these friends would be talking about him as they were talking about his wife. (There weren't many friends, it must be said. The social circle had always been narrow (neither parent could be described as gregarious; having the mutant son in residence also imposed certain constraints on the entertainment of guests, I'd say), and death had winnowed it to the brink of extinction.) I would sit with him and read; sometimes he read his paper or half-finished the crossword, but mostly he watched the birds in the trees or the traffic of the clouds or whatever other distraction might be available, and from time to time he'd speak. His utterances were brief and gloomy. 'It's meant to get better with time,' he said, 'but every morning she's gone again. It's the same day, over and over and over.' She'd died on a Tuesday. On the Wednesday they had been going to spend the day at Kew. They'd been talking about it, just before she went out to the post office. Some mornings, on waking up, for a second or two he'd think that they would be going to Kew that day.

Twice a week Janina would come round and cook a meal for him, and sometimes she'd stay all afternoon, talking to him as if he was on suicide watch. He didn't want to talk that much. The entirety of most days were spent inside the house. Then came the week of his birthday. Celia came over to see him, and stayed for five days, and each afternoon she went for a walk with him. This became a new routine for him, after she'd gone: every afternoon, regardless of the weather, he'd take half a dozen circuits of the park. These walks brought a slight lightening of the gloom. 'Grey,' he'd answer, when I asked how he was feeling; very occasionally 'light grey'. This new candour, by the way, did not betoken a new intimacy between us – had there been a lodger in the house I think he might have said the same to him. In bereavement he could no longer be bothered with the effort of keeping his thoughts to himself.

One lukewarm August evening my father said to me: 'I'm feeling very grey. I'm going to bed. See you at breakfast.' It was still not perfectly dark. In the morning I waited until eight-thirty before knocking on his door. There was no answer, and I knew what I was about to see. There was no sign of distress on his face. It was if he'd finally wound down and stopped. So my father, at least, had what used to be known as a good death, or so it appeared. From his mouth might have issued a scroll inscribed: *In manus tuas, Domine, commendu spiritum meum*. I held his hand and sat with him for an hour, then I rang Celia.

In his *Physiologie du goût* the epicure Jean Anthelme Brillat-Savarin records that General Baptiste-Pierre-François Bisson drank eight bottles of wine every day. The general was immensely corpulent, he writes. Nevertheless – eight bottles?

'Be in the world, but not of it' – or, for some of us, vice very much versa.

Freddie rings: he's deluged with work, so he's going to have to be in the office on Saturday. Charlie takes the call, but Janina goes out into the hall and grabs the phone. 'This is not acceptable,' we hear her hiss, like a boss to a useless underling who has finally gone too far. And: 'No, no, no – that's simply not good enough.' Charlie comes back into the living room to report that Freddie will not be coming. 'This has been on the cards for a while,' he whispers. Livid Janina goes upstairs immediately, without so much as a Goodnight.

I step out of bed and pain impales me, vertically, as if a two-foot spike has shot up through the pelvis. The after-shocks last for hours.

It has been discovered that Petru has a magnificent voice: his employer, lured by a sweet high tenor to the vicinity of the swimming pool, found Petru skimming debris off the water and singing to himself while he worked. This is moderately interesting, I tell her, but what I want to know is whether or not she's back with Mauro. A pause supplies the answer. 'Now don't you go all Charlie on me,' she orders. She knows exactly what can and cannot be expected of Mauro. 'It's just a bit of fun,' she says, and she can't be too choosy now she's at an age where everything depends on high-grade lingerie and low-level lighting.

JONATHAN BUCKLEY

Celia and Mauro went to Bologna last weekend. It was enjoyable: the hotel (refurbished this year, which was a principal reason for the trip – Mauro visits hotels the way other people drop into new bars or shops) was as excellent as Mauro had expected it to be, and they took a slow stroll up to the basilica on Colle della Guardia, which used to be one of her favourite spots in the city. The weather was perfect, with a gorgeous Bolognese dusk to round off the day, suffusing the old brick walls with the roseate flush that she always loved so much. In the evening they went to a restaurant that was a favourite with herself and Maria. The moment she opened the door she recognised the boss. His name then occurred to her as well, and it was as if the force of the sudden recollection of his name obliged her to utter it: 'Ciao Tino.' She had to explain why she knew him, and Tino did a good job of pretending to remember her.

It was a really wonderful evening, says Celia, but the cadence of her voice implies that the weekend with Mauro in Bologna was not as much fun as she'd expected it to be. 'But?' I prompt. 'No "but". It was terrific,' she says. The restaurant, the whole weekend – she had a great time. 'But? But? But?' The meal was exceptional, she insists, and Mauro was on top form. He's taken delivery of a new Aston Martin, and when he called for her on Friday evening she found on the passenger seat a Pucci shirt he'd bought for her. And yet – now we come to it – perhaps it had been a mistake to go back to one of her old haunts. As they were walking back to the hotel from the restaurant, a wave of sadness broke over her – that's really what it was like, the impact of a wave. The restaurant had hardly changed since she had last been there, and neither, it now seemed to Celia, had she: she was still doing the same sort of work as she had been doing when she lived in

Bologna all those years ago, for the same sort of money; she was living more or less the same life, albeit – temporarily – with a man of considerably more substantial means than his predecessors; and now she was two decades older – that was the only difference. She counted the years, and was horrified.

The next day, walking up to the basilica, she was caught in the backwash of her wave of gloom. Sitting on the parapet on which she had so often sat with Maria, she tried to recall days that they had spent together in Bologna, and it was terrible that so few came to mind. She had lived in this city for a long time; she had been happy here; she had met Maria; yet all those hours – hundreds and hundreds of them, replete with good experiences – seemed to have left almost no residue. 'It's as if they never happened,' she says. And she knows that, ten years from now, almost every minute of what's happening now will have evaporated too. She has a great time with Mauro. Their brains aren't in perfect harmony, but you can't have everything, can you? The sex is as good as she's ever had; he makes her laugh, and vice versa. And yet, and yet . . . At times, when she's not with Mauro, she wonders if she hasn't permanently lost something. She seems to need Mauro to give her life some zest, and that's what's wrong – something's gone seriously awry if she's enjoying herself most acutely with a man she doesn't love. Perhaps this dulling is inevitable, as one grows older, but she can't bear to think that it is.

At Sunday lunchtime Mauro had to meet someone for a business conversation, so Celia took herself off to Fidenza, a town she had never visited before. As the train pulled out of Bologna station she could feel the mood of ennui beginning to dissipate. An expectation of pleasure arose. Until recently, the first stages of engaging with a new locality have been one of life's dependable satisfactions for Celia. The gratification of walking though unknown streets is of such richness that, to ensure maximum piquancy, she has often promised herself, while still in the thick of those hours of discovery, that she will never again return to this place – a promise that in many cases she has kept. And Celia's afternoon in unfamiliar Fidenza did indeed prove to be pleasurable. The unique townscape of Fidenza composed itself around her as she walked from the station. The duomo presented itself in powerful sunlight, against a sky of crystalline blue. It was beautiful, really beautiful, she could see that – and yet it was as though the church were some sort of gigantic exhibit with a label that read *A Beautiful Church*, and she could see that the label was accurate, in the way a label bearing the text *A Large Building Made of Stone and Brick* would have been true. She went inside: her eyes received the light from a variety of things that should have pleased, and she felt almost nothing. Her thoughts, if they could be called thoughts, were as drab as postcards. Novelty had failed to have its customary revivifying effect – it felt, instead, like yet another repetition of the experience of being somewhere new. And the failure of Fidenza had an air of high crisis. The problem may be Italy – or rather, Celia in Italy. She has become dangerously jaded, she concludes, and the only way to refresh her faculties is to make a drastic change.

The solution, she would have me believe, is England, the country that once bored her. She's been in exile so long, so the argument goes, that the motherland has become a semi-foreign country. Her career (she actually uses the word) is going nowhere, she says. Back in London she could get a far better job than any she's going to get in Italy. Back in London, I point out, she couldn't afford any accommodation much larger than a kennel, unless she were to live in the limbo of deep suburbia. The riposte to this is a story about the travails of getting something done about the state of the road outside her flat. If she were a pal of a local politico, she tells me, it would have been repaired six months ago. 'I think I've had enough, Dan,' she says. 'In the end it wears you down.' By this time next year, she insists, she'll be back in London. But I'm not to say a word to Charlie – it's one thing to concede defeat on the school, but she doesn't want him thinking that he's been right about everything.

Newly posted at Tat2.co.uk: pictures of a young woman who calls herself Ainj. A vermilion and turquoise shark swerves around her navel; a red starfish lies on the front of a shoulder; her left arm is sheathed in variously blue-green whorls and torcs of Celtic derivation, intertwined with seaweedish tendrils. *Trix did a genius job, yeah?* Ainj writes. *Next we do the other arm, and then a chest plate to tie it all in. Gonna hurt like fuck but you gotta suffer for your art, right?*

A most splendid day: sunlight flowing up and down the hills; magnificent accretions of cloud, in multifarious tones of white; lengthy solos from a blackbird on a nearby TV aerial. Ellen enters, with a face I've seen on so many hospital visitors: fearful and humble, as if they are walking through an ogre's palace but might get out alive if they watch their behaviour. All those doors, and death behind every one. The air moaning in the lift-shaft like the ogre's sigh. Ellen puts a hand on mine. 'How are you?' she asks. 'In despair,' I answer. And he who dies in despair has lived his whole life in vain. Not sure if I said this. 'But a hospice would have been worse.' I did say this. Janina and Charlie, says Ellen, would never have contemplated a hospice – they would never have let me die alone. 'Everyone dies alone,' I almost say. I feel a compulsion to be wise. Ellen commends my bravery. It's in the job description, I tell her. Ever heard of anyone losing a cowardly fight with cancer?

Introduced to Ellen, Peter doesn't know at first whether to shake her hand or hug her like one of the family, but he picks up a cue from her and does a little jump forward to give her a kiss on the cheek. They both go the same way and almost crack foreheads; he blushes brightly. As soon as his jacket is off, his mother takes him out into the garden for a talk. It's obvious that Freddie is the subject. Much shrugging from Peter, as if to say that his brother is a hopeless case. He's looking podgy and quite pale – insufficient exercise and sunlight. And the hair is already thinning too. After an hour, he comes up to my room.

Freddie's weakness for the white stuff, it appears, is putting his relationship with Valerie in jeopardy – indeed, Peter thinks they may have passed the point of no return. Screaming arguments have become frequent, and Valerie has delivered more than one ultimatum. Valerie has a volcanic temper, Peter says, but Freddie's behaviour has been so erratic of late that even a vicar would be tempted to take a knife to him. Off his face in a Piccadilly bar, he came within a syllable of starting a fight with a similarly disoriented individual who – as any sober idiot could have seen – would have been capable of removing half of his teeth for him with a single blow. Even more severely scrambled one night last month, he permitted his hands to skim a curvaceous and unfamiliar posterior that presented itself to him in the crush around the bar. Valerie decanted a quantity of iced water onto his groin, and swore that a repetition of this misdemeanour would be the last offence he ever committed against her. Last night Peter and Freddie went out for a drink. Much of the talk was about Valerie: she's the best thing that ever happened to him, says Freddie. He's besotted with her. There's not a sexier girl in London, and he doesn't know what he'd do if she weren't around. But she needs to understand that these are the best years of their lives and it's just too soon to get all domestic. This would appear to mean, says Peter, that Valerie simply thinks it's healthy to get to bed before 2 a.m. at least three times a week, and has doubts about the long-term sustainability of a cocaine-based diet. After the pub Freddie announced that he was going on somewhere – 'Not your kind of place,' he told Peter, chucking him a key to his flat. Peter had half a mind to tag along, mainly to prove that he wasn't quite the slipper-guy his brother took him to be, partly to keep an eye on him (Valerie wouldn't be there), but questioning revealed that the bar in question really wasn't Peter's kind of place, and they had more or less run out of things to talk about anyway. (Not that talking would have been feasible where Freddie was going – the music was loud, he warned, which meant it would be the sort of din that impairs your hearing into the following week.)

When Peter got up this morning his brother had still not returned, so he rang him on the mobile, which put him onto voicemail, as it did again ten minutes later. On the third attempt Freddie answered: he said he was at the office, but the background noise didn't sound right – Peter heard footsteps on a wooden floor, and there are no wooden floors where Freddie works. He was immediately tempted to ring the office landline to check if Freddie really was there, but then was dismayed that he should be reduced to trying to prove his brother a liar. 'I'm sorry,' says Peter, defeatedly. 'He should be here. He has to stop messing people about,' he says, in a tone that could be his father's.

An object known as the Exceptional Lie Group E_8 has given Peter great excitement recently. Exceptional Lie Group E_8 is a 248-dimensional structure, and the mapping of it took four years of work, he explains. The final computation – more than three days' processing time for a supercomputer – churned out in excess of two hundred billion entries, and by 'entries' we mean not mere digits but complex equations. 'That's so much data,' he enthuses, 'that if all the numbers were typed out they'd cover an area the size of Manhattan.'

'Four dimensions has always been my limit,' I tell him. Undeterred, he endeavours to explicate in the language of the laity the meaning of this inconceivably symmetrical creation and what its discovery might mean for supergravity and string theory and the work that Peter does. In this context, I don't even understand what 'discovery' means, but I endeavour to simulate a partial comprehension. Peter knows that I'm putting on a show, just as he is, to an extent, in compensation for the absence of the feckless brother. But his 248-dimensional entity does delight him. 'This is as complicated as symmetry gets,' he tells me, with the hazy smile of a boy who has tasted ambrosia.

'So, how is it here?' he asks at last.

The views, I tell him, have begun to pall.

He tells me about a theory espoused by some crackpot American scientist – that we could all be reborn in a computer simulation at the end of time. An instant after we die, we could wake up again, billions and billions of years in the future, in a world sustained by code.

'I'd want to see the terms and conditions,' I answer. But I appreciate that this might be good news.

Ellen likes Peter very much, she tells me. Charlie told her that Peter is a genius, but she'd never have guessed that he was a genius – and she means this in a good way, I must understand. She would have liked to have kids, she says. Why has she never mentioned this before? 'Well, I'm not going to go around complaining about my situation, am I? In the circumstances,' she says. Maybe she will have kids, I tell her. 'Too late,' she answers. I remind her that Stephen's folks were late starters; she nods, as if acknowledging a fact that's of no relevance to her.

Thinking again of the hoopoe I saw with Celia. Some facts: the cry of the hoopoe is a 'soft repeated "poop"' – very similar to the sound produced by blowing across the mouth of a milk bottle, and not unlike the first component of the bird's remarkably euphonious ornithological name, Upupa epops. The hoopoe was once known as the dung bird; it was said to make its nest in human faeces.

Mr Ridley is crossing the road, unaccompanied, when a young man appears on a Vespa. Young man pulls up in front of Ridley, removes helmet and commences conversation which elicits not only laughter from the ogre but also an affectionate-seeming application of claw to young shoulder, in manner that suggests congratulation. I am not the only one to be surprised: the woman across the road, looking up from her ironing in the front bedroom, observes the remarkable interaction and, losing concentration, slides the hot iron onto a fingertip. Mouth movements and facial expression suggestive of bad language.

Celia calls again – the patient's condition is giving cause for concern, evidently. She chats to Ellen for quite a time; Ellen afterwards is overcast. Is it Roy? She says it's not Roy. It's nothing, she says. Two hours later, the truth is revealed. While talking to Celia, Ellen had mentioned that she'd spoken to Stephen yesterday, and that Stephen was excited about going to Japan. 'You once thought of going to live in Japan, didn't you?' she asked Celia, who answered that at some time or another she'd considered going to live in virtually every country north of Antarctica. Ellen says she must have got the wrong end of the stick, but didn't Celia strike up a friendship with one of her Japanese students, when she was working in London? Well, Celia replied, there were some nice Japanese kids, but nobody in particular stood out, as far as she recalled. Ellen reminded her about the Japanese businessmen lying drunk on the floor of the bar, foot to foot. This rang no bells.

Celia has a memory like a sieve, I tell Ellen. Of course there had been a favourite Japanese student: her name was Kachiko and she had a sister called Yuko. I couldn't count the number of the times I've remembered incidents from Celia's life more clearly than she did. 'Next time you talk to Celia, remind her of Kachiko. The name will come back to her.'

'OK,' says Ellen. It would appear, however, that more things than merely the story of Kachiko began to unravel during her conversation with Celia.

'Want to tell me what else Celia said?' I ask.

'It's not important,' she says. Her face, I suggest, says otherwise.

'For God's sake, Ellen, what's the bloody problem?' I groan.

'There's no problem,' she says, with a brightness that only makes things worse.

'Yes there is.'

She's holding a towel stretched tight between her out-stretched hands; she studies it as though it's a printed page and she's scanning a story that doesn't quite make sense. 'All it is,' she says at last, 'is that she thought it was funny, the idea of the drunk businessmen lying on the floor. But I don't think she'd forgotten it. I think it was the first time she'd ever heard it.'

'Well, it's true,' I tell her.

'OK,' she says.

'Look,' I say. 'It happened. The salarymen on the floor – I didn't make it up. Perhaps Kachiko's father wasn't one of them, but that isn't important. It happened.'

'So it isn't true?'

'Yes, it's true. I just told you.'

'But it didn't happen to this girl's father?'

'I think it did.'

'But maybe not?'

'Maybe not.'

'OK,' she says, scrutinising my eyes with a look of gentle disappointment that makes me want to start hurling large objects. 'I understand now,' she says, and she goes into the bathroom to cram the towel into its drawer.

'What does it matter?' I shout after her. 'What the fuck does it matter?'

'It doesn't matter,' she calls.

311

'Why are you so worked up about a bunch of pissed Japanese engineers?'

'I'm not worked up,' she says calmly, coming back into the room. 'You're the one who's worked up.'

Of course she's right, but it's pleasant to lose my temper; a lovers' tiff must feel similar. 'It amused you, didn't it?' I yell, though I'm already losing conviction. 'It amused me. So what's the problem?'

'There is no problem. I'm just a bit confused, that's all.'

'What the fuck is there to be confused about?'

She points out that I had expected her to tell me what was going on with Roy, and in the end she'd told me. In fact, as she recalled, I was the one who'd talked about how important it was that we were open and honest with each other.

'I did?'

'Yes, you did. As you know perfectly well. So I thought that you were being straight with me, all the time. I misunderstood.'

'So I put in a dash of local colour. So I tightened things up a bit. I'd have thought that was obvious. I wasn't there. I don't have tapes.'

'I know that.'

'I put words into people's mouths.'

She looks at me steadily, and I see wounded affection. 'It's all right, Daniel. Really. Like you say, it doesn't matter,' she says, then she leaves.

At bathtime, having apologised yet again, I ask: 'Was I very unpleasant? Did you dislike me for a minute?'

'For a minute.'

'Only a minute? Are you being honest, Ellen?'

'Two minutes,' she says.

I smack my hands together in what is intended as a gesture of delight. 'God knows I've tried to be as horrible as the next man,' I tell her.

We go downstairs to watch a film with Charles and Janina. I'm swiftly asleep.

I Still Cannot Get My Head Around This Absolute Beatiful Babe – I Could Never Beleave Theres Such A Woman In This World – Have I Died And Am Looking At An Angel Or A Godess?? I Love U Soozie And I Wish 4 U All The Best Things – I Give U Thanx For Brightning Up My Life For This Time.

God help us all.

Reading in the living room. From time to time Ellen glances at me over the top of the page. A spiral of hair, slipping out from a purple plastic hairslide, swings in front of her face; cross-eyed she examines the fallen lock, then tucks it back. For some reason I find this extremely touching. The smell of molten solder comes into the living room; turns out that it's the smell of rosemary in hot oil. Ellen sniffs: 'Sorry,' she says, 'it smells like rosemary to me.' Since our argument there has been an infinitesimal cooling between us. I've told her, more than once, that everything I've written for her is true, essentially. She nods, and talks about something else.

'I'm going to have a nap now,' I tell her. 'Please do not disturb, unless I start rattling.'

'Sweet dreams,' she says.

I dream of sitting in the living room, reading with Ellen; what a waste of unconsciousness.

As Ellen administers the night-time dose, I remark that this is the worst pain I have ever experienced. This is quite probably true. But I can't know that it's true, because I cannot remember a previous pain as I remember the hoopoe, or being in a taxi in London with Celia and Stephen. I recall that I was in pain, but not the pain itself.

'What were you thinking, Daniel?' asks Ellen. 'Nothing in particular,' I answer, too tired for more. *Cumulus – stratocumulus – Stratocaster – Jimi Hendrix – Hey Joe – Voodoo Chile – voodoo – Haiti – Papa Doc Duvalier – Maurice Chevalier – little girls – boater – bloater – ichthus – Jesus – mosaics – Ravenna – Constantinople – Cefalù – cephalopod – celadon – poison – poisson – Poissons d'or – Debussy – Eastbourne – East of Java – East of Eden – James Dean – Nicholas Ray – Fay Wray – King Kong – King Vidor – King Zog – King of the Road – Roger Miller – King Roger – Roger Dodger – Roy Rogers – Wyatt Earp – Virgil Earp – Virgil – Aeneas in the Underworld – Orpheus in the Underworld – Kathleen Ferrier – furrier – farrier – blacksmith – Vulcan's forge – Venus – breasts – what's-her-name Myers – Russ Meyer – Russ Conway – Conway Twitty – Tweety Pie – pie in the sky – toad-in-the-hole – spotted dick – syphilis – Naples – Vesuvius – Pompeii – Pompey – Julius Caesar – Marlon Brando – Mutiny on the Bounty – the Pirates of Penzance – Pirates of the Caribbean – treasure chest – cabinet of curiosities – Kunstkammer – Rudolph II – Rudolph the Red-Nosed Reindeer – moose – caribou – elk – Elke Sommer – Britt Ekland – Wicker Man – Man of Straw – man-of-war – U-boats – torpedoes – Hedy Lamarr – Hedwig Eva Maria – Ave Maria – the Queen of Heaven – Heaven Can Wait – Heaven's Gate – Forest Gate – Forest Hill – New Forest – Rufus – Chaka Khan – Kubla Khan – morphine – curare – tree frogs – bullfrogs – Jeremiah was a bullfrog – Lamentations of Jeremiah – Skeets Nehemiah – clay pigeons – homing pigeons –*

carrier pigeons – pigeons pigeons pigeons – Trafalgar Square – Trafalgar Square with Celia. That's what I was thinking, El.

Oceanic stupor and lurid dreams, which evaporate before I can get them down. Describing dreams like describing a piece of music. A vivid memory breaks in: Celia's decrepit old blue Mini. The sunburnt paintwork felt like polished chalk and the interior smelt of hot engine oil and damp leather.

Again the bowling green, more or less the usual script. Then a jump-cut and I'm looking out from a ground-floor window of a house that is submerged in water as clear as arctic air. But I don't know it's water until, high above the house, a horse steps out from a bank of grass and ripples spread from its hooves. The line of vision is 30 to 45 degrees from the vertical, so I can see the rider: he's a Mongol warrior, clad in scaly armour, with a round leather shield and domed helmet. Horsemen troop out onto the water: many lances are in evidence; much flapping of scarlet silk pennants. All eyes are trained in one direction, but so many horses that the surface of the water quickly becomes choppy and opaque. Hooves cover it like lily-pads. When the water settles there's nothing to see but the bank of grass and the sun. Dreams: the bubbling scum or froth of the fancy.

Charlie brings up a bottle of Château Taillefer, 1990, one of his favourites. J & E join us. A toast proposed by the moribund: 'Thank you very much for having me.' Janina a paragon of self-control; never lovelier. Wine tastes of mucus. Later, when we're alone, I remark to Ellen that most people, not being ready, leave a mess behind when they go. In my case, however, everything is in order. There are no loose strands. I know how my story ends. 'No,' says Ellen. 'If someone is thinking of you, it hasn't ended. Nobody knows how it ends.'

Memory: watching a zombie film with Zoë. Her squealing at the dismemberments and eviscerations – disgusted-thrilled, like a small boy finding a dog turd churning with maggots. I can hear her voice in the room. Without this body, might something have happened with Zoë? But without it, I would never have met her.

A plane enters the window and crosses it on a course parallel to the frame, at precisely the line of the Golden Section. Below its condensation trail, a long reef of smoke from a bonfire at the farm. Behind, scribbles of cirrus. It looks like a sketch of a sky, abandoned. At the crack of a backfiring engine the sheep sprint in unison across the field and abruptly stop together, like a platoon of automata disabled all at once by power failure.

Imagine it: after the cremation, all gathering downstairs. Janina, the most obviously upset member of the party, busies herself in the kitchen. Stephen is talking to her, and she keeps breaking into tears. Dr G is there? Perhaps. Celia whispers to Ellen that the weeping is beginning to get on her nerves. 'Want to go for a walk?' she asks, and they go for a stroll by the stream. Ellen and Celia come to the spot where we saw the heron. Ellen tells her about it, and she recalls the heron. She watches Celia, who watches the smoke from her cigarette as it drifts over the stream.

In the evening, Ellen is in my room. She has the laptop, her inheritance. Tucked into a pocket on the outside of the laptop's case there's a postcard. She takes it out, hoping there's some sort of message for her, and dreading it too. There isn't one. She switches on the laptop and reads two or three pages. She reads a description of herself. 'True enough,' she thinks. Or 'That's not nice.' She looks out of the window. There's nothing to see, except a big silver Mercedes arriving. Celia comes up to check that she's all right, and within a minute she's in tears and Ellen is comforting her. Ellen has the composure of a bishop.

A year later. This room has been repainted and the books have all gone to Stephen and thence who knows where. There is no trace of me here, other than a scuffing of the carpet where the chair was, and a faint mark left by the tripod of the telescope. Celia and Ellen sit on the riverbank, a few yards apart, not talking much. Yes, Ellen is a frequent visitor. Celia lights a cigarette. For a few months she'd managed to give up, she says, but not smoking didn't agree with her – she'd become too twitchy and too crabby. 'And too fat,' she adds, squeezing a thigh. Is she still with Mauro? Yes, she's still with Mauro and it's going well, she says, with a smile that signifies that she doesn't quite understand how she's come to be in this situation, but isn't going to worry about it too much. 'What about you?' she asks, and Ellen tells her what? Ellen says she might have started seeing someone. She isn't quite sure what the situation is, so she's taking it slowly, but she likes him and she thinks he likes her. 'Good for you, El,' says Celia. She's delighted, or a better actress than Ellen ever thought she was. Celia's friend Maria has moved to Livorno because her husband (name??) has landed a good job there, so Celia is seeing Maria quite frequently. The school where Celia's working now is a good one. She's rid herself of Christine, who's had her affair with whatever his name was, and might still be having it now, for all Celia knows.

Perhaps she has seen Petru? Yes, she's seen Petru, crouched against a wall in an alleyway, beside a pile of discarded cables, winding a length of wire around a stick. Behind him there was a supermarket trolley loaded with spools and lengths of copper piping. His hair looked as if he'd poured oil over it. She watched him winding the wire, slowly, grimly, as if making a bomb; to Ellen she confesses that she couldn't bring herself to talk to him.

They talk about what I have written. There are things here that Celia isn't happy about – the Taussigs weren't really like this, and the portrait of Mauro is off-beam as well. Having read this description of Mauro you might be able to pick him out at a party, but Daniel's version of him is too crude. And often she can't recognise herself in the woman called Celia. 'More Danny than me,' she says; this is what Charlie will say as well. Janina will never read a word of it.

How long will Ellen remain in contact with the family? Many years, I think. I hope. *Dum spero spiro*.

Roy. What about Roy? Pissed for the eighty-fifth day in succession, he drives into a phone box at two o'clock in the morning. Car is a write-off, but Roy survives. Lightly injured: a broken ankle and a cracked wrist. That'll do for Roy.

Wake up to find Janina and Ellen kneeling beside the bed – an Adoration of the Shepherds. Beatitude of the almost dead. Janina says they are thinking of installing a carp pond. Ellen admits to having a grudge against fish. Janina laughs – so she knows quite a bit about Roy, it seems. One day, says Janina, she may run for a seat on the local council. More news: Freddie is coming next week.

A night of constant rain, then a morning of radiant overcast: the sky a glowing porridge. Long pools have formed in the fields: bright offcuts of sky lying in the mud.

So much more to write. Dissolving in pain.

Tomorrow Stephen